REVEALING THE TRUTH

AGENTS OF ESPIONAGE
BOOK ONE

LORRI DUDLEY

WILD HEART BOOKS

Cover design by: Carpe Librum Book Design

ISBN-13: 978-1-942265-74-0

Though one may be overpowered,
  two can defend themselves.
A cord of three strands is not quickly broken.

— ECCLESIASTES 4:12

CHAPTER 1

The hard slap of footfalls running outside the stable broke through the fog of her brain. Katherine Ainsley Jenkins, the Countess of Dysart, inched along the edge of the stall past her favorite mare, who nudged her newly born colt to a stand.

The head groom lifted his cap and wiped his forehead. "'Twas a long night, but mama and baby are doin' fine." He plopped his hat back on his head and dipped the corner. "Much obliged for your aid, Lady Dysart."

Katherine mustered a weak smile and tightened the sash of her dressing robe. Distressed naying from her mare had roused her in the night, and the responsibilities of Steepleton Manor demanded she look into the disturbance. The delivery of the baby foal had been long and labored, and Katherine's presence had been needed to calm the wearied mother.

Hay clung to Katherine's hem as she stepped out of the stall, and she must smell like the stable, but she'd done it. Steepleton Manor welcomed its first new addition to their pedigree family since her parents' passing. "Please let this be the beginning of Steepleton's revival," she whispered to the sunlight streaming in through the loft window. How many hours had she spent pouring over horse breeding books trying to keep her papa's legacy of the famous Jenkins Lipizzaner horses going?

Denton, the butler, skidded past the open stable doors into view. His highly polished shoes slid on the loose gravel, and he flailed his arms before coming to a halt. The whoosh of air swirled the sweet scent of hay under her nose. He righted himself with haste and tugged at the bottom of his jacket, dislodging any wrinkles.

Several of her father's Lipizzaner horses leaned their necks out of the stall openings to see who approached.

It was uncharacteristic of her dignified butler to hurry. Her stomach twisted. The only other time she'd witnessed Denton this flustered had been the day he sought her out with the news of the deadly carriage accident that killed her parents. *Please let Claire be safe.* She placed a hand on a nearby post for her knees threatened to crumple. The second worst day after burying her parents had been packing Claire off to finishing school. As much as Katherine desired to hold her sister and continue to mourn their parents together, Claire deserved a chance to marry and lead a normal socialite's life.

"Mr. Bainbridge has arrived early, my lady." Denton stood at attention. The only sign of his recent sprint to the barn was his chest's quick rise and fall.

Her grip on the post tightened, and although she wanted to lean against it with relief, there was too much to do. "Already? His letter stated he'd arrive at week's end." Her mind whirled in a thousand directions. Why had he come? What could he possibly want after shirking his guardianship duties for three years? One question screamed louder than the rest. Would he still act as crazed as he had after Madeline's funeral?

"Inform the staff of his presence." Katherine mentally listed all the tasks to be done for their new guest. "And make certain they have finished preparing the larger guest room to accommodate him."

"Yes, my lady, right away."

"Did you seat him in the rose salon?"

Denton cleared his throat. "I escorted him there, but he insisted he would wait for you in your father's study. I wanted your approval before forcibly escorting him out."

The gleam in the butler's eye revealed his protective nature. It seemed he would enjoy throwing her cousin out on his ear. "No, Denton. I will see to him right away."

Katherine dreaded facing her troublesome cousin on her own, but since her parents' deaths, there was much she'd had to face alone. As she crossed the expanse of yard, morning dew soaked her slippers and the hem of her dressing robe. The grass had grown longer than to what Steepleton's sprawling lands was traditionally accustomed. A sheep had wandered through the broken rock wall where a large oak tree branch had fallen. The groundskeeper was supposed to have the branch cut into firewood and the wall repaired but heavy rains had flooded the garden, and he was busy saving his plantings from drowning. All the items begging her attention cluttered her mind as she hastened through the portico entrance, up the back stairs and down the hall to her room.

Her maid helped her change into a cream day gown of light cotton, but Katherine declined her maid's attempt at fixing her hair, for there wasn't enough time to restyle it. Katherine twisted it into a loose bun as she hurried down the hall and stairs toward the study. Her mother's voice echoed in her head, "Ladies never rush or run. They walk with grace, poise, and if necessary, a hint of purpose." Mama would always add the last part with a wicked smile, which made Katherine bubble with unladylike giggles. Katherine's gait was faster than what her mother would consider "a hint of purpose," but her cousin shouldn't be snooping around her father's study unobserved.

She paused at the door and inhaled a deep breath to steady herself, taking a nostalgic whiff of her father's cigars that still lingered long after his passing. Pasting a welcoming smile across her face, she entered the room. "Good afternoon, dear cousin. How delightful of you to visit."

Horace lounged in her papa's favorite chair. "Yes, well"—he flashed a beguiling smile— "we are family. And family takes care of one another. Do they not?"

Katherine forced her tight smile to relax. He was her guest, after all. Horace was seven years her senior, and he'd aged since she'd last seen him. His previously jet-black hair was edged with gray from the temples down. He had been considered a handsome man in his youth, but the carefree man her older cousin had married ten years before had faded away. Despite his relaxed posture, permanent lines of sorrow now creased his brow and dulled his once twinkling gaze. He appeared to have matured a decade in the past three years.

He stood and opened his arms to her. "Come here and give your cousin a proper welcome." His smile fractured his dour appearance.

She willed her legs to edge around the desk and stood still as he placed a kiss on each cheek. The musky scent of his cologne and a hint of gin invaded her senses. She closed her eyes and mentally counted the seconds before he stepped back.

"How I've missed you and Claire." His hands slid over her shoulders.

Katherine's jacket sleeves protected her from shuddering. "To what do I owe this visit?"

"I've come to the realization that I've been neglecting my duties as your nearest relative and guardian." He released her and flopped into her papa's chair once again, gesturing for her to sit on the adjacent stool.

How *kind* of him to offer her a seat in her own home. His audacity set her teeth on edge.

"I was still caught up in my grief over Madeline when your parents died, and I failed to recognize my familial obligation. I've come to rectify the situation." He smiled, but it didn't reach his eyes.

Rectify?

"I'm unaware as to how you've been able to manage these past three years, but I'm here now, and I'm going to ease your burden."

Katherine's mouth dropped open, but ingrained manners snapped it back closed. For three years, she'd managed her parents' estate. During that time, her cousin had never written a single note to inquire about how she and Claire were faring. Why the sudden interest? Did he *now* feel guilty? Was he truly offering her his support?

Katherine dug deep into her heart for a smidgen of grace. It would be nice to share the burden of this large estate. And he had been grief-stricken at the time of Mama and Papa's deaths. Perhaps he was trying to make amends?

She lifted her chin. "I would appreciate any assistance you'd be willing to give. I think you'd be proud of what I've accomplished, keeping everything running and maintaining orderly bookkeep—"

"It's settled then." He slapped the mahogany desktop. "I will inform my valet to bring in my trunks and shall meet with you in the morning to review the ledgers. I'm fortunate to have such a level-headed cousin." He stood, and his chair slid backward, tapping a small tower of periodicals Katherine had meant to file. They cascaded like a paper waterfall over the rug and across his path.

"What is this?" He pushed at the papers with his booted toe.

"Papa's medical journals." She bent down to gather them. "He was fascinated by new medicines and advances in technology. He used to read to me from them." She'd loved those times when she sat curled up on her father's footstool and listened to his baritone voice reverberating with enthusiasm. He would read about this new elixir or that discovery and then stop and say, "Incredible, my child. Think of the potential." The future had seemed budding with possibilities, but now her opportunities looked limited. Without a season, she feared she'd become a spinster, forgotten and alone in this vast house.

"Throw out that old rubbish." He shoved the pile out of his way with the side of his foot.

Katherine gasped. They were her father's journals and of great sentimental value to her. How dare he suggest they be discarded?

He grasped her arm, hefting her upright, and the papers she collected fell back to the floor. He ushered her to the door. "There is much for us to review, but let's get settled first."

She peered over her shoulder at the disarray littering the floor. She'd need to ring for a maid to tidy up.

He paused just outside the door and cupped her elbows. "You have been brave, but I'm here now." Her cousin's tone sounded pleasant, but his grip was too firm, tempting Katherine to rip her arm from his hold. "I'm going to make everything all better. You can go back to doing embroidery and taking daily rides. You'll no longer have all the burden of responsibility on your shoulders. Do you even remember what it was like to be carefree?"

What was he suggesting? Did he mean to offer his guidance? Steward the finances? Take on some of the hiring? As much as she desired to climb onto the life raft that he offered, a warning in her head caused her to pause. Why would he suddenly want to help?

He raised her chin with his index finger to meet his gaze. "Of course you don't, but that will change. I will take charge, my dear. Everything is going to be fine. You run along and rest up. We shall dine at eight."

He pressed a light kiss on her forehead, and with a firm

hand on her lower back, guided her a few steps down the hall-way. Should she be angry at Horace's forwardness or relieved to relinquish some of the burden? Managing a large estate had a steep learning curve, and at first, she'd made plenty of mistakes. She could have questioned her lawyers, but most issues had needed an immediate response. By the time she penned a letter, had it couriered to London, and received a reply, their answer would invariably be too late. Horace had managed his wife's estate. His social connections and advice on tenant disputes and the constant appeals of the aristocracy to purchase Papa's prized Lipizzaner horses would have been helpful.

Horace stopped walking, but she continued to drift down the hall. What she wouldn't give to pursue once again the things she'd enjoyed before her parents' accident, like reading a novel, visiting with friends, or attending a ball.

But what caused her cousin's change of heart, and why now? The last time he'd visited was ten years ago, when she was in leading strings. Would he have the best interests of Steepleton Manor in mind?

On the other hand, he was a relative and family could be trusted, right?

Four years ago, she would have said yes along with her parents, but he'd changed after Madeline's death. His easy-going manner might resemble his old nature, but the jaded look in his eyes and the bitter edge in his voice stirred doubts.

"Katherine," he called from behind her. "I forgot to mention that we can be married as early as Friday. I've obtained a special license. Then, you can have your coming-out season, and I can present you at court. Won't that be nice?"

She froze— "Pardon?"— and spun on her heel in time to watch him saunter into the study as if he'd merely commented on the weather.

Katherine marched to the open doorway.

"You heard what I said." He didn't bother to look up from the ledgers.

"Married?"

"Indeed." He leaned back in her papa's chair and had the audacity to put his boots up on the desktop. He flashed her a brash, self-assured smile. "Now that you are of a marriageable age and I am widowed, we cannot reside in the same residence. Think of the scandal." He tapped his fingertips together. "It's the logical thing to do. This way, I can manage the estates from here, and not only can I continue to provide for you as your guardian, but I can also do so as your husband." He crossed his arms over his chest and tilted the chair on its hind legs. "Besides, who else is going to have you since the Turner boy backed out?"

Katherine willed herself to let the pain roll off her, but it remained fresh even after three years.

He sighed as if disappointed. "It's what your parents would have wanted. You and Claire will be provided for and given the protection of my name, which is in your best interest. Wouldn't they have wanted what was most advantageous for you?"

A tremor shook her knees and ran up her spine. She curled her hands into fists to keep the quaking from becoming visible. "This is unbelievable."

"No, it's inevitable." His tone remained flat.

Inevitable? What was he talking about? The warmth of the room suffocated her. The walls pressed in, crowding the whirling thoughts in her mind.

"I beg your pardon, but I'd rather not."

He waved a dismissive hand. "I understand that you need some time to adjust to the idea, but you'll come around. Go rest up and we can discuss the arrangement over the evening meal."

What rights did she have? Could she refuse? Papa had named her cousin Madeline as her guardian in his will and had neglected to update it after Madeline died. Did that make

Madeline's husband Katherine's official guardian? Did it give Cousin Horace the right to tell her who and when she would marry?

Blood roared in her ears, and blackness crept into her periphery. She feared she might faint. Turning to the door, she forced one foot in front of the other and stumbled from the room. In a daze, she staggered down the hall toward the terrace, desperate for fresh air.

"You have a few days to see reason." Horace shouted before she could twist the door handle and escape to the veranda. "The vicar shall arrive on Friday."

CHAPTER 2

*L*ord Stephen Hartington stared out the study window of his London townhouse. Ominous clouds loomed overhead, threatening to burst with rain at any moment. People on the sidewalk below scurried about like rats in the rookeries, intent on completing their errands before the heavens let loose.

"Agent Scar has been monitoring a ring of horse thieves and wants you to bait them into the open." Agent Jacob Warren kept his voice flat, but the sound of him rubbing his palms together hinted that the case was nearing a breakthrough.

"I've yet to meet this mysterious handler of ours." Stephen tore his gaze from the dreary scene and turned to Jacob, who was relaxing in the leather seat near the mahogany paneled hearth as if he'd asked Stephen about his plans for the evening and not for Stephen to endanger his family. "My dabbling in spying for the Home Office has been fine in London but bringing it home to my elderly parents and small village is out of the question."

Jacob pulled up on the expensive nankeen fabric of his tailored breeches and leaned forward on the armrests of his chair, his square chin jutting out. "I hate to inform you, but they've already infiltrated your town. Agent Scar has a man deep undercover who's gone dark, but before he disappeared, he had some startling revelations about plans to smuggle pedigree horses through Wales and onto France."

Stephen rubbed his temples. Perhaps he should return home. With Father's leg injury, he struggled to keep up with the daily running of Willowstone Farm. Stephen already sent his earnings to help pay for physicians and upkeep. If he went home, he could earn a commission and help with the farm.

"The question is whether you want to be present to keep your village safe or stay here in London and miss the action." Jacob arched an eyebrow and hit him with the same I-dare-you glint that had originally convinced Stephen to try his hand in espionage.

"I promised Miss Julia Napier that I'd attend the Rutherford Masquerade."

Jacob shrugged. "I don't see why this would stop you."

Stephen rubbed his lower jaw. He and Jacob knew that cases didn't always run that smoothly.

"You and Miss Julia are getting serious?" Jacob leaned back and tented his fingers.

"It's past time I settled down." Stephen lowered into his chair behind his library table desk. "And as far as London debutantes go, I find her the most bearable. Miss Julia states her mind, and she's not hiding a secret life."

"You're not still hung up on the incident in Belgium, are you?" Jacob swiped his hand through the air. "She was a beaut of a double agent. Hard to see a woman like that hang."

Stephen's jaw tightened. *Especially when you'd promised her a future together.* He shook off the memory.

"When do you plan to"—Jacob grimaced as if he'd swallowed soured ale— "become leg shackled?"

"I haven't spoken to her father yet, but soon—after this case."

A smile broke across Jacob's sharp features. "Good, so you're saying you're in."

"I accept." Stephen pointed at his friend and colleague. "But this will be the last case. I plan to marry, and a good marriage cannot be built on secrets."

Jacob snorted, but whether at the prospect of marriage or not keeping secrets, Stephen couldn't be certain. Jacob rose. "We'll take it one day at a time for now."

A knock sounded on the door.

Jacob shifted into a ready stance, his gaze riveted on Stephen.

"Nothing to fret," Stephen said. "I was waiting on a missive and told the butler to interrupt us if it arrived."

Jacob's shoulders eased, and he adjusted the cuff of his sleeve while Stephen opened the door.

Wilson stood in the doorway and cleared his throat. "A message has arrived for you, my lord." The butler held out the letter.

Unfolding it, Stephen recognized Julia's feminine scrawl and scanned its contents. He shook his head and muttered, "It's a shame. This could have been the perfect opportunity to propose." Stephen stuffed the message into his jacket pocket. "That will be all, Wilson."

The butler turned and strode down the hall, but not before Stephen caught the spark in Wilson's eye.

"I'd place bets on your butler being up to something with that last look." Jacob snorted.

Both Wilson, Stephen's butler, and his housekeeper, Mrs. Bevel, prided themselves on knowledge of family matters. "I have no doubt Wilson is about to lord that juicy tidbit of information over Mrs. Bevel."

Jacob's lips twitched.

"You laugh, but their rivalry is exasperating. Last week they badgered a poor maid to tears over which held a brighter shine, the polished marble floors or the silver service."

His smile widened. "I'm certain Miss Julia will set things to rights. She's sacked quite a few maids and footmen who've displeased her."

Stephen hadn't heard about Julia terminating staff on a whim, and the notion didn't settle well.

"If you pack and leave within the hour," Jacob said, "you can make it to your parents' estate before nightfall. I'll pen some letters from your steward inviting investors to Willowstone Farm to view your prime blood thoroughbreds. I'll highlight the pedigree potential in hopes of drawing the ringleader's attention."

Stephen gulped. Was he doing the right thing? Or would this put his family in danger?

"By the way..." Jacob clapped Stephen on the arm. "My money is on your housekeeper. The floor shine is blinding. Best of luck to you with Miss Julia Napier." He snorted. "Better you than me." He strutted down the hallway, turning to wink at a passing maid.

Stephen watched his friend's retreating form. Was he talking about the institution of marriage—or Julia specifically?

Stephen strolled through the lush ornamental gardens of Hyde Park and sat on the park bench where Julia suggested they meet. She wouldn't be pleased about his visiting his parents' estate. Stretching out his long legs, he laced his fingers behind his head. The prospect of going home settled him. He'd feel better being near his family to protect them and their holdings, knowing there were horse thieves and blackguards in the area. It would be best to draw out the perpetrators, collect his substantial fee, and launch his endeavor to train horses. All he needed to begin his new life was to finish this assignment and return to London to claim his future spouse, and Julia seemed the best candidate.

A slow smile stretched his lips. He had life figured out, and his plan was logical and solid. He would marry, he and his wife would move to the country, and they'd raise five—no, maybe six, children. She would teach his daughters to sew and play piano, and he would instruct his sons to ride and shoot. His parents would dote on their grandchildren as they had him.

He caught sight of a pale blue umbrella past the passersby and rose to his feet, knowing the occupant underneath was Julia. She favored the pale blue color because it made her eyes appear a darker cobalt blue, and she tended to wear clothing in that color. Which was all right for Stephen. A little boring perhaps, but it added to her femininity.

Would he tire of pale blue?

Stephen pushed the thought aside as Julia came into view and extended her gloved hand.

"Miss Julia." His gaze roved over her curvaceous form as he bowed. She was what the *ton* would call a classic beauty with blond hair and porcelain skin. He pressed a kiss on her satin glove and reverted to her given name. "Julia, you look lovely as always."

Her lips curved into a demure smile, but her demeanor changed as she snapped her umbrella shut. "What is this about you leaving?"

Word traveled fast. It seemed Julia had a spy of her own among his staff. He wasn't certain whether to be furious or impressed.

She puffed her lower lip into an angry pout. "Who will be my dance partner at the Rutherford Masquerade?"

"It's a masquerade." Stephen cupped her chin between his thumb and forefinger. "You're not supposed to know the identity of your dance partner." He flashed a smile to soften his chide. "I'm hoping not to be gone for more than a fortnight. There's a new thoroughbred being delivered to the estate, and I must be there for its arrival." He leaned in and whispered in her ear, "But it's nice to know I'll be missed."

She huffed and plopped down on the park bench. "Don't think you can talk me out of being mad at you." She clutched the umbrella and sulked, staring off to the side in a small form of rebellion.

"I would never do that." Stephen laced his tone thick with sarcasm and lowered onto the bench with a chuckle. He passed her a velvet box. "Especially, when gifts are much more affective."

"Oh!" Julia snatched the box from his fingers and opened it to find a strand of perfectly set pearls. "It's lovely." She held it up and turned her back for him to do the honor of placing it around her neck.

He'd hoped she would like it. It cost him a fair sum, but if he wanted to woo Julia, he knew she would expect expensive gifts. He hooked the catch.

She turned and smiled at him, one hand on the necklace. "You do know how to make me happy."

"I hope to make you even happier when I return."

Her eyes widened. "Only a fortnight, you gave me your word."

Stephen chuckled as he aided her to stand so he could escort her home. "I will do my best to return posthaste."

A ball crashed into her side. "Ow." Julia rubbed her hip.

A little tow-headed boy chased after it, skidding to a stop in front of them. "Sorry, guv'nor, me ball got away."

Julia inspected her dress for dirt, snapping, "Watch what you're doing."

"Now, Julia." Stephen's brows knit together, and he picked

up the ball. "I'm sure it was an accident." He spun the toy a couple of times in his hand and tossed it back to the boy.

"Thank you, guv'nor." The boy grinned at Stephen, exposing a gap earmarked for his two front teeth.

"Harrumph." Julia scowled at the dirt stain marring her gown and tucked her arm around Stephen's.

Her overreaction to the child's mistake darkened the sun like the clouds that threatened to rain. When he returned, they'd have a discussion about children and her plans on raising them before he proposed.

As they continued down the stone path through the park, a smile tugged at the corners of Stephen's lips. The image of the toothless, tow-headed boy stayed in his head. It was time he set up a nursery.

"I cannot marry him." Katherine spoke to herself as she twisted her mass of curls into a bun without bothering to summon her lady's maid. She didn't need a fancy coiffure to decline what might be her only chance at marriage, but spinsterhood would be preferable to a life with such an ill-mannered man. Tears sprang to her eyes, and her reflection in the mirror blurred, fracturing the colors of her bedchamber like a kaleidoscope. She blinked them away and stuck out her chin.

"Get a hold of yourself, Katherine." She straightened. "You've been in charge of an entire estate. You've taken the servants to task when they needed it, and you even fired the stable boy when he harassed the scullery maid. You should be proud of how assertive you've become in the past couple of years." Her shoulders slumped. Taking a stable boy to task was different than refusing her cousin's offer. She'd successfully avoided her cousin for two days since their interaction at his arrival, but Friday was approaching. The mere thought of confronting Horace caused her palms to perspire and her tongue to feel thick and cumbersome in her mouth. There was no guessing what his reaction would be.

"I'll just go down there and tell him that I respectfully decline. I've been caring for myself for three years now, and I will continue doing so." She plucked the miniature painting of her parents off her painted white bureau. Her index finger traced their outlines. "They wouldn't have wanted me to marry the likes of him. I know it."

Katherine's thoughts strayed to memories of her loving parents and how her papa had snuggled deep in her blanket tent, telling her a bedtime story, complete with a prince who would come to her rescue and whisk her away to his castle. Her mama had smiled and laughed when young Katherine tried to curtsy, dressed in one of Mama's ball gowns, with yards and yards of fabric swallowing her whole. Mama had brushed an unruly lock of hair from Katherine's forehead and said, "Too soon, you'll be grown and will marry a man as wonderful as your papa."

Katherine traced her mama's face with her finger. She resembled her mother with her long eyelashes and wide-set eyes, but their vivid green color came from her father, which she hoped compensated for the mass of untamable brown hair she'd also inherited from him. She'd often wished her hair was blond like Claire's. The gossip columns declared blond was all the rage this season.

Her bun didn't hold, so she scraped the large mass of waves off her face and secured them with a ribbon. She pinched her cheeks, hoping the rosy color would supersede the blackish-blue smudges under her eyes. Since her cousin's arrival, sleep had eluded her. In the dark of night, her cousin's voice echoed in her mind, *I forgot to mention we can be married on Friday*, and *Who else will have you since the Turner boy backed out?*

"You can do this." She set her jaw. "You *have* to do this."

With a deep breath to bolster her courage, Katherine raised

her chin and headed downstairs, but the quiet sound of her swishing skirts whispered, *you'll be alone.*

She found her butler, who informed her Horace was in the billiard room with a business partner. When she approached, their voices were muffled by the closed door. She knocked.

"Come in."

Katherine entered to find Horace seated with a stiff-looking fellow in a dark overcoat and a luxurious red silk waistcoat.

"They'll bring in a pretty penny before being shipped to France." Cousin Horace glanced up. "Ah, Katherine, my soon-to-be-bride." Horace extended his arm and waved her over. "I hope you have a special gown chosen for our big day tomorrow." He and his guest placed their hands of cards facedown. "Let me introduce you to my colleague, Lord Pewitt."

"Lady Dysart." Lord Pewitt nodded, his gaze lingering on her figure.

Heat warmed her cheeks from such scrutiny, and she hid her face with a slow curtsy.

"I haven't seen your sister, Claire. I'm assuming she'll be attending the wedding?"

Katherine forced her expression to remain blank, but her body released a silent sigh. Claire remained safe at finishing school, and he couldn't worry her if he didn't know her location. "Claire is visiting with friends." It wasn't a lie. She had friends at school.

"But the wedding is tomorrow. Surely she'll be here to see you walk down the aisle?"

"I'm afraid she won't be back in time."

"Pity. I know the two of you are quite close."

"Mr. Bainbridge." Katherine eyed Lord Pewitt before returning her gaze to her cousin. "I was hoping for a moment of your time."

"Of course, my dear." He flashed her a version of the grin that had won her cousin Madeline's heart. "But call me Horace.

We are, after all, to be married." He leaned back in his chair and crossed his arms over his chest.

Katherine glanced in Lord Pewitt's direction.

"I haven't all day." Horace also peered at his comrade, and her cousin's expression hardened before he turned to Katherine. "Whatever you have to say can be said in front of Lord Pewitt."

"Cousin Horace, I-I appreciate your offer, but I must respectfully decline."

His lips thinned and a muscle twitched in his jaw. "You merely have marriage jitters. It's understandable."

"It's not—"

"An old man like yourself, Bainbridge"—Lord Pewitt clapped his friend on the shoulder— "doesn't appeal to such a pretty, young thing. You may have been a Corinthian in your day, but the years have made you soft." His lips curled in a smirk. "You have options, my dear." Lord Pewitt removed his hand from Cousin Horace and adjusted his gold cufflink. "I understand they are limited since the Turner boy jilted you, but Bainbridge here is willing to step up and see to his duty." His eyes moved down over her curves. "Now that I've had a look at you, I might even be willing to sacrifice myself on the altar of marriage."

"See here." Horace twisted to face his associate. "I'm her guardian and will determine what is in Katherine's best interests."

Lord Pewitt's jaw tensed, and his gaze drifted from Katherine to Horace.

Her cousin's hand curled into a fist out of Lord Pewitt's view. A moment passed before Horace relaxed and used his formerly fisted hand to lightly brush his knuckle down the skin under her capped sleeve. "I realize this is sudden, but I'm marrying you for your own good. Your parents would have thanked me for my thoughtfulness." Horace glanced in Lord

Pewitt's direction as if to gauge his reaction. "You *will* obey me in this."

What power did Lord Pewitt hold over him?

It didn't matter. She wasn't interested in being manipulated by either man. "I have designed to be a spinster and will manage the estate on my own."

"Don't be a fool." Horace leapt from his seat and yanked her toward the doorway as if changing his mind and seeking privacy to finish their conversation. "You are a woman. You can't manage an estate as large as this without a husband."

Lord Pewitt cleared his throat and Horace halted between the bookshelf and the door.

"I've done—"

"This place is barely holding together." He leaned over her.

Katherine's jaw dropped. Barely holding together? How dare he? She gritted her teeth. "I've done more than merely keep my home intact. I had the fields properly irrigated, the horse fences mended, and I handled all the needs of the staff. And I did it on my own, without your help." Her chest heaved. "You didn't even bother to come to my parents' funeral."

Horace's face drained of color.

Katherine cupped her hand over her mouth. She'd gone too far.

His gaze flicked to Lord Pewitt, and his eyes grew wild. Katherine thought she saw a flash of fear in their depths.

He slapped her.

The force sent her sprawling across the floor. Sparks of light danced in her periphery, and her face burned like a lump of hot coal. She placed a hand on her cheek and felt the throbbing heat. There'd be swelling or a nasty bruise. Most likely both.

Never had anyone laid a hand on her person.

A wave of cold fear washed over her. Her instincts told her to flee. She grabbed her skirts and scrambled to get to her feet, but she wasn't fast enough. Her cousin grabbed her by the collar of her day dress and lifted her into the air. He slammed her against the wall with enough force to drive the air from her lungs, nearly missing the bookshelf.

He held her there, his hot breath blowing against her face. "You ungrateful brat."

Her tightened collar choked the air from her lungs, and she tugged at his grip.

"You will marry me tomorrow." His lips trembled, and his gaze skittered again to Lord Pewitt. "Or else..." He peered at the floor for a moment as if seeking a proper punishment. "I will compromise you here and now with Lord Pewitt as a witness." He finished as if proud of thinking up such a horrid consequence. His voice turned sinister. "Either way, you will marry me, whether you like it or not."

Lord Pewitt sat at the card table with an amused expression. He raised his glass to take a sip, neither voicing protest nor moving to aid her.

"Do you understand what I'm saying?"

Katherine snapped her gaze to Horace and either nodded or trembled. Whichever, it was enough for Horace, who relaxed his grip. Her feet touched the floor, and she pressed her palms against the papered wall to keep her knees steady.

"Now run along and don a pretty gown because we shall be dining with Lord Pewitt tonight." He turned her toward the door and smacked her backside to send her on her way.

Katherine's stomach rolled. What kind of hideous monster strikes a defenseless woman and threatens to ravish her publicly? Who uses manipulation to force a marriage? She resisted the urge to run. Instead, she tipped her chin in the air and walked with poise until she rounded the corner and bolted for the safety of her chamber.

Once she'd closed and locked the door, Katherine pressed her palms to her temples. Her world was falling apart. She paced the length of her bedchamber, trying to come up with a plan. She'd ask Denton to gather the footmen and throw both Horace and Lord Pewitt out on their ears. She strode to the door, placed a hand on the handle, and paused. Denton came from a long line of butlers who'd served the Dysart Earldom. If Cousin Horace was officially her guardian, then he could dismiss Denton. What would their faithful butler do then? Where would he go without a reference? Dysart's staff was her responsibility. Would she be forcing Denton into a life of destitution.

It was too much. How had her situation become so dire, so fast? How was she supposed to resolve a nightmare? She racked her brain. Who could she turn to? Her father's attorneys? They were in London. The town constable? From what she remembered, he was a close friend of Horace's. The servants couldn't protect her from her guardian without risking termination, and her only family was Claire who was a mere ten and seven years of age and over a day's ride away.

You can't do anything without help. The critical voice of her fiancée's mother taunted her.

Former fiancée. Alfred had cried their engagement off.

She strode to her jewelry box and emptied its contents into her reticule, along with all the pin money she'd put aside to provide her sister with a new trousseau for her season in London.

She gazed at the bedchamber she'd had since childhood, with its bright cheery yellow papered walls and lace curtains. The dolls she and Claire used to play with as young girls still sat in a chair in the corner. After her parents' deaths, she and Claire had slept curled on her canopy bed and dried each other's tears. They even learned to find laughter once more.

Their crazed cousin shouldn't be able to saunter in and steal their home and safe haven. She would find a way to prevent it even if it meant leaving temporarily. She wiped the moisture from her eyes.

The attorneys seemed her best bet. She'd ride to London and request a meeting to determine if Horace was her true guardian, and if so, what controls he held over her. If she remembered properly, there were certain funds he couldn't touch without the consent of her attorneys. Apprising them of his actions could delay or prevent Cousin Horace's access, and as a last resort, she could stay in hiding until she turned five and twenty and his guardianship ended.

Katherine donned her pelisse and kid gloves. As an afterthought, she grabbed the miniature picture of her parents and tucked it away into the pocket of her coat. With one last look, she bid the room a silent farewell and crept down to the front door.

Denton stood erect at his post. Katherine yanked down on the rim of her bonnet and held it tight against her face to keep him from noticing the red mark brandishing her cheek. She sashayed sideways up to the front entrance. If Denton learned of recent events, he may take action to defend her, and she needed him to remain here and ensure Steepleton Manor was protected.

"Good afternoon, Lady Dysart. May I say what a nice day for a carriage ride?"

"Denton, I know I can confide in you." She tugged his arm, and he leaned closer. "I must go away for a while. Stay here and keep things running smoothly. You must do whatever you must to look after the staff and Steepleton as your family has done for ages. I hope not to be gone long but keep a leery eye on Mr. Bainbridge and his companion. If he asks, inform him I have gone to visit Lady Frances for the afternoon. That I hoped to borrow her daughter's dress."

"Yes, my lady." The man straightened to stand proud as a ship's mast. "May I ask, is everything all right?"

Everything is wretched, her mind screamed, *I'm being threatened and forced to flee. Other than the solicitors in London, I don't know where to turn and I don't know how Steepleton will hold up in my absence.* Katherine swallowed past the lump in her throat and cast a glance back at the empty foyer. The responsibility of Steepleton had fallen upon her shoulders, and it was her duty to keep up appearances even if the walls crumbled around her. "I'm fine," she said and crossed over the threshold. After a few steps, she stilled on the stone landing. Denton was her butler but also her friend. How could she leave without saying goodbye? She grabbed his hand, keeping her head bowed. "Denton, I want you to know you're the most loyal butler a family could ask for. Keep the house safe while I'm out."

Denton puffed out his chest and stood straighter if that was even possible. "Thank you, my lady. It is my pleasure to be in your service."

Did she detect a hint of sadness in his tone? She longed to check his expression but needed to keep the nasty bruise hidden.

She strode to the stable instead of having a carriage pulled around but stopped at the sound of Lord Pewitt's voice resonating from around the back of the barn.

"Your temper got the better of you and has set us back a week. We'll have to wait for her bruising to fade before the vicar marries you."

She ducked into an open stall and crouched down.

They entered the stable and her cousin's voice lowered to a whisper. "We should have just stolen the horses. Forget this whole business of marrying the chit."

Katherine's lips parted in a silent gasp. Her papa's legacy was his Lipizzaner horses. .

"Pedigrees are worth rot without the papers." Lord Pewitt's tone sharpened. "Forgeries won't suffice. You don't want to upset these buyers."

"I don't see a way around her lawyers. They manage the Jenkins' fortune at least until the countess turns five and twenty or marries. Less questions are raised if the horses are transferred via marriage, but your plan isn't working."

"Then you need to become more convincing. Either woo her into marriage or force her hand by taking her to your bed. I don't care which but do it quickly."

Their voices grew distant as they passed and exited the stables. Katherine slipped out of the stall and trailed behind them to hear the rest of the conversation. She dared to peek through a window. Horace paused in the yard and said something she couldn't discern.

"If you want out, then go." Lord Pewitt's voice rose. "But since your bad luck at the tables, you don't even have a pocket to let. It seems to me that you have no choice but to chase after your cousin's inheritance. Unless you'd prefer debtor's prison."

Horace glanced around as if nervous someone overheard.

Katherine ducked below the window.

"I'm in." Her cousin's lips curled. "If getting my hands on the Jenkins Lipizzaner stallions wipes out my debts entirely."

Cousin Horace was in debt?

Lord Pewitt rumbled a low chuckle. "Perhaps, but the deal isn't done yet."

A young groom rode back from exercising one of the horses. "What ken I do for ya, my lady?"

She peeked at her cousin and Lord Pewitt to make certain they were far enough away not to hear her. She waited a moment for them to reach the house. "I'd like a carriage readied and be quick about it."

He bowed. "Right away, my lady. Let me wake the coachman. He takes a quick nap in the hay loft after the noon meal." He climbed the ladder and stirred the sleeping man.

She cast a few nervous glances at the house, but all remained silent. Twisting the strings on her reticule, she scanned her family's sprawling estate. Her father's prized horses grazed in the field. A few of the Lipizzaner stallions drank from the nearby creek bed, their coats glistening in the afternoon sun while others romped in the tall grass. Her favorite mare, Sugar-and-Spice, must have caught wind of her because her ears perked up as she raised her head toward Katherine. Her tiny foal suckled at her teat. Katherine lifted a hand in farewell but resisted the urge to walk over and give the horse one last loving pat.

The groom opened the coach door and waited to assist Katherine to her seat. The carriage pulled away, and the only home she'd ever known faded into the distance. A sob escaped her throat, but she gave herself a mental shake. She had to be brave and keep a clear head for what would come next.

She was on her own.

CHAPTER 3

*K*atherine tapped on the roof of the coach, and the driver slowed the team. In front of the groom, she'd instructed him to drive her to Lady Frances's to borrow a gown in case the groom was questioned about her whereabouts later. But now, she informed the driver that the London offices of her papa's attorneys would be her destination.

Should she go to the authorities first? Would they help her or take her cousin's side? What would she tell them? That they should arrest the man because he wanted to force her hand in marriage? The chances of anyone listening to her, much less believing her story, were slim, especially since Cousin Horace was friendly with the constable. The best course of action would be to first seek legal counsel.

She snuggled into the coach cushions. Out the window, an embankment sloped down to a river running parallel to the road. It swirled in its torrent. The waters were bursting over their banks from all the rain they'd had of late. Trees flashed by as the coach picked up speed. She closed her eyes to block out the dizzying spin of the debacle her life had become. Let the feeling be due to motion sickness and not the case of nerves she'd been fighting since her encounter with her cousin. Why were men so unpredictable? Other than her own father, the few men she'd known left her life in upheaval.

A gunshot pierced the air. The horses whinnied, and the coach lurched. Katherine dropped to the floor. A cold sweat broke over her body. Had Horace sent someone after her? Was the gunshot a warning to get the driver's attention?

I will not marry a monster.

She pulled herself up to peek through the back curtain, fearing she'd see her deranged cousin. Instead, three men on horseback with kerchiefs over their faces galloped at full speed, attempting to overtake the coach.

"Highwaymen?" She crouched on the floorboards and dumped the contents of her reticule onto the seat cushion. Leaving a few coins behind to throw off suspicion, she stuffed the majority of her pin money down the front of her dress. She would need the funds if she and her sister were to stand a chance of survival. She prayed the robbers wouldn't check her person.

The coach shook from its breakneck pace, and she braced herself as it rocked on two wheels. Keeping low, she stretched to pull aside the curtain and see how the footman fared. Another shot rang out, and the driver's body jolted. Blood spilled before he pitched over the side. His lifeless body rolled down the steep embankment.

Mr. Lewis! Katherine clapped a hand over her mouth to suppress her scream. She inched upward to gauge the road ahead. With no one driving the coach, how would she slow the horses? And if she could somehow slow them, what then—die at the hands of highwaymen like her faithful driver?

The frightened horses barreled forward. A sharp turn lay directly in their path, and the horses would have to slow to make the turn. She had to jump. That may be her only chance to escape.

The bandits drew up along the coach's right side. One swiped at the horse's reins but missed. *Please let them be too preoccupied to notice her sneaking out the other side.* She gripped the handle and struggled to open the door against the airflow.

The turn approached fast, and Katherine wedged the coach door open. The ground rushed under her feet, and the wind ripped at her bonnet. Tendrils of her hair whipped about her face. She would be lucky to survive this.

Who would care for her sister? Would Horace try the same ploy with Claire as he had with her? She couldn't let that happen. Someone had to warn her.

I can't die, not now. Lord, help me.

With an abrupt lurch, the coach tilted on two wheels and dragged the horses off the side of the road, where they lost their footing on the steep embankment. Katherine's grip on the door tore away, and she soared through the air. She hit the embankment and the impact shot pain through her side, jarring her spine and sending excruciating shock waves up her neck. She wrapped her arms to protect her face as she rolled down the steep slope for several yards before sliding feet-first toward a river. Buried rocks bruised her back as Katherine searched for anything to slow her descent. A low branching pine tree was her only hope before she'd be thrown into the rushing water below. Using all her strength, Katherine flung herself toward the pine tree. She seized one of the limbs. The force nearly ripped her arms from their sockets, but she jerked to a stop as her legs skidded over the embankment's edge. The river rushed beneath her, splashing droplets of water onto her boots and hem. Pine needles jabbed her hands and wrists, but she clung to the branch and scrambled for a foothold amid the tree's emerging roots.

A loud splash sounded about a field's length ahead to her

right. Her carriage plunged into the river. The horses's hooves clawed at the steep, muddy embankment as the heavy coach sank.

The muscles in her arms stung under the load of her own weight. Her feet flailed in the air until one caught a tree root. She hand-over-hand pulled herself up the branch and heaved the lower half of her body onto flat land under the pine tree. She grabbed ahold of the tree trunk and squeezed it like a frightened child hugging a beloved doll. Exhausted, she lay there, listening to her heart pounding and rapid breaths.

Nothing felt broken. Her hands were badly scratched and bleeding, and her dress was dirty and torn. She ached everywhere, but she would survive.

I'm alive. Thank you, Lord. She pressed her forehead against the rough bark and let tears trail down her cheeks. She rested a few moments to gain her bearings.

Rocks tumbled past, clunking off roots and other larger rocks before splashing into the water below. She held perfectly still.

"I don't see anything this way," one of the bandits yelled to another. "She must still be in the coach." The man skidded to a stop a few feet from her.

Katherine hugged the tree's trunk closer, praying the dense, low-lying evergreen branches would hide her from view. A black beetle crawled over her hand, tickling her skin, but she dared not move for fear of giving away her position.

A splash sounded and a man yelled. "She's not in the coach."

"Blast." Another voice yelled, "Get them 'orses before they drown and keep an eye on the water. If Pewitt finds out we lost 'er, we won't live long enough to tell about it. If we can't bring 'er back, then we need proof she's dead."

Lord Pewitt. Her cousin *had* sent the bandits. He wanted her dead. The blood in her veins turned colder than a northern winter, and she gritted her teeth to keep them from chattering.

"With this current, 'er body could be a mile downstream," shouted the man a mere foot from her. His square-toed boots kicked at the loose dirt, sending more stones into the river and puffing a small dust cloud into Katherine's face. She stifled a cough.

A third voice yelled, "Search downriver, but keep a lookout for any signs of 'er. I swear I saw somethin' when the carriage went over."

The men picked their way up the embankment. As the last of them disappeared around the bend, Katherine dared to catch her breath.

Her cousin had sent men to kill her.

Were there no lengths to which Horace wouldn't go?

She remained in her hideaway for what felt like hours afraid they might return.

Finally, she pulled herself upright and stood to test her legs. Her right foot tingled with pins and needles from the lack of blood flow, and her left leg ached when she put all her weight on it, but she must press through. She crawled up the embankment and peeked around a bush for any sign of the hired assassins.

Birds squawked at her, flitting from tree to tree. Katherine hobbled down the road. It wasn't long before she reached the fork in the bend. The right path led toward Lady Frances's house, but she chose the left, leading out of town toward her sister in Sherborne. Hopefully, Horace would assume she was either dead or had taken refuge at the elderly woman's estate.

If her cousin believed her dead, would he next go after Claire? Was Claire in immediate peril? She must warn her sister before Horace or Pewitt found her. Katherine picked up her pace ignoring the pain in her ankle. Cousin Horace didn't know where Claire attended school. The only people who'd know the school she attended was her lady's maid, who went with Claire to attend to Claire's needs while at school, and then Mr. Lewis who'd driven her, but they'd killed him.

Bile rose in her throat at the remembrance of his limp body pitching over the carriage and sliding down the embankment.

Several times, Katherine hid in the underbrush as a carriage passed. She dared not summon anyone for help for fear they would notify the constable, who'd return her to her cousin. Sherborne stood a day's ride by carriage, but it would take much longer by foot. If she could trek a couple towns over, it might then be safe to ask for help, otherwise she'd have to find a barn or someplace safe to sleep for the night unnoticed. Thankfully, no one stopped or even slowed on the rural road. Afternoon slid into evening, and the once beautiful bright blue sky now eerily glowed red and purple. Clouds moved in. The air smelled heavy of rain, and the wind picked up. Katherine's ankle throbbed from exertion, and she scowled at the impending storm clouds.

Distant thunder rumbled in response. She tugged her pelisse tighter around her shoulders. The sun had just set when the sky opened, and a torrent of rain poured out, soaking her in seconds. Katherine's bonnet flopped in her face. The wind whipped her skirts, and she fought against it with bones that protested her exhaustion and a stomach that growled in hunger. At least the cold numbed the aching pain of her ankle to a dull throb, but it hindered her walking. Several times she stumbled. Her falls coated her knees and hem in mud.

Night settled and visibility declined. She needed to find shelter before she froze. In the distance, an echoing of horses' hooves pounded the road. She spun in the direction of the sound and wiped the rainwater from her face to clear her vision.

A lantern floated in the darkness approaching like a specter in a vision, but when she blinked, it was gone.

Find a place to hide.

Her feet no longer cooperated.

A large boulder came into view, and she stumbled toward it. Her boot caught in the hem of her gown. She raised her hands to protect her head from the rock, but she was too slow, too late. A sickening thud, a flash of light, and blinding pain propelled her into darkness.

---

*T*he shaking of the ground stirred Katherine. What was that shaking? A carriage? She needed to hide. But when she tried to move, pain seared her head. Rainwater puddled around her. She must get up or she'd drown. She had to warn Claire.

"There was a girl." A woman's voice rose above the pounding rain. "I saw her in the flash of lightning."

"No one in their right mind would be out in this weather." The man's sharp tone cautioned Katherine to run. "Maybe you should get a pair of spectacles."

Katherine tried to stir, but her movements felt sluggish and nauseating dizziness swept over her as she attempted to lift her head.

She must get to Claire. She must.

"I know what I saw, Charles," The woman's voice yelled over the rain.

Were the strangers friends of Cousin Horace's—sent to finish her off?

"Are you out of your mind?" The man said. "Get back in the coach." Boots splashed into a puddle, and Katherine forced her eyes to open a sliver and followed the glow. Lantern light reflected off a multitude of tiny raindrops, but she couldn't tell if the shadows were people, trees, or rocks until they moved.

"Over there. Shine the light over by that rock," said the female voice.

"Well, I'll be. It *is* a woman." The man called Charles bellowed for someone to follow him.

The woman crouched close and placed a warm gloved hand on Katherine's arm. "Don't fret, dear. We've got you. Help is here."

Katherine struggled against eyelids that wanted to close.

"Hold the carriage door open." Warm arms wrapped Katherine in a tight hold as she was carried to a coach and laid across a seat.

"She must be frozen solid, poor thing," said the woman. "Let's get her home quickly."

A cane tapped on the carriage's rooftop, and the conveyance sprung to life. Katherine's head threatened to split apart by the jostling, and she struggled to remain conscious.

"Something terrible must have happened. Look at that ugly bruise on her cheek and the bump on her head. Oh, Charles— look at her hands. They're cut and scratched." She clicked her tongue. "The poor thing." A warm hand cradled Katherine's cheek. "There, there, dearie, everything is going to be all right. You're with us now, and we'll take care of you."

Darkness sucked Katherine under, much like the churning river had pulled under her carriage.

CHAPTER 4

Katherine bid her mama and papa farewell, and they each pressed a gentle kiss onto her forehead. Her mother's smile held the same radiance as the diamond bracelet shining from her gloved wrist. Mama blew her one more kiss and climbed into the coach after Papa. They waved at Katherine from the window, and the coach rumbled off down the lane.

Katherine hiked up her skirts and ran after it "I love you." Her legs pumped as hard as they could. Her lungs burned from exertion, but she wasn't gaining any ground. She continued to drag her un-cooperating feet as if through thick mud, but the coach pulled farther away.

Dark shadows materialized from the gully to her left. Three ominous men on horseback galloped off after the coach. She screamed, "*Mama! Papa!*" but the tightness in her throat, like a hangman's noose, strangled her words. A sob escaped and tears burned her eyes as the coach and riders drifted out of sight.

Katherine turned her head into the pillow and willed herself to wake from her nightmare. A calm woman's voice whispered close by, and Katherine stilled.

"Lord God, please place a healing hand on this young woman. Be with her. Help her to know she is safe. I lift her up to you, God. When she wakes, please reassure her that she is in your care."

Katherine fluttered her eyelids open, curious about who was praying and desperate to believe the soothing words. She blinked, squinting at the cheery sunlight streaming through a nearby window. Outside the paned glass, the world blurred pinks and greens. She blinked again, and the branches of a blossoming cherry tree came into focus. She turned her head but doing so brought white-hot streaks of pain over the left side of her skull. She winced and closed her eyes.

"You have a bit of a lump on your head. The doctor bandaged it but said you'd have quite a headache when you woke up."

Katherine dared to open one eye and then the other and saw a sweet round face with gentle blue eyes crinkled with laugh lines. The woman's peppered white and gray hair was loosely knotted in a bun.

"There now, you take it easy and rest." Her hand smoothed several strands of hair off of Katherine's face.

Katherine relaxed into the warmth of the coverlet. "Where am I?"

"Willowstone Farm."

She struggled to sit up, but the woman stilled her with a wrinkled hand. "You're our guest and welcome to stay as long as you like."

Mustering a weak smile she hoped would show her appreciation, Katherine asked, "Do I know you?"

"Oh, heavens, where are my manners? I'm Lady Felton."

Katherine recognized the name. The Earl of Felton resided several towns away. She'd made it farther than she realized. Mama had mentioned the earl and his wife and what a pity that they hadn't traveled to London for the season in over a decade, something about an injury making traveling difficult. "Pleasure to meet you." Katherine's voice sounded like she eaten coarse sandpaper. She coughed and cleared her throat.

"You gave us quite a scare." Lady Felton patted the coverlet. "We found you unconscious by the side of the road."

Unconscious. She remembered the wind-driven rain and, in her plight, succumbing to total exhaustion. She tried to remember what happened but pounding like a marching infantry thrummed inside her head, and she winced.

"Oh, I beg your pardon. I shouldn't have troubled you so. You needn't worry about a thing, merely rest." Lady Felton held out a cup. "Here, try to swallow a bit of tea."

Katherine eased herself up on the pillows, cautious not to jar her head. She accepted the cup and maneuvered it with bandaged hands. Someone had addressed all the scratches from her slide down the embankment.

"I've introduced myself, but I still don't know who you are." Lady Felton tilted her head. "What is your name, dear?"

The teacup froze halfway to Katherine's lips. Katherine's mind whirled. She wanted to trust Lady Felton but look where trust had gotten her in the past. What if Lady Felton knew Cousin Horace? She'd be obligated to send for him. The throbbing in Katherine's head increased. She didn't contain the strength to face him. If only she could hide here, wherever here is, for a few days to regain her energy. But what about Claire? Would she be in danger? No, her cousin wouldn't know where to find Claire. Thank heaven the Sherborne Finishing School for Young Ladies Decorum was too long to write, and she'd abbreviated any notations in the ledgers as FS. If Katherine could pen her sister to warn her, then maybe they both could remain safe from their wretched cousin.

Katherine's lips parted to speak but she closed them. Surely Lady Felton would recognize the Jenkins name and send her back to her guardian. Should Katherine make up a name or speak the truth? The throbbing increased to pounding. Thinking wrapped her skull in a band of pain, and tears of exhaustion sprang to her eyes. Should she tell the truth, refuse to say, or lie about her identity? "I'm..." She looked away. "I'm..."

Lady Felton's hand covered her mouth. "Oh my. You poor dear. Your head injury might be worse than the doctor thought." She shook her head. "I've heard of this sort of thing before. I had a distant relative who endured something similar. He was unseated from his horse and landed on his head. After that, he didn't know who he was and couldn't recognize his family—not a one. The doctor called it amnesia. My heavens, you might be suffering from memory loss."

Lady Felton stood and paced, tapping her index finger on her chin and looking up at the ceiling. "I believe his memory returned after a week or two, which may mean it's merely temporary, but I'll send again for the physician. Don't fret about a thing, dear. You rest up."

Katherine fumbled for words. Should she correct her and tell the truth? Or pretend to suffer from amnesia until she could weigh her situation and options?

Amnesia would be convenient. Thank heavens she'd listened when her father prodded on about new findings and studies in his medical journals. He'd read several articles on amnesia, and she frantically tried to recall the symptoms.

Lady Felton tucked the covers around Katherine and bestowed a loving smile. "God is watching over you, and I'm praying you rest in His care." She patted Katherine on the leg, then stepped out of the room.

God. Katherine had frantically pleaded for His protection yesterday. Before that, though, she hadn't thought about Him in years, not since her parents' deaths. They had taken her to church every Sunday and dutifully said the mealtime and bedtime prayers, but once they passed, Katherine found she couldn't pray anymore. How could she pray to a God that allowed her parents to be taken from her? Instead, she lashed out at Him as she cried a flood of tears, *why did He let them die?* But God hadn't answered, so Katherine had busied herself with taking care of her sister and the management of the estate.

God is watching over you.

Would Lady Felton still think He was watching over her if she knew how Cousin Horace had attacked her and sent hired men to kill her? Katherine considered herself fortunate to have survived being thrown from the carriage, only nearly to freeze to death in the rain. If God was watching over her, He was doing a poor job.

A yawn forced its way out, stretching her mouth, and her eyelids became heavy. It wasn't her fault that Lady Felton made a hasty conclusion about amnesia. She hadn't lied, merely allowed for a misunderstanding. But misleading such a sweet woman didn't feel right. How would she keep up the charade? And for how long?

Then again, maybe the misconception was a fortunate boon. It would allow her identity and whereabouts to remain secret. She just needed to post a letter to Claire to stay put, and no matter what, not to trust their cousin. Or would it be best not to frighten her and write to warn Madame Lamoureux, the headmistress, of their cousin's misdeeds? The school would have the staff to keep Claire safe. The pain wracking Katherine's head sapped the last of her energy and sleep overtook her. Katherine's last thoughts were that, maybe, God did do her a small favor.

Or maybe He just wanted a good laugh.

---

*K*atherine awoke to a sigh and tapping of fingernails on hardwood. She pretended to sleep, but curiosity got the best of her. She cracked open one eyelid the tiniest bit and tried to identify her mysterious company by peeking through her eyelashes.

"Oh, good. You're awake."

Caught. Katherine opened her eyes.

A perky brunette sat in a chair next to the bed. Straight, dark-mahogany hair hung down past her shoulders with a few loose finger-curls at the ends. She appeared slightly older than Katherine, and a gold band circling the non-tapping finger revealed she was of a marriageable age.

Katherine's own hair must look atrocious, and her hand itched to smooth it into place.

Long eyelashes framed the woman's wideset ice-blue eyes, which inspected Katherine as if she'd never seen another human being before.

"Mother told me to check on you but not to wake you," the pretty brunette said. "So, I've been patiently waiting for you to wake up. Unfortunately, patience is not a virtue God gave me much of, so I'm pleased you're awake."

Katherine chuckled. The woman's impatient tapping of her fingernail had woken her.

Her rosy lips broke into a warm smile. "I'm Abigail, but everyone calls me Abby. Mother says you may have am... am..." Her eyebrows drew together. "Am-something."

"Amnesia?"

"Amnesia, yes. See, your memory must be improving. It's already better than mine." She laughed, and Katherine instantly took to the young woman.

"So, what should we call you?" Abby asked.

To what extent did amnesia affect a person's memory? Katherine's pulse picked up its pace. Would a person forget her own name? Lady Felton had seemed to believe so.

Abby leaned forward in her chair, inspecting Katherine's face. "Hmm, let's see. Do you look like a Rebecca?" She pursed her lips. "Becca? No, I don't think so. How about Elizabeth?

Betty? Hmm, maybe Mary Frances." She frowned slightly. "No, not Mary. Maybe Katie or Kate?"

Katherine's lips parted in a silent gasp at the nickname her sister used for her.

"Kate. Yes. You absolutely look like a Kate, so that's what we'll call you." Abby's grin widened. "When you're feeling up for it, maybe tomorrow or the next day, we can take a stroll, and I'll show you around the farm."

"This is a farm?"

"A horse farm. You probably thought it was awfully quiet for an animal farm." She giggled. "Papa and my brother dapple in breeding and training horses. Not so much Papa since his accident, but we have a new thoroughbred coming in this week, and my brother will be home to oversee things."

A wave of homesickness washed over Katherine. How long would she be away from Steepleton Manor and its stables? Mr. Peters, the head groom, would be doing double duty without her help. Would he be able to keep the horses active in her absence?

"Abigail." Lady Felton's voice rang from the door. "Didn't I tell you not to wake our guest?"

"I didn't." She put her hand over her heart. "I promise." She stood and stepped aside, giving her mother a clear view of Katherine. "We decided she shall be called Kate."

Lady Felton glanced at Katherine to confirm it was a joint decision.

Katherine hoped her approval showed in her eyes because her head still ached too much to nod.

"Kate is a fine name. At least until she remembers her true one." Lady Felton waved her daughter out of the room. "Abby, why don't you let Kate get some rest?"

"Yes, Mama."

Lady Felton hung a muslin day gown in the wardrobe. "Here's a dress Abby has outgrown. I believe you're slightly smaller than she, so it may be a tad long, but we can have it hemmed."

"Couldn't you at least find her something a little more fashionable?" Abby frowned at the gown. "Waistlines have dropped at least two inches since I wore that."

Lady Felton closed the wardrobe doors. "I didn't want to take any of the dresses you still wear without permission."

"Don't worry, Kate." Abby patted Katherine's hand. "I'll find you some fashionable gowns." She rose and strode from the room on a mission.

"Abby has always been excitable. She moves like a whirlwind and has never been able to sit in one place long." Lady Felton sighed, but a loving smile touched the corners of her lips. "Tonight, I'll have you take dinner in your room, but tomorrow, if you feel up for it, we'd be delighted to have you join us downstairs for breakfast."

"That would be lovely." A lump formed in Katherine's throat. How considerate of them to include her, a stranger. She had nothing to offer them in return, yet they treated her like family. The sting of missing her parents magnified.

Lady Felton patted her on the leg, "All right then, get some rest. I'll come and check on you later."

Katherine waited until the door closed with a click before she eased out of bed. Every muscle in her body ached, and her head spun, but standing felt good. She padded on bare feet across the room, favoring her ankle, and opened the wardrobe. Thank goodness her clothes hung there beside Abby's highwaisted gown. She fumbled through the pockets. During her long walk, she'd fished her petty cash out of her bodice and settled it into her pocket next to the picture of her parents. Her fingers encountered a corner of the small frame and the hard mound of her purse, and her muscles relaxed.

A light knock sounded, and the door cracked open. "I forgot."

Katherine froze.

Lady Felton poked her head around the corner. "I came upstairs to mention that the physician will be here..." She peered at the empty bed. "Kate?" She spied Katherine with her hands in the pockets of her ruined clothes. "Is everything all right?" Lady Felton's forehead wrinkled.

"Quite," Katherine replied with a bit too much enthusiasm. She lowered the volume of her voice. "I was merely looking to see if anything in the pockets might help trigger my memory."

Lady Felton stared at Katherine. "Did you find anything?"

Katherine swallowed and shook her head. She hated lying, but there was no way around this one.

"You checked all the pockets?"

She nodded. She couldn't show Lady Felton what was hidden in her pelisse. At the very least, she'd wonder what a young woman was doing with so much money on her person. Worse, she'd recognize the picture of her parents and send her back home to her cousin.

"There wasn't anything?"

Had the servant who'd undressed her in her unconscious state discovered the contents and reported it to Lady Felton? "Uh, no." Her tone wavered with the lack of confidence. "No such luck."

"I see." Her expression remained tight. "Well then, get some rest. I'll wake you when our physician arrives."

Katherine nodded and clasped her hands together to keep them from shaking. She wanted to crawl under the covers and hide there for the rest of the day.

Lady Felton left, closing the door behind her, and Katherine padded to a small desk on the other side of the room by the window. She needed to write to Madame Lamoureux to warn her to keep Claire safe under the care of the finishing school until Katherine could come for her. She pulled open the drawers and peeked through their contents. Spying writing paper and a quill, she let out a quiet "hurrah," and sat in the chair, and quickly penned her letter.

Dear Madame Lamoureux,

There has been a severe turn of events. Our cousin, Mr. Horace Bainbridge, has tried to lay claim to our estate, and has attempted to have me killed. I'm writing to you because I don't want to worry Claire. I am safe, but I fear he may come for Claire. He is not to be trusted. I feel Claire will be safest under the strict watch of the finishing school, but please, do not allow any visitors to call upon her until further notice. Horace Bainbridge is well connected, and we can no longer be certain of who is friend or foe. Under no circumstances should Claire leave the premises or wander alone. Until further notice, please send correspondences to the postmaster under the name of Miss Sweetgoer. I will come for Claire as soon as possible. In the meantime, keep her safe under your directive.

Sincerely,
Countess of Dysart

Katherine removed another sheet of paper to write to Claire because her sister would be expecting to hear from her. Katherine tugged on her bottom lip. How much should she tell her? She didn't want to frighten her sister or cause her undo worry, but Claire needed to be on her guard and not write home giving away her location. Katherine dipped the quill and wrote that their cousin was staying at Steepleton, temporarily managing the estate while she handled an issue a few towns over and instructed her to send her letters to the postmaster.

A third letter, she addressed to their solicitors apprising

them of the circumstances and asked them to contact her immediately, once again, giving the postmaster as an address. She folded the letters and addressed them. Dripping wax from a nearby candle, she sealed their contents and allowed them to cool before tucking them into the pocket of her pelisse in the wardrobe. After she set the small desk in order, she climbed into the soft bed and pulled the covers to her chin. How was she going to mail the letters? Her convenient amnesia story did not allow her to recall the names and addresses of loved ones. She needed a creative excuse to go into town and secretly post them.

Time was of the essence.

CHAPTER 5

Stephen clenched his teeth and pulled out his pocket watch, growling under his breath. His lead horse had picked up a stone, which had set them back several hours. A half day had been lost searching for a blacksmith, seeing the hoof set to rights, and giving the horse time to recover.

His carriage rolled up the drive of Willowstone Manor, but he'd misplaced the key to his parents' home, and now it was well past midnight. He wished his mother weren't so insistent upon locking the doors each night. Since his father's accident, she'd needed a little extra reassurance. "It's merely a deterrent to keep someone from the temptation of sinning," she'd say. His mother was a light sleeper. If he aroused the staff, she would surely wake from her slumber and create a ruckus.

The horses were brought around to the stables, and two young groomsmen woke, blinking heavy eyelids, to rub down the horses.

Henderson, his valet, alighted from his perch next to the coachman, but Stephen stopped him before he unloaded his trunks. "Wait here while I find a way inside."

"Certainly, my lord." Henderson nodded and stretched his old joints after the long ride.

Stephen headed toward the servant's entrance of the house. If it wasn't unlocked, then perhaps he could rouse a scullery maid who might be sleeping near the hearth to unlock it. He inhaled a deep breath, savoring the aromas of horseflesh, wet dew on the grass, and his mother's lilac bushes with all their syrupy sweetness.

The house was dark, but the full moon lit up the cobblestone walkway. Crickets chirped comforting night music, and owls called out in a hooting duet. Nostalgia crept over him like morning fog in the glen. How different this was from the hubbub of the city. He'd resided in London for over four years, periodically traveling home to maintain, train, and breed horses as the reginal Cotswold's sheep herding and trading dwindled. Since most of their tenants had been sheep farmers, times had gotten tough, and his family needed to subsidize the lost income. His constant traveling back and forth grew weary. It was time to move home.

He missed his family and the horses. Now that he'd established enough connections in London, saved a small pot from his spying commissions, and built up a reputation for the farm, he could run things from Willowstone Manor with minimal visits to London. He merely hoped he'd heard God correctly on the new direction to take the farm.

Stephen neared the ivy-covered stone house and tested the servant's entrance door. Locked. He raised his hand to lightly knock, but an idea surfaced—the cherry tree. A half smile tugged the corner of his mouth. He used to sneak in and out of the house as a mischievous young buck on holiday from Eton but hadn't climbed its branches in an age.

He wandered past the back portico to the guest wing and spied the old cherry tree intact. *Thank God for small favors.*

Surprisingly, his father had never bothered to have it

chopped down or its branches trimmed. Stephen inspected its limbs for the best approach and scaled the trunk, careful to put his weight on only the thickest sections. He weighed a few stones heavier than the scrawny boy of his youth.

Reaching the house's second floor, he side-stepped his way down the branch, judged the distance, and mapped out his landing before he sucked in a deep breath and leapt to the small ledge. The roof line cut into his upper chest, and his fingers gripped at the rake boards underneath. His left foot slipped on some small pebbles, and he thrust his body toward the house, hugging the exterior wall.

Adrenaline surged through him in pulsing shockwaves, tingling his fingertips.

That was close.

His well-polished boots scraped over dirt and broken slate roof tiles as he inched along to the window. He leaned his weight against the wall once more, and he held his breath as his fingers fiddled with the sash. A gentle breeze washed over him, ruffling his hair and cooling the beads of sweat on his forehead.

Finally, he raised the sash and sent up a silent prayer of thanks before easing himself inside.

Strange noises pulled Katherine from a deep sleep. She ran her hands up the smooth sheets of the bed and frowned when the scabs on her palms caught on the material. The physician had removed her bandages that afternoon, but she forgot about her injuries in her hazy dream state until the scabs threatened to pull off and bleed. She folded her hands, tucking them under her pillow. She'd started to drift back to sleep when the scratching noise began again.

Her eyelids shot open, and she sat up in bed. Her ears

strained against the silence, waiting for another sound and hoping she'd hear it over the pounding of her heart. The branches of the cherry tree rustled and scraped the glass panes with an unearthly sound. She'd almost convinced herself the wind had caused the noise—until something thudded against the exterior wall, followed by a grunt.

A man's grunt.

Someone was on the ledge outside the window.

She threw back the covers and sprang to her feet, refusing to let dizziness overtake her. A large silver candlestick rested on the small desk, and she snatched it up, wielding it over her head. Pressing herself flat against the wall with the window on her right, she prayed she was out of view. Had one of her cousin's hitmen found her and come to finish the deed?

Should she cry for help? Was her bedchamber close enough for someone to get to her before the bandit? Or should she stay quiet and try to hide? The wardrobe across the room beckoned. Could she make it? Would she fit?

The window squeaked and the sill raised.

A scream stuck in her throat.

A tall, hulking form of a man squeezed through.

His back was toward her. She held her breath and willed him not to notice her. He tossed the curtains aside and stepped into the chamber. His head swiveled toward the disheveled bedclothes, and her stomach plummeted like a barrel over a waterfall. The bright moon illuminated the man's chiseled features and square jawline. She watched his brows draw together as if perplexed.

Wind rustled the curtains, and the movement drew his attention. He glanced in her direction. *Drat!* Katherine brought the candlestick crashing down with all her might.

"Who...?" With quick reflexes, his arm flew up to deflect the brunt of the blow. "Ow!" He grabbed the candlestick with his other hand and jerked it forward, throwing Katherine off balance.

She sailed across the floor, landing face-first on the bed.

The man pounced. He pinned her arms behind her. When she struggled and cried out, he put his knee in the small of her back and used his free hand to push her head into the covers.

Katherine screamed, but the bed swallowed the sound. She bucked with all her might but didn't stand a chance against his brute strength.

"Settle down." He spoke into her ear with a deep masculine voice.

She writhed and twisted, determined to die fighting.

"I promise to let you up if you promise not to scream."

Katherine stilled, and he lessened the pressure on her head. She nodded to buy herself time to think. True to his word, he released her and stood, backing away a step.

Katherine rolled to face her assailant and pushed off the bed, inhaling to release her loudest scream. Only a tiny squeak escaped before he cupped his hand over her mouth and pressed her face into his hard chest.

Her teeth sank into the fleshy part of his hand, and she thrashed against his hard frame with all her might.

He tightened his hold. "Listen."

Her meager attempts to free herself didn't seem to do anything but upset him.

"I don't know who you are or what you're doing in my parents' house, but I'd like to get to the bottom of this without disturbing their sleep. Hold still and keep quiet."

Katherine froze. *His parents' house?*

CHAPTER 6

*T*he words jarred Katherine into compliance. Abby had mentioned her twin brother ran the farm and had been expected to arrive that day. Had she just attacked the son of her hospitable hosts?

He slowly removed his hand but kept a firm grip on her shoulder. With his thumb and index finger, he tilted her face toward him. His chiseled features were drawn into harsh lines and angles highlighted by the glow of moonlight. His jaw clenched, and a blazing inferno flared in his eyes.

Her muscles tensed with the instinct to flee, and she eyed the doorway.

"Don't even think about it." He reached for the desk, slightly dipping her, and grabbed a match from the drawer. His gaze remained on hers, and he raised a single eyebrow that distinctly told her not to move as he bent to retrieve the candlestick and candle that had tumbled onto the floor.

Her chest heaved from exertion, and she focused on slowing her breaths while he lit the candle and held it in one hand.

Pulling a chair next to the bed, he gestured for her to sit.

She complied but chose to perch on the very edge of the mattress in case she needed to make a quick run for it.

He set the candle on the desk, yanked the chair from underneath, and lowered onto the seat. Crossing his ankle over his knee, he closed his eyes and rubbed his palm where she'd bit him. "My apologies for frightening you. I try not to make it a habit to scare the guests."

She nodded. At least she hoped she did, but it might have been her body trembling. In the additional light, he didn't look quite as frightening. His hair was the color of dark chocolate, his face tanned from the sun. He was impeccably dressed in a white cambric shirt and buckskin breeches. She should have been able to relax now that she wasn't in immediate danger, but her pulse thumped at a quick pace and her skin tingled. Something about him set her on edge. His masculine presence changed the air in the room, and the panther-like way he moved made her stomach flutter like the leaves on the trees before a storm.

Dropping his hands to his sides, he opened his eyes and peered at her.

Katherine bit her lip so she wouldn't gasp. His eyes, the same stunning, ice-blue as his sister's, held her in check. His eyelashes were thick, and the contrast of the dark eyelashes with the light eye color drew her like a candle flame. He was quite handsome.

His gaze dropped lower and then leapt back up to her face.

Katherine gasped, and heat flooded her face. She was sitting there in nothing but borrowed nightclothes. She snatched the closest blanket and pulled it around herself like a cocoon, clutching the ends to her chest so only her head and neck remained exposed.

He seemed amused by her modesty and issued a vexing half-smile. "Who are you?" His penetrating gaze never left hers.

"I'm..." Her dizziness returned with force, leaving her off-balance. Rational thought eluded her like a hot air balloon floating into the clouds. What had Abby called her? "Oh yes, I'm Kate."

"Kate?" he repeated, with a half smirk, half grin.

A lady wouldn't use her given name with a stranger. Katherine swallowed, realizing her error too late, but she said nothing to correct it.

"Are you a house guest of my parents?"

Katherine raised her chin in the slightest of nods.

He leaned forward, resting his forearms on his thighs. His face was only a few inches from hers.

She bit her bottom lip and leaned away, afraid his closeness would cause her to lose her train of thought altogether.

"I'm Stephen Hartington, Lord and Lady Felton's son. Pardon my intrusion. My coach was delayed, and instead of waking my parents at such a late hour, I decided to sneak through the window. Had I known they had company, I would have found another way." He glanced at his forearm and gently massaged it. "I fear I shall be sporting a nice bruise come morning." A smug smile twitched the corners of his lips. "I never anticipated being attacked by a candlestick." He smiled fully then, producing straight rows of white teeth.

Katherine blinked and gave herself a mental shake. "It was all I could find to defend myself on short notice."

He chuckled. "I'd hate to think of what kind of condition I'd be in if you'd been better prepared."

He peered at the red marks on his palm. Slight imprints from her teeth marred his skin. "What are you anyway, part wildcat?"

"You threw me onto the bed." She crossed her arms and sat up straighter. "I had no idea what your intentions were."

He raised both palms "Merely to gain entrance to my home, I assure you."

"Have you heard of using a key?" Her cynical remark

sounded strange to her ears. It must have been due to the lateness of the hour.

"It has been a trying day." He closed his eyes and rubbed his temples. "Somewhere between London and here, I've misplaced it."

Maybe she'd pushed him too far. "I beg your apology. I didn't mean to lash out. I'm still a little shaken."

He examined her with nonchalant arrogance. "Understandably so."

She must look atrocious but suppressed the urge to tame her unruly curls.

The room fell still, except for the pounding of her heart and the rise and fall of her breath. He sat a foot away, but she could feel the heat radiating from his body. He smelled of leather and cedar with a hint of citrus, and she reveled in the scent.

He cleared his throat. "I should be going." He placed his hands on his knees to push to a stand. "Please accept my sincerest apology for disturbing your sleep and..." His eyes narrowed, and his gaze shifted to her cheek. He cupped her face in his hand.

She tried to pull away, but he leaned with her, gently rubbing his thumb over the bruise on her cheek. His featherlike touch sent tingles down her spine and caused the hair on her arms to stand on end.

"I didn't do that, did I?"

He appeared so concerned that Katherine lifted her hand to her face. Her fingers brushed his, and he pulled his away.

She cleared her throat. "That was there before."

His eyes searched hers, waiting for further explanation. When she offered none, he continued to study her with those ice-blue eyes. "Are you a friend of my sister?"

Katherine stilled. Could this man, with his intense gaze, expose her secrets and see through her farce? Unable to determine a decent answer, she replied, "Sort of."

His brows snapped together. "Sort of?"

"The hour is late. May we discuss this in the morning?"

"Indeed." He rose to his feet and scooped up his bag. "I must apologize again for my intrusion and disturbing your slumber." He strode to the door.

Katherine stood, bringing the blanket with her.

He paused at the door and turned. "I'm truly sorry to have frightened you."

All traces of flippancy had disappeared, and a sincerity showed in his eyes that startled her. She held his gaze. "And I apologize for attacking you with a candlestick."

He nodded as a form of acknowledgement. "Good night, Miss..." he started. "Good night—*Kate*," he amended, boldly using her given name. In a flash, his cocky smile reappeared, and with it, the twinkle of laughter in his eyes. He turned down the hall and disappeared in the inky darkness.

How dare he be so forward as to use her given name, and to say it with a cheeky smile. Granted it had been the only name she'd offered, but plain Miss would have sufficed. Either Lord Hartington was a rogue or the man was purposely trying to draw a rise out of her. Katherine padded to the door and closed it. She crawled into bed, murmuring, "Lord Hartington, it serves you right that you'll be sporting a bruise tomorrow." She tossed one way, then another, but sleep was long in coming. Her thoughts kept turning to the events of a particularly intriguing midnight intruder.

---

*S*unlight danced through the windowpane, warming Katherine's face. She winced at the bright light and rolled over, squeezing her eyes closed. *It can't be morning yet, can it?* The hall clock chimed nine times as if to answer. She threw aside the covers and slid her legs off the bed.

Heavens. She'd overslept. According to Lady Felton, it was customary for them to share breakfast at precisely nine. Her late awakening was all Lord Harrington's fault, but she couldn't point the blame at him. If anyone learned that a man had been in her bedchamber, her reputation would be in tatters.

She'd best hurry, then.

True to her word, Abby had left several day dresses for her to wear. From the wardrobe, Katherine selected a light blue muslin gown with a darker blue ribbon accentuating the lower and tighter waistline. It had a square neckline and little puffed sleeves that capped her shoulders. Her fingers fumbled with the hard-to-reach buttons. How accustomed she'd become to having a lady's maid. She quickly tied her hair into a neat top knot and donned her well-worn kid boots. Pausing to examine her appearance in the mirror, she ran her hand down the fabric. The dress fit her well except that the hem was a tad long, but it would hide the poor condition of her shoes.

Katherine opened the door and hurried in the direction of the aroma of salty-sweet bacon. The wainscoted hallway lined with glided framed paintings of horses was atypical for a mere farmhouse and better suited for a manor which would be expected of an earl. Several large Willow trees drooped with budding leaves outside of a large, mullioned window. It seemed farm was the only misnomer in Willowstone Farm's name. She descended the grand staircase to the main level, where a footman opened a set of doors and stepped aside for her to pass. But instead of a formal dining area, she was ushered into an airy white paneled room where Lady Felton, Abigail, and a man whom Katherine believed to be Lord Felton sat at an oak table. The older man rose at her entrance, leaning heavily on his cane.

"Kate, I was wondering if you were coming." Abby gestured for her to sit in the empty chair next to her.

"Abigail, where are your manners?" Lady Felton frowned at

her daughter before turning to Katherine. "I'm glad you decided to join us. We've just sat, and you'll have to excuse us for not hosting the morning meal in the dining room. Over the years, we've preferred the intimacy of informal eating. This room is much more accommodating to our small family, and in the winter, it is less drafty than the dining room."

A footman pulled a chair out for her, and Katherine smiled a greeting as she sat beside Abby.

"I don't believe you've met my husband. Charles, this is Kate. Kate, my husband, Lord Felton."

He resumed his seat. "Pleased to meet you Miss... ah..." He glanced at his wife for help determining what polite society would deem appropriate, for it wasn't proper to call a young woman by her first name.

Abby piped in, "Didn't you say you found her on Vernon Road? Why don't we unofficially call her Miss Kate Vernon until we learn otherwise? I think that's as good a name as any." Her gaze searched faces for any dissenters.

"Miss Vernon or Kate is lovely." Katherine dipped her chin. "It's a pleasure to meet you, Lord Felton. Thank you for your hospitality and for sharing your table with me. I owe you a great debt of gratitude."

"The pleasure is all ours." He sipped from a steaming cup of chocolate. "I do hope you are feeling hale?"

"Much improved." Katherine slid her napkin into her lap.

A footman entered and served plates heaped with toast, bacon, and fried eggs, while another brought Katherine a cup of chocolate to drink.

"Are you feeling up for a stroll of the grounds after breakfast?" Abby clasped her hands. "I'd love to show you around."

Her breath caught at the opportunity to get her bearings. Her ankle hadn't pained her when she'd descended the stairs, and this might be her chance to figure out a way to post a letter to Claire. "That would be lovely."

"Do not overdo yourself, young lady." Lady Felton picked up her fork and knife and cut a bite of egg. She eyed her daughter. "And don't push our guest too hard. She is still recovering. Although, I think some fresh air might do her good. Make sure you both bring a shawl. The sky is bright and sunny, but it is springtime, and when the wind blows, there's a nip in the air."

The door behind Katherine opened with a slight squeak. Lady Felton gasped, and her fork froze halfway to her lips.

Katherine's heart leapt into her throat. Was it Cousin Horace? She closed her eyes and clutched the table, her nails digging into the wood.

Please God, don't let him hurt these nice people.

"Stephen!" Abby's arm brushed Katherine's as she shifted in her seat.

Katherine's eyes sprung open, and she peeked over her shoulder. Her midnight intruder casually leaned against the doorframe with the same crooked smile on his lips. The tension in her muscles melted like the warm butter on her toast. It wasn't Cousin Horace or his henchmen. Merely the Feltons' oldest son, who seemed to have a knack for surprising people.

Lady Felton scooted around the table and wrapped her son in a warm embrace.

"It's so good to see you. We didn't expect you until later in the week."

Lord Hartington pecked a kiss on her cheek before she released him. "It's good to see you too, Mother. I had to move up the delivery of the thoroughbred. Its owner had plans to travel to Scotland at the end of the month, and it turned out to be more convenient for both of us."

Abby rose from the table. Lord Hartington lovingly kissed her forehead and tickled her side with his fingers.

"Stop it." Abby jumped aside and attempted to retaliate, but Lord Hartington grabbed her hands in one of his. He wiggled his fingers close to her stomach as if to tickle her something fierce.

"Enough." Lord Felton's tone was stern as he stood, but his smile revealed his love. "Our guest is going to think we lack good breeding. You haven't been here for more than two minutes, and the two of you are already teasing." He gripped his son's hand in a firm handshake, and they both gave each other a hearty clap on the back. "It's good to see you, son."

"And you, Father." Lord Hartington smiled.

"Come and have a seat. We just started to break our fast."

His gaze locked on Katherine. "Good morning." He flashed her an easy yet disarming smile.

Her insides warmed as if she'd sipped from the steaming cup of chocolate the footman had placed in front of her, but it yet remained untouched.

"Oh, Stephen, forgive us." His mother pressed her hand against her bosom. "I was so surprised I neglected to introduce our guest. This is Miss Kate Vernon."

Lord Hartington's eyes held hers with a teasing glint. "'Tis a pleasure to make your acquaintance, Miss Vernon." He pulled out a chair and sat.

A footman set an extra place for the new arrival and heaped a large quantity of eggs upon his plate. The young lord's gaze fell upon his family with such fondness that Katherine longed to be a member of their intimate group.

"There's not much of a resemblance besides our coloring, but Stephen and I are twins." Abby's eyes held a twinkle of mischief, and he cocked an eyebrow as if to warn her he'd seek revenge for whatever she was plotting.

An unladylike giggle welled up in Katherine at their unspoken body language. They may be unidentical, but their demeanor were similar. She wiped her mouth with her napkin to cover her grin.

"I decided her name." Abby's face beamed. "It's quite clever, if I must say so myself."

His brow furrowed. "You named her?"

"She has amn... amn..." A dimple appeared on Abby's left cheek, and she glanced at her mother for help. "Amn-something."

"Amnesia," Lady Felton corrected.

"Which means she can't remember anything—not even her name. Mama and Papa were lucky to happen upon her before she froze to death the other evening. You know, the night of the big rainstorm that chilled everyone to the bone." Abby ran her sentences together. "She'd had an accident, and they found her on the side of the road unconscious and half-dead with a big lump above her temple." Abby paused to breathe and checked Stephen's reaction.

His smile fell. "Why were you on the side of the road?"

Katherine blinked. How should someone with memory loss respond? With a shrug? *I beg your pardon, but I don't recall?*

"That remains a mystery because she can't remember." Abby raised her palms. "The physician told Mama it's probably retro... retrograde amnesia... which is the most common form of amnesia and can be brought on by head trauma. The physician said in most cases it's temporary, and she needs lots of rest."

His ice-blue gaze scrutinized Katherine as if to determine the truth of the situation. She fought the heat of a blush rising in her cheeks. Beneath the table linen, she pinned her hands between her knees to keep them from shaking and fought with all her willpower not to squirm under his intense gaze.

"I hope my family has taken good care of you."

"They have been wonderful." Katherine forced a steady tone. "I owe them my life."

Lady Felton leaned over the edge of her plate. "We are thankful God brought us to your aid when He did." She turned to Stephen. "I didn't hear you come in last night."

Katherine dropped her fork, and it clattered onto her plate. All gazes swerved to her.

Lord Hartington shot her a warning glare that could freeze the sun.

"My apologies." She retrieved her fork.

"Oh, sweetie, are your hands still bothering you?" Lines of concern wrinkled Lady Felton's forehead.

"I'm fine. Just a little clumsy." She kept her gaze lowered.

"I was going to show Kate Willowstone's grounds today." Abby slathered a liberal amount of jam onto her toast. "Would you be able to join us?"

"Unfortunately, I have work to do this morning." Lord Hartington leaned back in his chair. "However, I can make time for a round of cards this evening."

Abby's butter knife stilled. "You still owe me two farthings from our last game."

"I thought it was *you* who owed *me* the two farthings."

"Indeed." Her tone dripped with sarcasm. "If you recall, I had a stupendous comeback in the last hand."

Lord Hartington glanced at the coffered ceiling and scratched his cheek.

"Stephen, what happened to your hand?" Lady Felton gasped. "It looks like something bit you."

Katherine's fork clattered onto her plate again, and everyone glanced in her direction before peering at Stephen. The tips of her ears burned. What was wrong with her? She drew her hands back under the table and sat on them. Problem solved.

Lord Hartington pinned her to her chair with another warning gaze.

Her breathing stilled as she waited for his answer. He knew as much as she the scandal that would ensue if it became known he'd entered her private quarters late at night. Despite the innocence of it all, she'd surely be turned out.

He inspected his palm and rubbed it with his thumb. "It's nothing, a little mark."

The rest of the meal passed without issue and reminded Katherine of times when her parents were still alive, how they used to chat about exciting things that had happened the day before. Lord Hartington and his father discussed horses, while Abby and Lady Felton planned a trip into town.

That just might be an opportunity to post her letters.

"It will also be a good time for us to stop by and pay Mrs. Emerson a visit," Lady Felton said.

"That would be nice." Abby nodded, but her countenance changed. She picked up her fork and pushed her food around on her plate but didn't bother to eat it.

By the time everyone had their fill and the footmen had removed the dishes, Abby appeared to be in better spirits.

"Are you ready for me to show you the grounds?" Abby rose. "It's finally warm enough to go outside, and I am dying to get some fresh air. I've been cooped inside all winter."

Katherine stood. "We should probably get our coats."

Abby sighed with a dramatic droop as if it might take too long and the sun would disappear before they enjoyed it.

Lady Felton chuckled and issued Katherine a side glance. "I think you could be a good influence on my impatient daughter."

"Mama." Abby sent her mother a reproachful look before grabbing Katherine and pulling her out of the room. "If we're getting jackets, we might as well change into riding habits in case we decide to ride." She lowered her voice. "I'll meet you in your room. I need to ask you a question about Stephen."

The blood drained from Katherine's face, cooling her over-heated cheeks.

CHAPTER 7

*G*olden rays warmed Katherine's skin and raised her spirits. Abby threaded her arm through Katherine's and pulled her down the front steps.

"It's such a beautiful day." Abby peeked at the azure sky. "Springtime is my favorite time of the year. Everything comes back to life. The frozen gray earth becomes vibrant in full color. Don't you love days like today? It's like God is renewing hope and letting us know there will be good days ahead."

Although the overly bright sun hurt Katherine's eyes, she laughed at Abby's enthusiasm and succumbed to her contagious mood. Still, the situation of evading her cousin and protecting her sister hung like a dark cloud in the background.

They walked up the front drive a few yards before Abby turned to face the house.

"So, this is Willowstone Farm." With a broad sweep of her arm, she proudly displayed a large, Julian-style house that had two wings scrolling out in opposite directions. Ivy vines climbed their way up the sides of the honey-colored stone front, accentuating its rustic beauty. White fences sprawled out endlessly into the distance, and a large stable with four dormers sat nestled off to the side.

Willowstone held a rustic quality unlike her family's sleek Greek Revival home. The wings appeared to have been additions added later due to the brighter coloring of the stone which made Willowstone comparable in size to Steepleton Manor. It was the rolling green pastures and the large stable in the background that flooded Katherine with homesickness. She blinked away the sting of tears before Abby could notice.

"The manor and grounds are beautiful." Katherine nudged Abby. "I can't believe you call this a farm. You misled me."

Abby giggled. "My father has always referred to it as a farm, and we do breed horses. He's the Earl of Felton, but he and my mother are very humble. They say everything is God's, and we must be good caretakers. Come on." She tugged on Katherine's arm. "I'll show you the stables." Together they strolled across the manicured lawn.

Katherine's stomach fluttered. Papa had often compared their horse barn to the earl's. Perhaps she could see how they manage their horses and incorporate some of their methods? A pain stabbed her heart. If her horses were still hers.

Sunlight reflected off floating dust particles, and the sweet scent of hay permeated the air. Stalls lined either side of the barn, and a couple of horses peeked their heads out and snorted their greetings.

"We have an indoor ring for training and about twenty stalls with sixteen horses." Abby stopped, and a groomsman slid a heavy wooden stall door open. "This is Amethyst."

A chestnut filly with a white star on her nose raised her head and perked her ears as Abby stroked the horse's neck and snout.

"Over here is her sire, Dominion." A shiny stallion, who had to be seventeen hands tall, whinnied in response to his name. "He's a smart one, and frisky too. I don't dare saddle him. Only

Stephen rides the wilder ones. I prefer my sweetgoer, Duchess, over here."

Abby pointed and strode over to a dark bay mare raising its head and straining to prod Abby with its nose. She reached into her coat pocket and pulled out a bag of carrots. She held one out for Duchess, who gently nuzzled Abby's hand before mouthing the carrot.

"Would you like to give a carrot to Amethyst?" Abby held one out.

Katherine accepted it and walked toward the chestnut.

Dominion had other ideas. He stomped his foot and kicked his stall door.

Katherine laughed. "I know, pecking order and all that. Here you go, big fellow." She held the carrot out in the palm of her hand, and the rowdy sire snapped the carrot up.

"Dominion, no." Abby crossed her arms. "I'm always fearful he's going to bite my fingers."

"That's what he wants you to think." Katherine turned to the horse. "He's just trying to show me who the real master is." Katherine scratched Dominion under his chin, careful to avoid any horse-carrot slobber, and addressed the stallion. "Aren't you?"

"It sounds like you might know something about horses."

"I might." Katherine bit her bottom lip and admired the stallion. "Could we try riding?"

"A slow walk or trot would be okay."

"Splendid." Katherine clasped her hands to refrain from clapping.

The stable hands saddled up Amethyst and Duchess and helped both ladies into the saddle. As the groomsmen adjusted the stirrups, Dominion whinnied.

"Perhaps we shall go for a ride sometime soon," she whispered under her breath, following Abby into the exterior ring.

Abby clutched the reins and rode stiff in the saddle as they circled the perimeter. Katherine put Amethyst into a trot and pulled alongside Abby. "Is something the matter?"

Abby laughed, but it sounded pinched and nervous. "I need to warm up a bit."

"We don't have to ride if you don't want to." Katherine slowed her mount.

"Don't worry about me. I'm being silly, especially for living on a horse farm, but I was thrown from the saddle a few years ago. It gave me quite a scare and a broken arm. Ever since then, I've been a little hesitant. I'll be all right in a few minutes."

Katherine stayed close to Abby as they circled the ring several times. Perhaps her nearness could ease Abby's fear. After a few more laps, Abby's confidence built, and she relinquished her tight grip on the reins.

*S*tephen set aside his growing list of townsfolk to question regarding theft in the area or any suspicious activity amid their stables. He leaned back in his chair, drew aside the curtain, and peeked out the window at the two women circling the ring. He tried to return to business, but his mind wandered to the strange woman with haunting green eyes. They reminded him of the color of dew-drenched leaves, and he had the odd desire to find some to prove it.

Kate. She was a complete conundrum—one moment all fiery and tempestuous, and the next shy and reticent. She piqued his curiosity, but no one, not even she, knew anything about her. Even the best spy needed some sort of clue to follow. Her gowns were borrowed from Abby and her hands were scraped and scabbed making it challenging to tell if they'd even seen a day's hard work. She spoke like one trained by a governess and carried herself as one highborn, but why had she been found alone on the side of the road? What possibly could have happened? The sight of that ugly bruise on her cheek had caused his own to ache. Stephen's heart clenched at the images that swam before his eyes—a horrific accident, robbery, or assault?

He shut down the ill direction of his thoughts and peered at his notes, attempting to concentrate—to no avail. He spread out a local map, dotting the areas where there'd been a reported horse stolen in the last ten years. The scattered points didn't register any sort of pattern—at least not yet. He particularly enjoyed piecing mysteries together. Events, connections, or items appeared unrelated until something triggered an epiphany, and a pattern became apparent. He'd miss the rush and clarity of mind that happens during those inspirational moments once he quit domestically spying for the Home Office after this operation. But if he continued, he'd feel morally obligated to postpone his plans to marry and set up a nursery, because the thought of keeping a separate life hidden from his future wife soured his hopes for their future. He stared at the plotted points one more time and allowed his thoughts to drift. His gaze roved out the window.

Kate kept to his sister's careful canter. Was she timid around horses like Abby or unaccustomed to a mount? For some reason, he longed to see her riding free with her wild mane of curls flowing in the wind behind her. He pictured the gleam of her smile and the sparkle in her eyes as she enjoyed the thrill of the horse's brisk pace.

He shook his head to clear the vision, seeing again the two cautious women easing their way around the ring.

Pity.

He should be thinking of Julia, but she preferred to ride in a carriage or curricle, not on the back of some filthy animal. Perhaps his thoughts strayed at the hope for companionship on his daily rides. Nothing compared to the freedom of an early morning gallop through the green hillsides, nor the feeling of straining muscles and horseflesh as he rode at a breakneck pace toward an unknown destination. Maybe that was what he needed, a good, hard ride to regain his focus and he could visit the closest townsfolk on his list. He rolled up the map and stalked out to the stables with a purposeful stride.

---

atherine held Amethyst under tight restraint. Despite the dull ache in her head, she itched to ride across the plain with the wind whipping her face and feel the weightlessness that would come if she jumped the stream and small rock wall.

"Why don't we ride down the path a little way?" Abby gestured toward a worn dirt trail that wound around bushes and led to a copse of trees. "I'll show you a bit more of the grounds."

"Are you certain you're up for it?"

"I'm fine. God didn't give me a spirit of fear." Abby spoke the words in a determined tone. "Sometimes it takes me a few moments to remind myself of that."

A groom opened the gate, and she followed Abby down a path leading toward a small grouping of trees.

"May I ask what happened for you to have been thrown from the horse?" Katherine sat deep and relaxed in the saddle.

"My overconfidence." Abby sighed. "Stephen and I had finished racing, and when we came to rest, I thumbed my nose at Stephen because he was being a braggart about winning. I think a snake slithered in front of my horse and startled it. The horse reared and bolted. I clung to its mane until it jumped a fallen log and threw me. I ricocheted off a tree trunk, breaking my left arm and badly bruising the left side of my body."

Katherine gasped. "How terrible."

"Stephen was beside himself. It's endearing to know he

cares for my well-being, but he didn't want to leave me alone in the woods. He screamed for help, but no one heard. Eventually, he galloped back as fast as possible and returned with Mama, two groomsmen, and a stretcher. He didn't leave my side for a week."

The assessing ice-blue of Lord Hartington's eyes flashed in Katherine's memory, how he'd so easily unarmed her physically and emotionally. It was hard to picture him as the doting older brother, but then again, she'd witnessed the loving way he teased Abby during breakfast. It was as if the man was a two-sided coin.

"I should have gotten back in the saddle as soon as I was better, but I let fear have its way. Soon, it controlled me. You should have seen it. I would shake uncontrollably just being near a horse, which is dreadful when you live on a horse farm. It spilled over into other areas of my life too. I couldn't ride in a carriage or go into town. My world shrunk as I became captive to fear."

"What did you do? How are you able to seat a horse now?"

"It's entirely God. My mother had me memorize scripture as it pertained to fear. It says in 2 Timothy, 'For God hath not given us the spirit of fear; but of power, and of love, and of a sound mind.' I repeat several scriptures whenever my worries surface, and God gives me the strength to overcome them. It didn't happen right away, mind you. Courage is a habit." She released a sigh. "My faith grew one step at a time." She snorted. "Or should I say one canter at a time, and eventually my fears receded."

Abby trotted down the path. She wasn't precisely galloping off into the sunset, but something perked up in Katherine. She admired Abby's trust in God. It offered her...

Hope.

"There's a small stream up ahead. I know a nice place

where we can sit and have a bite to eat. I snuck some cheese and bread out of the kitchen for us to nibble on."

Abby led them to a clearing beside a bubbling stream, and they tied their horses to a nearby tree. A sunbeam spotlighted an area where the plants and wildflowers sprouted. She removed a small basket and a blanket from her saddle bag and spread the cloth where the least number of rocks protruded. She plopped down, crisscrossing her legs under her billowing skirts. Katherine did the same.

Abby pulled out the cheese and bread, and Katherine relished the warm sun on her face. Everything was so peaceful here. Maybe not when Lord Hartington was present, but for the most part, Willowstone Farm was serene, and the Hartingtons were a loving and caring family. It reminded her of how things used to be before her parents passed. She longed to savor it, but precious time was being wasted. She needed to post her letters and warn her sister. But how?

"Do you think I could accompany you into town tomorrow?" Katherine held her breath.

"I don't see why not." Abby's face perked up. "Actually, I would love the company. You might be the distraction I need."

"Distraction from what?"

"We can discuss it another time." She swiped her hand through the air. "I want to talk about a different kind of distraction." Abby's eyes sparkled with mischief. "What do you think about my brother?"

"Um, well, he's intense. I mean serious." She remembered his teasing in the breakfast room. Would Abby wonder how she obtained that impression? "But not really. It's obvious he loves you and your family, and I'm sure women swoon because he's handsome in a mysterious sort of way." *You're making a cake of yourself.* "Truly, I don't know him at all. Only what I saw of him at breakfast, which was not enough to form of an opinion." She re-lived the featherlike touch of his thumb as he brushed the bruise on her cheek, the concern in his voice. *I didn't do that, did I?*

A giggle escaped Abby's lips. "Silly. I merely wanted to see if you would be up for playing a prank on him."

Heat poured into Katherine's cheeks.

"He *can* be intimidating, and the prank won't work if you swoon in the middle of it." Abby put her index finger to her lips. "On second thought, swooning might be a good distraction."

Katherine could almost see the thoughts spinning in Abby's head.

"I need to be certain you aren't enamored with him like some women are." Abby giggled. "Once I saw a woman completely lose all coherent speech when Stephen asked her a simple question. She just kept blinking and making vowel sounds... uh, eh, ih, ah. I felt bad for the poor chit. It was quite humiliating. Women can find it overwhelming to be near an eligible man who's handsome *and* titled." She shrugged. "The combination gives some women the vapors." Abby bit into her slice of cheese. "What do you think? Can you handle it?"

Katherine wanted to avoid Stephen Hartington, but Abby's question had cornered her. If she said she wasn't up for the challenge, it would sound like she was enamored by him, and that was the last thing she wanted.

"Of course." Katherine tried to sound nonchalant. "For you."

"Splendid." She clapped her hands. "He always beats me at cards, but I have a plan to best him. I need you to distract him while I cheat. Nothing dramatic, merely make him look away for a second so that I can deal from the bottom of the deck."

"Where did you learn such a thing?" Aghast, Katherine stared at her friend.

Abby leaned in. A sly smile curved her lips. It reminded Katherine of the look Stephen issued her before he left her chamber last night. "Henry, our footman, is teaching me. His wife put him on a diet, so he's been teaching me how to cheat at cards in exchange for me smuggling him sweets."

Katherine broke out laughing. "You're incorrigible."

"You sound like Mama." Abby chuckled with Katherine. "She's always after me about my ridiculous ideas, exasperating daydreams, constant fidgeting, and other unladylike habits."

"Besides being a card 'sharp,' what other unladylike pursuits do you have?" Katherine asked.

"When I was a young girl, Mama frowned on me wearing boys knickers, riding straddle, balancing on rock walls, and climbing trees."

Katherine, too, had climbed trees when she was young. She used to challenge her sister to see who could ascend the highest, and Katherine usually won. In fact, one of the gardeners used to call her part monkey.

A light breeze rustled the leaves of a nearby maple. Its copious low-lying branches made it perfect for climbing.

Abby's gaze grew distant. "I used to race Stephen and his friend, Nicholas, to the top of that maple."

"How did you fare?"

"Considering they were a head taller and could reach much higher branches than I"—she sighed and her mouth broke into a full-fledged grin—"quite well, actually."

Abby removed her slippers and stockings.

"What are you doing?" Katherine didn't like the determined look on Abby's face.

"I climb much better barefoot. I wouldn't want to risk slipping and falling to my death." She rose and moved to the tree.

"Is this wise?"

"Probably not, but I want to see if I still can reach that high." Abby gripped a branch and peered at Katherine over her shoulder. "Besides, I can't have you believing me scared after seeing how timid I am on a horse." She pulled herself up onto the first branch.

"I don't think that at all." Katherine rose and moved to stand near the tree.

"You stay put." She eyed Katherine with a warning glare. "Mama would box my ears if I allowed you to hit your head again." Abby shimmed herself up to the uppermost branches of the tree with the agility of a treecreeper bird.

Katherine shaded her eyes from the sun to keep her friend in view.

"Drat." Abby appeared frozen near the top.

"Is something amiss?" Katherine gripped the first branch.

"I'm caught." Abby held onto the tree with one hand and reached behind to unhook a tie on the back of her gown from a limb.

"Can you reach it?"

Abby switched hands and attempted to dislodge her tie from a different direction. Several minutes passed as she floundered.

"Careful." Katherine tugged on her bottom lip with her front teeth.

"I'm afraid it's bested me." Abby rested her head against the narrow upper trunk. "I'm stuck."

"Hold on. I'm coming." Katherine pulled off her kid boots and stockings and hoped the dizzy spells would keep at bay. Starting from the opposite side of the tree, she picked her way up branch after branch until she reached a similar height.

"Hold tight. I couldn't bear it if you fell." Abby's expression held more concern for Katherine than for herself.

Katherine drew alongside Abby on a nearby branch and smiled to ease her tension. "Perhaps a fall would knock some memories back into me."

"I think the wait-and-see method is a better approach."

"Agreed." Katherine unhooked the tie that had looped

around the end of a small but thick branch. "There. I've restored your freedom."

"Thank heaven."

A gust of wind swayed the treetop, and Katherine gripped the tree tighter.

Abby laughed. "What a sight we must pose. Two big buzzards perched on branches."

A strong breeze sent a shiver through Katherine, and goose pimples formed on her arms. "It's a bit chilly. We should head down."

Abby agreed, but instead of carefully picking her way down, she swung from one branch to another until she landed like a cat on the path below.

"Abigail Hartington Emerson!" A baritone voice yelled. "What do you think you're doing?"

CHAPTER 8

*S*tephen reigned his horse to a halt and dismounted. He rounded on Abby with a scowl, widening his stance and crossing his arms. "Women, especially of your age, do not go about climbing trees."

Abby's nostrils flared. "Are you calling me an old spinster?"

"You are no longer a child." Stephen raised his chin, daring her to disagree.

Her expression grew mutinous. "You instructed me to get outside and live a little instead of pining for Nicholas's return."

Leaves rustled behind him, and he turned.

"Too old to climb trees, eh?"

Kate? A pair of feminine feet, along with a trim set of ankles, stepped onto a branch eye-level with his chin. She sat on the branch and curled her toes under the hem of her dress, looking like a queen perched on a throne. She held her chin high as she peered down at him with one arched eyebrow that set him in his place as a reminder, he'd climbed a cherry tree just last night.

Stephen's blood quickened. Her hair had fallen partially

loose from her tight chignon, and tendrils of chestnut curls framed her face like little tongues of amber fire. Her eyes glowed a lighter spring-green color in the daylight as they challenged his own. The fresh air pinkened her cheeks, and her full lips curled up at the corners in a defiant smile. She was spirit and quick wit wrapped up in a beautiful package, and he must stay on his guard, or he'd become lost in her green pastures.

"I should have known you were behind all this." He raised his hands and plucked her off the tree branch. She yelped with surprise and clung to his shoulders for support, but she didn't resist him. The scent of sunshine and lavender floated over him, and springs of silken curls tickled his face and lips.

Her warmth radiated through her riding habit, and his skin tingled in a peculiar way where her hands rested. She swayed on her feet and gripped the sleeves of his jacket tighter. He held onto her until she steadied, and a moment longer than necessary, lost in the depths of her eyes. Who was this strange beauty who had interrupted his life?

Who is Kate Vernon, truly?

"Ahem." Abby interrupted his thoughts. He released Kate and stepped back to set some distance between them. He didn't miss the quizzical look his sister flashed him. If he knew his sister—and he did—wrong conclusions were already forming in her mind.

"I'm merely looking out for you."

"Harrumph." Abby crossed her arms and glowered at him. "Looking out for us or badgering?"

He hadn't come to pick a fight. In fact, the day was lovely, and he'd been in better spirits after his ride. He didn't want to taint the moment with petty bickering. "I'm not here to upset you. I, too, was out enjoying the nice weather. I will leave you to your pursuits. Just be cautious." He eyed her with an older brother's reproof, even though he was only older by five minutes.

"I will see you at supper." In one swoop, he mounted his horse and steered it toward the pasture. He'd been meaning to check to see if the groundskeeper mended the fence properly. "I wouldn't mention this to Mother. If she learned of your climbing escapades, she'd likely swoon." He nodded to his sister and then Kate. "Miss Vernon." He held her gaze until he clicked his heels and set the horse into motion.

*K*atherine refused to squirm despite feeling like a baby rabbit in the sights of a circling hawk. Where had her cheekiness come from? Why would she dare to take his lordship to task over his hypocritical tree climbing?

When he'd passed and ridden out of sight, Abby said, "We should probably head back also." She donned her stocking and shoes and fetched the blanket.

"Your brother called you Abigail Emerson." Katherine glanced at the simple gold band on Abby's finger. "You're married?"

Abby's eyes clouded. She turned and neatly folded the blanket, tucking it into Duchess's saddle bag.

Katherine hadn't known Abby long, but careful movements seemed out of character. It also was odd that no one had mentioned her husband. "If you don't wish to speak of it..."

She turned, and a far-off expression softened her face. "I was married to a wonderful man named Nicholas Emerson."

Emerson. "Is he related to the same Mrs. Emerson your mother wishes for you to visit?"

"She's my mother-in-law. "Nicholas was declared dead by the crown, a casualty of war."

Katherine gasped. "I'm so sorry. I didn't mean to bring up painful memories."

"It's good for me to talk about it." Abby smiled, but it

appeared more as a half-smile, half-wince. "I don't often get the chance. My friends won't bring it up. They whisper when they think I can't hear. I know they're putting on a good show for me, but..." Her gaze lowered.

Katherine squeezed Abby's hand. What would she have done if she hadn't had Claire with whom to mourn their parents' death? It had bonded them as sisters.

Abby flipped over a rock with the toe of her boot. "Seven years ago, the day after our wedding, Nick left to serve in the royal army. He had enlisted with some far-fetched plan to gain a title through exceptional service to his majesty. I had begged him not to go." Abby's gaze turned hollow. "But it was too late. He'd given his word and wouldn't go back on it. He told me he was doing it for me and that he loved me. It was the last time I saw him." Abby fiddled with the tie on her riding habit. "I kept thinking he would show up on my doorstep someday, but the notion has dwindled over the years. I haven't the heart to begin courting again, and now I'm considered 'on the shelf.'"

"I'm so sorry. I know what it's like to lose someone you love —er—I can imagine, I mean." *You can't know. You're not supposed to remember.*

Abby didn't seem to notice Katherine's slip. "I think the hardest thing was not knowing, but that is in the past. I'm moving forward with God's help. Who knows, maybe some gent will come looking for a spinster."

"You are hardly a spinster. I'm certain that, once you let society know that you are ready for the marriage mart, gentlemen will be lining up at your front door, just for the chance of courting someone as lovely and kind as you."

"Oh, Kate." A tremor wriggled Abby's shoulders as if shaking off negative thoughts, and she sighed. "I'm delighted you are here. I just know you and I are going to become close friends."

"That sounds splendid." Katherine's heart clenched,

knowing her stay would only be temporary. The thought of disappointing Abby, who'd already been through so much, was another unintended consequence. She never meant to hurt anybody with her falsehood, but she must protect her sister and herself.

"I have some things I need to attend to before dinner." Abby walked her horse to a nearby rock for the extra leverage and mounted Duchess. "Or should I say, for after the evening meal?" A mischievous smile donned her lips. "I usually don't condone cheating, but he is my brother, and I would like, for once, to beat him soundly."

Katherine slid her foot into Amethyst's stirrup. "I can see it means a lot to you. I will do my best to be of help, but I'm not sure what kind of distraction I can pose." She pulled herself up into the saddle.

"Oh, it's simple." Abby pulled on the reins. "Ask him about God or horses, and he'll lose track of everything else."

Easier said than done when the man turned her into a jittery squirrel. They cantered back to the barn and dismounted. A fresh breeze fluttered the strings of her bonnet like little slaps of warning not to forget her objective, and the letters tucked into her corset poked her as if to remind her of her priorities.

In the barn, Dominion neighed and kicked the stable door, seeking attention. "Do you mind if I stay and ride a bit more? I'd like to enjoy the warm weather and fresh air a bit longer."

"Make yourself at home." Abby squeezed Katherine's fingers. "Thank you for listening." She strode in the direction of the main house. Part way, she turned. "Don't forget to arrive on time for the evening meal. We hold country hours and eat at six sharp."

"Most definitely." Katherine waved and waited until Abby entered the house. By the look of the sun, it was a little past noon. If Katherine left now and used the fastest horse possible, she could ride to town, find a postmaster, and get her message on its way to her sister today. If she was lucky, the letters would be in the attorneys, Madame Lamoureux, and Claire's hands on the morrow. She flagged the groomsman who'd led Amethyst away for a rub down and asked him to saddle Dominion. She'd need a fast mount.

"Are yer certain? Ol' Dominion has quite a feisty streak."

"Which direction is town?" She had no time for explanations.

"Down the lane and take a left. It will lead ya straight there in under a half hour's ride."

He finished saddling Dominion and helped her mount. "If you'll wait a moment, I'll ready me horse fer the ride."

"I won't be needing a groom." She clicked her tongue, and Dominion sprang to life, leaving the poor groomsman helpless in the dust. Whereas Amethyst was dainty and well-tempered, Dominion was power ready to be unleashed. His spiritedness reminded her of Sugar's spicy disposition, and she coaxed the horse as she would have her own reveling in the splendor of the wind whipping her face.

Dominion galloped full speed down the narrow lane. The exhilarating pace threatened to swipe her bonnet off her head, so she pushed it down to dangle on her back. She leaned forward into Dominion's sheer muscle and strength, and he increased his speed as if releasing weeks of pent-up energy. Katherine guessed he was enjoying this ride as much as she. She inhaled the scent of horseflesh and polished leather. If she closed her eyes, she could almost pretend she was home enjoying her daily ride on Sugar.

The wind tugged at her hair. With one hand, she reached back and pulled out the pins. Her curls would have been disheveled anyway. If she remembered correctly, Lady Felton mentioned it was less than a twenty-minute ride into town.

Plenty of time to tend to her business and return before her absence was noticed.

---

*S*tephen trotted into the stables. He felt more at peace after the hard ride, and now he could refocus his energy. A groomsman took the horse's reins, and Stephen dismounted. He turned to leave but paused at an empty stall.

"Where's Dominion?" He figured the groomsman had taken him out for some exercise or grooming.

"Miss Vernon took 'em for a ride, m'lord."

Stephen whipped around to face the young lad. "She *what*?"

The groom stepped back and swallowed.

"Who's escorting her?"

"Ahhhh... no-one, m'lord." The boy took off his cap and twisted it in his hands. "She said she didn't want a groomsman."

"Of all the bird-witted, foolish... Which way did she go?"

"Toward town, m'lord."

Stephen snapped the reins, and his horse leapt into a full gallop, leaving the groomsman in a cloud of dust.

Hoofbeats hammered the road in a steady drumbeat. Stephen drove his horse down the lane. Earlier, he'd chosen the newest horse to train, the stallion was fast but slow to obey his commands.

He thought of Miss Vernon on the powerful steed, and his heart thudded. He'd preferred a spirited horse and purposefully left Dominion on the wilder side. Only a skilled horseman could handle the like. He prayed the timid behavior he'd witnessed earlier was her holding back because of Abby's fear of horses. Could her amnesia cause her to forget how to handle a horse? Stephen pictured her clinging to Dominion's back to keep from being tossed off.

Lord, help her. The woman was a menace to herself.

The road turned a sharp left, and Stephen steered his horse to the inside, maintaining the vigorous pace with ease. As he rounded the corner, Miss Vernon and Dominion emerged into view over a few hundred or so yards ahead. He dug in his knees and urged the horse to quicken its already swift pace.

---

*A*pproaching hoofbeats thundered behind Katherine, conjuring dreaded images of her cousin's assassins riding alongside the coach, shots ringing out, and the coachman slumping over in his seat. What if they had inquired about a woman who fit her description and had been sent to find her? She snapped the reins and dug in her heels, demanding the horse increase its speed. Whoever followed would have to be an expert horseman to keep up.

Beads of perspiration formed on her brow as she mentally willed Dominion to move faster.

The tenacious rider kept up the pace. She peered over her shoulder, but her hair whipped her face and blocked her view. *Please let the rider be Abby.* Maybe she'd been lying about her fear of horses.

Or perhaps it was the groomsman, despite her decline of his escort.

She spared another glance. The shape of a large man bearing down on her wasn't the young boy who worked the Hartington stables. A shiver turned her blood to ice, tingling her hands and legs.

Think, Katherine. It was only one man. If she could lose him, she could circle back to the house. A large path veered off the main road into the woods ahead. When she applied the slightest pressure, Dominion changed course.

Moments later, so did the other rider. He had gained

precious ground, narrowing the gap down to a several hundred yards.

A whimper tore from her throat. There was no mistaking it. The rider wasn't merely in a hurry to get to town.

He was pursuing her.

Dominion maneuvered the well-worn path with amazing agility, but no matter what tricks she tried, she could not lose the mysterious neck-or-nothing rider. She'd vaulted over downed trees and a small creek. Dominion anticipated her slightest movement and easily flew over obstacles, but the jarring landings restored the pounding ache in her head.

She wasn't going down without a fight, even if her hunter had the advantage of seeming to know the terrain and also not having to ride side-saddle. She turned the horse off the narrow path and into the dense woods. Maybe he wouldn't give chase. She raced toward a low-lying tree branch and ducked at the last minute, hoping the rider wouldn't notice in time to do the same. The other rider, however, wasn't fooled. He yelled, but the hoofbeats drowned out the sound. Or had it been her imagination?

She broke out of the woods into a clearing, but a new sound penetrated her fear. A gurgling roar.

River.

She yanked the reins to the side to turn the horse. Mud splattered. Katherine braced and closed her eyes.

"*L*ook out!" Stephen waited for the splash.

Miss Vernon turned Dominion an instant before the horse would have plunged into the river.

When she'd glanced back during his pursuit of her, a look of sheer terror had marred her face. He could only imagine the fright she must be feeling, out of control, nearly missing a low hanging branch, clinging onto the reins for dear life. She could have been thrown to her death.

He cut his horse into the turn and coming within hearing distance of the other horse, yelled, "Whoa."

Dominion's ears turned toward the sound. Recognizing his master's voice, he slowed to a halt.

Instead of collapsing with relief, Kate tried to coax Dominion into a gallop, snapping the reins and commanding him in a stern voice. Her heels dug into his side as she bent low over the saddle. The faithful horse remained stock-still, waiting on his master's next command.

He snorted at the ridiculous sight and reined in alongside Dominion. She didn't appear relieved that the horse stopped.

Kate's eyes registered sheer terror for a suspended moment. Her face was drawn and pale despite her flushed cheeks. Recognition dawned like the sun over a grassy hill. She exhaled, her shoulders sagging as she whispered his name.

Not *my lord*, or *Lord Hartington*.

"Stephen."

Her use of his given name rippled like a current through his body, but the weight of what she'd done and how dangerous it had been hit him in the gut. "Are you mad? Do you have a death wish? What in heaven's name made you decide to switch to a horse like Dominion?"

She straightened, and sparks flashed in her green eyes. Her eyebrows dipped into an inverted deep V, and angry red splotches colored her cheeks. Once again, she'd reverted to the spitfire he'd remembered from their first encounter. "I'll have you know, I can handle myself quite well."

It dawned on Stephen just how well she had maneuvered the narrow trail, especially when Dominion jumped a fallen tree. She rode like a true horsewoman, expertly commanded the animal at fast speeds. After watching how close she'd stayed alongside his sister, he'd assumed she wasn't an equestrian. He'd expected to see someone afraid of riding, so he'd presumed he was witnessing a petrified woman clinging to a horse. When in fact, she was an adept horsewoman.

If not fear of the powerful steed, what had put that terror in her eyes?

CHAPTER 9

"*O*f all the nerve." Katherine's lips pinched together, and she had to force words past them. "Have you made it a habit of frightening helpless women?"

"What are you talking about?" Stephen snorted and his mouth twisted into a sardonic smile. "I was trying to save you from breaking your neck."

"I'll have you know I was doing fine until you scared me half to death. Do you always chase down lone women out for a leisurely ride?"

"Do you always gallivant off on someone else's horse without permission?"

"Abby said..." Katherine swallowed her words. She'd told Abby she was going for a ride, but she hadn't mentioned her intentions to ride Dominion.

"Abby said what?" His eyes flashed at her.

"Never mind." She clipped the word.

"Why did you ride like a timid beginner with my sister?"

"You were spying on us?" She mimicked his smug look.

His eyes widened, almost imperceivably, but he blinked, and his haughtiness returned. "I wouldn't call it spying."

"Abby's my host and friend, so I kept the same pace out of consideration for her. To do otherwise would have been bad manners."

Stephen turned and stared at the river's rippling waters. "How do you remember how to ride if you have amnesia?"

Katherine stopped breathing. He had her. The farce was over. What could she say? His question raced past her like the river's sweeping current, while the dull ache of her head slowed her thoughts as if moving through sludge.

Finally, a response came. She exhaled and relaxed in the saddle. "I haven't forgotten how to walk, now have I? Just because I have amnesia doesn't mean I can't remember basic things, like walking, talking, and riding."

Stephen accepted her logic with a curt nod.

Triumph burst in her chest. She sat up a little straighter.

Rather than argue, Stephen clicked his tongue, and Dominion started forward into a slow trot.

She floundered for a better grip on the reins.

Stephen's mouth curved into a smug smile.

He certainly knew how to grate her nerves. But she wasn't about to let him know it. Sitting up even straighter, she fluffed out the skirt of her riding habit as if nothing were amiss.

They rode in silence for a while alongside the river but back in the direction of Willowstone Farm. Katherine's headache receded, but the need to post her letters burned in her chest. He'd thwarted her plans. If she insisted they continue on into town, he'd surely want to know why. Could she say she needed something and had found some pin money in the pocket of her pelisse? Did that sound too far-fetched?

Would he see through her? Hadn't she lied enough already?

She studied the man who rode a pace ahead. Lord Hartington was very sure of himself, and why shouldn't he be? He was handsome. His family loved and adored him. He was titled, driven, and successful, but there was something else about him she couldn't quite put her finger on. His confidence wasn't prideful. It was more as if he knew his purpose.

He glanced back at her, and she quickly averted her eyes. "The horses should have cooled down by now," he said. "Let's rest here a moment and let them drink some water."

She nodded, and he dismounted. He held out his arms to aid her descent. Even though his gaze was gentle, his eyes, framed by those dark eyelashes, sent her pulse skidding. The dizziness returned in full force. She gripped the saddle to not lose her balance.

He watched her as if trying to read her thoughts.

Did her face give her sentiments away?

From the ground beside her, he raised a questioning eyebrow. "Come on, now. I won't bite. I promise."

Don't act like some ninnyhammer. She held out her hands and tried to grip his shoulders, but the world spun. Losing her balance, she slid out of the saddle at an awkward angle.

"Whoa." He caught her as if she weighed no more than a feather and set her feet on the ground. "Are you all right?"

His scent of leather and citrus surrounded her. His hands were warm and rough on her skin, and their masculine strength made her feel petite, feminine, and protected. "Just a bit of a dizzy spell. My head may not be fully recovered."

He set her feet on the ground and shrugged off his jacket, laying it over a nearby fallen tree trunk with half its roots sticking up out of the earth. "Sit for a moment and take it easy." He scooped up the horses' reins and led them to the river's edge.

A chill settled where his warm hands had held her steady, and Katherine hugged her midsection as she settled on the makeshift bench.

He removed a brush from his saddle bag and checked the horses for any injuries, brushing them with long efficient strokes as he whispered soothing words to the animals. They nuzzled his chest in appreciation, like children seeking attention from their father. He laughed, showing a gleam of white teeth. In the sunlight, his normally dark hair appeared more mahogany, his sharp features softer, almost boyishly playful.

While his domineering side set her nerve endings on edge, this softer side compelled her to want to know him. She shook that off. She was supposed to be furious with him. He'd given her a fright and thwarted her opportunity to post her letters. She wanted to scream and wave her fists, but how could she fault him for looking out for the well-being of his guest? Instead, she stared at him with an unexplainable urge to either tousle his hair or draw close and breathe in his intoxicating aroma. She pictured his stunned reaction if she did either of those, and her lips twitched.

Stephen caught her smile. She rolled her lips to subdue it, yet despite their earlier tension, he returned one of his own with ease. He approached, stopping only a few inches short of her seated on the fallen log. His bold gaze swept over her, sending shivers like a spring breeze across her skin. His smile faded, leaving Katherine with an odd sense of disappointment.

He fingered an untamed lock of hair and wound it around his index finger. "It's soft like silk." He grunted a pleased sound. "In the sun, it's the color of honey."

Katherine's breath caught.

His gaze searched hers. "Where did you come from?"

She didn't respond.

"You are an unexpected surprise." He tucked the lock behind her ear. He leaned in closer and reached behind her. When his hand returned, his fingers contained a twig.

She gasped and felt for any other extraneous objects from her brisk ride. Her hair must be a complete bird's nest—twigs and all. She quickly twisted it into a bun.

Stephen's low chuckle rumbled. "You should leave it down."

His fingers stroked her face along the edge of her hairline. "It's beautiful. It reminds me of barley."

"Barley?" His nearness left her out of balance and off kilter. She pictured her head with stalks of barley sticking out in all directions like a scarecrow. How could that be appealing?

"Well, the color of barley." His gaze grew distant. "More like the color of barley at dusk when the breeze ripples it into waves."

Warmth swirled in her stomach at the husky tone of his voice. She hated the mousey-brown color of her hair, but the way he spoke of it made it sound desirable. If she'd thought as much growing up, it would have done amazing things for her self-image.

A sigh escaped her lips. She looked away so she wouldn't appear like some besotted fool. Whenever he was around, her world tilted. Her emotions tumbled down an embankment while she tried to grasp something solid so she wouldn't lose herself in his gaze.

She focused on brushing the wrinkles out of her borrowed dress, but the heat of his fixed stare bore into the top of her head. Stephen seemed like a logical man. One who weighed his options and formed quick opinions. What if he found her lacking? The risk was hurt and misery, but what were her chances of reward? Slim to none. To him, she was an unknown, no history, no background. For a man of the Quality, seeking the attention of such a woman would be a regrettable mistake. If only she could tell him the truth.

He leaned against the felled tree and stared out at the sparkling water.

Katherine cleared her throat and searched for a safe topic of conversation to break the silence. "Dominion is well trained. It was almost as if he could sense my next command."

"My father and I take great pride in our work." Stephen flashed her a sideways glance. Silence once again fell between them. His eyes grew distant, and one corner of his mouth drew up in a half smile. "In everything we do, we try to carry it out wholeheartedly, as if to the Lord."

She shifted on her perch to face him. "You train horses for God?"

"You could phrase it that way." He chuckled. "We do our best as if working for God, not for man. God rewards those who love Him and serve Him with their whole hearts."

"Your family has a strong faith." She remembered the prayers Lady Felton had prayed by her bedside.

"My parents are longtime believers." Conviction resounded in his voice. "They've been tried and tested, and their faith has become even stronger because of it. They love God, and it shows in all they do." His expression softened as he spoke of his family.

"Is it the same for you and Abby?"

He let out a deep breath. "Abby and I are believers. But even though we grew up in a loving God-fearing family, I'm afraid we're baby Christians." He pushed off the trunk to a full stand. "God is doing a work in both of us, refining us by fire, like purifying gold. We will come out better for it on the other end, but the process is tough."

"Does Abby's refining have to do with Nicholas Emerson's disappearance?"

Stephen peered at his hands. "It does, but I know God will get her through this."

There was a long, silent pause. The sad look in Stephen's eyes conveyed his compassion for his sister.

"And what about you?"

Stephen regarded her closely. "You certainly are full of questions."

Heat filled Katherine's cheeks. In the past few years, most of her interactions had been with servants, direct and to the point. She hadn't always been so forthright.

He chuckled as he turned to stare at the water, but his expression grew serious. "I chose to walk away from God while at Oxford. My parents raised me in church and prayed daily, but I was doing it more for them than me. When I left for school, I put God on a shelf and pursued worldly interests. I traveled abroad, looking to experience the world. I fell in with a dubious crowd and watched someone hang for her poor decisions." He exhaled a deep heavy sound. "At that moment, I realized there had to be something more, some bigger purpose for my life. I prayed a prayer for the first time that came from my heart." The slap of the back of his hand into his other palm added emphasis to his point. "I wasn't just repeating words or praying what I thought my parents wanted to hear. I prayed out of a deep longing for God to give me direction. I asked him to take control of my life." He cleared his throat and loosely laced his fingers. "It's a testimony to my parents' devoted prayers for my salvation that I found my way back."

"You have a remarkable family."

"God has surrounded me with a wonderful family and friends." He tilted his head up, and although his lips didn't move, she could almost hear a whispered, *thank you.*

She stayed quiet as he remained lost in his thoughts.

A rabbit hopped out of the woods and nibbled on some clover. When Dominion snorted, the tiny creature darted for cover.

Stephen rubbed the back of his neck. "When I returned to London, an old friend from Oxford and his new wife had purchased the flat next door to my bachelor's lodgings. Seeing the changes God had made in my friend's life stirred something inside me. I wanted that sort of life for myself—a wife and a family."

Her heart ached to the point of weeping. She, too, had longed for those things, even more so after her parents passed, but when her betrothed backed out and the responsibilities of her home and holdings fell into her lap, her dreams fizzled. She wouldn't let the same happen to Claire.

"I don't know why I'm telling you this." He exhaled. "I shouldn't bore you so."

"Not at all." She shook her head. "Quite the opposite."

An appreciative smile curved his lips, and he peered out at the water. A light breeze ruffled his hair and danced a loose curl about her face.

"Have you and your family always trained horses?" Would he have heard of the Jenkins's prized horse stock?

"We used to only breed them, but after my father's accident, I specially trained a horse just for him and had the idea to train horses for injured people." A sparkle lit his eyes. "Life took on new meaning, so I approached my father, and he liked the idea. We both worked on the regimen together. I spent a significant amount of time researching and getting our name out there. Like you saw with Dominion, we school the horses so well that they sense what you want them to do by the slightest movement. I purposefully left Dominion a bit on the wilder side since he's my personal mount."

Katherine tilted her head. "You have a lovely story."

"It is rather remarkable." He laced his fingers and stretched, cracking his knuckles.

"What's remarkable"—she fought down a teasing grin— "is that you can go from nighttime prowler to daytime pursuer to charitable defender of the weak."

"Weak?" A mischievous gleam lit his eyes. "Since when are wildcats weak?"

Her wide smile matched his as they locked gazes and held. The river's rushing grew faint until all she could hear was her heartbeat.

Stephen's eyes darkened and held the anticipation of a pending storm. "We should head back." He spoke the words but didn't move or release her from his gaze.

He knew nothing about her, and she understood very little of him, but contentment surrounded him, and her guard slipped in his presence as if they'd known each other for years. He teased her the way he did his sister, yet it was different. He held a magnetic pull that captivated her and exasperated her at the same time.

"Lord Hartington?" Her voice was barely a whisper.

"Stephen." He leaned closer. The solid strength of his body standing so near heated her skin like a hearth's fire.

His citrus and leather scent teased her senses. His shoulders dimmed the sunlight and she stared at their broad expanse encased in a well-fitted, wool frock coat. How easily such confidence and strength could help shoulder the responsibilities that buried her. "Stephen."

"I didn't expect you." His voice held a tone of reverent awe that curled her toes.

Was this how courting felt—courageous like ivy climbing to reach the sun, thirsty like willow tree near a stream, awake like black coffee, and alive like a sunflower tilting its head toward the sun?

Her eyes fluttered to a close, and her world spun. She tilted, leaning against his chest. His arms encircled her, and the letters stuffed in the bodice of her gown crinkled. Her breath caught. Had he heard?

She pulled back, but his hands moved to cup her face.

"Who are you, Kate Vernon?" His ice-blue eyes smoldered. "Why did you flee me as if the devil himself were in pursuit? What are you afraid of?" His eyes dropped to her lips. "I can help. Let me protect you."

Help? Her parents were supposed to protect her, but they'd died. Alfred was supposed to care for her but he reneged. Cousin Horace was her official guardian, yet he attempted to kill her. She pushed him away, off the log and to her feet. What had she been thinking? She must protect herself—this time against temptation. "It's getting late."

Stephen ran a hand over his head and through his thick hair. He squeezed his eyes closed and shook his head. "You're right." When he opened them, he no longer met her gaze. "We should return." He rose and gathered the horses.

She barely knew Stephen Hartington, and she may not know much about flirting and courting, but she was certain he'd been about to kiss her. And if she hadn't come to her senses, she would have let him. Her cheeks burst into flames, and homesickness washed over her like a bout of nausea. She wanted nothing more than to crawl under the covers in her own room at Steepleton Manor and pretend she'd never woken up the morning her cousin arrived. She hastened to Dominion's side and waited for Stephen to assist her in a leg-up.

He cleared his throat, and his hands encircled her waist. She refused to acknowledge their strength, the ease at which he lifted her into the saddle, or the tenderness with which they had held her only moments before.

She followed his lead as they rode a different route back toward Willowstone. Green rolling hills dotted with white sheep graced the far bank of the river.

"Were you able to become acquainted with the grounds?" He spoke over his shoulder.

"Only a small portion."

He pointed out the far border of their lands in the distance and some of the tenant cottages as they passed. Gone was the adoring gentleman with endearing platitudes. An aloof, businesslike gentleman lingered in his stead.

The groomsman's shoulders sagged with relief as they rode into the barn. He held the reins for Stephen to dismount, and Stephen aided Katherine down from her horse. She gripped his upper arms for support and gritted her teeth until her feet touched the ground, but when she tried to turn away, he tightened his hold on her waist. Katherine raised her chin and forced her gaze to meet his.

"Miss Vernon, what happened back there was poorly done of me." He frowned. "I forgot myself, but it won't happen again."

She blinked at his detached tone and the glacial look in his eyes. Had she misread his feelings? Her cheeks flushed with heat, and her stomach soured. She bit her lip and issued him a curt nod. She had grown accustomed to rejection.

Stephen relinquished his hold.

Katherine strode from the barn, and once out of his line of sight, fled for the safety of her bed chamber.

CHAPTER 10

*S*tephen's family and their guest supped together in the formal dining room. Footmen refilled their long-stemmed crystal glasses and set out dishes of food drizzled with creamy sauces. This time of day had always been his favorite—the time when they gathered and broke bread together, swapping stories of past and present. Tonight, however, he struggled to focus. The vision of Kate's rosy cheeks contrasting with the sparking liquid emerald color of her eyes captivated his thoughts. He could still feel the soft warmth of her fitted against him. Even now, as she sat across from him avoiding his gaze, his fingers ached to reach out, drag her into his arms.

He was a cad.

One moment, he had been talking about being a Christ-follower and the next acting like some libertine, forgetting he was a gentleman. *For heaven's sake.* He'd been considering proposing to another woman. What had come over him to allow his emotions to supplant reason? He spared a glance above the rim of his glass and received his answer—an enchanting pair of eyes that peered at him as if he were the only man on earth.

What did it say about his character, that since he'd returned home, Julia hadn't even come to mind until now? Stephen rested his fork on the side of his plate. He needed to focus on his mission—prepare for the delivery of prime blood horses to be used as bait for the serial horse thieves and protect his family while he waited for the bandits to make their move.

The same tenacious lock of hair fell across Kate's face, and she tucked it behind her ear with long graceful fingers. She'd looked terribly frightened barreling through the woods with her long curls streaming behind her, and he never received her answer as to why she'd been so scared. Why didn't he inquire further? How could he have missed the way she'd expertly maneuvered his horse? Had he learned nothing from his time at the Home Office?

Look at all the angles.

He rubbed one eyebrow. An expert horsewoman appears out of nowhere a few days before the arrival of the prized steeds.

She claims amnesia and cannot recall her name or any other information regarding herself and her past.

She rides off on Dominion for town.

Could she have been stealing his horse or testing to see how observant the groomsmen and staff were?

If so, he was up against professionals, and Kate Vernon was excellent at her trade, made all the more so with her air of innocence and angelic face. He would need to keep a close watch on her and call-in recruits for undercover reinforcements. He'd post a letter to the Home Office tomorrow.

Kate had avoided eye contact with him all evening. His father made her task easy by dominating the conversation, retelling some of their childhood feats. Abby tried to change the subject, but their father persisted. It wasn't long before

Mother and Abby added to the stories, and they all were talking over each other.

Kate's eyes sparked as she laughed at their antics, sending his traitorous pulse racing. She wasn't trying to impress him or his family. She didn't hold an uppity air of criticism as did most of his acquaintances. Kate seemed happy merely to be in their presence. He prayed she wasn't in line with horse thieves. He'd hate to see someone so full of life hang for such a crime.

A shiver ran down his spine, and he blocked the memories pushing to resurface.

Those gathered at the table whooped with laughter to the point of tears as Father related the story of his and Abby's feats of climbing from their cribs. His belly shook as he described how their mother had set up an all-night surveillance of the children's room.

"Poor Sarah thought she was turning as mad as a hatter," his father said, "for she'd come in to check on them, and they'd be in each other's cribs or together in the same one." Father slapped his good knee and smiled at Mother.

Kate sat forward in her seat, absorbed in his father's tale. There was a loneliness to how she hung on every word. If she did have amnesia, was her family looking for her? Did she have a family, and did they care about the empty chair at their table? If a lady of the *ton* had gone missing, it would make the papers or at least the gossip columns. He'd check in town or set Jacob on the task.

Kate's tentative grin broke wide over something Abby said. Kate made such a captivating picture that Stephen's lips lifted into a smile too.

Mother caught his gaze, and a warm gleam settled in her eyes. She leaned over and whispered, "She stands out, doesn't she?"

Stephen turned his attention to the floral centerpiece. He hadn't yet told his parents about Julia. Would they enjoy having the fashionable socialite as their daughter-in-law. While Julia was refined, elegant, and haughty, Kate appeared down-to-earth, natural, and wholesome.

And potentially a horse thief.

"I know you're puzzled by her, but some people don't always fall into neat categories."

Stephen pretended not to hear. Mother was always after him about not making snap judgments about people, but in his line of work, it was necessary to size people up and make quick decisions regarding their character.

"My poor wife posted the servants and me at various ungodly hours of the night"—His father leaned back in his chair and propped his bad leg up on a nearby stool— "to keep watch and discover how the twins were mysteriously switching cribs. Stephen would heave himself over the rail, crawl across a bureau, and dive into Abby's crib. He would then assist Abby out so she could do the same." His fingers wrapped around the wooden armrests of his chair as he guffawed another hard belly laugh. A twinkle lit Father's eyes as he regained his composure. "God has blessed us with two delightful, intelligent children."

"I'd add inventive and incorrigible to that list," Mother said, and they all laughed. Pride for her children glowed on her face.

"Well, my beautiful bride, it's getting late. I think it's about time we retire for the evening." Father leaned heavily on the table and struggled to a stand.

"Good night, darlings." Mother smiled as she rose and handed her husband his cane. She placed a kiss on each of her children's foreheads.

Stephen jolted as his mother turned and kissed the top of Katherine's head, bidding her goodnight. His family had taken to the stranger, and they'd be heartbroken if she turned out to have less than good intentions. All the more reason to get to the bottom of the thieving ring quickly and keep his spy work on a professional level.

"*G*ood night," Katherine squeaked in reply. She hadn't felt the tenderness of a motherly kiss in years. Seeing the Hartington family and how they interacted had raised a lump in her throat that she'd struggled to swallow around.

Lady Felton lovingly brushed her fingers down Katherine's cheek before she turned and followed in her husband's wake.

"How about a nice game of cards?" A wolfish smile swept over Abby's face.

Stephen raised both brows in a challenge. "You're a glutton for punishment."

Katherine had successfully avoided speaking to Stephen at dinner, and the idea of conversing with him now stirred her stomach to the point of casting up her accounts. There must be a way to get out of Abby's devious plan.

What if she faked a yawn? "I think I might—"

"Of course you should join us, Kate." Abby cut her off. "I could use the moral support playing against such a worthy opponent." Her eyes pleaded with Katherine, and Katherine didn't have the heart to disappoint her friend.

They adjourned to the gaming room, and Abby whispered, "Remember, distract him so he doesn't notice me dealing from the bottom of the deck."

"How exactly?"

"Get him talking about God or horses. Maybe bat your eyelashes."

She stopped short and leveled Abby with a deadly stare, but her friend giggled and pushed her into the room.

This was a terrible idea.

A hardy blaze burned in the hearth, and mahogany tables surrounded by low-backed chairs were stationed in corners. Chess games already in progress awaited the return of their players. The Hartington family must spend many evenings together, much as her family had.

A deep ache created a vacuum in Katherine's heart. She missed her family and the way they loved and laughed. Her sister was all she had, but she only got to see Claire when she was on holiday from finishing school. When she completed the courses, Claire would debut to society. Some fortunate gentlemen would ask her to be his wife, and Katherine would be alone. Strange how being in the Hartingtons' presence made her loneliness more cognizant.

If she'd been able to have a family of her own, she would have wanted it to be like the Hartington household—happy, loving, and filled with laughter. However, to have a family meant she must marry. If that prospect hadn't looked bleak before, her cousin's disastrous visit made it abysmal. Her dowry, estate, and inheritance could all be lost to a blackguard.

While Abby located the deck of cards, Katherine wandered over to a chess board and picked up the knight chess piece pretending to admire its fine carvings. Her cousin could be sitting at her father's desk right now, selling off her family's heirlooms to pay down his debts. He could be ruining the legacy she'd worked the past five years to save, which her father, grandfather, and great-grandfather had spent their lives developing.

Stephen removed the chess board and set it on the sideboard. "Let me take that from you before you snap the poor horse's head off."

Katherine blinked. "I beg your pardon?"

Stephen stood over her, his very nearness sending her off kilter. He tugged the chess piece she held, and she loosened her tight grip. He placed it back on the board.

"I'm sorry. I was woolgathering." Katherine forced a smile.

He pulled out a chair at the empty table and gestured for her to sit. Abby seated herself and shuffled the cards.

Stephen lowered into a chair and scooted closer to the table. "What does one with amnesia gather wool about?" He stretched out his long legs and laced his fingers behind his head. His steady gaze held hers as if her answer was of the utmost importance.

So much for avoiding eye contact. Katherine's skin warmed under his scrutiny, and flashbacks of their interlude in the woods jostled her thoughts. "God and...and horses."

Abby paused in her shuffling and shot Katherine a glare that said *don't give us away.* Abby had suggested she talk about those things, but Katherine could have been more subtle, slipping them into conversation instead of blurting the topics together. She met Stephen's gaze and shrugged as if everyone woolgathered about such things.

Abby bridged the cards and set them on the table. "I'll deal first."

Stephen nodded for her to go ahead and focused on Katherine. "God and horses, eh?"

She scrambled for a response. "Horses are such majestic creatures that I was thinking God must have some in heaven. Don't you think?"

She sounded like a henwit.

Abby bridged the cards one last time and started to deal.

"You seem to have an affinity for horses, and you've proven to be an excellent horsewoman." He casually slanted toward one arm of the chair and crossed an ankle over his knee. "Where did you learn such skills?"

Katherine's lips parted to tell him her papa had taught her, but hesitated. Someone with amnesia wouldn't remember.

His gaze searched hers.

Odd. Was that eagerness in his eyes?

She shrugged once more, but this time with the strange sensation that she was a fish who dodged a hook.

Stephen watched a few cards slide across the table before

he grabbed a well-worn Bible from a nearby table, flipped near the end, and read, "And I saw Heaven opened, and behold a white horse; and He that sat upon Him was called Faithful and True, and in righteousness He doth judge and make war." He paused. "There you have it. Revelation describes Jesus coming back on a white horse."

His eyes narrowed and he studied his sister's fingers for an instant.

Katherine gripped the edge of her seat. Her distraction wasn't working. "How did you know where to look?"

He flipped the book shut, and his fingers slid down over the binding. "My parents read to us from the Bible every night since I was a child. I guess some things stuck." He picked up his hand, and Katherine did the same. He arranged his cards and laid one down.

"Have you read the entire Bible?"

"A few times."

Katherine's family Bible had rested on a pedestal in her father's office. She'd opened it a couple of times, but the snatches of words she'd read from Leviticus and Numbers eluded her. "It made sense to you?" She played her card and Abby picked it up discarding a five of diamonds.

Stephen chuckled. "At first I understood the gist of things, mostly the childhood versions of Noah's ark and Jonah being swallowed by the whale, but the more I read, the more things are revealed to me. I pray to God to help my understanding and to speak to me through His Word, and suddenly the same story I've read many times over will have a whole new meaning."

It was Stephen's turn again, and he tossed a card into the discard pile.

"Do you have a favorite Bible story?" She asked more out of curiosity than to aid Abby's trickery.

He rubbed his lips with two fingers. "I'd say the story of

Shadrack, Meshach, and Abednego being thrown into the fiery furnace."

Her expression must have shown her horror for he chuckled.

"Not a hair on their heads was burned, and they walked out of the furnace not even smelling of smoke. While others believed they were at the mercy of King Nebuchadnezzar, they decided to put their trust in God." A crooked grin spread across his face. "There's something comforting about Jesus being with them in the fire."

If only Jesus had been with her in the billiard room before her cousin had knocked her to the floor.

Abby spread her hand on the table and Katherine and Stephen followed suit.

"I win." Abby's voice rang with pride.

"Your game has improved." Stephen said with such a tone of appreciation that Katherine shifted in her seat to ease the weight of their duplicity.

His twin's chest swelled with triumph. "I'll deal again since the two of you are enjoying a lovely chat." She scooped up the cards and shuffled once more.

"Indeed." Stephen arched a brow at Katherine "You must have heard about the story of Samson, right?"

"Wasn't he the strongest man in the world?" She neatened the cards in front of her and picked them up sorting them by suit.

Stephen flashed her a boyish grin with two rows of even white teeth. "His arrogance was his downfall, leading to Delilah cutting his hair and the Philistines gorging out his eyes."

Katherine grimaced.

He picked up his cards and fanned out his hand. "God allowed Samson's strength to return." Stephen narrowed his gaze on Abby. "But Samson *never* regained his eyesight. If God's moral laws are broken, a penalty that cannot be overlooked will be paid."

Abby moved her hand of cards closer to her chest and warily eyed her brother.

"Think of it like Sir Isaac Newton's laws of physics." He placed a hand on the armrest and scooted forward in his chair. "How an action causes a reaction. God's moral laws are the same. If we step out of a second-story window, we expect to hit the ground, but how many times have we sinned and expected to get away with it?"

His gaze turned on Abby's with an intensity as if to communicate a hidden message. "Our actions have consequences."

Katherine swallowed hard, thinking about the deception she was living. What sort of price was she going to pay for her lies?

"Your turn, Kate." Abby's pitch sounded a tad high, and her face had paled.

Katherine discarded, and Abby quickly snatched up her card and called the hand.

"And, dear sister, what might the consequences be for cheating?"

Abby laid down a pair of aces, which trumped both their hands. But there was no triumph in the action. "How did you know?"

"Let's just say I prefer my hand being dealt from the top of the deck." He tossed down his cards on the table and laced his fingers behind his head. "You can't get away with anything. I will find you out."

His words targeted Abby, but he flicked a warning look in Katherine's direction.

I will find you out.

Did Stephen know she was lying? How? And if so, what did he plan to do about it?

CHAPTER 11

The weather was unseasonably warm the following morning as Katherine rode in the stuffy private carriage with Lady Felton and Abby into town. The bright sun shone between the branches of the blossoming trees and filled the air with their sweet fragrance. Petals sprinkled the road, turning the lane into a whimsical fairytale land. The letter in her pocket kept Katherine grounded in reality.

Today should be less eventful than yesterday with its horse chase, near kiss, and a disturbing game of cards. Lord Hartington had seemed determined to create a rise in her. How easily she'd succumbed to his nearness, losing herself in the intensity of his gaze by the riverside. The last thing she *needed* was to lose her heart to Lord Hartington. There was no time to entertain the possibility. She needed to focus on getting her letters posted and then work on a plan to gain back her father's estate. One that didn't require sacrificing herself on the altar of matrimony to her wretched cousin.

As their carriage clattered over a stone bridge and rolled into town, Katherine scanned every building for a messenger service or postmaster to send her missive to her sister. It seemed a simple enough task, but what had her cousin done since her disappearance? Would her name be written in every newspaper and signs posted notifying the town of her missing person? She must keep her head down and not draw attention.

Lady Felton tilted her head. "Does anything look familiar?"

Katherine sighed and could honestly say, "I'm afraid not."

There was a quaint rustic charm to the honey-colored stone buildings with slate roofs. The square's convenient location drew crowds from various towns to sell their sheep and other wares, and people bustled in and out of shops. Street vendors called out to entice buyers. All sorts of delicious smells wafted into the air, like fresh baked bread and spices. Sheep filed down the narrow side streets to market, led by their shepherd. Ladies in bright colored dresses and parasols strolled arm in arm past the shops. Despite growing up less than a day's ride away, Katherine couldn't recall a time she'd ever visited here.

Her stomach twisted. What was the likelihood of Horace or his henchmen patrolling the streets? He was friends with the constable. What would she do if either one spotted her?

She pulled and twisted the thumb portion of her glove. She would rather die than live under the cruelty she would suffer at the hand of Cousin Horace. She recalled her cousin's face, enraged and shaking with uncontrolled fury as he pinned her up against the wall of the billiard room. His threats echoed in her head *"You ungrateful brat. You are going to marry me tomorrow, or else I will compromise you here and now with Lord Pewitt as a witness."*

Despite the heat, a shiver ran through her.

The carriage drew to a stop, and nausea washed over Katherine. All the things that could go wrong ate at her until she was afraid the contents of her breakfast were about to make a reappearance.

Abby awaited the footman to open the carriage door. "I have a dress fitting. Then, we can look at some of the latest arrivals while Mama stops to buy some jams to take over to Mrs. Emerson's." She glanced at Katherine. "Are you all right? You're as pale as a ghost."

Lady Felton stared at Katherine, awaiting an answer.

"I'm fine." She squirmed under the weight of such scrutiny. "Truly. I feel much better now the carriage has stopped. Perhaps I suffer from motion sickness."

"Sit and rest for a spell." Lady Felton fussed over her like a sick patient. Holding her palm up to Katherine's forehead, she tested to see if she felt warm. "Your color is coming back. You very well could have an aversion to riding in a closed carriage." Lady Felton patted her knee. "If necessary, we can hire an open carriage to return to the farm."

"Oh, no, I should be fine now." The last thing she needed was to parade about in an open carriage for all to see. She might as well broadcast her whereabouts. *I'm residing at the Willowstone Farm. Come and kill me.* "You don't need to hire another carriage on my account. Now that I know what the problem is, I'll make certain I look forward instead of watching the scenery pass."

Lady Felton nodded, but her brow remained furrowed.

Katherine put her hand over Lady Felton's. "Thank you for your kindness. It's nice to be fussed over."

Lady Felton looked at her in a way that reminded Katherine of her mother. "It is my pleasure, dear. If you change your mind, don't hesitate to ask."

After alighting from the carriage, Katherine pulled her bonnet tighter around her face and peeked out from underneath its wide brim. To her right, she spotted a sign for a postmaster's office. Now, she needed to devise an excuse to escape for a few moments.

"I'm going to the mercantile to purchase the jams and other items." Lady Felton pointed in the shop's direction. "Shall I meet you here in about an hour?"

"An hour should give us plenty of time for my fitting." Abby hooked her arm through Katherine's and pulled her toward the closest dress shop. "We'll even have time to see what kinds of dresses other guests have ordered for the Rutherford Masquerade." Excitement lit her face. "I love masquerades. They're intriguing. Half the time you can easily guess who your dance partner is, but it's the other half that makes them so thrilling." Her eyes turned distant and wistful. "It may be sad, but sometimes during these masquerades, I pretend that the gentleman behind the mask is Nicholas."

Katherine's heart twisted for her friend.

Abby blinked and was back to her bubbly self. "This year, I originally wanted to go as Viola from Shakespeare's *Twelfth Night,* since she also had a twin, but Viola dressed as a boy to hide her identity, and Mama didn't think it appropriate for me to do likewise, so she ruled it out. Instead, she convinced me to go as Juliet Capulet from *Romeo and Juliet.*"

Abby captured both of Katherine's hands in hers. "You must come with me to the masquerade as my guest."

Katherine hesitated. She didn't plan to intrude upon the Hartington family long. Plus, a masquerade meant being around hundreds of people. She needed an excuse. "I don't have a dress."

Her friend's face glowed with enthusiasm. "You can wear my costume from last year. I didn't get to attend the ball because I was in mourning for Nicholas." Her face tightened. "I still don't believe he's gone. There's something in my spirit that can't accept it's true." Like the switch between night and day, her face beamed once again. "Oh, Kate, say you'll come. It will be so much fun. We'll be anonymous together. Maybe after the unveiling, someone will recognize you and help you remember who you really are."

"I don't think..."

"Please, for me. People have acted strange around me since

Nicholas's disappearance. They mean well, but my presence makes them uncomfortable. Having you there would be a godsend. Do tell me you'll come."

Katherine's mind screamed *no* but her head nodded against her will.

Abby wrapped her in a tight embrace. "You've made my day. I can't wait to tell Mother. Come on." She grabbed Katherine's arm and pulled her into the dress shop. "You can help me look for a Juliet mask."

Vibrant fabrics spilled from every usable inch of floor space like elegant waterfalls of color. Several young women stood in the fitting areas as the sales associates held up various recommendations and measured them. It reminded Katherine of an artist she'd once seen who'd dab a bit of color here and there on the white canvass until a beautiful picture emerged.

She fingered the soft silken fabrics and mused over the last time her mother had brought her to a dress shop for a fitting. Gowns were being ordered in preparation for her coming out season. The plan was to have most of the gowns made and ready for when she graduated from finishing school. Her mother thought it wise to beat the season's rush and order them a year in advance, reserving a few in case trends changed. All Mama's work had been premature. After the accident, Katherine never had a season, nor did she complete finishing school. Claire would wear some of the dresses for her debut next season, if her cousin's actions didn't ruin her chances. Katherine would do everything in her power to ensure he didn't. She peeked out the window at the postmaster's office across the street.

"Isn't this divine?" Abby held up a shimmering burgundy material. "It's similar material to my costume."

"It's lovely."

"My fitting will be a few moments." Abby followed a seamstress and paused at the curtain. "Would you like to come in?"

This was her opportunity. "I'm going to keep looking around. You go on ahead." She waited for the curtain to close behind Abby and the seamstress before she bolted for the door. Keeping her bonnet down, she ignored the stares as she hurried to the postmaster's office in a most unladylike fashion. Her mother's voice rang in her head. "Ladies never rush or run. They walk with grace, poise, and if necessary, a hint of purpose." *Forgive me, Mama. These are desperate matters.*

She paused for a carriage to pass and darted across the street. A horse whinnied, and its snort ruffled her bonnet. She gasped at the large dark stallion she hadn't seen on the other side of the passing carriage. The horse reared, and Katherine cringed as his hoofs flopped in the air above her head. The rider turned the horse barely in time. Katherine gathered her wits and skirts with shaking hands and sprinted the rest of the way.

You won't do yourself any good if you get yourself killed.

She leapt up the small set of steps and burst into the quaint office, leaving the door wide open in her wake.

"Well, good day, my dear." An elderly gentleman stood with great effort from his chair. His rheumy eyes gleamed with kindness, and the sunburst lines beside them deepened as a smile broke across his face. "What may I do for you?"

"I need to post a few letters." She gasped between pants and slid her letters onto the counter. "These two go to the Sherbourne Finishing School for Ladies' Decorum. Here is the address."

"Sherbourne? That will be two shillings."

"When can I expect it to be delivered?"

"Well, let's see." He opened his log book and calendar. "Charlie is heading out today... oops, but he's headed east. Ah, let's see Henry is leaving... Oh, when is Henry due back...?" He grabbed another logbook off a shelf.

Katherine's fingernails dug into her palms even through the thin material of her gloves.

He pushed the book into its slot. "No, not that one." His fingers traced the writing on the spines. "Here it is."

Her toes curled in her kid boots. "It's all right. I must go. I'm in a bit of a hurry." She pushed the letter to her solicitors toward the postmaster, and it teetered on the edge of the counter. "It should go to Whitmer and Collins Attorneys at Law on Mayhew Street in London. Please make certain it arrives." She sprinted for the door.

The clerk yelled after her. "Don't worry, my dear. I stake my name on it."

"Whoa, fella." Stephen tugged on the reins and fought to calm his frightened horse. Dominion snorted and stomped his foot but obeyed. Stephen's heart bludgeoned his chest as if to break out of his ribs. He, too, had quite a scare. The blasted woman could have been trampled. If Dominion wasn't so well trained, someone would be fetching the physician or the undertaker.

Dominion shook its mane, letting out a loud whinny of discontent.

Stephen furrowed his brow. There had been something familiar about the woman, but he couldn't quite put his finger on it. She needed a good lesson on the hazards of dashing across a street without looking. It could save her foolish life. He jumped down from Dominion and tied him to a nearby hitching post, securing the reins.

"Mighty good of ya to come in tah town, millord." Mr. Johnston, the local saddler, tipped his hat from the entrance of his shop. His long apron hung down to his ankles.

"Good day, Mr. Johnston." Stephen touched the brim of his. "How's the missis?"

"She's busy with grandkids. Got twelve now and count'n."

"Twelve." Stephen whistled. "God bless your families."

"Mighty kind of ya. Children are a reward from the Lord. Blessed is the man whose quiver is full of them."

Stephen had been praying for a quiver full of children. He wasn't prone to worry, but his own parents had struggled with conceiving and had he and Abby later in years. Julia was one of six children and being from a prolific family was one of the items he'd listed in an ideal spouse. His parents loved each other very much, and he and Julia would come to love each other in a similar fashion over time. Kate's image, with the sun backlighting her hair in a warm honey color, flashed through his mind, but he pushed it aside.

He stepped onto the shop's porch and waved Mr. Johnston over. "When is the local horse fair?"

"Coming up in a fortnight." The man rocked on his heels. The fair was a profitable time for the saddler. "Will you be selling or buying any bloods?"

"Both." Stephen leaned close and lowered his voice a tad. "I have a purebred stallion that just arrived that I'm training to sell, and I'm always looking to pick up a young blood. Could you let me know if you hear of anyone who wants to be on the other end of the financial transaction?"

"Rightly will." He scrunched up his face. "There was a fellow a sennight ago lookin' to sell and then buy a sweetgoer for his fiancée as a wedding gift. Gibbons was his name. I mentioned you to him. Has he come by the farm?"

"Not yet." Could Gibbons be part of the horse ring and putting out feelers? Did he and his so-called fiancée work as cohorts? "I appreciate the referral."

After Mr. Johnston shuffled back inside the shop, Stephen

strode toward the postmaster's office to courier his request to the Home Office for an additional undercover agent.

Could Kate be involved with Mr. Gibbons? Stephen's jaw tightened. Was she the fiancée?

The door of the postmaster's office flung wide, and the same figure who'd darted in front of his horse ran out. Her head was turned to acknowledge the parting remarks the clerk yelled at her.

Stephen had a split second to brace himself.

CHAPTER 12

$\mathcal{K}$atherine deflected off a hard surface. She would have tumbled backward if not for two strong hands grabbing her upper arms and holding her steady.

"Kate?"

She peered up at the hard line of Stephen's chiseled jaw. His eyes burned like blue fire, and she winced.

"Where are you going? You almost got yourself killed a moment ago by darting in front of my horse, and now this. What has gotten into you?"

"That was *you* on the horse?" Her cheeks heated like the coals in the nearby blacksmith's shop.

"Are you in danger?" He gave her a tiny shake. "Where are Mother and Abby?" His head turned, peering up and down the lane.

"They're fine." Her voice registered a strangled pitch. "I, uh... I thought I saw someone I recognized, so I was running to find out if they knew me."

He glanced over her shoulder at the postmaster's office.

The lies tasted bitter in her mouth and tightened her stomach into a knot. How much longer could she continue with this charade? She'd created a horrible mess, but now there seemed no turning back. As soon as the Hartingtons realized she'd been lying to them about not knowing her identity, they would surely turn her out.

"Did they?"

"Did they what?" She blinked to bring her mind to the present.

Stephen issued her an odd look. "Did they recognize you?"

"Ah, no. No, she didn't."

"How unfortunate." His eyes narrowed. "Where are my mother and sister? Why aren't you with them?"

Katherine's fingernails dug into the palms of her hands. She was irritated with herself and wanted to kick Stephen in the shins for his questions and for showing up at the most inconvenient time. She needed to return before Abby noticed her disappearance. "Your mother is at the mercantile, and Abby is across the way at the dress shop getting fitted for the masquerade."

He released her.

Katherine stepped back and raised her chin. "Good day, Lord Harington." She forced a dismissive tone hoping he would leave her alone. With a farewell nod she strode toward the dress shop.

Stephen caught up with her, his long stride casually matching her rapid one. "There's no reason to be so sensitive."

Had she been? She paused, opening her mouth to snap at him, but then stopped herself. She continued toward the shop.

"What no quick retort?" He goaded her as if trying to fly her into the boughs. "No witty response?" One side of his mouth twisted into a sardonic smile.

He dogged her every step until she turned with an annoyed huff. "Are you going to follow me all the way? Don't you have business to attend?"

He broke into a full-blown grin, and his eyes sparkled with merriment. "I did, until I realized how much you needed me."

She stopped at his remark, crossing her arms, displaying what she hoped was an exasperated expression meant to say, *explain yourself*.

"Someone has to ward off the oncoming traffic, call, 'Look out, vexed woman plowing through.'"

"Incorrigible." She tilted her face toward the sky, complaining to God, before facing Stephen with an upturned chin. "Your mama was right. You are *completely* incorrigible."

Stephen chuckled and continued trailing her into the dress shop.

"There you are." Abigail stood in her Juliette costume with a pinned hem. "I was beginning to think someone abducted you." She turned to Stephen. "I should have known you'd be involved. You're always trouble."

Katherine flipped him an *I-told-you-so* look over her shoulder.

Stephen pretended to be offended. "First incorrigible, now trouble—how in the world do you put up with me?"

Abby frowned and eyed them both with questions before holding the sides of her skirt out. "What do you think of the dress?"

Katherine stepped back to take in the full effect.

Burgundy satin fabric, the color of crushed roses. Similarly colored braided rope crisscrossed over her chest and led down toward the V waist that accentuated her hips. The gently puffed sleeves narrowed and elongated into points over the backs of her hands. On the crown of her head was a similar braided circle with miniature fabric roses entwined. A sheer veil cascaded down to her mid-back. She looked magnificent. Katherine's heart clenched for her loss of Nicholas, *Where for art thou, Romeo?* It seemed too fitting. A warning sting of tears brewed behind her lids. "It's stunning."

"You look incredible." Brotherly love shone in Stephen's eyes, and the tears that had burned behind Katherine's eyelids threatened to spill over. She quickly wiped them away before anyone noticed. What had come over her? Recently she'd been on the verge of tears at any given moment. The strain of living a falsehood must be taking its toll, keeping her in a fragile emotional state.

"Well then." Abby beamed. "I'll change out of this and will be just a moment." She whirled into the dressing room, leaving Stephen and Katherine alone together. An awkward silence followed, and Katherine pretended to busy herself admiring the fabrics. Her hand grazed lightly over emerald-green silk.

"That color matches your eyes."

Katherine startled and glanced up to find him watching her.

"They're a lovely color, you know."

She froze as he moved closer. Transfixed by his gaze, she didn't dare breathe. A foot or so of distance separated them, but his body heat radiated as if he had replaced the sun.

"Your eyes are the color of morning dew on wet leaves, and when you're angry, they glitter like emeralds." His brows lowered and he leaned in for a closer look. "Except for the tiny gold flecks around the center."

He stood back, but the air continued to crackle between them. Heat flowed up her neck. The heady scent of citrus and leather surrounded her like a mist, holding her captive. He stoked the heat with his disarming smile, similar to the one he'd displayed beside the riverbank when the sun shone off his hair and bronzed skin.

"I'd hate to think of how many poor beaus are waiting for you, wondering where you've gone and when you'll return."

His words broke the spell, and her mind jolted back to reality. "What beaus?" She stepped aside to put space between them and process his words.

Stephen laughed. "They're going to be disappointed you

haven't recalled a single one of them." His husky voice ran over her skin like silk. "I, for one, am *not* disappointed."

Her lips parted.

He propped his shoulder against the nearby window frame and focused his attention outside as if he hadn't just addled her wits.

She moved on to another table piled with fabrics, these sturdy cottons suitable for daily tasks. Had he been flirting with her? Was he toying with her to see if she was a respectful woman or one he could dally with? She bit her bottom lip and cringed at how enamored she'd behaved at the riverbank. Hadn't Abby said that women swoon in his presence? How embarrassing that she'd gotten dizzy and lost her balance, falling into his chest. It was probably a common occurrence for the son of an earl. Mama would roll over in her grave if she knew her daughter had behaved in such a fashion.

"If you plan on going to the masquerade as a pheasant crossed with a pumpkin, that is a perfect choice."

Katherine jumped, surprised he'd spoken when he appeared engrossed in the scenery outside the window. She stared at the hideous material clutched in her fingers. It slipped to the floor. She scooped up the mass of bows, plumes, and ruffles in a horrid shade of rusty orange and frowned at its unsightly appearance.

"I always thought fashion sense was inherent in a woman, much like *walking* and *riding horses*." He taunted her with her own words. "But now I see it's a learned social skill."

She held the fabric up under her chin. "You mean this isn't all the rage right now?" She feigned an innocent expression.

"It looks like the skin of a tiger still eating a peacock."

Katherine burst out laughing.

---

*S*tephen stepped away from the window, reveling in the melodious sound of Kate's mirth. What was it about her that intrigued him? The woman was a conundrum of refined poise and authentic wholesomeness, timid intellect and unabandoned passion. Perhaps she'd been a governess? He shook his head. No, why would someone so lovely attain such a position? From what he knew, wives typically didn't hire beautiful live-in governesses. Kate carried herself like someone highborn, which ruled out her having been a servant. He'd glimpsed her hands during their morning meal, and they were still healing from the scrapes and scratches, making it hard to discern whether they'd ever scrubbed a floor with lye. Her dignified air said not, but her nervousness ruined the effect. Was she running from someone abusive—a father, husband— or ringleader? She didn't wear a wedding band, but she could have taken it off.

What was she afraid of?

Something wasn't right, but he couldn't put his finger on it.

His higher-ups had trained him at the Home Office to suspect everyone and weigh all options, but his heart struggled to connect with the possibility that she could be a horse thief. Even her being a woman logically made it less likely. Women didn't buy and sell horses. Buyers would be skeptical of being duped. They'd fear her father or husband wouldn't have approved of the sale and come collect their property. If Kate Vernon was a horse thief, she wouldn't be in it alone. Of course, the Home Office suspected there was a whole gang of horse thieves, and she could play a part in their operation.

Stephen would stay sharp and watch her every move. If she was involved, it was only a matter of time before she'd drop her defenses or slip up, and he'd unlock her mystery. Every riddle had an answer, and the sooner this one was solved, the sooner his life could carry on.

Abby reappeared from the fitting rooms and smiled at Kate —or whatever her real name was. His sister was taken with their new guest. He hadn't seen his sister in such good spirits since before Nicholas's disappearance. He was grateful Abby had found a friend, but was Kate good for Abby? Hard to tell since she couldn't—or wouldn't—disclose the truth about herself.

He shifted to lean against the window frame and observed Kate and Abby's interaction. He didn't want his sister's frail state of happiness to be disturbed, which was another reason he must discover Kate's secret. He wouldn't allow his trusting sister to be hurt again. He'd discover Kate's true identity and intentions. To do so, he'd need to spend more time with her. If she was lying, eventually, she'd make a mistake, and when she did, he'd be waiting.

"I'm ready for the masquerade," Abby said. "Let's go find Mama, and then we'll visit Mrs. Emerson." She turned to Stephen. "And what plans do you have, dear brother?"

"I was hoping to join you."

Abby's lips parted, and she blinked. "You *want* to join us?"

"It's past time I visited Mrs. Emerson. She was the mother of one of my closest friends."

Abby flinched at his use of past tense. "You've never shown interest before."

Kate backed up a step. The heel of her boot slid on a scrap of fabric that had fallen on the floor and she started to topple. Stephen's arm snaked around her waist to steady her.

Kate placed a hand on his chest, and his muscles leapt under her touch, stealing his breath. Her green eyes held his, and her lips parted in a silent gasp.

"Thank you." She stepped out of his reach. "That could have been a bad spill."

He cleared his throat. "Indeed."

Abby's face illuminated, and her eyes twinkled like a matchmaker's. "Of course, you should join us." Her lips curved into an impish smile. It's about time you visited Mrs. Emerson, and you can show Kate some of the town's highlights on our way there."

Stephen's jaw twitched. His sister had gotten the wrong impression. Lord help them if she started playing cupid. Knowing his sister and how her mind worked, she would intervene, using the situation to her advantage, in an attempt to bring the two of them together. Then again, that could prove to be beneficial in uncovering the truth about Miss Kate Vernon.

Abby bounded out of the shop. Left with no choice but to escort Kate in the wake of his scheming sister, he held up his arm for her to take. Her gloved fingers slid over his jacket, and his hair rose on end at her light touch. Even reason couldn't shake the queer effect she had on him. She was nothing like the women who'd caught his interest in the past. Yet, her slightest touch stirred up feelings within him he'd preferred to have remained dormant.

*K*atherine slowed her breathing and forced her thoughts from the distracting man beside her as they met up with Lady Felton and strolled to Mrs. Emerson's residence. The house was on the outskirts of the main part of town, close enough to walk to but far from the hustle and bustle. It was nestled in the beginnings of a thick wood, creating a rustic atmosphere.

Large willow trees with drooping branches shaded a quaint bubbling stream that ran through the yard. The manor-style house was much smaller than Steepleton Manor and Willowstone Farm but still very grand with its large windows and high peaked roofline. Overgrown ivy covered its entire front face, and chimneys puffed out billowing smoke, giving the house a warm and inviting feel.

A cheerful housekeeper greeted the foursome and asked them to follow her to the solarium. As she filed down the hallway, Katherine's gait slowed. Portraits hung prominently on the walls of each room, and she peered inside, curious to catch a glimpse of Nicholas. Above a fireplace in a blue salon rested a picture of a young man with his dog. The painting held remarkable detail. The artist captured the sparkle of mischief in the young man's eyes and the half smile on his lips. Katherine dared not look at the painting overly long for the rest of the party continued down the hall.

In contrast to the dark wood paneling of the rooms she'd passed, the solarium was bright and colorful, with flowers galore. Mrs. Emerson hunched over a plant with a watering can in one hand and pruning shears in the other. She set down the objects and straightened, a kind smile gracing her lips.

"How good of you to visit your old mother-in-law. I'm so happy to see you. You grow more beautiful every day." She pressed a kiss to each of Abby's cheeks, then turned to Lady Felton. "And, Sarah, I'm so pleased you came calling. How are things at Willowstone farm?"

"Very well, especially since Stephen is home." Lady Felton passed a loving glance at her son.

"Stephen." The fine lines on the corners of Mrs. Emerson's eyes deepened. "How you've matured. It's hard to believe that my Nick would have been your age." Her gaze flickered to Katherine. "And who might this lovely lady be? Someone you fancy, I suppose?"

Katherine's ears burned.

Stephen's hand moved to Katherine's back without acknowledging the second question and lightly pressed her forward. "Mrs. Emerson, may I present Miss Kate Vernon. She is visiting with us for the present time."

"Nice to meet you, my dear. Your eyes remind me of the Scottish Highlands. I've never beheld a more vivid green."

"Thank you, Mrs. Emerson." Katherine's mother was Scottish. The words perched on the edge of her tongue, but she caught herself before the tell-tale slip escaped. Katherine dipped a small curtsy. "I'm pleased to meet you."

"Do have a seat, everyone, and I'll ring for tea. Oh, and, Abigail." She paused before pulling the cord. "I have someone I'd like for you to meet. My nephew is visiting for a cricket tournament, and I've told him about you. He'll join us shortly."

"Ahem." A male voice spoke from the doorway.

Mrs. Emerson turned toward the sound. "There he is now."

A large muscular man entered the room. The front button of his jacket stretched the corresponding hole above his puffed chest, but he wore a pleasant smile.

"I'd like for you to meet my nephew, Mr. Fredrick Wilson. He's the eldest son of my youngest brother from Davenport."

Mr. Wilson stood a good three inches shorter than Stephen with a wide stance and an eager glint in his eyes. Broad shoulders and a crooked nose alluded to a tough exterior, but rosy cheeks gave him a boyishly handsome quality. He acknowledged everyone in the room, but Katherine noticed his eyes lingered a trifle longer on Abby.

Mrs. Emerson sat on the green velvet sofa, with Abby to her right. Mr. Wilson and Stephen held out damask patterned bishop's chairs for Lady Felton and Katherine on either side of the sofa, before seating themselves, Stephen opposite Abby, in tufted chairs. The housekeeper returned with the tea service, and Mrs. Emerson chatted amicably about Fredrick's athletic accomplishments as she let the tea seep. "Do you take one lump or two?" she asked Katherine.

"Two, please."

Mrs. Emerson dropped two cubes of sugar into the teacup and stirred. "Abby, dear, I know you prefer your tea sweet." She poured another cup and prattled on about Abby's fondness for sweetened tea and sweet breads. Mrs. Emerson dropped four cubes of sugar into Katherine's cup instead of Abby's and stirred. She turned to Lady Felton, who stared at Katherine's teacup. "How about you dear? One lump or two?"

"I'll just have a little lemon, please."

Lady Felton joined Mrs. Emerson's boasting and listed all of Abby's talents as if she were up for bid at auction. Mrs. Emerson passed Lady Felton her cup and Abby hers, but she hesitated before handing Katherine's hers. "Did I...?" She grabbed the tongs and plopped two more sugar cubes into Katherine's tea.

Katherine opened her mouth to protest but the sugar was already dissolving in the tea. She accepted the cup Mrs. Emerson offered to her, while Mrs. Emerson prattled on about Abby's interests and Lady Felton joined in.

Mr. Wilson leaned forward in his chair, seemingly enraptured by the conversation.

Abby frowned at her mother, but Lady Felton either didn't notice or pretended not to.

Katherine knew hers would be sweet, but as the sugar flavor filled her mouth with a touch of tea, her first impulse was to spit it into the cup. Instead, she swallowed the granular syrup consistency not to appear rude.

"Is everything all right, Miss Vernon?" Stephen asked, a hint of mockery in his tone.

"Quite." Katherine resisted reaching for the teapot for a liquid to wash the thick molasses-like tea down. "I must have swallowed wrong."

Stephen pinched his lips to smother mirth.

Mrs. Emerson shifted in her seat to ask Stephen how he'd like his tea. He coughed to cover his laughter and cleared his throat. "Plain, please."

Katherine shot him a look that said, *afraid?*

He glanced at her cup and snorted, his raised brow signaling, *undoubtably.*

Mrs. Emerson, none the wiser, handed him his cup while she touched upon one topic and then another.

Katherine struggled to finish her tea and follow Mrs. Emerson's train of thought.

Stephen eyed Mr. Wilson with a questioning brow as the young buck stole repeated glances at his sister.

"I was thinking." Mrs. Emerson sipped from her cup. "Fredrick should join you young folks for an outing."

Lady Felton's face brightened. "I'm sure they would love that, and I think a picnic would be perfect for them to get acquainted. What do you think, Abby?"

Abby blinked. "I'm not..."

Her mother elbowed her in the ribs.

"A picnic would be lovely," Abby finished with a smile.

"Tomorrow, then." Mrs. Emerson patted her hands together.

Stephen crossed his arms, his gaze roving over Mrs. Emerson's nephew as if deciphering whether Mr. Wilson would be beneficial or detrimental to his sister's well-being.

The siblings might tease each other, but when it came down to it, Stephen's surly expression made it clear that he would do anything to see to his sister's happiness.

Woe to Mr. Fredrick Wilson if he misstepped.

---

*T*he following morning, Katherine grew dizzy sitting on a tufted couch across from Lady Felton, watching Abby pace in front of her mother.

"I can't believe you are joining in on her matchmaking antics." Abby raised her palms. "I am not ready and dislike being forced into things."

"Quit complaining, dear. Go out and have a good time. Fredrick seems like a nice young gentleman. It won't hurt you to spend a little time with him." Lady Felton's brow furrowed. "Mrs. Emerson feels responsible for you since Nicholas's passing."

"*Missing.* He's missing, Mama. There is *still* a chance he could be alive out there somewhere."

"Sweetheart, it's been seven years. I don't want to destroy your hope, but that is the reality. I don't want you to miss out on life, nor does Mrs. Emerson. We both love you and desire to see you happy. Mrs. Emerson believes she's helping you move on by introducing you to her closest nephew. Mr. Wilson's eligible, handsome, and quite a catch. She believes he's the next best thing."

"I don't want the next best thing," Abby grumbled.

Katherine ached for her friend.

"Give him a chance," Lady Felton said. "That's all I ask."

Abby heaved a sigh and nodded, but her stiff body language displayed her displeasure.

The Felton's butler, Weston, announced a Mr. Fredrick Wilson had arrived. Lady Felton issued her daughter a motherly *behave-yourself* look and asked the butler to see him in.

Fredrick strutted into the room, his hat in his hand. A tuft of light brown hair stood on end from his hat's hasty removal. "Good afternoon, ladies. Lovely day, isn't it?"

Katherine nodded while Abby eyed her mother.

"Wonderful suggestion to hold a picnic. Right much fun, indeed." He delivered Abby a half grin.

She bestowed him with a bright smile, but Katherine could tell it didn't quite reach her eyes.

Stephen strode into the room, and Katherine's pulse quickened. Why must her traitorous body have such a reaction? The infuriating man flustered her and fascinated her at the same time. Next to Stephen, Fredrick appeared boyish and awkward.

The way Stephen dominated a room merely by his presence set her nerves on edge. Lord and Lady Felton had been gracious to take her in, but her heart warned her she was truly at Lord Hartington's mercy.

He placed a light kiss on his mother's and sister's cheeks, and the tightness in her stomach eased. How could someone appear threatening one moment and devoted and loving the next? He nodded at Fredrick before turning the full weight of his gaze upon her. A competitive glint flashed in his eyes as if letting her know he was up for a challenge.

She blinked. Why did she feel like she was the opponent he meant to conquer?

"Shall we be off?" Stephen directed his question to everyone, but only Fredrick answered.

"Indeed. Let's get this match started."

Did Mr. Wilson associate their picnic with a cricket match or a boxing match?

Stephen grabbed the picnic lunch Lady Felton had packed for the outing and stepped aside to hold the door for the ladies. "I suggest we ride to the clearing." Stephen followed them into the hall and out the back door. "It's the most scenic spot and has both shade and sun this time of day."

At the stables, the groomsmen saddled their horses while Fredrick and Stephen conversed about boxing. Katherine twisted the thumb of her borrowed riding glove. How could she be going on a picnic while her cousin posed a threat to her life, her sister's, and their home? At least she'd been able to post her letters. It was time to plan her next move—a meeting with her attorneys to seek legal counsel over her rights to her inheritance. Her letters should arrive by the latest tomorrow and then two to three days for a response. If Horace turned out to be her guardian, would her lawyers advocate for her or only offer their services to her cousin? Her gaze slid to Stephen's profile. How much easier this would be if she had someone to run her plan by, but she'd made that impossible, pretending to have amnesia.

What a hobble.

Stephen's jacket strained across his shoulders as he assisted one of the grooms with saddling Dominion.

While he was busy, Abby leaned in and whispered, "Doesn't Stephen look handsome today?"

Katherine dropped her gaze to her hands and didn't respond.

"I think the two of you would do nicely together," Abby added in a hushed tone.

"What? I... he..." Katherine's gaze flew to Abby's face. "We-we don't even get along."

Abby giggled. "How can you think that? You are exactly what Stephen needs."

Katherine wanted to question her further, but Fredrick assisted Abby in a leg up to mount Duchess. Stephen turned to Katherine and offered her the same onto Amethyst.

She swallowed. *Why did he fluster her so?*

CHAPTER 13

*S*tephen rode beside Kate. They kept a good pace down the path through the woods. A small smile quirked the corner of Kate's mouth, and her face glowed. She moved naturally with the horse's rhythm. How had he ever believed she couldn't ride? Her look of sheer joy when she sat upon a horse was enough proof.

Stephen slowed Dominion and looked at her with admiration in his eyes. "I'm sorry I questioned your abilities on a horse."

"It's exhilarating to be out riding. I daresay there's nothing I enjoy more."

"You'll have to demonstrate your skills with a race later."

Her lips twisted into a smile, and she accepted his challenge. Then, she glanced over her shoulder, and Stephen did the same to see how Abby was faring. Abby had dropped behind with the trailing footman. Fredrick rode a couple of lengths ahead but also looked back to see what was keeping her. Stephen and Kate stopped to wait for Fredrick and Abby to catch up.

Without the added noise of the horse's hoof beats,

Fredrick's voice rang out full of frustration. "Miss Emerson, I beg you. Please, hurry up. We are lagging behind, and I hate being a laggard." Fredrick waved for her to move faster.

Abby glared at the man, and if looks were a weapon, Fredrick would be meeting his maker right now. Perhaps it was Fredrick who needed his sympathy, not Abby.

Abby eased the horse into a canter to catch up, clinging tight to her mount with her knees. It was clear her patience with Fredrick was diminishing. On the other hand, Fredrick appeared oblivious to Abby's anger and angst. He'd yelled to Stephen to maintain their earlier discussion of sports while motioning for Abby to hurry.

Abby bowed in what appeared to be a silent prayer, clicked her tongue, and dug in her heels. Her horse leapt into a gallop. She crouched low over the horse's back and effortlessly flew past Fredrick, then Stephen and Kate. Her horse's hooves kicked up the soft earth as they plowed through the woods. She kept up the pace until she reached the clearing. Stephen followed with Kate close behind and met Abby at the picnic spot a few seconds later.

Stephen sprung from the saddle before Dominion came to a complete stop. He grabbed Abby by the waist, pulled her off Duchess, and spun her around in the air. "I can't believe it." He laughed and lowered her to the ground.

Abby beamed.

Kate clapped her hands with a wide grin.

"See?" Fredrick entered the clearing with a raised chin and chest pushed out like a red robin. "A little prodding was all she needed." He dismounted and sauntered toward Abby. "Glad to be of service, Mrs. Emerson."

Abby's mouth gaped.

Fredrick didn't appear to notice. "I daresay the bowler, Tilton, will have the upper hand in the next match. I'd bet ten shillings on it."

Stephen forced his gaze to Fredrick. Was he truly going to converse about cricket? Could the bloke be that oblivious?

The footman laid out the blanket, and Abby and Kate set out the food.

Stephen cooled the horses with Fredrick's assistance, who changed the topic to racing.

After a few minutes, the ladies called them over to eat. They headed that way and sat while Fredrick continued to monopolize the conversation. Did the man not stop? Stephen enjoyed discussing everything from horse racing to boxing, but even he had his limits. Poor Abby must be miserable.

"Kate and Abby." Stephen attempted to draw the women into the conversation. "Which cricket team do you believe has the best chance of winning the tournament?"

"Women don't have opinions in this sort of thing." Fredrick glanced in Abby's direction. "They know best about fashion, embroidery, and the like."

Abby's brows rose. "Actually, I believe Wrentham will beat Davenport. They have better batsmen, and their bowler has a good bite to his dipper pitch."

Fredrick's eyes widened, and his mouth dropped open. He promptly shut it. Awe sparked in his gaze.

Stephen swallowed his laughter. If he had to guess, Fredrick fell in love with Abby at that very moment.

atherine hesitated to pass Abby a glass of lemonade. The way her friend's nostrils flared caused Katherine to fear she'd toss it in Fredrick's face.

"I must agree with my sister on Wrentham walking away with the win." Stephen drew Fredrick's attention.

Katherine leaned toward Abby while the men discussed

cricket. "How are you faring? You were so fearless taking the horse to full gallop."

"Thank you." Abby nibbled on her finger sandwich. "I prayed for the strength." She cast an annoyed look at Fredrick. "It was Mr. Wilson who offered the motivation." Her tone dripped with cynicism.

"Did you hear about the fight between Rodheimer and Cappavelli?" Fredrick finished his last bite of bread and cheese. Had he truly moved on to boxing?

"I heard it was a set-up." Stephen's gaze met Katherine's, and he glanced heavenward as if to say, *the bloke doesn't take a hint.*

"I know I'm supposed to find the good in everyone." Abby's voice was low. She sipped her lemonade, then added. "Love your neighbor and all that, but some people make it harder than others."

Katherine hid a giggle behind her napkin. "When you showed him your knowledge about the game of cricket, I think he vowed to marry you. If a man could swoon, he would have done so."

Abby harrumphed. "He might have good intentions, but he's sorely lacking knowledge about women."

Fredrick's volume increased with his fervor. "Then Cappavelli gave him a one-two punch."

"At least he's enthusiastic." Katherine ate the last bite of her sandwich.

"Would you care for more lemonade?" Abby asked.

Katherine nodded, and Abby passed Katherine's glass to the footman to refill.

"Rodheimer followed with a right uppercut, then a couple of jabs with his left." Fredrick raised his fists to mimic the motions.

"Would either of you like some lemonade?" Abby scooted toward the men and reached for Stephen's empty glass.

"Then he gave him a thundering right hook."

A sickening sound of knuckles connecting with flesh thudded, followed by Abby's wail. She covered her face with her hands and rocked back and forth.

Katherine gasped and wrapped her arms around her friend to comfort her. "Abby are you all right?"

Fredrick jumped to his feet. "I didn't mean to hit her." His eyes flicked between Abby's rocking form and Stephen's menacing grimace. "I'm terribly sorry. You must believe me. I would never hurt a woman. It was an accident. I got carried away." He bent down toward Abby. "Miss Emerson, please tell me you're not injured."

Abby stopped rocking and removed her hands from her face to impale Fredrick with a lethal stare. Her left eye was already swelling shut.

"Let me have a look at it." Katherine gently tilted Abby's face in her direction. She tried not to cringe at Abby's puffy eyelid and the purplish-red bruise growing on her cheek.

"How bad is it?" she asked.

"It's not that bad," she lied. Funny how they flowed from her lips now.

"The look on your face says otherwise." Abby blinked as if she might cry.

"It's bruised, and there's some swelling. You'll need to put some meat on it to keep the inflammation down. You may end up with a black eye" She grabbed a linen napkin and dabbed at a tiny cut near Abby's eyebrow to stop the bleeding. "But your demi-mask will cover it at the masquerade."

Abby groaned.

"I'm truly sorry, Miss Emerson." Fredrick's horrified expression looked so distraught that Katherine's heart went out to him. "Let me walk you to the house."

"I'll help." Katherine packed up the picnic as Stephen rose.

Abby glanced at Stephen, then at Katherine, and held up

her palms. "It's all right. Fredrick can take me." The cords of her neck strained as she swallowed. "I'm sure he can get me to the house without further injury." A smile wobbled on her lips. "You two stay here and finish the picnic." She extended her palm farther to hold Stephen and her in place.

Fredrick lifted Abby into her horse's saddle as if she were as fragile as a paper doll. He seized the reins and walked the horses back the way they came.

"Do you think she'll be all right?" Katherine asked as she and Stephen watched their retreating forms.

"I had half a mind to plant a facer in the bloke's nose until I saw the horror on his face." Stephen snorted as he sat back on the blanket and draped his arm over the top of his knee. "However, after looking at Abby, I'm more concerned for Fredrick's safety. I've never seen her more furious."

Katherine smothered a giggle. She passed Stephen some bread and cheese. The breeze ruffled his hair and added a ruggedness to his looks.

He appeared so at ease as he stared off into the woods that she held her words and admired him in her periphery, pretending to nibble a piece of cheese. He'd rolled up his sleeves, showing his tanned forearms, and his face was bronzed from the sun. Much like his steed, he exuded a controlled, authoritative air, but on occasion, she'd catch a wildness in his eyes. His lashes were thick for a man's. Women wished for such lashes, but on him, they looked masculine and added to the intensity of his gaze. His nose was straight, and his jawline square, adding to the confidence that radiated from his being, as if he had life all figured out.

"A penny for your thoughts?" Stephen said.

Katherine startled. "I was merely thinking about how sure of themselves men are. It may be unintentional, but Fredrick came off as extremely egotistical, and Abby appeared put off by it."

"By now, she's probably taken his ego down a notch"—Stephen grunted— "if she hasn't murdered him already."

Kathrine's intended, Alfred, had been conceited. More than once, she'd seen him admiring himself when he passed a mirror. She'd been fortunate not to have married him, spared from a life of misery. "Why is it that all men seem to be born with arrogance? Is it a requirement to be male?"

He raised a haughty brow. "I'm not arrogant."

"Ha." The scoff came out louder than she'd intended. "Such a statement rings with arrogance."

"I'm not arrogant." Stephen's gaze captured hers. "I'm confident. There's a difference."

Katherine laughed in a mocking tone. "Do explain."

"Arrogance is having too high of an opinion in one's self, otherwise known as putting on airs. Confidence is humbly knowing who you are and what you can do through Christ Jesus. I am confident."

"You're splitting hairs." It seemed very strange to know someone who put their trust in God so completely that they based their capabilities on Him.

They sat in comfortable silence while they finished their bread and cheese. From one of the tenant's cottages, violin notes carried on the gentle breeze.

"I know you like horses and can climb a tree like a monkey, but there's not much else I know about you." Stephen picked up a small stone, flipping it over in his hand, and then gave it a hard toss into the woods. "I'm curious about who Kate Vernon is, but I can't ask you to tell me about yourself because you'll say you can't remember."

Katherine brushed a bit of grass off the blanket. A hint of frustration laced his tone, but was it because he couldn't get answers, or was he doubting her having amnesia? She longed to tell him about her past and to share the weight of her burden to protect her sister, herself, and their inheritance. She wanted to rest her head on his shoulder and absorb his inner strength. The urge was so strong she shivered.

"What excites you, Kate? Do you like to sing? Do you dance?"

She shrugged.

"Let's find out." He rose and held out his hand.

She stared at his long fingers, and then her eyes snapped to his face. He was serious.

"What are you doing?"

"Experimenting. Take my hand."

She accepted his assistance, and he pulled her into his arms.

"We're going to dance." His tone dared her to refuse.

"Here?"

He tilted his head and cupped his ear. "Don't you hear that?"

The combination of the sweet violin, chirping birds, and croaking frogs filled the air.

He placed his palm over his heart and tapped the iambic pentameter rhythm of a heartbeat, and then raised a challenging eyebrow at her.

He was silently ordering her to bend to his will, and Katherine didn't particularly like being commanded. She pulled away, but he whisked her into his arms and propelled her around the clearing in a waltz. There was no time for her to feel silly about dancing in a meadow or worry that she hadn't been approved by the *ton's* patronesses to dance these steps yet. It was all she could do to keep up with him. Her feet hardly touched the ground. The grass was difficult to move in, but Katherine adjusted. Before long, she spun and glided through the glen as if it were a ballroom. She silently thanked her mother for all the dance instruction she'd insisted on.

Stephen spun her in an endless loop of twirls and caught her in his arms when the world continued to spin. Dizziness washed over her as he held her close, and they swayed to an imaginary beat.

"You are light on your feet. You must hold your own in the most prestigious ballrooms." His eyes bored into hers as if he peered directly into her soul.

Lightheadedness flooded her and she swayed, but with either nervous anxiety, anticipation, or from the continued after-effects of hitting her head, she wasn't sure which.

He pulled her closer into the warmth of his embrace. Her cheek rested against his chest as his arms encircled her, cloaking her with his heat.

Propriety demanded she step away. The footman tending the horses was surely witnessing this inappropriate display, but she'd craved the sense of security she found in Stephen's embrace.

Stephen's heartbeat thudded next to her ear, and his fingers curved around her side. Her body warmed at his touch, stirring a deliciously sweet dizziness as if her blood had turned to honey.

---

*S*tephen peered down at the beauty in his arms. Kate appeared unaware of the contented sigh that escaped from her lips. An aching desire to have her always exude such contentment seized him. He never again wanted to witness her frantic expression like the one she'd worn galloping through the woods or darting across the street in front of his horse.

Who was she running from?

He'd paid the postmaster a visit after leaving Mrs. Emerson's home the day before. Kate's behavior had struck him as odd. She'd attributed her reckless dash across the street to seeing someone she thought she knew, but when Stephen questioned Mr. Wesley, he said she had posted several letters.

When the elderly man had been distracted by another customer, Stephen had rifled through his logs. There'd been one entry during the time Kate had entered the courier's office —two letters sent to the Sherbourne Finishing School for Young Ladies' Decorum.

By the way Kate danced and behaved with polish, he'd guess that she'd attended finishing school. It would be one thing for her to remember what she'd learned there despite her amnesia. Quite another for her to remember the name and address of the school.

She'd lied to him. To all of them. Why? What was she hiding or hiding from?

Kate was a liar, but was she also a thief?

Her timing seemed intentional—appearing right as new horses were scheduled to arrive, and after Jacob intentionally wrote letters, dropping hints that prime bloods were being purchased to bait the horse thieving ring. Stephen swallowed, still rocking with Kate to an imaginary rhythm. It seemed odd for a refined woman to be involved with horse-thieving bandits, and his instincts screamed that she was innocent. However, he would have to alert Jacob when he arrived to his suspicions about Kate and the incontrovertible evidence of her lying to him, Abby, and his family.

Why then did an overwhelming need to protect this slight wisp of a woman grip him? Had Kate fallen on hard times and gotten over her head with the wrong crowd? Hadn't he learned his lesson from Daphne? The image of her come-hither smile blurred into the memory of her lifeless body dangling from a hangman's noose.

The remembrance choked Stephen's breath, and his arms tightened their hold on Kate. Why did she evoke these irrational feelings? He'd only known her for a few days, but already she relegated his feelings for Julia to what now felt like a business transaction.

His thumb caressed the ridge of her spine, and he prayed. *Lord, what would you have me do? Give me wisdom. Help me to know your will in this matter. Please let me...*

He broke off mid-prayer. What had he begun to ask God for? To please let him have her? *As a wife?*

What if she was part of the horse-thieving ring? A spy couldn't marry the enemy. Hadn't he learned that lesson? Could he get her out? Pay off her associates or those she worked for? He barely knew anything about her. Being a thief would be a black mark on her character. How deep would she have to be involved for his feelings for her to wane? His family had accepted her wholeheartedly. She would have to be a good little actress to fool all of them, but if she was, how much devastation would her lies cause?

His misgivings destroyed the magic of the moment.

He straightened. His involvement would remain strictly business. "So you've danced the waltz when you haven't had your coming out season yet?" He teased her but also hoped to catch her in a slip.

Kate stiffened. "How would you know if I have or haven't been out for a season?" A blush deepened the pink hue of her cheeks, and she pushed against his chest with her palm, forcing him to release her.

But his answer was easy. "Because, I would have remembered you."

CHAPTER 14

*K*atherine gaped at him. His tone had sounded flippant, but his eyes were sober. "Pardon?"

"I would have remembered you."

Heat swirled her stomach at the huskiness in his voice, and the weight of his stare rooted her to the spot. She was going mad, certifiably insane. That was all there was to it. She couldn't understand this man's sudden mood swings. One minute he chided her like an elder brother, and the next, he'd say something romantic and make her heart somersault. He danced with her and then pushed her away. Actually, she'd done the pushing, but only because she'd felt a shift in his demeanor. He tested her as if to catch her in a lie, and in the next moment, he complimented her. He kept her on edge and off balance, and she didn't like it. Was a little predictability too much to ask?

She narrowed her eyes. "Why would you remember me?"

"I'd remember those eyes, that green the color of wet moss."

Moss? Not exactly the most romantic image.

A half smile spread over Stephen's lips. "But when you're angry, they glitter like emeralds."

Much better, if only she could forget the 'when you're angry part.' Was he trying to upset her?

He tucked a strand of hair behind her ear. "I wouldn't forget how your hair always seems to escape your coiffure."

His compliments were getting worse.

"You leave an impression."

Warmth spread through her chest. She'd always considered herself ordinary, but here was a handsome heir telling her she was different, maybe even special. She couldn't stop a small smile from forming on her lips and bit her lower lip to disguise it.

"I just haven't decided whether it's a good or bad impression."

Her smile died, and she smacked him on the arm—*hard.* Her hand stung.

"You also pack a good wallop. That's the second time you've struck me." He rubbed his arm.

"Both well deserved," she muttered under her breath.

His face grew serious. "You're beautiful, witty, and spirited. I merely wish..."

A group of children burst through the clearing, stopping at the sight of Stephen and Katherine, except one young lad who wasn't watching and crashed into the rest with a resounding thud. A domino effect ensued. Most of the kids fell, a couple recovered their balance and jumped to stand at attention, but their eyes never strayed from Stephen.

Katherine rushed to right a couple of toppled children from the pile. She dusted them off and pulled grass shoots out of their hair. One of the girls began to cry, and Kate used the bottom corner of her riding jacket, to wipe the child's tears and a smudge of dirt off her face.

"There now, all better." Katherine smiled. "What's your name?"

"Marisa McLaughlin." The child's voice was timid. She

stared at Katherine with big brown eyes and a heavy mop of hair she brushed away from her face with both hands. "You're pretty."

"That's a very nice compliment coming from a lovely girl such as you."

Marisa blushed. Her chin was practically resting on her chest as she peered up at Katherine with a shy smile.

"We're going to play cricket," Marisa whispered. "You can be on my team." Her tiny hand slid into Katherine's palm, and her small fingers curled around hers. Katherine glanced at Stephen. They should be heading back but how could she turn down the child's offer?

In the midst of the chaos, a pigskin ball had popped out of a child's grip and rolled to a stop in front of Stephen's feet. Stephen bent over and scooped up the ball. "Afternoon, Henry." Stephen tossed the ball to the tallest boy in the group. "How's your family?"

"Doin' right well. We were thinkin' we'd play a game of cricket 'ere, but we'll move it elsewhere. Sorry for disturbin' ye." He dipped his cap and turned, motioning for the kids to leave but Marisa hung back.

"Hold up." Stephen called, and five of the children turned in unison.

Stephen's gaze met Katherine's, and he tilted a questioning eyebrow.

She squeezed Marisa's hand and nodded her agreement.

"We don't mind if you play here." Stephen crossed his arms. "Need a coach or referee?"

Henry's face brightened. "Yessir, we do."

"All right then, let's set up."

A couple of the boys put out their shoes for boundaries as Henry called out the teams.

When Marisa was picked, she held up Katherine's hand.

"She's on my team." She tugged Katherine along with her, but Henry examined Katherine with a dubious look.

The game began well enough, with Marisa and Katherine's team up first. Stephen stood next to a tree stump they used as a wicket to call the plays fair or foul. Several boys had good hits, and their team was ahead by a few runs. Marisa was up next. As she moved into position, the boys groaned and Marisa's shoulders slumped.

"Wait, one minute." Katherine signaled to Stephen and strode to Marisa's side. She whispered, "Don't let them intimidate you. There's an open spot right in between those two boys. Hit the ball lightly between them and run as fast as you can without looking back."

Marisa squared her shoulders and nodded. She was ready.

After Katherine stepped away, the bowler rolled the ball, and Marisa did exactly what Katherine instructed. Marisa sprinted to the tree stump while the other side scrambled to get to the ball. The whole team cheered, and Marisa beamed with pride.

The game continued with both teams equally matched. Katherine couldn't remember having so much fun. She had played cricket as a young girl with the grooms in the side yard, and the rules came back to her quickly. On occasion, she caught Stephen watching her, a lazy smile spread on his face as if pleased. He tossed the ball to Henry with a perfect arc. Katherine admired his athleticism. No matter how far off the mark the children threw it, his quick agility reined it in. Stephen tousled a boy's hair and chided Henry but winked at her to show he was kidding. Katherine had witnessed Stephen's playful side with Abby but seeing his tenderness with the children plucked her heartstrings and sent strange vibrations reverberating through her.

She'd been granted an opportunity to meet a gentleman of her liking, and she'd ruined it by not being honest. Should she come clean? Would he understand her situation or condemn her for her falsehood? Could he protect her as he'd offered by the river? Would his clout as nobility stand up against her well-connected cousin if the law was on her cousin's side? Or would Stephen have no choice but to send her home to a forced marriage or her death?

---

*T*he match grew close to the final game-winning points, and Stephen called for the next at bat. Kate was up.

The children took to her, especially Marisa, who the kids saw as Henry's annoying tagalong sister. Children could be cruel, particularly to Marisa, but not so with Kate around. She championed Marisa and boosted her confidence. That was the kind of mother a child deserved, and not the type who would pass a child to a nursemaid or governess to raise. A good mother showed her love, encouraged her children to excel, and picked them up when they fall.

Stephen wanted a wife like her.

Blast! He wanted Kate.

He didn't just want to know Kate's past, he wanted to discover her future, and he wanted it to be with him.

"Watch out!"

A ball crashed into the side of Stephen's skull. A white light flashed behind his eyelids, and a ringing sounded in his ears. He fell to his hands and knees and shook his head to silence the bell noise.

Kate dropped to his side. "I didn't mean to hit you." She cradled his face in her hands. "I thought you saw me throw it to you. I'm dreadfully sorry." Her brow furrowed, and the pained expression on her face appeared woefully apologetic.

Stephen couldn't resist. With his best blank stare, he said, "Do I know you?"

The color drained from her face, and her hand flew to her mouth. She grabbed the material of his shirt and shook him. "Stephen, it's me, Katherine."

"Who's Stephen?" A smile twitched the corners of his lips.

"I should throttle you." Kate sat back on her heels.

His shoulders shook with mirth, and he wiped a hand over his mouth to smother his laughter.

Kate pushed off his chest and stood, attempting to hide her smile by looking away. Stephen wasn't fooled, and it made him laugh all the harder. The other kids chimed in. Their peels of squeaky giggles overwhelming Kate. She covered her mouth with her hand, but everyone heard her smothered laugh.

"Well, I think that's enough for today." Stephen rose and dusted off his hands.

The children's shoulders slumped, and Henry pleaded. "One more game?"

"Miss Vernon and I must be getting back." He glanced at the sky as if to determine the hour. "It looks like it's getting late. You will need to be getting home soon, too, unless you want your mamas to give you a thrashing for being late for supper." At his words, the children's eyes widened, and they disappeared into the woods.

Stephen and Kate rode together, laughing over the game's highlights.

"Did you see how seriously little Timothy took his job?" Kate asked. "I thought the poor child was going to throw his arm out of its socket, And he was so intent on getting the batter out. I worried he might come to blows with Henry, who was taking it easy on him at bat."

Stephen chuckled. "At least he was trying his hardest to play. Did you see young Isaac in the outfield? Every time I looked, the boy was picking daisies."

Kate flashed him a wide grin. "At least his mother will have a nice bouquet."

Stephen shook his head. When was the last time he'd felt this relaxed? He slowed the horses, not wanting the lovely day to end, but the sky reminded him of the lateness of the hour. If they didn't return soon, there wouldn't be enough time to dress for dinner. He pictured his mother's disapproving glare if they arrived for the evening meal with grass stains on their clothes and dirt smudges on their faces. "Are you still up for a race?"

Kate's eyes flared. "Of course."

Stephen slowed his horse to a stop, and Kate did the same. "Through the field." He pointed out their path. "Clear to where the horse fencing begins near the stables." He gestured to the right where their route would turn.

Kate leaned to see where he was pointing, and her leg brushed his.

How easy it would be to pull her into his saddle and kiss her until those haunting green eyes burned with passion.

She looked at him, head tilting to the side. Springy curls danced in the breeze about her rosy cheeks. He reached out and brushed the back of his glove down her cheek.

Kate closed her eyes and clutched the reins. "Ready. Go." She spurred her horse into a full gallop, leaving Stephen to chase. Laughing, she peeked back at him, the sound dying when she saw how near he was.

He closed in on her lead. Dominion soared over the ground. Hoofs thundered as they rounded the bend. Kate peered over her shoulder once more, and her eyes widened. Stephen drove Dominion hard around the turn and stayed on her flank. As the stables came into view, Kate whooped as if victory was in sight, but Stephen bore down and breezed ahead of her horse before they reached the finish line.

When their horses came to rest, Kate shifted to face him. "I do believe it was a tie."

Stephen laughed. "You, my dear, are daft if you believe that. Your start alone was disputable."

"I didn't see anything wrong with the start. I clearly said, 'Ready. Go.'"

"I tell you what. I will decree it a tie, but only with the promise of a rematch tomorrow morning to determine the true winner. Agreed?"

Kate eyed him with a discreet grin. "Agreed."

They trotted into the stables, where a groom assisted Kate from her saddle and took the horses for a cool down and good rub. Stephen guided her toward the house.

They were nearly there when Kate's gaze lowered to the ground. A faint blush stained her cheeks. "Lord Hartington."

He slowed and faced her.

"I had a lovely time." She peeked up. "Thank you."

Stephen cupped her chin with a curved index finger and raised an eyebrow. "I liked it better when you called me Stephen."

Her pink cheeks deepened to red. She nodded and hurried into the house.

Stephen watched her go, unable to tear his eyes from her retreating form. He was beginning to develop a strong liking for a lithe, lean type of figure, along with liquid green eyes that compelled him to want to take off his shoes and run barefoot in the grass. He smiled, recalling her reaction to his feigned amnesia. Panic had marred her features as she'd said, *Stephen, it's me. Katherine.*

His smile pulled into a frown. He'd inadvertently gotten a bit of truth out of her.

She had called herself Katherine.

CHAPTER 15

*T*he next morning, Katherine awoke to the sun streaming in through her window. Donning one of Abby's old riding habits, she strode into the breakfast room, eager for her rematch with Stephen.

Lady Felton sat at the table, her glasses perched on the bridge of her nose as she read a scandal sheet. Spying Katherine, she pushed the paper aside and shook her head.

"I don't know why I read these horrible things. I feel like it's my only link to London and the goings on of the *ton*, but these columnists rarely have anything nice to say about anyone." She smiled. "Good morning, my dear. You look refreshed. I pray you slept well?"

"Very well, thank you." Katherine sat in the chair pulled out by their footman, who after draping her napkin in her lap, brought her food and a cup of steaming chocolate.

"I'm grateful for your company. Charles and Stephen have long since been up and eaten. They're out supervising the training of a young mare that arrived early this morning. Abigail is still sleeping and will probably do so until late morning, and even then, I fear her black eye may put her in foul spirits." She patted Katherine's hand. "So it's just you and I this morning. Did you have any plans for the day?"

Katherine swallowed her bite of eggs and blood sausage. Should she ask for a second trip into town? What would be her reasoning, and how would she sneak off this time to see if Claire or the attorneys had replied to her letters? Katherine sipped her chocolate, searching for ideas but came up with none. "Stephen offered to take me out riding this morning."

"How splendid." Lady Felton perked up in her chair. "It's such a lovely day. I think the two of you will enjoy yourselves. I have some leftover material I need to have taken to one of the tenant's homes. There's a delightful woman, Mary McLaughlin, who makes the most beautiful quilts you've ever seen. I try to donate as much fabric to her as I can. She made the quilt that's on your bed. They fetch a pretty penny, and her daughter Marisa is now helping."

"I met Marisa yesterday." Katherine sipped her chocolate and set it down. "Stephen and I played a fierce game of cricket with the children in the clearing."

"Truly?" Lady Felton peered above her spectacles with renewed interest.

Katherine relayed yesterday's events, skipping over Stephen and her dancing in the glen. When she was finished, she stared into her swirling cup. "Thank you for taking me in. You didn't have to. You could have sent me on my way or to a hostel, but you didn't. Instead, you have fed and clothed me and made me feel at home and"—Katherine struggled for the right word—"safe. I feel very safe here. Thank you for all your kindness. I wish there were some way to repay you."

"Pish posh, dear, it is our pleasure. You are a delightful addition to our family, and you're welcome to stay as long as you like."

"Thank you."

Lady Felton's astute eyes clouded. "I do wonder why you

chose the word safe." She leaned over her cup of tea. "Was there a time you felt unsafe? Have any memories stirred?"

A bite of egg stuck in Katherine's throat, and she inwardly scolded herself for carelessness. "I meant welcomed. Very welcomed."

A movement outside the window drew Katherine's attention. Stephen stood in the outdoor ring. He lifted his hands toward a skittish young horse that bucked and tossed its head. Stephen held his ground, the epitome of maleness in fawn breaches and boots. His tanned skin contrasted with the creamy whiteness of his loose-fitting shirt. He circled the beautiful mare, her brown coat shimmering in the morning light. She trotted past him shaking her mane with defiance and hopping a bit with her front feet as if threatening to rear. Stephen raised his palm. Easing forward, he placed his hand on the mare's nose and gripped her bridle with the other. He must have whispered something soothing because the mare stilled. In one graceful swoop, he mounted the horse bareback and held her to a tight cantor around the ring.

Katherine's lips parted at the drastic change in the horse's behavior.

"Stephen's a miracle worker with those horses." Lady Felton sipped from her cup.

"He speaks to them,"—Katherine grunted— "and they do his bidding."

"Stephen knows it's a heart condition."

"How so?"

"Most people try to modify the horses' behavior. They focus on discipline and rewards to get the horse to do what it needs to do. In some cases, it works, but they don't have the same success rate as Stephen. Stephen gets the horse to trust him first. Essentially, the horse will give itself over to Stephen, and they'll do anything for him. When their heart is conditioned, they trust he won't steer them wrong."

Lady Felton exhaled a whoosh of breath. "It's the same with people. We think we can change our behavior to fix our lives." A warmth lit her eyes, and a fond smile touched her lips. "What we really need is to trust God and let Him change our hearts." She glanced toward the empty hallway. "It's like that with Abigail's fears. She has done remarkably well. Praying and reciting scripture have helped her come a long way, but she hasn't entirely been freed from it. She'll continue to struggle until she gives it to God and trusts Him to change her heart from the inside out."

Lady Felton's eyes filled with a mix of love and sorrow. "Abigail holds onto her fear as if she owns it. However, when you hold onto fear, you don't own it. It owns you. I continue to pray for her to let go and trust God so He can work in her."

Lady Felton searched the depths of Katherine's gaze and Katherine gripped the edge of her seat to keep from squirming.

Trust God.

It seemed so foreign. She wasn't sure she could trust anyone. It sounded simple, but the doing was the bigger issue. How could her heart trust again after the loss of her parents, the desertion of her so-called fiancé, and the attempt made on her life by her cousin? By the time her Cousin Horace showed up, she'd almost expected deceptive behavior. Lady Felton said to put her trust in a God whom she couldn't see or hear, who left her utterly alone to fend for herself.

On the other hand, the Hartingtons believed and trusted God. Their lives weren't perfect, but they were peaceful and happy.

Lady Felton rose from the table. "I guess we all could stand to let go and let God do a little work in us."

"How?" The pressure to know wedged like an air bubble under Katherine's ribs. "How do we do that?"

"You just ask Him." The corners of her eyes crinkled with her smile. She paused as if expecting Katherine to say more.

But when she didn't, she patted Katherine on the arm and excused herself.

The footman collected their plates and disappeared into the kitchen.

What if Lady Felton was right? What if all she had to do was ask? She folded her hands together and bowed her head. The position felt awkward and strange. She hadn't prayed since before her parents' passing, when her small family had made its Sunday outing to the little town chapel. It wasn't a trip they made every Sunday, but she did remember her mother placing more importance on their regular attendance before they died.

Katherine closed her eyes and cleared her throat. "Lord," she whispered. "It's Katherine. If You are listening, please help me to know who to trust. I want to trust in You, but I've been so hurt. I can't handle this all on my own. Please, protect Claire and the Hartingtons...and me. I'm scared." Her voice cracked, and tears sprang to her eyes. "I want to let go and trust You, but it's hard. There's so much at stake. Help me to trust You."

She waited as if God would answer her, but a few minutes passed, and nothing miraculous happened. Wiping the tears from her eyes before anyone caught her weeping at the table, she stood and smoothed out the wrinkles from her borrowed riding habit. Inhaling a deep breath, she wandered outside into the bright morning sun in search of Stephen.

"Good morning." The rich timbre of Stephen's husky voice boomed, clear and crisp like the morning air.

Katherine squinted and raised her hand over her eyes to block the sun's blinding rays. As her eyes adjusted, Stephen dismounted and passed the young mare to a stable boy. He strode with long purposeful strides toward her. His skin glistened with perspiration, and he brushed his hands on his breaches, causing the dust particles to sparkle around him as the specks reflected the sun.

"Ready for our ride?"

Katherine nodded.

"Go and select a mount while I clean up a bit." He walked away but turned as if rethinking his order. With a tiny shake of his head, he continued to the house.

Did he fear she'd select Dominion and leave him with a boring, docile horse? She strolled into the stables. The stable boy labored to move the resistant new mare into its stall while she attempted to bite him. The lad cursed under his breath. "Sorry 'bout that, mum. This beast is mean-spirited"—he jabbed his index finger toward the horse— "and if ya don't start mindin' yer manners. I'll convince the master to send ya to the town butcher."

The horse shook her mane and dug in her heels. Its muscles twitched, and her eyes shone wild with fear. The mare looked back and forth between Katherine and the groom, and her eyes rolled back in her head.

"Watch out!" Katherine yelled.

The horse twisted and kicked. The groom jumped to the side just in time. The rear hoof broke a board inches to the left of where the groomsmen's head had been.

"Thanks fer the warnin', mum." He gritted his teeth and pulled on the horses' bit.

The horse's eyes glazed over. Katherine's heart went out to the poor creature. It had been delivered to a new stable with different horses and strange people, unsure who was friend or foe. Feeling a kinship with the mare, Katherine stepped forward and whispered soothing words as she had witnessed Stephen do. Katherine's Sugar had been as obstinate when she first arrived at their stables. "It's all right. Everything shall be fine."

"Stand back, miss." The groom tugged on the reins, and the mare bucked.

Katherine stayed the groom with a reproving look and reached for the reins. He shook his head, but Katherine remained firm, continuing to speak soothing words to the horse.

The groom finally relented, and Katherine patted the horse's neck. "I know it's a strange place, and you don't quite know who to trust. I'm also far from home and missing my parents." She stroked beside the horse's crest down to her point of shoulder. "But the Hartingtons are wonderful people. They have good hearts and your best interests in mind."

Step by slow step, she guided the now docile mare into the stable. "You remind me of my horse at home." She remained by the mare's side, stroking her mane like a mother combing her daughter's hair.

The stunned groom looked on.

Katherine knew she, too, must learn to trust. Here, the horse had already blindly placed confidence in her because of a few kind words. Katherine had been in the presence of the Hartingtons, who'd shown her every kindness, yet she still held back revealing who she was. It was past time she told them the truth. No more secrets. They deserved as much.

"Kate?" Stephen entered the stables.

"Over here." She spoke a bit too loudly, forgetting about the skittish horse, who tensed.

Stephen rounded the corner and froze.

She smiled at him and patted the mare. "She's beautiful."

Stephen reached toward her. "Kate, I need for you to slowly walk to me."

"It's fine. She and I are friends. We have a lot in common." Her fingers stroked the mare's dark mane. Her muscles rippled as if enjoying the touch. "This is who I was talking about. I know you're acquainted with Stephen already, and I applaud your decision to trust him."

Stephen eyed someone behind her and nodded.

Before she could see who was there, the horse's reins were snatched out of her hands.

Startled, Katherine screamed.

The frightened mare kicked.

The groom toppled over the backside of the half wall as the mare slammed its hooves into the side.

The reins tugged, and the horse reared.

Katherine covered her face with her arms and braced for impact. The horse's hooves descended.

Stephen's fast grip yanked her out of harm's way.

They hit the dirt floor hard, Stephen taking the impact.

The groom slid the stall door in place before the horse kicked it, splintering the wood and causing the hinges to shake.

Stephen lay on his side, his arms cradling her against his chest. He released a deep breath but didn't move.

The rapid beat of his heart thundered in her ear.

"Thank God." He whispered the words in a ragged voice.

She opened her mouth to thank him for his rescue, but he squeezed her tighter, and she mumbled the thank-you into his chest.

He'd box her ears for pulling such a stunt once his relief wore off. Everything would have been fine if the overexcited groom hadn't frightened the mare. They remained there lying on the ground longer than necessary. Katherine braced herself for a fierce reprimand. She opened one eye and peered up at Stephen.

He relaxed his hold and lifted his head. "Are you hurt?" Instead of anger, his eyes shone with heartfelt concern.

A lump formed in her throat, and she nodded.

He sat up, cradling her in his lap, and searched her eyes. He pushed her out to arms' length and examined the rest of her for any scratches or bruises.

Her cheeks grew warm under such scrutiny, and she lowered her gaze.

Stephen stood helping her to her feet as he did so. His hands lingered until she regained her balance.

Katherine straightened and pulled away to shake out her skirt, but Stephen maintained a firm, almost possessive grip on her waist.

He yelled to the groom to saddle up Duchess and Dominion. Katherine's head snapped up, but his face was an expressionless mask.

He still planned to ride?

A groom peeked down from the hayloft, and several more stood motionless with muck shovels suspended in midair, watching what would unfold.

Her insides deflated.

A tongue lashing was still coming, just not in front of prying eyes.

Would Stephen understand that he'd been trying to help? Lady Turners voice echoed in her head. *You're useless and can't do anything right.* She'd failed in keeping her papa's legacy going, holding onto their inheritance, keeping her sister safe, and now with trying to help here.

CHAPTER 16

$\mathcal{T}$he farther they rode down the path, the tighter Stephen squeezed the reins. Instead of resuming its usual pace, his heart beat erratically, and he couldn't subdue the cold tingle icing the back of his head. Kate could have died. She was his responsibility, yet she seemed to have an affinity for near disasters.

Once they were out of hearing distance from the staff, Stephen found his voice, halted the horses with a shaky command, and rounded on her. "What in heaven's name were you thinking?" The pressure of this morning's upheaval exploded. "Do you not have any regard for your own life? You could have been trampled. Crushed. Killed."

"I was trying to help."

He'd expected her to cry or recoil in fear at his attack, but Kate held her ground.

"I watched how you calmed the horse earlier, and when the stable boy was having trouble, I stepped in to soothe her."

She'd been watching him? A spark lit in his chest, but the rolling flames inside him smothered it. "Did anyone ask for your help?"

She shook her head.

As heir apparent, Stephen had learned to size up women and guarded himself with a tough exterior. Julia was an easy read. He knew who exactly she was. From the beginning, she'd been forthright, stating she was seeking an advantageous match, and he'd admired her for her honesty.

Then along came Kate, and his carefully constructed logic sank faster than a leaky boat. One look from her doe-like eyes pierced his armor. He'd tried to size up this tiny, fragile woman, categorize her into the neat, judicious groupings where he'd placed most women, but she continued to surprise him. Her strange arrival, knowledge of horses, and the suspicious claim she had amnesia but remembered addresses pointed to her being an accomplice in a horse thieving ring. What reason could she have going in the new mare's stall? A person might be curious about a new arrival but would keep a safe distance. Had she been sizing up the horse?

His heart screamed she was innocent. She could be a self-defending wildcat wielding a candlestick, a sophisticated dancer waltzing in a meadow, a carefree angel playing cricket with the neighboring children, or a damsel needing his rescue, but she couldn't be a horse thief. It wasn't in her demeanor. She made him feel things he didn't want to feel. He was losing the careful control of his emotions that he'd kept tightly contained after losing Daphne.

His vulnerability set him on edge and cast kerosene on the fire within. "I don't need nor want your help."

She gasped, and the words hung in the air, stilling the normal woodland sounds. Even the horses quieted and turned their ears to hear better.

He closed his eyes. He shouldn't have said that.

If only he could take the words back.

He opened his eyes as Kate's turned away, but not fast enough for him to miss the welling tears in her eyes.

"I'm sorry." He inhaled a steadying breath. "I didn't mean any of it—

not a word."

Kate sat poised with a stiff back and high chin.

He dismounted and placed a hand over hers in hopes she would look at him. "I panicked. I kept seeing images of you trampled underfoot. I couldn't live with myself if anything happened to you."

Tears dripped from her eyes, and her shoulders crumpled.

He pulled her down from her mount and into his embrace.

She buried her face against his neck, her hair tickling his throat, and let loose racking sobs that shook her entire body.

"I'm not useless y-you know," she said with quiet firmness even though her body still trembled with uncontrollable sobs. "I c-can do things."

"I know you can, love." He tipped her face up with his index finger and the deep pain haunting her eyes pierced his chest. "I didn't mean what I said." He brushed his lips to her cheek to wipe away the tears that spilled and trailed his hand up and down her spine, aching to take away the hurt he caused her. "Can you forgive me?"

She peered up at him with red-rimmed, shimmering green eyes, and her slight nod was his undoing. He kissed away a glistening tear from her other cheek, wanting to heal the hurt he'd caused and trailed more along the smooth skin of her jaw line. Her eyes closed and she clung to him, tilting her head up to him. He claimed her mouth in a searing kiss desiring her forgiveness, longing for her acceptance, and craving her love. Her lips were soft and pliable forming to his with a sweetness that caused his body to tremble. She tasted of salty tears and chocolate, and she smelled of spring and sunshine. When she didn't pull away, he slowed his kiss to savor the feel of her. Her fingertips kneading his back and the intimacy of it only increased his need to discern the mystery of Kate Vernon.

Warmth radiated from her body, surrounding him in a euphoric cocoon. His blood sang with the sweetness of her.

He pulled back before he forgot himself. He'd already taken more liberties than a gentleman should. His ragged breath matched her own.

She stared at him with a dazed expression, her lips swollen from their kiss and her color high.

"My word," he whispered unable to hide the awed reverence in his voice. "I never anticipated you...this." He breathed her in one last time and forced his feet to step back and his fingers to untangle from her hair. He swallowed and his Adam's apple strained against the tightness of his cravat. Clearing his throat, he said, "We should ride."

She blinked away the passionate haze in her eyes and turned toward Duchess, but he gripped her arm to stop her.

"Promise me you won't put yourself in harm's way like that again."

She nodded, but it wasn't enough.

"I need to know I can trust you on this. I don't want you hurt." His gaze locked on hers.

"Can I trust you?"

She opened her mouth to respond, but nothing came.

Why didn't she speak? Did she not realize the danger she'd posed to herself? Was she admitting that she couldn't be trusted? What was he to think of that—an honest liar?

Straightening, he stepped away and grabbed the reins. He slapped the leather straps into the palm of his glove. By Jove, the woman frustrated him, but if he continued to argue with her, she would never open up to him. It was time to change tactics. Flashing her a sideways smile, he said, "It's time for a rematch. Why don't you show me how capable you are by beating me in a fair horse race?"

She eyed him warily. "Only if you ride Duchess and allow me to ride Dominion."

Laughter burst through Stephen's lips. By all that was holy, she had spirit.

He reworked the saddles and verbally laid down the path of the race, pointing out the markers down the lane where two tall oak trees stood.

He let Kate call the start, and she burst out in front, crouching low over her mount, racing with the skill and agility of a true horsewoman.

Stephen drove Duchess until she was head-to-head with Dominion, but instead of passing her in the last leg of the race, which he easily could have done, he eased up, allowing Kate a slight lead for the win.

Kate whooped when she crossed the finish line. She turned Dominion in a tight circle, beaming a proud smile at her opponent.

He grinned at the joy on her face.

Her elation faded into a fierce frown. "You let me win."

"What makes you say that?"

"You are much too competitive not to show the slightest displeasure over losing. You let me win."

Laughter rumbled in his chest. "I can't get anything past you." He shifted in his saddle as warning alarms sounded in his head. It appeared she could read him well enough. Would that he could read her so easily.

They rode on, enjoying being out in the fresh air. Stephen couldn't help but glance her way often. Her cheeks were flushed from the ride, and springy curls bounced with the horse's gait. They stopped by Marisa's mother's house and delivered the material for her quilting. She waved them inside, but Stephen declined. It might be pure selfishness, but he didn't want to share Kate's attention with anyone right now. They promised to come by on another occasion.

Beams of sunlight filtered through the canopy of trees as they rode beneath, and Stephen inhaled the musky scent of rich earth, sweet pine, and moist leaves. "Smell that," he said. "There is no better fragrance. You don't get this in London. The pungent city smell takes a few days to get out of my lungs and clothes. The first thing I do when I come home is inhale a deep breath as if I'd been holding mine for a long time."

"You're not a city man?" Kate angled her head for a better view of him.

"London serves its purpose, but no. I'm a country gent. I plan to move back here as soon as my work there is finished." A small rabbit jumped out from the underbrush and raced across their path into the woods. "I'll miss my friends and my neighbors."

"Where do you reside?"

"I have a bachelor's lodging on Mount Street in Mayfair near Hyde Park. You can't beat the area for rubbing noses with the right people. It's come in handy for business." And for collecting foreign and domestic intelligence. "When I'm not there, I'm here on the farm, ensuring the training school is successful."

Kate prodded him with questions about his business dealings and London's social scene. Her inquiry even extended to his townhouse and Willowstone Farm, specifically how they were managed. Was she digging for information to pass along to her accomplices? He carefully phrased his answers, cautious not to blow his cover or reveal the quantity of staff and when or where they might be posted. However, her questions leaned more toward the practical side as if she one day hoped to run an estate. Refreshed by her interest in things he too enjoyed, he relaxed in his saddle and spoke freely of his belief that God had nudged him to take a risk in writing a check to start the special training of horses for people with injuries, like his father.

"That's a big undertaking." She pulled Dominion away from a tuft of grass he was intent on munching, and they sauntered along the path. "But you have such tremendous skill with horses, and you undoubtedly have the knowledge and proper motivation because of your father's injury. I don't believe there is a more capable person."

"I don't want to be just some titled fop who attends balls or gambles his inheritance away. It may sound arrogant, but I feel called to a greater purpose."

"It shows in your actions and the way you treat your family and others." Kate smiled. "You're different."

The significance of her words and the way she looked at him with her shy grin made his heart race as if he'd ridden Dominion at a full gallop across the meadow. Kate listened and spoke from her heart, and she wasn't out to impress him or gain his favor. She asked him questions, not growing impatient for him to finish so she could talk about herself.

They slowed the horses to a stop so she could recapture the errant curls that had escaped her coiffure. She frowned as more fell loose, wrestling to get the springy tendrils in order. Sun backlit her head, giving her a halo of light. *Was the sun this bright yesterday?* He inhaled, filling his nose with the scent of dew in the meadow and his lungs with fresh air. *Was the sky this blue?* He clicked his tongue and turned the reins to let the horses meander through the woods.

Kate inquired about his childhood as he pointed out forts and tree houses he'd built when he was a boy, and spoke of the feats he'd accomplished, like sailing a boat he'd made himself down the river for a hundred yards before sinking. Her curiosity seeming unsatiable, and she laughed at the antics he related.

"Is there anything you don't do well?" She stared at him as if he was some aberration. "Something you're not proud of?"

Daphne's face entered his head, and he told himself not to mention her. He hadn't spoken of Daphne or his infatuation to his parents or Abby. He pinched his lips to keep them shut, but Kate's open expression tugged at his heart. He swallowed to keep the words down, but under the weight of those appealing green eyes, pressure built in his chest. It choked out his air, and a voice in his heart whispered, *you can trust her*.

"I fancied a woman who turned out to be a spy for France." His chest deflated as if he'd been holding his breath, but he felt lighter. "I was fresh out of university and attending sessions in the House of Lords on my father's behalf because of his injury. She pretended to be a young widow who'd been forced to marry an old gent she never loved and who recently passed. Her widow status allowed her freedom, and she used it to her advantage. The real reason she'd had an interest in me was because of my connections."

"How awful." Kate seemed truly horrified.

He shrugged. "The War Office approached me about their suspicions and asked me to intercept a letter she'd written to warn Bonaparte about how the House of Lords planned to strategically fund Prussian troops in the north. She was hung for treason." He swallowed. "The King instructed me to be there, and I was cheered for my hand in her capture, but I will never get the image of her..." He rubbed his eyes to block out the image of Daphne, her body turning limp, her head slumped at an odd angle. "I had tried to get her to confess, to repent. I even begged the House of Lords for leniency, but her judgement had been settled."

"Your actions probably saved many lives." Her brow furrowed. "But that is a great weight to bear on your conscious."

Kate's compassion alleviated much of his pain. He exhaled, and the pressure dissipated. He needed to lighten the somber mood. "My mother once told me that she used to pray I'd get caught when I misbehaved, like sneaking grapes from the neighbor's vineyard, so I'd learn about consequences. She preferred my character getting developed over me getting away with something. God was listening, because I got caught a lot."

"Really?" Astonishment rang in the squeak of her response.

"One time, I put a frog in Abigail's stockings. She found me out and retaliated by sliding a snake in my shoe." Stephen chuckled. "I had to be pried off the chandelier. Mama found out we'd had 'ungodly' creatures in the house and rang a peel over both of us."

"Remind me to stay in your parents' good graces."

"There was also the time Nick and I thought it would be funny to lure a bunch of geese into the schoolhouse. One of the younger kids spotted us and tattled. While all the other kids spent the rest of the day learning under the willow tree, Nick and I scrubbed goose droppings off the floors and desks."

While Kate laughed, Stephen admired the smooth line of her neck. "What about you? I can imagine you were a mischievous child, always getting underfoot."

Kate's laughter died.

He'd asked the question out of honest curiosity, not as a trap, but she scrutinized his face as if wondering about his intentions.

Those green eyes wavered, a rainbow of emotions coloring her expressive face in hues of anger, regret, sorrow, and surrender. Her lips quivered and parted.

He stopped breathing. Kate was going to tell him the truth. He knew it as well as he knew the sun would rise tomorrow. He could read her like he could his sister. Such a connection wouldn't be unheard of with twins, but it seemed strange to feel a similar bond with a woman he'd only known for a few short days. The air hung thick with foreboding. Twice Kate opened her mouth to speak, but her breath grew ragged, and her head lowered. "I suppose."

He'd just borne his darkest secrets, but she didn't trust him to do the same. He clenched his teeth. *Blast!* What had he been thinking? She wouldn't reveal her connections to the horse-thieving ring after he'd confessed to sending a woman to the gallows. What kind of an operative would set himself back like that?

He needed to put her at ease, so he forced a wry smile. "I guess since we're unable to say what you did as a child, I'll just have to guess. I'm sure you must have ridden horses. You ride like you were born in the saddle."

Dominic snorted as if in agreement.

Kate lowered her chin and stared at her gloved hands.

"You must have had a tree house by your climbing ability. I can picture you scrambling up and, once in the tree house, having a proper tea party."

Kate burst out laughing, and he knew he'd called it right. "What else?" she prodded and relaxed in the saddle.

"Let's see." He rubbed his chin. "I bet you were a friendly and curious child who dogged people's steps, asking questions. I imagine you were a carefree young girl, innocent and imaginative, always daydreaming. And, as you grew into a proper lady, you were surrounded by men seeking your hand, but I know you'd never been kissed."

His words stained her cheeks a rose color, indicating she, too, was remembering their kiss.

"How would you know?"

The innocent way her lips had parted under his left little doubt, but the longing swimming in those green eyes beneath her fan of dark lashes was nearly his undoing. He forced himself to ignore the question.

He chose a more somber tone. "There's a heaviness in your eyes like you've had to carry a burden." His horse shifted, and his leg brushed Kate's. She sat so close, yet a chasm gaped between them. "I can tell you work hard and feel responsible. You're proud but not boastful."

Kate stared at him as if under a spell.

"You're a fighter. You haven't been beaten down by life or

taken out by obstacles. Even though I would guess that you've seen a few of them by the condition my parents found you in."

Kate's mouth fell open, but no words came out.

"Despite all that, you have a kind and caring heart." Movement in his periphery drew his attention.

A large doe stepped into the clearing, looking directly at them before nibbling on some grass.

"Shh." Stephen gestured to the corner of the clearing and the animal.

Kate followed his gaze to the edge of the dense woods. "She's beautiful."

Indeed, she is, but he wasn't looking at the doe. He chose to accept his feelings for Kate as he would gravity. He loved how she laughed, how she listened. She didn't have weighty expectations for him to surmount. He pictured their lives together, growing old with one another—having children together. If she was somehow wrapped up with thieves, he would convince her to change her ways. He must.

Not for one second did he believe she'd willingly joined a life of thieving. Circumstances must have driven her to it. He could help her escape.

He lowered his voice to a whisper. "You remind me of a doe with your soft, wide-set eyes. You're graceful and skittish too. I fear you'll bolt at any moment." When she looked back at him from the doe, he continued. "It's engaging and infuriating at the same time. I pride myself on being a good judge of character, but you are a puzzle. I can't neatly lump you into a specific category. You're not a social climber, a spoiled swell mort, a hoyden, or a naive green girl. You're a natural beauty, gentle and kindhearted, yet a fiery titan when incented. You're openly curious but not ignorant."

The more time he spent trying to learn Kate's secrets, the less he cared about them and the more he cared about her.

The doe made her way through the clearing, stopping once to nibble on grass.

Kate chewed on her bottom lip, her cheeks bright with two red splotches. "What's that over there?" She pointed to a marker of some sort buried by overgrown thistles.

Stephen shook his head to clear it and swiveled to where she pointed at the vines and weeds covering a rounded stone. His muscles reflexively tensed and Dominion's ears perked up in response. It had been a mistake to ride in this direction. "It's a gravestone."

"What is it doing way out here?"

A bitter taste filled his mouth. "It's here because the woman couldn't be buried in the family plot."

---

*C*urious, Katherine nudged her horse closer.

Stephen followed a few steps behind.

Though he was close, she missed the comfort of his presence and peered at him over her shoulder. Tenderness welled in his eyes, and her heart beat faster.

Other than playful teasing by the boys in town, no man had singled her out. She'd never been courted or wooed. Even Alfred Turner, the man to whom her parents had betrothed her to as a child, had never paid her any mind. Stephen's strong arms had wrapped around her, and he absorbed her loneliness, enticing her with a taste of being wanted—desirable. How was she to return to normal life after this?

She kept trying not to be attracted to him but failed miserably. It was the small things that touched her, how he whispered words of encouragement to a young mare, smiled at her in that confident way of his. It was the loving look he held as he addressed his mother or teased his sister. It was the intensity with which he held her gaze.

Now was the time to tell him the truth. She'd tried earlier to force the words past the warnings screaming in her mind, but since then she'd sensed a change in him. She no longer feared he'd throw her out. He'd be angry, yes, but he cared for her.

Please God, help him to understand.

"Stephen, I..." She paused a few feet from the grave, noticing how it had been left isolated and uncared for. It bothered her. If she couldn't return home, would this be what would become of her parents' graves? "Who is buried here?"

His countenance changed. His eyes grew cold, and a muscle twitched in his cheek. When he spoke, his voice sounded flat. "My aunt."

Katherine's heart clenched at the thought of this lost soul shunned by her family, neglected, and isolated, but such lack of caring seemed inconsistent with the Hartingtons' character. She dismounted and brushed away some of the vines until she read the headstone:

Lady Marie Cameron Bove
Born: 1756 Died: 1782

Katherine examined the dates and summed the years in her head. Lady Bove had been a mere six and twenty when she died, only a few years older than herself. How could the family leave her all alone in this desolate spot? Katherine bent down and pulled at the weeds as if the small effort might compensate for the injustice. She yanked at the plants, splashing chucks of dirt over her skirt and hands.

How could they forget about Lady Bove forgotten all alone out here?

Was she to suffer a similar fate as a spinster? Would Claire move on with her family and life, and Katherine would be left behind to rattle around Steepleton Manor as the overgrown

grass and weeds from her inability to keep up with its maintenance hid her from the world?

"Kate. Don't." Stephen's tone was harsh as he jumped down
from his horse.

She froze in mid-pull, leafy vines and twigs protruding from
her clenched palm. Torn between acquiescing and defiance,
Katherine sought his eyes.

He stared at the tombstone as if it were a venomous snake.

The weeds fell loosely from her fingers.

"She's the reason my dad's leg has withered." His voice held
an edge, and pain brandished his eyes. "She's the reason my
once prominent family now struggles financially." He stared at
the gravestone in disgust. "It was an arranged marriage, but my
uncle fell helplessly in love with her. She was quite beautiful,
and their marriage brought them both joy, or so we thought.
Shortly after they were married, her waist started to grow, and
my uncle was never happier. He spoke of his wife and the baby
to anyone who would listen.

"The truth came out that the baby was not his. She had
known she was with child before they were married. My uncle
was devastated. Her deception ate at him day and night. He
turned to spirits to dull the pain and drank himself to death
one night. The scandal that followed affected my entire family.
The *ton* didn't outright reject my parents, but whispers were
everywhere. Lady Bove was shunned by polite society, unable
to show her face in public. My parents offered her love and
kindness. They visited her frequently, but her will to live faded.

"One day, my parents visited, and she wasn't home. A
servant said she'd gone for a walk, so they headed down the
path in the direction she'd taken. They found her on the verge
of a precipice, her toes protruding over the edge. They begged
her to move away, to think of the baby she carried. She turned,
giving my father time to inch his way over to her. He talked to
her with soothing words, calming her hysterics. She appeared

to be responding, but when my father was close enough to reach her, she looked him in the eyes and fell backward to her death.

"My father reached for her and lost his footing. Thank God, he landed on a low ledge about twenty feet down, but he landed poorly, breaking his fall with his right leg, which never healed correctly despite the qualified physicians we paid to see him."

A hollowness darkened Stephen's gaze. "Her lies killed my uncle and maimed my father. I know we are supposed to forgive, but part of me believes she deserved what happened to her."

The woods grew silent. Even the birds stopped singing.

Katherine's chest ached at the pain in Stephen's voice and for the woman whose life ended in tragedy.

They remounted their horses and headed toward the house, each left to their thoughts. Katherine understood his pain, but her heart ached for herself also. Would Stephen equate her lies with those of his aunt? What if he rejected her without listening to her defense? His vehement hatred of his aunt shook her confidence. Deceit had left Stephen with wounds that hadn't yet healed, from his aunt to the French spy. Would he be able to forgive Katherine, or would he send her back to her cousin?

A chill ran through her veins.

Look where deception had gotten them. Lady Bove was dead and forgotten in a neglected grave, and the French spy had danced at the end of a hangman's noose.

Was Katherine headed down the same path?

Her head pounded. If she told the truth, she'd lose her heart, for she'd fallen for Stephen, and he would hate her. But if she kept her secrets, she could suffer an even worse fate.

*D*espite returning after their first ride together in a somber mood, their daily rides became Stephen's favorite pastime. Good horse stock had arrived the day before, and he spent his afternoons either training or spreading the word through his connections. Intelligence from the Home Office led the agency to believe the ring had illegally gotten pureblood horses and were seeking a buyer, which caused Stephen to switch tactics. He now emphasized he was seeking to purchase good stock, specifically thoroughbreds. Jacob and another trusted agent rotated, traveling to local horse markets and keeping watch in Willowstone's stables, but Stephen didn't dare relax regarding his family's safety. Rotations had been set for lookouts with Stephen in the mix, and he was still a bit groggy after manning the two to nine shift this morning.

Even though he knew Kate was harboring a secret, he started to doubt his assumptions. She had a thorough knowledge of horses but lacked malicious intent, and there had been no sign of criminal activity in the area. But was his regard for Kate clouding his judgment? His feelings continued to intensify the more time they spent together—along with the weight of her secrets.

If only she would trust him.

It was day four of their morning rides, when Stephen approached her from behind as she strolled into the barn. "Ready?"

She jumped and whirled.

"Sorry, I didn't mean to frighten you." He flashed a smile, not at all contrite. He hoped, over time, she'd open up. She'd been skittish since their first meeting, jumping at every shadow, and he couldn't resist teasing her about it.

Kate smirked. "If you didn't intend to scare me, why are you smiling so?"

He chuckled. "You practically leapt out of your skin."

"Very funny." She hoisted herself into the saddle without his assistance.

Stephen had grown accustomed to the smile glued to his lips as of late.

And why not? His family had already grown to love and adore her in the past weeks.

Thank you, Lord, for putting Kate in my life.

Whatever hesitancy he'd had toward her melted away. He wasn't quite certain what caused the change in his attitude, but he no longer cared about her secretive past or why she pretended not to remember. She'd made no further attempts to post any letters, but he had eyes on her. If she had been awaiting a response, enough time had passed that she would attempt to slip into town to make contact again soon. He hung onto the hope that the letter she'd sent was a final farewell to any attachments she might have once had.

A smile touched his lips as he considered life with Kate. It would never be dull. Kate questioned him about everything, especially his training of the horses. She knew how to tease him and make him laugh. He loved the sparks that shone in her eyes when he goaded her. With Kate by his side, he would rouse each morning, anticipating what the day would bring.

He'd extended his trip home, for he hadn't finished his mission. If he routed out the horse thieving ring the additional funds would ease his financial burdens, plus the time spent training the horses while undercover would give him a head start with his own business. His future plans had always felt like items to cross off a checklist, but now his skin tingled at the prospect of what was to come. Kate was never far from his thoughts, and it was time he told her his feelings. He was almost certain she felt the same. Her affection showed in her eyes, in the little glances she gave him without knowing he was watching. Soon. He would tell her soon.

The bright sun promised a glorious day. He eased into a

cantor. During their brisk ride, Kate's bonnet slid off, and a mass of honey brown curls shone in the mid-morning sun. Willowstone manor peeked into view between the poplar trees.

Suddenly, Kate jerked on the reins, bringing her horse to an abrupt stop. Duchess reared in protest, but Kate swung her around. Both horse and rider tensed.

Stephen turned his mount. "What's the matter?"

"Were you expecting someone at the house?" Kate moved the horse in a tight circle.

"The horses I anticipated arrived yesterday, and I'm not expecting any more until next week." He craned his neck. Sure enough, a carriage sat in the drive.

Kate's face had drained of color, and her eyes widened. Her reaction could only mean one thing. She was running from someone—someone of whom she was very much afraid. He rode nearer and took the reins from her hands. She barely paid him any mind as she handed them over. She bit her lower lip, gaze never straying from that stranger's carriage.

Stephen dismounted, wrapped an arm around her waist, and gently pulled her from her mount.

He looped her horse's reins over a branch behind some overgrown brush.

He crouched to peer straight in her eyes. "Everything is going to be all right. Wait here." He'd defend her at any price.

Her bottom lip trembled, and she clutched his sleeves.

His heart clenched at her vulnerability, and he pulled her into his arms. She clung to him like a child, and a shudder ran through her. A fierce possessiveness like he had never known swept over him. Much as he hated to leave her, it was time to discover from who she was hiding. He reluctantly pulled away and lifted her chin with his fingers until a pair of watery emerald eyes met his.

"I'm not going to let anything happen to you." His eyes remained locked on hers until she nodded. He swiftly remounted. With a click of his heels, he charged into the open ready for battle.

But his stomach plummeted, recognizing the emblem on the coach.

Thunder and turf.

CHAPTER 17

*a*n elegant town coach with six brilliant white horses and the Napier crest on top rested in the drive.

Stephen should have guessed.

A sour taste filled his mouth as a footman, holding a pale blue parasol, offered his hand and helped a curvaceous, blond-haired woman wearing all blue alight the steps.

"Julia." He whispered her name under his breath. It would have been impossible for her to hear, but she turned and spotted Stephen as he approached. Her hand raised in a proper wave, and he had no choice but to ride down the hill and greet her.

She smiled a wide grin before her lips turned down in a pretty little pout. "What happened to a sennight?"

"I was detained." He dismounted and approached. A stable boy ran out to tend to Dominion and the travel-weary carriage horses.

She extended her hand for him to take, and Stephen, remembering his manners, brushed a kiss on the top of her glove.

178

"It's good to see you, Julia, but why, may I ask, are you here? Didn't you get my note?"

Her head tilted to the side. "What note?"

His jaw clenched. He'd sent Julia a note letting her know he'd been delayed. He'd considered writing her about Kate, but he had still been working out his feelings and hadn't known exactly how to explain what he felt.

"I feared something was amiss when you didn't return. I was going to visit with my sister and had the marvelous idea to stop by and pay a visit to you and your family since you're practically on the way."

Her sister's residence was more than a day's ride south of Willowstone Farm, nowhere near on the way.

Mrs. Napier, Julia's mother, climbed out of the coach with the assistance of a footman. "How lovely to stretch my legs after a long ride. I daresay I could use a warm bath to ease the ache. Good day to you, Lord Hartington."

He greeted her and bowed low.

"You've dawdled for too long in the country." The older version of Julia with white-gold hair and deep frown lines pursed her lips at him. "The season is far from over."

Julia glared her mother into silence before turning and batting her eyelashes at him. "You promised to take me to the Rutherford Masquerade. I couldn't let you break your promise."

Blast. He'd forgotten about the masquerade in a few days.

Julia watched him with those wide eyes as if awaiting something.

He glanced into the wood where he'd left Kate. How would he explain Julia's visit to her?

Julia cleared her throat. "You...um, look well."

He rather doubted that, at least if he appeared anything like how he felt internally. "Come inside, and I'll introduce you to Mother."

Mrs. Napier had already marched up the front steps and rapped on the door with the end of her parasol.

Their butler ushered her in, but Julia stilled Stephen with a hand.

"I've missed you." She glanced at the stable boy and coach driver, whose backs were turned. Rising on her toes, she wound her arms around his neck and pressed a kiss to his cheek.

Astonished by her boldness, Stephen tensed. It wasn't like Julia to show affection. She must have genuinely missed him.

A stab of guilt twisted his heart.

"Julia." He took her hands from behind his neck and lowered them.

"You're right, but I couldn't resist. I've missed you so."

He stepped back. "I have much to discuss with you, but let's not keep my mother waiting."

*K*atherine crouched low behind the dense underbrush. Her racing heartbeat slowed, but her mind remained on high alert. She'd assumed the worst, envisioning Horace or Lord Pewitt stepping out of the coach, brandishing a loaded pistol. In her premonition, it had been aimed straight at Stephen's forehead, demanding he reveal her whereabouts.

Be rational.

Most likely, this was a friend coming to visit Lady Felton. However, as the minutes ticked by, her thoughts plagued her. What if he was in danger? Her fingers twitched. She needed to assess the situation for her sanity. Looping Duchess's reins on a limb, Katherine gripped the trunk of a tree and rose to peek above the thick underbrush, keeping hidden from view in case someone glanced in her direction.

Standing at the entrance to the house stood Stephen, alive

and well, and two women. One slipped into the house guided by Weston, the Hartington Butler, who was probably taking her coat. The other dressed in a pale traveling gown twisted her arms around Stephen in a lover's embrace and pressed her lips to his cheek.

Pain sliced through Katherine's heart. The two seemed to cling to each other for a long moment before Stephen ushered her inside.

Katherine turned and pressed against the tree trunk. The bark scratched her skin through her riding habit. She shut her eyes as if it could erase what she'd just witnessed.

How could I have done this to myself again? She'd longed to feel desired, wanted, and in Stephen's case even loved, so badly that she'd become disillusioned once more. He was devoted to someone else. She lightly banged her head against the rough bark. *First Alfred, now Stephen.* How stupid could she be? She squeezed her eyes tight against the painful memory flooding back of Alfred informing her the betrothal was off. Why hadn't she learned her lesson?

Her throat constricted, and tears burned the back of her eyes, but she couldn't cry. She'd cried enough over the loss of her parents and Alfred backing out, and she refused to weep from finding Stephen in another woman's arms.

How could she have misinterpreted his intentions? Had it been her imagination, like how she used to dream of Alfred rescuing her after the death of her parents? Had Stephen merely been looking for a friend and confidant, or had he been looking for someone to trifle with and her appearance made her a convenient proposition to seduce into his bed?

Stephen looked at her like she was the only one who mattered. She couldn't have imagined that, could she? She had so little experience where men were concerned. Maybe they were all like that. Maybe her father had been an exception.

Katherine grabbed Duchess's reins and stalked toward the

LORRI DUDLEY

stables. No matter what the reason Stephen had for embracing the woman, it was apparent he'd completely forgotten about her waiting in the woods. His rejection stung. Katherine's steps slowed, and her limbs felt heavy, but entering the stable, she lifted her chin, unwilling to acknowledge, even to herself, just how much his betrayal hurt.

———

*S*tephen instructed Weston to fetch his mother and escorted Julia and Mrs. Napier into the drawing room. He gestured for them to be seated, but his twitching nerves caused him to lean against the high-backed chair's headrest and steal glances out the window.

Julia prattled about the goings-on in London. Her eyes sparkled, and her face grew animated as she caught him up on the recent happenings among the Quality. He couldn't have cared less. In the past, he'd humored her as she rambled, but now he found her gossip irritating.

Mrs. Napier nodded off, her head leaning against the wing of the other high-backed chair.

What in heaven's name was taking Mother so long? He shifted his weight and stilled his hand to keep his fingers from drumming the armrest.

"Mrs. Napier, Miss Julia, what a surprise." Mother greeted Julia and her mother with a tight smile and entered the room. "How lovely to finally meet. Stephen speaks highly of you both."

He furrowed his brow. Her words were pleasant, but usually, Mother greeted people with enthusiasm.

"This is quite unexpected. I would have had tea and scones prepared had I known you were coming. Please be patient with us as Cook musters up something in the kitchen." She rang for tea and settled herself between Julia and her son. "How are you and your family?"

Before Julia had the chance to answer, Stephen stood and stepped forward. "Please excuse me, Mrs. Napier." He turned and bowed to Julia. "Miss Julia. I have some unfinished business I must attend to, and I will return as soon as I am able."

Julia's thin brows snapped together.

He nodded to his mother and retreated. He exited the house through the back door and scrambled up the hill to where he'd left Kate. "Kate, where are you?" He scoured the woods, but there was no sign of her. He ran a hand over the top of his head. How did he get into this situation? How was he going to explain Julia to Kate? Right now, he couldn't explain his feelings for Kate to himself. How could he have forgotten entirely about Julia after being on the verge of proposing? Did he still want to marry her? His heart retorted a firm no, even though logically, it seemed the rational thing to do. She came from money. She was beautiful and had a figure made for childbearing.

But Kate listened and laughed. They enjoyed each other's company. Or was he merely caught up in the enigma that Kate represented?

God, I need some clarity. In this matter, I can't trust my head or my heart.

Katherine let herself in through the side door and attempted to slip unnoticed up the front stairs to her chamber.

"You have other company?" A light feminine voice carried into the hallway. The woman in pale blue had spoken. She sat beside Lady Felton in the drawing room across from the stairs.

Katherine put her head down and climbed the first couple

of steps, holding her breath and willing them not to call her in for introductions. She needed the privacy of her room to get her teetering emotions under control and regain her courage.

"Kate, is that you?"

Lady Felton's voice sounded strained. Katherine stopped, but she didn't turn. She would pretend she hadn't heard Lady Felton's call, but Mama's voice rang in her head. *I taught you better manners than that.*

After all the kindness Lady Felton had shown her, Katherine was obligated to answer her summons. Closing her eyes and gritting her teeth, Katherine slinked down the stairs. She inhaled a deep breath and crossed into the drawing room.

"Kate, there you are. Let me introduce you to Miss Julia Napier and her mother Mrs. Napier."

Katherine dropped into a proper curtsy, and Miss Julia acknowledged it with a slight bow of her head.

"Miss Julia, this is Miss Kate Vernon."

"Are you a relative of the Hartingtons?" Miss Julia folded her hands over her knees, striking a becoming pose.

The woman was even lovelier up close perched on her chair with her skirts fanned. Dressed in a traveling gown with matching boots and kid gloves, Miss Julia Napier reminded Katherine of one of her mother's prize-winning blue-bell flowers. Her smooth complexion, light blue eyes, and blond hair, which was perfectly set in its coiffure without a single strand out of place, relegated Katherine to a shadow in her borrowed gray riding habit. No wonder Stephen forgot about her in the woods. Miss Julia Napier was a nonpareil.

The last drop of hope bled out of Katherine's heart.

Miss Julia's assessing eyes flicked over Katherine's form, waiting for her answer.

"I'm not a relative. The Hartingtons were kind enough to—"

"She's become a dear friend of the family." A fond smile illuminated Lady Felton's eyes.

"I see." The corners of Julia's lips turned down.

Katherine stepped closer to Lady Felton. "Are you feeling all right? Your voice sounds strained. May I get you something? Perhaps I could ring for tea?"

"Oh no, dear." Lady Felton took Katherine's hand and gently patted it. "It is very sweet of you to worry over me. Tea is already on the way, and I'm sure it will be just the thing."

Quiet fell over the room. Katherine wet her lips and turned to Miss Julia. "You must be a close friend of the family, too?"

"Stephen and I are...well...a match." She looped her index finger around a strand of perfectly round pearls and tilted her chin up, giving Katherine a view of her long, graceful neck. "Stephen gave these to me right before he came here."

Acid churned in Katherine's stomach. How could Stephen kiss her in the glen when he was already attached to another woman? Had he used her for amusement? Did he think so lowly of the lost stray they'd picked up on the side of the road that he could toy with her emotions and discard her when he was finished?

Katherine glanced at Lady Felton. Had she known the extent of Miss Julia's and Stephen's relationship? If so, Katherine was a poor reader of people, for she'd had the impression that Lady Felton and Abby were attempting to push she and Stephen together. The tea service arrived, and Lady Felton focused on steeping the tea and pouring the cups.

Katherine struggled to keep her voice from cracking. "How wonderful for you both. I'm sure everyone is delighted by your visit."

She needed a hasty exit, for her knees turned as watery as the tea. "If you'll excuse me, I need to freshen up. Delightful to meet you, Mrs. Napier." She bobbed a curtsy. "Miss Julia."

"It was our pleasure, Miss..."

Silence lapsed. *Drat.* The new revelations had addled her wits to the point that she couldn't even remember her surname.

LORRI DUDLEY

"Vernon, Miss Vernon," Lady Felton said.

"How could I have forgotten." Miss Julia offered her a stunning smile. "Miss Vernon. It was a pleasure."

Katherine curtsied and hurried out of the room. Unshed tears blurred her way up the stairs, so she placed a hand on the wall to guide her to the safety of her bedchamber.

*K*atherine listened to Miss Julia dominating the dinner conversation, raving about the magnificent balls Stephen and she attended. She elaborated on how he'd escorted her to the theatre every Thursday and the important people with whom they frequently dined. Each time she referred to Stephen, she peered at him and batted her lashes, not in a vapid girlie way but with a long, graceful sweep. She'd perfected the art.

Katherine pushed the food around on her plate with her fork, wanting to retch.

Stephen focused on eating his meat pie and occasionally conversed with his father regarding the new mare that had taken to its training. He glanced down the table at Katherine a couple of times, offering an apologetic look, but she wouldn't hold his gaze.

Otherwise, he spent the meal in a pensive mood.

Lady Felton and Abby also remained quiet. On occasion, they would issue her a sympathetic smile, but scrutinized Stephen's interactions with Julia.

Katherine had grown accustomed to the family's playful banter, but that was missing during dinner. Miss Julia did her best to draw everyone's attention, especially Stephen's, with grand stories. "Stephen, who was that lovely couple at the Warwick ball?" or "What was that strange food the prince regent asked to have served?"

Other than single-word responses, Stephen didn't contribute to the dinner conversation, which was unlike him. After dinner, the men retired for a quick cheroot, and the women adjourned to the sitting room to continue their conversation. Abby and Lady Felton sat on either side of the fire. Julia fanned out her skirts and sat in a low-back chair beside her mother. Katherine settled on an adjacent tufted settee.

"Miss Vernon." Miss Julia broke from talking about her gay exploits in London and turned her steely focus on Katherine. "I don't recall having made your acquaintance. When was your coming out?"

"I haven't had a season." Too late, Katherine tried to swallow the words. "Not that I can recall, at least." *Phew.* She'd almost blown it.

Julia's peel of musical laughter floated through the room, and she focused on Lady Felton. "Where did you find such a dear? She is adorable." She turned back to Katherine. "Oh my, you *are* green." Miss Julia placed a hand to her bosom. "Believe me. You would remember if you'd had a season."

Abby spoke up in her defense. "Kate truly can't recall whether she's had a season or not." She scooted to the edge of her seat. "There was an accident. She received a blow to the head, and she can't remember anything from her past. Our physician called it amnesia."

Miss Julia pressed back in her chair as if Katherine had a contagious disease. "How terrible for you."

"You haven't told us how your sister is faring after the baby?" Lady Felton flashed Katherine a don't-you-fret look before drawing Julia's attention.

Julia launched into another monologue, and Abby's eyes quickly glazed over. She stared over Miss Julia's head out the window into the night sky. Her brows tilted in a wistful expression as if hoping to sprout wings and escape the mundane chatter.

Katherine smothered a giggle. She longed to wrap her friend in a fierce hug.

The room quieted.

"You *do* realize women will say or do anything to get your son trapped into matrimony." Mrs. Napier leaned in Lady Felton's direction and lowered her voice.

Lady Felton straightened, her hands folded in her lap.

A few indecipherable sentences passed until Katherine heard the whisper of her name and strained to hear.

"I'm not insinuating Miss Vernon is that sort." Mrs. Napier peeked at Katherine. "I see it all the time in London, especially once they discover he's in line to be an earl."

Lady Felton shook her head. "I don't think—"

"I'd *hate* to believe women are now chasing him into the country too." Mrs. Napier glanced Katherine's way again, but Katherine pretended to be interested in fishing out a speck of dust from her teacup.

"What is all the whispering about?" Abby snapped out of her stupor and frowned at her mother.

"Indeed." Lady Felton stiffened. "We don't abide gossiping servants, and especially as ladies, we shouldn't fall prey to chin-wagging either.

An aghast look crossed Mrs. Napier's expression, but the men returned, cutting off what Katherine assumed would have been a shocked—feigned—reaction.

The group reconvened in front of the piano except for Stephen who chose to linger by the fireplace.

Stephen's presence once again choked the air from the room, and Katherine hated that her traitorous gaze strayed in his direction. He grabbed a poker and stabbed at the logs in the grate, sending red sparks into the flue.

She was not going to covet another woman's... How had Miss Julia referred to him? Her match? Katherine would put

Stephen from her mind and focus on finding a way to sneak back into town to see if her letters received any response.

Lady and Lord Felton excused themselves to retire for the evening, and Mrs. Napier followed shortly thereafter. Katherine opened her mouth to excuse herself also.

Abby stilled her with a hand. "Shall we play a round of cards?" Abby flashed a wicked smile at Katherine.

Stephen issued his sister a don't-you-dare-cheat look.

Julia sighed. "I'm not really in the mood for cards."

Abby snorted.

Was it wrong to have wished for Abby to trounce Julia at cards?

"How about charades?"

Julia declined that game as well.

Abby slumped in her chair. "What would *you* like to do, Julia?" Her voice bordered on sarcasm.

Julia smiled a sweet, coy smile and turned to Stephen. "I was hoping we could talk. Stephen and I have *so* much to catch up on."

Stephen settled into the corner of the settee on which Katherine sat perched on the far edge. He crossed his ankle over his knee and, with his cravat dangling loosely from his collar, looked the epitome of casual indifference. He flicked his hand toward Julia as if to say, *Go right ahead.*

Was he that uncaring? Had Katherine imagined those shared moments between them? Were her feelings for Stephen so disillusioned that she'd manufactured feelings on his part? He could at least appear flustered while sitting with his soon-to-be intended on one side and herself on his other.

Mrs. Napier's prior whispered remark churned up a thundercloud inside Katherine. She wasn't after Stephen's title. She already had a title, and she certainly hadn't followed him into the countryside to throw herself at him. *He* was the one who kissed *her.*

She *hadn't* imagined that.

They'd spent countless hours this past week together while she waited for enough time to pass for returned correspondence from the school and her attorneys. Something had developed between them, and it couldn't honestly be called friendship. She might be green in the ways of men, but she wasn't naïve enough to believe friends shared passionate kisses.

Julia prattled on about her and Stephen's future endeavors. "We'll have to sell your place in Mayfair. I do hope we can find a place more uptown."

She spoke as if they were already engaged. Katherine cast Stephen one last side glance, and although his expression remained bland, Miss Julia held his concentration.

Katherine had been forgotten.

Miss Julia fanned herself and batted her eyes. "I cannot wait for what surprises the spring has in store."

Enough. She didn't have to sit here and endure this.

Sitting up a little straighter, she waited for Miss Julia to breathe between sentences so she could excuse herself.

Stephen's warm hand came to rest on her midback. Tingles flooded her spine. She pulled away, but his hand shifted to the curve of her lower back. The seconds stretched into minutes before he retracted his arm back to his side. Had Julia witnessed his touch? She prattled on about a gown she intended to purchase for the season and described the French style to Abby.

Had he anticipated her readying to leave and was asking her to stay? A moment before, he hadn't appeared to remember she was in the room. Had he been aware of her as she'd been aware of him?

His small gesture didn't justify the torture of listening for another minute. When an opportunity presented itself, Katherine faked a yawn. "I'm not accustomed to the late hour. I must beg your pardon so I may retire."

Abby yawned as well, but the couple would be without a chaperone if she left. She sighed and squeezed Katherine's hand. "Good night. I'd like to speak with you in the morning."

Katherine bid Stephen and his *match* a good night and slipped off in the direction of her room. She paused at the library. The hour was still early, and she wasn't a bit tired. A good read would be the perfect thing to take her mind off Stephen and Julia and calm her nerves so she could sleep. She opened the door and walked inside, breathing in the wonderful scent of weathered pages and leather bindings on the books that lined the walls. She chose one on Egyptian history and attempted to read, but the words blurred, and her mind refused to focus.

The image of Julia wrapped in Stephen's embrace taunted her.

Footsteps jogged down the corridor. Katherine closed the book and stepped into the shadows, not wanting to be around anyone at the moment. Stephen passed briefly, peeking into the room, but didn't spy her.

That had been close.

Katherine pressed her palms to her face hating the loving remembrance of his touch, kiss, and words, *I hadn't anticipated you...this.* Why was she such a fool when it came to men?

The walls of the library pressed in around her. She longed for her mama. Mama would wipe her tears and listen to her woebegone heart. She would sit Katherine down, stroke her head, and whisper words of encouragement.

Katherine wanted to go home, to be in familiar surroundings, but even the house where all her memories resided had been taken from her.

She moved to the window and peeked into a night as bleak and unrecognizable as her future. She pulled the curtain farther aside, and the glow of lantern light from the stable beckoned her.

How had the new mare that she'd whispered words of reassurance to settled into its unfamiliar home? Perhaps she'd check on her—sneak a quick visit. They could offer each other comfort.

No one would be the wiser.

CHAPTER 18

The previous day's events ran through Stephen's head like a bad play, repeating the same dramatic act over and over. He tossed and turned, wishing he'd done things differently. But as pink streaks formed in the morning sky, he abandoned his efforts to sleep and threw the covers aside. Kneeling at the foot of his bed, he prayed.

Lord, I thought I knew Your will, but now I wonder if it was my own that I was following. Guide me and give me wisdom for this situation. Help Kate to forgive me...and Julia. I didn't mean to be a cad. He prayed until words no longer seemed adequate and stumbled downstairs to prepare for the day.

He entered the breakfast room where his mother sipped a cup of steaming coffee.

"You're up early." She motioned for another cup of the brew to be brought for Stephen.

"I couldn't sleep." He plopped into the chair next to his mother.

She offered him a sympathetic smile. "You have a lot on your mind, I presume."

He sucked in a deep breath and blew it out. "You could say that."

His mother studied him over the rim of her cup.

Stephen propped his elbow on the armrest and rested his face between his thumb and index finger. His vision clouded as he stared across the room, trying to shake the haunting look of hurt in Kate's eyes. He could feel his mother's gaze on him.

"Business decisions come so easily to me." He rubbed the lower half of his jaw. "But women are another matter. They're very complicated." His gaze flicked to his mother's face. "No offense."

"We are complex creatures. I presume you're having a difficult time now that Miss Julia has arrived."

"I had been convinced that Julia was the right woman for me, but now I'm not sure."

"What has changed?"

He rubbed his face with both hands. "I seem to have developed feelings for Miss Vernon."

Mother's lips curled into a small smile, but her eyes pitied him.

"Julia was the logical choice." He stared at the cream swirling in the coffee the footman set in front of him. "She's from a wealthy family of good breeding and social standing, and her cousin is the Viscount of Phelps. She's also one of four siblings and seems suitable for childbearing."

"You sound like you're purchasing a horse, not deciding who you want to spend the rest of your life with." She raised a questioning eyebrow and drew her coffee cup to her lips.

"I'm trying to be wise. I'm ready to settle down and set up a nursery, but I must consider all aspects."

"Have you taken your heart into consideration?" She patted his arm. "I know you take the weight of your responsibilities seriously, and more often than not, members of the peerage marry based on titles or for financial gain. Your father and I, however, don't want that for you. We want you to marry the woman God has chosen for you—someone who will love you and respect you. I know you worry about our financial situation, but God will provide. He always does."

"I'm trying to be a good steward."

"What do you find appealing about Kate?"

Stephen crossed his arms. "She's exasperating." His gaze drifted out the window to the hint of a sunrise. "Kate has an innocent outlook on life, like she is discovering everything for the first time. She loves children and is gentle." He looked at his mother for emphasis. "But she has spirit, too, and won't let people push her around. She's intelligent and a quick learner—not to mention beautiful, and those eyes..."

Mama pinched her lips together, but it didn't hide her smile.

"She seems to be of good character, but she's riddled with secrets. How can someone be of good moral fiber and not forthcoming?" He tilted his palms up. "I know she hit her head and supposedly has amnesia, but I caught her posting letters to a finishing school. If she has amnesia, then how would she know an address? She's using the amnesia as an excuse to hide her secrets."

"She's being cautious." A flicker of sadness darkened his mother's light eyes. "Some people, like Abby, jump into things with their entire being, but others,"—she quirked a half-smile at him—"like yourself, hold their cards close to their chest until they know it's safe."

His palm dropped to the table with a slap. "Shouldn't she trust us by now?"

Mother shrugged one shoulder, but he read the look in her eyes. Kate had been progressing, but Julia's surprise visit had set them back.

"Blast it all. I'm tired of this gammon. I want the truth, and I can't make certain decisions until I've gotten it."

LORRI DUDLEY

"Do you recall Paul's first letter to the Corinthians, chapter thirteen?"

Stephen lowered his brows. Where was she going with this? "You mean 'Love is patient, love is kind...'"

"That's the one, but where it states, 'Love rejoices in truth... Love gives the benefit of the doubt; it believes all things and endures all things.'"

"Are you saying I should go along with her charade? I should believe her lies?"

"That's not what I'm saying."

"What *are* you saying?" Stephen's voice sounded calm, but a tense muscle twitched in his jaw.

"The best way to make someone *trustworthy* is to *trust* them."

Her advice was the antithesis of what the Home Office had taught him. *Trust no one.*

She searched his eyes. "And conversely, the fastest way to make someone *untrustworthy* is to *not* trust them." She paused a moment as if to let it sink in.

He shouldn't have held back on telling Kate his feelings. His suspicions might have been cleared up if only he'd confronted her about knowing any links to the horse thieves? And then there was Julia, who he should have mentioned, but figured he'd have more time.

"Kate, I'm sure, has a good reason for not telling us everything." Mother sighed. "I think she's afraid of something, and it's her fear keeping her silent. Once she knows she can trust in God, and she can trust us, she'll come around. We'll get the whole story. Be patient."

"So, I should throw over Julia and trust Kate will eventually share her secrets?"

"You need to ask God for guidance and to reveal His will for your life. He is faithful and will show you the right path to choose. Just be certain to keep your eyes and heart open." She finished her coffee and stood, then leaned over and placed a light kiss on his cheek. "Remember, love *isn't* out to catch someone doing wrong. Love delights in catching someone doing right." As she left the room, she quietly sighed. "I'll be praying too."

---

*K*atherine snuck out of the house and headed to the stables earlier than usual. If she hurried, she could have Duchess saddled and be out on her ride before Stephen arrived—assuming he even came. This could be her chance to ride into town and check with the postmaster on her correspondences.

Why did things change in a flash? She'd been going about her life when a knock sounded on the door and Denton had stood before her, his face solemn, to tell her there had been a carriage accident and her parents would not be coming home. Then, her intended had cried-off her. Two years later, she'd finally started to put the shattered pieces of her world back together when her cousin arrived. And now, when Katherine had started to hope for her future, Miss Julia Napier appeared, and Katherine's life, once again, felt as if it had upended.

The smell of hay and morning dew hung in the air as she entered the stables. The new mare raised its snout, and Katherine held out her palm with a couple of sugar cubes. The barn stood quiet this morning, so she whispered, "Good morning, my friend." She picked up a brush and continued where she'd left off the night before. "Soon, you'll let me ride you."

Voices spoke from outside the stable window as men approached. "I heard of raids happenin' just north of here." She recognized the lilt of the head groom's voice. "Keep a closer eye on her. We found footprints of the female variety enterin' the stable that hadn't been there when I started my rounds last

197

night. I questioned, Philip, who'd been on watch. He said he hadn't seen anyone, but I'm taking him out of the rotation because he keeps dosin' off durin' his watch. I'll bet she's scopin' out the grounds and passing messages to the leader."

Two long shadows stretched from the stable's entrance, and Katherine's hand stilled.

"She's not a thief."

Stephen. One of the shadows shifted.

They suspected one of the staff of being a thief? A woman? Katherine considered the housekeeper and all the maids she'd met. Could one of them—?

"She's not who she says she is. Don't be losin' your head over a pretty face. You've got a good thing goin' with yer bluebell."

Grooms weren't on such friendly terms with the lord of the manor. Who was this man?

"I need proof." Stephen's voice sounded weary. "I want to trust her."

The groom sighed. "We'll find out soon enough if Miss Vernon is in the middle of it."

A jolt ran through Katherine's body. They thought *she* was a horse thief?

"Be ready. If I were a bettin' man, I'd say they're gonna strike soon."

"Show me the break in the fence." The men moved away.

Dust particles sparkled in the sun's morning rays, spilling in through the open door where the shadows of the men had been a second ago.

"Good mornin', miss."

Katherine jumped and spun.

The mare whinnied, and her hackles rose.

A young groomsman climbed down from his sleeping quarters in the loft. "Shall I saddle Duchess for yer mornin' ride?" The groom reached to pull the saddle off the hook.

Katherine nodded and forced her breath to slow. She stroked the mare to calm her.

He pushed back his cap to see her better. "Will Lord Hartin'ton be joinin' ya?"

A woman he believes is a thief? Not likely. "I believe he'll ride at our normal time or a little after." *With Miss Julia.*

"Let me get a fresh blanket pad to put under the saddle and ready my mount to ride with you."

"I've learned my way around. I won't be needing an escort."

"It's the master's orders. I'll be right quick about it." The groom sauntered off into the far part of the stable.

The master's orders. Had Stephen been feigning the enjoyment of their time together merely to keep an eye on her in case she made off with her mount?

Dominion kicked the stall door, and Katherine was tempted to do the same.

"Good morning, Kate."

She jumped and grabbed the stall post to steady herself.

Stephen's husky voice reverberated from behind. She schooled her features and turned to face him.

His shoulder rested against the frame of the main door, and his gaze locked on her like a hunter with a doe in range. The material of the fitted jacket he wore strained against his shoulders as he pushed off the lintel post. He stepped out of the bright filter of the early morning sun and stood beside her. "Preparing for our daily ride?"

"But..." Her words trailed off.

"But I'm early?" That lopsided smile, the one she was becoming all too familiar with, softened his features. She nodded with a clenched jaw.

"I could say the same about you. I hope it's due to your eagerness to be in my presence."

She stalked past him into Duchess's stall, muttering under her breath. "Just the opposite."

"We have some things to discuss." He followed her and stood outside the door. "I thought we could ride down to the river's edge."

She needed an alternative, preferably someplace public, or someplace that could change his decision to come along. His betrayal burned too fresh, and she might lash out if left alone with him. *I want to trust her,* he'd said, but he didn't. It explained why he appeared when she and Abby had climbed that tree, while they were in town, and each morning she wanted to ride. She swallowed the bile in her throat. "I was hoping to stop in and visit Marisa. Mrs. McLaughlin invited us to see some of the quilts. I didn't want her to think I'd forgotten."

"I see." His smug expression didn't change, and he rested an arm on the post holding the horse tack. "While you're visiting with her, I can speak to Mr. McLaughlin. I've been meaning to check on his property but haven't had the opportunity."

Katherine forced a smile. "Well, then, let's be off." She cursed her traitorous heart for still desiring Stephen.

The groom set out a stool and aided her to mount as Stephen swung a leg over Dominion. She nudged Duchess out the door, and Stephen followed.

"Wait." A shrill voice squealed from the direction of the house.

Miss Julia stood on the terrace in a lovely, pale blue riding habit with a form-fitting jacket and flared skirt. She waived and scurried toward them, her other hand holding her hat in place. "Wait for me."

Katherine's grip tightened on the reins.

Stephen's face remained unreadable except for a tiny muscle twitch in his jaw. He ordered the groom to prepare another horse and dismounted as Miss Julia approached. She beamed a brilliant grin, and Stephen half-smiled in return. "Good of you to join us."

Katherine greeted Julia with a nod.

"I heard you ride every morning." Julia either didn't see Katherine or didn't care to acknowledge her. "I love a jaunt in the country. The fresh air does wonders for one's constitution. I was hoping to join you."

"You don't like to ride." Stephen moved the stool over for Julia as the groom led over another mount.

She waved a hand. "I don't like to ride in the city, but the country is a different matter."

"Here, let me assist you." Stephen lifted Julia into the saddle. She clung to him and flashed a dimpled smile through lowered lashes. "The day is quite lovely. It reminds me of the times we've gone riding together, you and I." She glanced at Katherine.

Was it too late to feign an illness?

"You mean the one time we rode through Hyde Park?" Stephen swung into the saddle. "Are we ready?"

"Wait."

Katherine leaned forward to see past Dominion's raised head and perked ears. Abby hurried in their direction wearing her riding habit.

"Abby? You're up early." Stephen's eyes narrowed, and he sat back in the saddle. "To ride with us?"

"It's a splendid day." Her gaze flicked among the three onlookers. Her black eye had dwindled to a yellow-colored smudge. "I thought I might enjoy the nice weather while it lasts." She mirrored Stephen's suspicious expression back to him. "Is there something wrong with that?"

"I should mark the day my sister rose at dawn." He shrugged. "The more, the merrier."

After helping Abby mount Amethyst, the group was ready to head off. Julia asked if they had a destination, and Stephen explained that they were going to visit Mrs. McLaughlin.

"Ho there."

Stephen's jaw tightened, and he lifted his hat to run a hand over the top of his head. His voice brimmed with sarcasm as he turned his horse, "Is all of England planning on riding this morning?"

"Lovely day, isn't it?" Fredrick cantered up the lane to meet them. "I just rode over to see how Miss Hartington was faring with her... He pointed to his eye. Mind if I join you?"

"Be our guest." Stephen's smile tightened. "Fredrick, you remember my sister and Miss Vernon. I don't believe you've made the acquaintance of Miss Julia Napier."

Julia's gaze roved over Mr. Wilson, as if assessing the fine quality of his clothes and freshly polished boots. If she was impressed, she offered no indication.

Fredrick's expression glazed over with a besotted look. "How do you do, Miss Julia Napier." He tipped his hat. "Fredrick Wilson. Delighted to make your acquaintance."

She returned a polite smile in his direction.

"*Now* are we ready?" Stephen's expression remained polite, but frustration spiked his tone.

Abby and Julia nodded, but Stephen hesitated and checked over his shoulder toward the house. When no one cried for them to wait, he clicked his tongue, and the party headed down the path toward the McLaughlin's cottage. Julia sidled up next to Stephen, and Fredrick flanked her other side, leaving Katherine and Abby together in the rear.

"Are you all right?" Abby whispered.

"I'm fine." She shrugged. "Why wouldn't I be?"

"I was livid when I found out Julia had schemed to join your morning ride. I wouldn't leave you to fend for yourself with the likes of her around. Do not be fooled by her angelic appearance. Her fangs hold venom."

Katherine snorted her agreement.

The trees opened up to a clearing, where sheep dotted the hillside like white clouds in a sky of green. Wildflowers bloomed along the path, and fat bumblebees danced around each blossom. Nature mocked her incongruent mood, not caring a wit about her woes. The strong rays of sun warmed their faces. Julia appeared oblivious to all of it except the sun. Her complaints to find shade promptly or else her delicate skin might freckle went unheeded, and she huffed a pretty pout at Stephen. He stared at the path ahead.

Julia scowled. "Stephen?"

"Beg your pardon." Stephen jolted and turned to her. "What did you say?"

She wiggled in the saddle like a bird ruffling its feathers. "Never mind." Turning her attention on poor Fredrick, she basked in the handsome Corinthian's attention, but Katherine caught Julia's gaze straying to Stephen each time she laughed at something Fredrick said.

Stephen glanced over his shoulder at Abby and Katherine. "You two faring well?"

"We're fine." Abby spurred her horse to close the gap between the groups of horses, and Katherine did the same.

Julia leveled Katherine with a glare like an animal protecting its territory.

"Stephen." Julia tilted her head in a becoming manner. "Would you be a dear and escort me into town tomorrow? I was hoping to do a little shopping."

Stephen stared off in the distance as if he hadn't heard.

Julia straightened and cleared her throat.

"I'd be happy to escort you, Miss Julia," Fredrick said.

She pretended not to hear. "Stephen?"

He glanced at her. "Hmm?"

"Fredrick offered to accompany me into town. I was hoping to do a little shopping and was about to tell him you'd prefer to be my escort."

"Actually"—Stephen leaned back to peer at Fredrick— "that would be grand of you, Fredrick. I have some work I need to tend to tomorrow. Miss Julia should enjoy her visit and not grow tired waiting for me."

Julia twisted her reins as if wringing out a rag.

Abby nudged Katherine. Her eyes brimmed with laughter, and her lips curled to pinch back her mirth.

Stephen had never been this distracted on morning rides with Katherine. Was he thinking about business or deciding whether to implicate her as a horse thief? Her chest tightened. Did he truly think so little of her?

Julia got him to remark on something she said, and Katherine was tempted to spur Duchess in another direction. How could she have been so green, so gullible? She wanted to believe the best of people, but her heart could no longer stand being broken.

She slowed Duchess's gait as the McLaughlin home came into view. Was it wise to visit Marisa? Mrs. McLaughlin would feel obliged to offer her guests food and drink, and now that the party of two had blossomed into a party of five, feeding such a crowd could cost the Mclaughlin family a week's wages, if not more.

As if sensing something amiss. Stephen glanced back. "Aren't you coming?" He slowed his horse.

She shook her head.

He frowned and turned his horse around. The others reined their horses to a stop and peered in her direction.

"What's wrong?"

"This is a bad idea." Katherine whispered, and felt the weight of the other's gazes on her.

Stephen raised a brow. "It was your idea."

"That was before, when it was the two of us. I think we'll be putting the McLaughlin family out. I don't want to burden them."

Stephen nodded and raised a hand to wave everyone away, but Mrs. McLaughlin and Marisa stepped onto the front porch.

He raised his arm higher, turning the signal into a greeting. "Too late now," he said under his breath. "If we don't go in they'll feel rejected. It's considered an honor when the Lord pays a tenant a visit."

Mr. McLaughlin, standing near the shed, set down a tool, wiped his hands on a rag, and hurried over to greet them.

Katherine raked her bottom lip with her front teeth but followed Stephen.

Mrs. McLaughlin welcomed them, holding a kicking baby in her arms, and invited the ladies inside. Stephen declined for himself, and Fredrick and he strode to see what Mr. McLaughlin was working on near the one-horse stable.

After they'd entered the quaint cottage, Marisa hugged Katherine's legs before grabbing her hand and insisting they tour their two-room house. She pointed up at a loft. "I sleep up there and climb the ladder all by myself."

Katherine climbed a couple rungs and peeked into the tiny room with a single mattress on the floor. Mrs. McLaughlin bid the ladies to sit after Marisa's quick tour and passed her daughter the baby. The sparse room was tidy with white-washed walls and a tufted sofa. Freshly picked flowers sat on the table in a vase with a hairline crack.

Abby pulled up a small stool and sat.

Julia scanned the couch as if for dust or crumbs before easing down and arranging her skirts in a fashionable presentation, taking up most of the sitting room.

Katherine eyed a lone high-backed chair but didn't want to use the last available seat and leave their poor hostess to stand. Instead, she perched precariously on the far edge of the stuffed couch where Julia's skirts didn't reach.

"I'm delighted to be paid the honor of such a visit." Mrs. McLaughlin smiled at her guests. "If I would have known ya were comin' I would have made some biscuits, but ya caught me unawares. I can offer a claret-cup of some of me husband's best wine." She ducked into the small alcove that served as a kitchen before anyone could decline and returned with a tray.

Katherine couldn't refuse the generous offer. "We didn't mean to burden you. I was merely hoping to take you up on your offer to show me some of your quilts."

"Ooch, it would be my pleasure." Mrs. Mclaughlin scurried into the only other room in the small dwelling. She returned, arms loaded with quilts, a smile stretched across her face. She spread out each quilt on top of a table, giving little tidbits of information or stories about each one. Mrs. McLaughlin pointed to a green square of fabric, and Katherine leaned forward to get a better look.

"This piece here. It was a bit o' fabric from Marisa's christenin' dress. See how I entwined the fabrics into a circle pattern. I'm plannin' on puttin' it in her hope chest for when the young'in gets herself married. The circles form weddin' rings locked together to remind her love is forever bound together." Mrs. McLaughlin had stitched each square, and a better quality couldn't be found in any boutique in London.

"You don't say." Fredrick's boisterous voice penetrated the thin glass panes of the window behind Katherine's head.

"Ran off with Mr. O'Malley's plow 'orse, they did. Unlocked my gate, too." Mr. McLaughlin's shadow blocked part of the sun streaming inside. "They would have taken our cart 'orse, but Marisa 'eard them and started wailin'. I think her cryin' scared them plum away. But that was..." He rubbed his jaw. "Probably six months ago, if not longer."

"If you hear or see anything, let me know." Stephen's husky voice vibrated Katherine's nerve endings, sending tingles to her toes. "Alert me even if a stranger passes through. We'll keep watch for one another."

"I'll 'ave you know when I was millin' some wheat in lower slaughter. A spruce of a fellow, seemed to me like a close shaver —and a trite mean-spirited—was at the mill tavern inquirin' about a woman who fits the description of yer guest." He jerked his thumb in the direction of the window. "Claimed she had curly 'air, green eyes, and a 'eart-shaped face."

Katherine choked on the claret and set the cup down.

Mrs. McLaughlin peered up from the quilt. "A bit strong fer ya?"

"It's delicious." She cleared her throat. "I merely swallowed wrong."

The women returned to their chatter, and Katherine mentally berated herself for having missed what else the men had to say. Mr. McLaughlin lowered his voice, and Katherine held her breath, straining to hear. "He said 'er wits might be addled, thinking 'er guardian meant 'er harm. Said there was a reward for 'er return."

"The description fits every lass of Scottish origins." Stephen chuckled, but it sounded forced. "He's not going to have a pocket to let if he pays out for information on every curly-haired woman. It's merely coincidence."

The men strolled toward the barn, and their shadows passed the window.

"Marisa, I'll take the babe." Mrs. McLaughlin extended her arms to the kicking baby. "Take a pitcher and glasses out to yer Papa and Lord Hartin'ton."

The baby cooed and grabbed at the kerchief that held her mother's hair back. Mrs. McLaughlin adeptly switched the baby to her other side.

"She's a handful, this one." Mrs. McLaughlin pulled the baby's hand down. "My first two were content to sleep or sit and watch from their swing, but this 'un is into everythin'. Once she gets 'er mind on somethin', there's no stoppin' her." She swiped the baby's nose with her index finger. "Isn't that right, lit'l 'un?"

Her soft, high voice drew a smile from Katherine.

A pot of water over the fire boiled over. "I can't be burnin' the noontime meal."

"Let me hold her." Katherine stood and took the baby, who looked up at her with big blue eyes, pumping her chubby little body in excitement. Katherine held out a finger, and the baby wrapped her pudgy hand around it and tried to draw it into her mouth. Katherine laughed at the sweet little bundle.

Mrs. Laughlin used her skirt to protect her fingers from the hot handle and drew the boiling pot away from the flames. After she had it settled, she moved to the window and edged the curtain farther aside. "Looky there, the men are headed back.

A moment later, the men crossed the threshold, Stephen's presence filling the room. His gaze scanned the faces, but he froze when he got to Katherine holding the babe. Warmth flashed in his eyes, slowly unfurling something in Katherine's stomach the way daylight opens morning glory petals.

Julia regarded the exchange with narrowed eyes and patted the sofa. "Join me?"

Marisa unhooked two kitchen chairs from the wall for the men to sit, and Mrs. McLaughlin refilled glasses with claret.

When Stephen didn't cross to Julia's side, Fredrick accepted the invitation, wedging his broad shoulders between her and Abby, while Stephen and Mr. McLaughlin took the wooden chairs.

Mr. McLaughlin was telling a story, and Stephen seemed to be attending to it, but several times his gaze strayed toward Katherine and the child she rocked. Was he wondering if she was the addled woman Mr. McLaughlin had heard about? Did he really think it common for women to have curly hair, green eyes, and a heart-shaped face, or was he covering for her? Would he seek out whoever was offering the reward, most likely her cousin, to learn who Kate Vernon truly was?

Her safe haven was crumbling. She needed legal counsel. She needed to make arrangements to get to Claire before their cousin got to her or Claire first.

The little one rubbed her face on Katherine's shoulder. Her eyelids became heavy, and her blinks longer in duration until she snuggled at Katherine's chest and fell asleep.

Mrs. McLaughlin pointed to a small crib in the corner. "Lay the child down or your arms will start to ache somethin' fierce."

Katherine did and tucked the blanket around her.

"A green-eyed woman?" Julia responded to something Fredrick said.

Katherine's hand stilled mid-tuck.

Julia's eyes narrowed on her. "With curly hair, he said?"

CHAPTER 19

Stephen bid the McLaughlins farewell, and their group remounted for the ride back to Willowstone Manor. Dominion followed the lichen-covered stone wall that marked the border of their land.

Behind him, Julia prattled on about how the city offers much more entertainment than the country. Fredrick added in his opinions, and Abby and Kate lagged behind, having their own conversation.

Seeing Kate cradling the sleeping child had halted Stephen's breathing. In that moment, their future stunned him with its clarity—the children God would give them to love and cherish, the life He would give them as they grew old together. How could God's Spirit tell him one thing when all streams of logic pointed in a different direction?

Kate had appeared after word had gotten out that prime blood horses were to arrive at the farm. She couldn't—or wouldn't—tell him who she was or anything about her past. Her footsteps had appeared near the stables the night that horse thieves were spotted in the area, and a man outside a horse market was looking for a woman who fit Kate's description.

Had she been roped into the horse-thieving ring and wanted out? Was she hiding at his estate to avoid the blackguards?

Could Stephen marry her—and heap that trouble upon his family?

He twisted in his saddle to face Julia. God forgive him, he didn't know what to do. "How do you feel about children?"

"Children?" Julia grimaced.

He examined her with the same intensity he'd often shown Katherine. Did Julia want the future he hoped to give his bride —life in the country, little ones filling his house with laughter? Did she want to be a mother like his had been—available, involved?

Julia blinked a couple of times. "Children are necessary to continue the family name, but of course, a nursemaid or nanny would tend to them."

Stephen faced forward again, and for a moment, the only sound was the clip-clop of the horses' hooves in the soft dirt.

Julia cleared her throat and rode up beside him. "I adore children." Enthusiasm poured out of her high-pitched tone. "Being from a large family, I want to have at least a half dozen."

He could picture a holiday meal with a table lined from oldest to youngest. He liked the image. "I've always envisioned teaching my boys how to ride and play catch and my wife cuddling with the babies and teaching the girls embroidery once they're old enough."

"Indeed." Her single word came out through tight lips raised in what he thought was supposed to be a smile.

He wanted to believe her words. Doing so would make it easier to lean his heart in her direction, but Kate had taken so naturally to the McLaughlin baby while Julia hadn't shown any interest. Maybe he wasn't giving Julia enough of a chance. One interaction wasn't enough to base a decision on.

Thanks, governor. The memory of the boy with the missing front teeth flashed through his mind. Julia had inspected her dress and rounded on the little boy. *Watch what you're doing.*

He remembered other interactions he'd witnessed between Julia and children.

"I've grown up taking care of my sister's children." Julia adjusted her horse to match Dominion's gait. "So it is second nature to me."

Fredrick nudged his horse in between them. "My sister has an entire brood of little ones. I bet an hour with her could train anyone. She's got them all marching like little soldiers." He mock saluted Julia. "Her youngest, though, gives her a time of it. The little fella's into everything. One day, he climbed out his window and onto the roof to see if he could fit down the chimney."

Stephen's grip tightened on the reins. "Did he make it?"

"Sure enough." Fredrick let out a hoot of laughter. "Slid down right quick and brought all the soot and ash along with him. My sister said it looked like a black storm cloud settled over her drawing room."

Julia gasped. "He ruined the furniture."

"Sure did, and they'd just had it imported from Paris too."

Julia's nostrils flared.

Stephen asked, "Was he hurt?"

"Walked away without a scratch." A crooked smile twisted the small scar on Fredrick's upper lip. "The boy bounces like a ball. My sister says, 'It's a good thing he's adorable.'"

Stephen thought he saw Julia grimace, but when he looked at her fully, she smiled. He slowed his horse and peered over his shoulder to ensure the rest of their party was keeping up. Abby and Kate had fallen several horse lengths behind. "Are you two coming?"

Abby waved for him to go ahead.

"Your sister will take care of Miss Vernon." Julia's voice purred like a gentle breeze. "However, I can understand your concern. Miss Vernon might lose herself and never find her way back. Isn't that how she ended up here in the first place?" She shook her head but then perked up in the saddle. "I'm excited about the upcoming masquerade. Aren't you?"

"Quite." At least he was happy it was one party Abby was willing to attend since Nicholas's death.

"The Rutherford masquerade?" Fredrick perked up. "Did you know old Lord Rutherford himself used to box?" Fredrick rambled on about boxing, and Julia interjected to speak about the ball.

Their prattle became background noise. As much as Stephen desired to settle down and start a family, he needed to remain focused and vigilant. The horse thieves had yet to strike, and the bait had been set. But where did Kate Vernon fit in the picture? Who was she? Culprit or victim?

He quashed the desire to beat his chest and pound her out of the walls of his heart. He couldn't afford a foolish love match. The new horses should bring in a pretty penny, but there were boards to be replaced in the horses' stalls. There were other expenses too. A cracked window in the east wing hall needed a new pane, and the roof over the kitchen should be re-shingled. The time had come to replace some old furniture, especially the worn sofa in the salon. Expenses added up. His contracted work for the Home Office would only pay if he brought down the horse-thieving ring. With the wool market being down, the rents collected from their tenants wouldn't be enough income to sustain his family in the lifestyle they knew. They'd be forced to sell heirlooms to make repairs.

He didn't care what polite society would say if it were just him without pockets to let. However, he did care when it came to his family and future children. He wanted to provide the best opportunities for his sons and daughters. Julia's dowry would be an excellent asset, but could he manage with her selfish tendencies?

Stephen valued logic. Reason had allowed him to deduce that Daphne was a French spy, and the Home Office sought him out because of his cognitive skills. Logic had helped him crack and resolve numerous assignments. He shouldn't allow desire to overlook reason now. Kate was a risky choice. On the other hand, Julia had social standing, prominence, funds, a known past, a solid reputation, and most importantly, she wasn't a thief.

This decision should be easy.

Perhaps paying a visit to the man looking for a curly-haired, green-eyed woman that Mr. McLaughlin mentioned could settle his mind.

---

*T*hat night, Katherine stirred in her sleep, tormented by dreams of Julia warning Stephen that Kate was just like his aunt—*her secrets will kill you*—and the sound of horses neighing and struggling to stay afloat while the carriage and strong current attempted to drag them under.

After finally drifting off to sleep, she awoke with her heart thundering against her ribs and surveyed the walls of her bedchamber in the Hartington household. Something was wrong. The fine hairs on the back of her neck rose, and a chill swept over her.

The moment reminded her of when Stephen had crept through her window. She pulled the covers tighter around her.

A horse neighed. *Dominion.*

She threw off the covers, donned her dressing robe, and knotted the sash as she strode to the window. Pushing aside the curtains, she squinted at the stables.

Another neigh sounded, higher pitched and longer than before, similar to that of Sugar when she was in labor. Dominion wouldn't be in labor, but he could be in pain or frightened. Where were the grooms? She opened the window and leaned out into the moonlit night, listening.

A flicker of light that could have been a firefly caught her attention near the stable's entrance. A shadow passed, and the light stayed constant. A lamp. She focused on the glow. Was it a groom? She couldn't make out the features, but he held a length of coiled rope.

She jerked away from the window. The overheard conversation between the head groom and Stephen screamed in her mind, *I heard of raids happenin' just north of here. We'll find out soon enough if Miss Vernon is one of them.*

Her breath caught.

Horse thieves.

She must warn Stephen.

Dashing down the hall to the west wing, she ran to the room she'd occasionally witnessed Stephen exit and rapped on the door. "Stephen." Her voice was a loud whisper. She tapped again. Lord help her if someone woke and witnessed her in her half-state of dress in the middle of the night knocking on a man's bedchamber door. "Wake up. There are noises from the stables."

The door yanked open, and Stephen with mussed hair and sleepy eyes, stuffed his arms into his shirt sleeves. "Kate? What's amiss?"

Katherine looked away. "The horses are upset, and I saw a man with a rope near the stables." Her reputation might suffer, but she understood the weight of responsibility he had for his horses, the same as she'd had at Steepleton.

He ducked into his room and returned a moment later, loading a shotgun. He tapped on the door to his dressing room, and a sleepy valet emerged. "Yes, milord?"

"Get your weapon and meet me out back. Be quick and quiet about it."

The valet straightened and disappeared into the dark room.

Stephen grabbed Katherine's hand and led her downstairs to the doors leading to the terrace. He pushed her behind a curtain and peeked outside. "Tell me what you saw."

"Only one man near the entrance of the stables, but there may be more. He was carrying a lantern and a coiled rope." She leaned closer for a better look and felt the tension rolling off Stephen's tightly wound muscles. "He's still there. By the pen enclosure."

"I see him. He has Duchess and Amethyst."

Stephen's valet crept up behind them, and Katherine startled.

"Henderson," Stephen said, "you and I will sneak around the side. I need to know how many we're dealing with."

"What happened to Mr. Warren?" The valet loaded his revolver as if he'd done so a hundred times.

"Not certain." Stephen quietly opened the door, and the cool night air rushed over the wooden floorboards. His whisper softened. "He could be tied up—or dead."

Katherine's hand flew to her mouth.

Stephen pulled her face into his chest. His lips touched her ear as he whispered, "Go upstairs, and if anyone wakes, keep them calm and quiet."

She nodded, and his grip on her loosened. She lightly touched the stubble on his jaw, her lips achingly close to his. "Be careful."

He nodded. She wasn't certain whether it was for her or a signal to his valet, but both men crouched as they snuck out the door and into the night air.

*S*tephen waved for Henderson to stay put under the stable window as he peeked through the other. In the dim light of the thieves' lantern, he could make out two men wrestling to get Dominion under control and another struggling not to get kicked by the new mare. A dark shape lay slumped at the end of the isle. Cross ties that held the horses for grooming had been used to bind him.

Was his friend hurt or worse? And where were the other two young grooms?

"Forget that 'un. 'elp me wit this beastie." The burlier of the thieves waved the other over.

Stephen crawled to his valet. "It looks like there's three of them. Two inside and one keeping guard out front." He pointed to a rain barrel. "Stay here, and if anyone suspicious exits the back door, shoot him."

"Yes, milord." A gulp sounded as Henderson swallowed.

In a half-crouched run to stay low beneath the windows, Stephen darted along the backside of the stables and crawled under the fence. He slowly lifted the latch to the side door and slid it open just wide enough for him to squeeze through. Hay tickled his nose as he crept toward Jacob on his hands and knees. His friend was bound and gagged, but his gaze held Stephen's.

Stephen set his shotgun down and pressed a finger to his lips. He tapped his chest to indicate himself and held up a finger, pointing out the door to inform Jacob he had one other outside. He removed a pocket knife and sawed through the ropes binding his friend.

Jacob yanked the gag from his mouth and held up three fingers, confirming the number of men Stephen had witnessed.

Stephen picked up his weapon, and Jacob reached into the back of his breeches, where he stowed a small revolver. Signaling toward the front entrance, Stephen directed Jacob to detain the man outside. Stephen would apprehend the two trying to steal his favored horse.

Jacob crouched low and rounded the edge of the stalls, stealthily moving toward the open stable doors.

Dominion, who must have caught a whiff of his master, calmed, and the burly thief tugged on his bit to pull him down the aisle. "Come on. Bring that other one." The thief pointed to the new mare.

Stephen rose from behind a hay bale and cocked his shotgun, pointing its end at the thief's back. "Don't move."

The thief froze, but Dominion reared, his front hoof knocking the man unconscious. The other thief used the distraction to run for the exit.

"Stop!" Stephen warned him.

A shot rang out into the night.

---

*K*atherine jolted away from the upstairs hall window at the sound of the weapon discharging. Julia's screamed and ran out of her chamber followed by her mother. Katherine shushed them with an index finger to her lips. "Stay quiet." *Lord, protect Stephen. Please, don't let him be hurt.*

Abby and Lady Felton ran into the corridor. Lord Felton hobbled behind them carrying his rifle.

"We heard a gunshot. Is everyone all right?" Lady Felton glanced around but Abby spoke the question in her mother's eyes. "Where's Stephen?"

"He's checking on the horses." Should she tell them about the men? "He told us to stay here and stay quiet."

Lord Felton cut through the women to see out the window. "A gunshot means trouble." He pushed back through and grabbed the railing to take the stairs.

Lady Felton grabbed Abby's arm and knelt on the floor bowing her head in prayer. Abby did likewise.

Mrs. Napier wobbled on her feet and pitched into a swoon.

Katherine jumped to catch Julia's mother, softening the blow before she hit the floor.

Lord Felton set down the gun and aided Katherine in getting Mrs. Napier to the narrow settee under the hall mirror. Mrs. Napier roused enough to not be dead weight.

Julia started to wail.

Katherine gripped Julia's shoulders. "Quiet down, or you'll get them and us killed." She grabbed a pillow off the settee and passed it to Julia to quiet her crying.

What if Stephen was hurt?

"Don't leave." Mrs. Napier clung to Lord Felton. "What if they come into the house? Who will defend us."

Julia's sobs grated on Katherine's nerves. She needed to do something instead of standing there helpless. "I'm going to peek and see what's happening." She darted down the stairs before anyone could stop her and stood at the same door Stephen had used to observe the stables. In everyone's haste, it had remained open, and the curtains billowed in the night breeze.

"Halt!" Stephen's voice bellowed.

A man sprinted for the safety of the garden. He was too slim of build to be Stephen and too tall to be any of the stable hands. He peeked over his shoulder and changed direction, skirting along the edge of the house. The thief would run right past her.

And then, he would get away.

She could stop him.

Katherine grabbed the wrought iron poker from the hearth and crept out the door. She stood behind one of the terrace's stone pillars. The pounding footfalls grew louder, along with the man's wheezing breaths.

"Stop him before he reaches the house," Stephen yelled to another man giving chase.

The thief glanced over his shoulder.

Katherine stepped out of hiding and swung the iron stick, crashing it into the man's chest. His feet flew out from under him, and he landed in the yard with a thud. His gun slid along the ground.

She raised the poker above her head to strike again, but the man held up his hands to protect his face from another blow.

Pounding footsteps drew up short. "Don't move." Stephen pointed his gun at the thief and stepped on the man's weapon.

The head groom yanked the thin man to his feet, slammed him into the stone pillar, and pinned his arms behind his back. "Henderson has the other two."

Stephen kept his gun on the thief but peered at Katherine. "You all right?"

She nodded.

"Thank you." He exhaled a deep breath. "But please don't do that again. When I saw you..." His voice hoarsened with emotion, and he cleared his throat. "My heart can't take it."

"I heard a gunshot."

"Henderson fired on the man but missed. Get inside and lock the door." He inclined his chin that direction. "We need a moment to tie these men up, and then I'll come tell everybody what happened."

She picked up the poker and turned to close the door.

"I assumed wrong." The head groom addressed Stephen. "She's obviously not a horse thief."

Katherine paused before the door clicked shut, relieved to no longer be associated with bandits.

The head groom shoved the thief in the direction of the barn, but she caught his next remark. "At least, not with this band of thieves."

CHAPTER 20

A weary Katherine stood in front of the hearth of the blue salon, bandaging the wound on the head groom's forehead while Lord Felton spoke to his son in the hall, and Abby and Lady Felton attempted to calm Mrs. Napier and Julia with cups of warm milk in the kitchen. "You took a good wallop."

"Knocked me out cold, they did. Next thing, I knew I was bound like a 'orse wit the cross ties." The man slipped back into his thick hackneyed cant, which had oddly disappeared when he'd been apprehending the thieves.

Thank God Stephen had had the wherewithal to apprehend a band of thieves. Had the Hartingtons had issues with horse thieves in the past? Is that why they were so suspicious of her after discovering she'd visited the stable the other night?

Feeling eyes watching her, she turned and found Stephen leaning against the fireplace mantel admiring her. Katherine's fingers froze in tying off the knot to hold the bandage in place.

A maid curtsied in the doorway behind Stephen. "Follow me, Mr. Warren. We have a warm meal and a cold drink waiting in the breakfast room."

"Pardon me." The groom's eyes traveled down the length of the young maid. "It's never good ta keep a lady waitin'."

Stephen nodded to him as he left and set his sights on Katherine. "You were a blessing tonight." Dirt smudged his cheek, and bits of hay protruded from his hair, but his eyes danced in the firelight.

The smoldering intensity in his eyes warmed her hotter than the fireplace, rendering her speechless. She swept her unruly curls over one shoulder but remained trapped under his gaze.

He stepped toward her. "Most women would have run from danger, especially when they weren't in their own home. You put your life at risk for my family. Thank you."

"I owe your family my life." Her voice emitted in a raspy whisper. "It's the least I could do." She cleared her throat. "Besides, everyone has done nothing but treat me like part of the family since I arrived, so in some ways, it feels like my home."

Stephen's face softened, and his lips hinted at the beginning of a smile. His eyes deepened to a darker hue, as dark as the smoke that billowed from the fire.

"It has been quite an evening." He stepped closer to the fire next to her. "You were very brave."

"My knees shook the whole time." She tried to smile but had no idea if she managed it. "But at least my aim has improved since I first wielded a candlestick."

He chuckled. "I can attest to you packing a good wallop." He rubbed his forearm where he'd deflected the blow. "And now, so can the thief."

She laughed, and it faded into a contented silence.

Katherine stood beside Stephen as they stared at the flames. Her lighthearted mood turned serious. "You and Henderson, stealing out into the night to face the attacker, now *that* was courageous."

"I do my best to protect what God has entrusted to me."

Weariness swept over her, and she swayed. Warmth from the fire and the faded rush of danger left her depleted. She suppressed the longing to lean into his strength and feel the security of his arms around her.

Lady Felton shuffled in, wrapped in a thick quilt. "Your father has already gone to bed, and I think I shall retire too. These old bones can't handle this much commotion in one night." She kissed Katherine cheek, then Stephen's, addressing him. "You may need to go and check on Miss Julia." She inclined her head toward the back hall.

Even though they stood apart, Katherine sensed Stephen stiffen. He leaned back to peer out the open door.

Julia's silhouette paced in the corridor. Her mama sat on a low-back chair, fanning herself, still recovering from her faint.

Fatigue weighed his eyelids, but he inhaled a deep breath. "Of course." He bowed. "Good-night, Mother. Good-night, Miss Vernon. Thank you again for your assistance. I pray you sleep well." He strode to tend to the frazzled women.

"May I aid you up the stairs?" Katherine raised her elbow toward Lady Felton.

"As tired as we are, we can lean on each other." Lady Felton laughed and curled her fingers around Katherine's arm.

They slipped past the front door, and Katherine overheard Julia's sobs as they mounted the stairs.

"Y-you left me. I was all alone and fr-frightened. I needed you."

Stephen shushed her. "I'm here now. I'm with you."

Was he being a gentleman, or was there something more to the tenderness in his reassurances? That evening, Katherine's emotions had traversed more ups and downs than the rolling hillsides of Cotswold.

As they reached the top of the stairs, Lady Felton patted Katherine on the arm, "Good-night, dear, get some rest."

Katherine smiled at the older woman, who appeared to have aged overnight. Her heart twisted. "Will you be able to slumber after all this excitement?"

Lady Felton released a sigh. "God will provide His peace. He always has. We will count ourselves blessed, for God spared everyone's lives, even the horses'."

He had, but how could Lady Felton have such reassurance? "How do you know when to trust God, especially when something horrific could happen?" Katherine held her breath, eager to hear the woman's answer.

"It starts with a small step of faith. Like a new foal on wobbly legs, we may fall, but God stands beside us, nudging us back up and letting us lean on Him as our faith grows." Her expression softened, and she gave Katherine's hand a gentle squeeze. "Trust the Lord with your heart and lean not on your own understanding. I've often found God will use these opportunities to open our eyes." Her gaze flickered toward the stairs. "Good-night, my dear." Lady Felton slipped into her room and closed the door behind her.

Katherine wandered to her chamber and climbed onto bed, but sleep was slow in coming. She stared out the window into the night. Had Lady Felton insinuated that God was opening Stephen's eyes, or hers?

The next day, the household moved slowly due to the lack of sleep. Purple smudges shadowed everyone's eyes. Very few words were spoken, as if everyone were conserving energy to survive the day.

Stephen accompanied the groomsmen to deliver the thieves to the proper authorities and promised to be back before the Rutherford masquerade the following day.

The next morning sunlight streamed in the windows like nourishment for the soul, and Katherine readied for a ride into town, donning the widest brimmed bonnet possible to hide her face. Although apologetic, Abby refused to ride out in public while still sporting a black eye. Good to his word, Fredrick arrived to escort Julia for their shopping trip, and Katherine asked to join them, bent on posting another letter to Claire and hoping to find one from her.

Julia relaxed during the excursion, likely due to the attention Fredrick lavished on her, or perhaps because Katherine had tagged along, leaving the only remaining female companionship for Stephen his mother, sister, and Julia's mother. Once in town, Fredrick offered Julia his arm, and the handsome couple strolled the cobblestone streets, relegating Katherine to walk behind like a paid chaperone. Julia playfully swatted Fredrick on the shoulder in response to something he'd said, and he threw back his head in boisterous laughter. The pair rambled on about fashion and their exploits in London, leaving Katherine alone to forge her plan.

As Fredrick held open the door to the hat shop, Katherine pointed to the postmaster's office. "I told Lady Hartington I would check to see if any letters were being held for her. I will join you shortly."

Katherine strolled into the postmaster's office. A bell chimed, and the same elderly man with the wire-rimmed glasses poked his head up from sorting letters. "Welcome, miss. A pleasure to see you again. Do you have another letter to post?"

She removed the letter to Claire she'd stuffed into the pocket of her walking dress and handed it over. "I was also wondering if any mail had arrived for Miss Sweetgoer?"

He shuffled behind a curtain, returning with two letters. "Indeed, I do."

She recognized her sister's handwriting. *Thank God.* Claire had received her letter. Was she safe? Had Cousin Horace attempted to find her? The second letter was addressed with a feminine script—most likely from the headmistress. No letter from her attorneys? Was the courier service to London running slow or had her first letter not made it to its intended address?

The postmaster opened a book toward her and dipped the pen in the ink well. "Sign for them in the book."

She snatched up the pen and scribbled Katherine Jenkins before thinking better of it.

Heavens.

Her hand froze. She was supposed to be Miss Sweetgoer. She tapped the quill to cause an ink blot over the letters and signed Mary Frances Sweetgoer next to it. Hopefully no one will take notice.

The postmaster flipped the book, read the name, and handed her the letters.

She thanked him and slid her thumbnail under the wax seal and unfolded Madame Lamoureux's missive first.

The Honorable Katherine Jenkins, Countess of Dysart,

Dear Countess,

I pray for your continued health and safety. Please do not fret over your sister, Miss Claire's safety. I assure you she is in good hands. The Sherbourne School is a fortress meant to protect its young ladies and their virtue and has done so for much of the nobility and even several princesses. We shall add additional staff and extra precautions to ensure her well-being and keep her where-abouts secret.

May God watch over you and protect you.

Headmistress Lamoureux

*K*atherine exhaled a shaky sigh and the tension she'd been carrying in her shoulders relaxed. She opened the letter from Claire.

Dearest Katherine,

I have so many questions I don't know where to begin. Why did you leave Steepleton? Has Cousin Horace's temperament improved? It must have if you left him in charge of our home. How long shall he be staying at Steepleton Manor and how are you faring with him being present? Is that the true reason for your departure? Is his company so miserable you needed to take the air in another town?

Either way, I'm grateful for you to have the opportunity to travel even if it is to handle issues. You've taken on so many burdens and handled them on your own, but please know that I am here for you. You have put me first all your life and I'm so grateful. It has been hard on us both being away from each other, but I'm now of an age where I, too, can be of assistance. When I return home, I'd like to share in some of the responsibilities, if you'd let me. You shouldn't need to go it alone any longer.

Please write again soon. I impatiently await your next letter for I miss you so.

Your Beloved,
Claire

*K*atherine blinked back tears as she refolded the letter. How she missed her sister. Thank God, Claire was safe, but for how long? What rights did Cousin Horace have if he was indeed their guardian? Could he withdraw her from the school? Their future rested in the hands of attorneys, Papa's will, and British law.

It's in God's hands.

The thought echoed in her mind so clearly that it had sounded spoken, but the postmaster sat at his desk cataloging letters with his head down. He hadn't said anything. In God's hands. That was a phrase Lady Felton would have used.

The postmaster looked up. "Anything else I can help you with today, Miss Sweetgoer?"

Katherine shook her head. "That will be all." She exited the building into the bright sunshine and pulled her bonnet tighter about her face. How long could she continue to impose on the Hartington's generosity? Should she give another day or two to hear back from her solicitors or start devising a plan to pay Whitmer and Collins Attorneys at Law a visit?

"Countess of Dysart drowns in tragic carriage accident."

She froze at the mention of her name and spun to face the young newspaper lad on the corner holding up a scandal sheet. She pulled out a shilling from her reticule and pressed it into the boy's palm, taking the newspaper.

She moved out of the way of foot traffic and scanned the article declaring her death and questioning if her family was cursed, since her parents had also died when their coach flipped. *Lady Katherine Jenkins is survived by her sister Claire Addison Jenkins, the new countess, and her guardian Horace Bainbridge. 'It is a shame for such a beautiful light to be snuffed out,' stated Bainbridge. 'It does seem like a calamitous cloud hangs over the Jenkins family.'*

A gasp clogged Katherine's throat at his ominous—seemingly innocuous—words, as if more disaster was still to come. She read his remarks as a threat that he would go after Claire next.

She returned the sheet to the newspaper boy to resell and

hurried back into the postmaster's office. Madame Lamoureux must know about this turn of events. The newspaper article sounded as if Cousin Horace had turned his sights on Claire. He'd claim Katherine's death and the need for Claire to take on the countess's role—including become his wife.

———————

*S*tephen leaned his head against the leather cushion of the highbacked office chair in his lodgings in Mayfair. He and Jacob had turned the horse thieves over to the Home Office to be prosecuted and handed their sentence.

Stephen laced his fingers behind his head and grinned at the ceiling.

Kate wasn't a horse thief.

Her actions had exonerated her and called into question other presumptions he'd made about her. Perhaps she did have amnesia. What if she had thought she'd seen someone she knew, and the postmaster had merely forgotten another customer posted the letter to a finishing school? Either way, Stephen was going to propose to Kate Vernon.

Julia would be upset by the news but eventually she'd realize that they envisioned different futures and wouldn't have made a good match. With her classic beauty, she'd have no problem finding a better-suited chap.

He rang for Wilson, and the door swung open seconds later.

"Good morning, milord." His butler stood at attention. "You look chipper. I take it business is going well?"

"Indeed." He scooted up in his chair. "Have the adjoining bedroom to the master freshened up and readied."

"Are we expecting a guest? Shall I inform Mrs. Bevel to order more goods and have the chef prepare meals for two or three?"

"Not yet." He held up his palm. "I may be getting ahead of myself, but if things go as planned, I'll be bringing a Lady Hartington here to be mistress of the house when we're in the city."

His butler failed in schooling his features. A hint of a smile curved his lips, and a glint lit his eyes. "I shall have the room readied immediately. The lady will be lucky to marry a man such as yourself, milord." He bowed and ducked out of the room.

Stephen pictured Kate's rosy glow as she warmed herself by the fire. Her actions had impressed him. She'd thought to wake him upon hearing the horses' distress. His parents spoke highly of her strength when she'd kept his family and Mrs. and Miss Napier calm. She'd bravely stepped into the thief's path to stop him from escaping, and when, as she'd stood by the hearth that night, she stated how she considered his family her own, she'd fused his heart to hers. His chest swelled. He couldn't wait to make her his.

But how did one marry someone with amnesia?

Could their marriage be official if she was using a made-up name?

He would have his attorney look into it, or perhaps Jacob would know. He'd investigated aliases, adoptions, and pseudonyms for the Home Office. He'd been the one to investigate the libertine who had multiple marriages and families in different countries. Jacob had had a time of it, determining which name the rogue should have been prosecuted under and which family received penance under British law.

He and Jacob would make a stop in the town of Lower Slaughter and interrogate the man Mr. McLaughlin described as a mean-spirited close shaver searching for a green-eyed woman with curly hair. The close shaver may have some useful information for them—hopefully Kate's real name and which of her side of the family should be invited to their wedding.

The bell rang, and Wilson knocked on the study door to announce the arrival of Mr. Jacob Warren.

"Send him in." Just the man he was hoping to see.

Jacob flopped into a chair, his clothes so wrinkled it appeared he'd slept in them. His cravat hung loosely around his neck, and his bottom lip was swollen and scabbed over.

"You look like the devil."

"I feel like I've been to his lair." Jacob rubbed his temples. "I was put on a new assignment."

"I take it the task didn't go well."

Jacob snorted. "A husband misunderstood my good intentions."

"And it ended in fisticuffs?"

"It ended in me jumping out a second-floor window, my jacket snagging on a nail, and me landing face first in the dirt."

"Ouch." Stephen managed to suppress his chuckle.

"That's not why I'm here." Jacob combed the top of his mussed hair into place with his fingers. "Agent Scar pulled me off that assignment and has us back on the case."

"But we caught the thieves."

"Common thieves. He doesn't believe they're associated with an underground ring. It seems the rogue agent briefly resurfaced. Something about a delay due to missing paperwork and a woman, but the mission is still in play."

"Blast." Stephen rubbed his bottom lip. He'd hoped to be done with his assignment and his dealings with the Home Office. This would delay his proposal to Kate.

His breath caught. Did that mean Kate could still be involved? Certainly not. He was done with that line of thinking. From now on, he would trust her.

"Do you mind?" Jacob gestured to the decanter on the shelf.

"Help yourself."

Jacob poured himself a drink, swirling the amber liquid in

LORRI DUDLEY

the crystal glass. "We're supposed to keep a sharp eye out specifically for sellers of Lipizzaner." He slammed back a large gulp. "We don't have specifics but, Scar's best estimate is that the exchange for the thoroughbreds will go down within the next week, so we must be ready."

CHAPTER 21

The following evening, as the clock chimed eight, Stephen found himself back at Willowstone Farm stuffed into a chair, discussing sporting events once again with Fredrick. Fredrick's jabber flowed past Stephen's ears with only the occasional word sticking to keep him abreast of the discussion. He tapped his demi mask on the arm of the chair and shifted in his seat. He was no longer interested in costumes, mysteries, or deceit. He was fed up with the lot of it. He'd hold to his word to escort Julia to the event and be done with it. A deep whoosh of air rushed past his lips. He rubbed his index finger across his forehead and nodded at something Fredrick said about a bad call.

Stephen glanced at the empty staircase and toward the clock, now showing quarter till nine. The trip to Lower Slaughter had been unsuccessful. The close shaver had left town, but he'd instructed the local tavern owner to take down information of the green-eyed girl's whereabouts. When the close shaver returned in a week, he'd pay the reward if the information led him to her. Stephen wasn't foolish enough to hand over his name and location and offered a throwaway address that couldn't be traced back to him, Kate, or his family.

Stephen tapped his foot on the polished marble floor, ready to get this night underway. The dead end regarding the close shaver left him restless. Something needed to come together with either the case or the truth about Kate. The puzzle pieces needed to start to fit. He rose to a stand, his patience threatening to snap when his mother and Mrs. Napier hurried down the stairs.

"Be ready." A wide grin donned his mother's lips.

Mrs. Napier clasped her hands at her bosom. "They're coming."

The older women stopped on either side of Stephen and turned to face the stairs.

Mother patted his arm and, leaning closer, whispered, "The wait will be worth it. Trust me."

He shot her a sideways glance meant to say, *Nothing could make up for the last forty-five minutes.*

She nodded toward the stairs, and Stephen beheld Julia dressed as a Grecian goddess. Her golden curls were half piled on top of her head, the rest left to cascade down her shoulders and back. She looked stunning in a gown of white zephyr, which clung to her figure and emphasized her hourglass shape. She descended the steps with the grace and confidence of one who was high-born.

Julia's mother clapped her hands and purred over her daughter's appearance.

Stephen glanced at Fredrick, who stood transfixed. His eyes looked like they might bulge out of their sockets, and if the man's mouth had been open, he would have been drooling.

Stephen forced a smile to show his appreciation, trying to strum up the emotion he'd always witnessed when his parents looked at each other. Shouldn't he be having a reaction similar to Fredrick's? Although Stephen admired Julia's beauty, his blood didn't stir, nor did his heart pound for the woman he had debated spending the rest of his life with. At best, he felt detached or slightly amused.

Julia's sultry eyes locked on Stephen, and she tucked her hand possessively into the crook of his arm.

Abby descended next, looking lovely as Juliet. Her high-waisted gown of wine-colored superfine richly enhanced her coloring. Her eyes sparkled, and she appeared happier than Stephen had seen her in a long time. His mother was right. The joy on his sister's face had been worth the wait. He gave his sister a grin. "You clean up nice."

Abby snorted and shook her head at his teasing, but a mischievous glint sparked in her eyes before she turned at the bottom of the stairs and peered up.

Stephen followed her line of vision to see Kate, hands clasped in front of her, shyly standing on the landing. His breath left his body as if he'd been punched in the gut.

It seemed he'd forgotten how to blink. All thoughts slipped from his mind.

She looked exquisite, like an orchid in bloom—natural, exotic, and alluring. She was dressed in a soft cambric fabric the color of the sky at dusk. The dress's skirt was a rich magenta pink at her waist that faded into a deep purple bodice, so dark that it was almost black. The dark top was dotted with tiny, jeweled stars, which shimmered in the light. They held no comparison to her eyes. Offset by the deep purple, their green depths conveyed an ethereal appearance. Her thick mass of hair had been pulled into a sleek French twist that hid her curls. Her skin was smooth like porcelain with a hint of pink in her cheeks. As she found everyone's attention on her, her color intensified to match the deep magenta of her dress.

She doesn't realize how beautiful she is.

Stephen's cheeks ached, and he subdued what must have been a goofy grin.

As Katherine descended the stairs, Julia stepped into his line of vision. "Can you guess who I am?" She spun in a circle stopping to pose.

"A Greek goddess?"

"Helen of Troy." She flashed him a coy look and straightened the lapel of his jacket. "But you aren't wrong. Helen was the daughter of Zeus, so she was part goddess."

Beyond Julia's shoulder, Kate joined Abby and his mother, who clucked over her like hens.

Abby caught his glance and studied him with a raised eyebrow. The older brother in him couldn't let it go and sent her a stay-out-of-it glare.

She shrugged a shoulder. "Remember when you used to dare me to walk the rail of the fence?"

"I do." What did that have to do with tonight?

"The chance of falling into the pen used to swirl my insides." She pressed a hand over her stomach. "I have that same tingling foreboding about tonight's masquerade."

His gaze skirted to Kate, and the same sensation rushed through him.

"I, too, have high hopes for the evening." Julia flashed him a seductive smile. "Let's be off, then."

Julia had been looking forward to the masquerade, and he'd uphold his promise to escort her. All he had to do was balance on the rail between the two women for one night, but heaven help him not to end up in a painful straddling of it.

***

The Italianate Palazzo of the Rutherford estate rested between the Cotswolds and London in the town of Aylesbury. The windows of the manor blazed with light as their carriages pulled up front. People in dazzling costumes crowded onto balconies and porches. Some guests meandered around the grounds. Music and laughter trickled around corners and out windows, creating an enticing atmosphere.

Katherine folded her hands as though she hadn't a care in the world, but her heart pounded. She practically pressed her face against the window to absorb the scene. This could be the only ball she ever attended for herself. Perhaps she'd be able to act as a chaperone for Claire for a couple of balls during her season if Katherine could get away from her responsibilities at Steepleton Hall. Assuming she ever got out of Horace's clutches.

Please let this night, her one chance, be magical.

"Time to put on our masks." Abby's eyes sparkled as she passed Katherine the final touch to her costume. "We wouldn't want anyone to recognize us."

Fredrick slid his loo mask down while Abby and Katherine secured each other's masks with pins.

Lord Felton tucked his into his coat pocket. "Why bother when I plan to remove the thing anyway."

Julia, Stephen, Mrs. Hartington, and Mrs. Napier all rode in the other carriage together, which had stopped in front of the Rutherford main entrance already. Stephen waited, Julia on his arm, for Fredrick's carriage to pull forward.

Julia pointed in the direction of the house and tugged on his sleeve, but Stephen stood his ground.

Fredrick exited and helped Abby alight the carriage steps with the assistance of several footmen standing by. He turned to assist Katherine.

She stared at the elegant people entering the Rutherford home. *What if I don't remember how to conduct myself? What if I can't remember the dances? What if...?*

Her palms perspired. This was a mistake. She wouldn't measure up to these people. She'd never completed attending finishing school, and her parents had passed before her coming out to society. It had been almost three years since her last dance and etiquette lesson.

A firm hand reached in and grasped hers, gently guiding her out of the coach. But instead of Fredrick's, it was Stephen's eyes that locked with hers. Her nervousness faded like the setting of the sun. Something stirred in the crystal blue depths of his eyes. Something she had not seen before—a sense of possessiveness and a hint of something she didn't recognize. The music, laughter, and house seemed to fall away until it was just the two of them.

"Have I told you that you look exquisite?" Stephen whispered in her ear.

His breath tickled her skin, and the fine hairs on her arms rose. Warmth flooded her, rushing to her cheeks, fingers, and toes.

Julia threaded her arm through Stephen's. "Are you ready to escort me to the masquerade?"

For an awkward moment, Stephen appeared uncertain about how to proceed.

"Oh dear, we appear to be short and escort." Julia signaled to Fredrick. "Mr. Wilson, will you be a dear and escort both Lady Emerson and Miss Vernon?"

Katherine issued Stephen a polite nod, and Stephen released her hand.

Fredrick gazed at Julia like a servant, eager to do whatever bidding the goddess needed, but whether he was in a love-struck trance or didn't hear Julia's request, he didn't raise his arm or move in Katherine's direction. An awkward moment passed with Katherine uncertain whether to take his arm or walk unescorted to the house. All the fears from the carriage rushed back.

Abby nudged Fredrick, who broke from his reverie.

"I'd consider myself fortunate to assist two beautiful women to the ball." Lord Felton offered one arm for Katherine to take and the other for his wife before Fredrick realized what he'd been tasked to do. "I shall be the envy of all the gents." He leaned heavily on his wife's arm. "Bear with me. These old legs can't keep up with the young bucks."

Katherine relaxed in the Hartingtons' presence. She would follow their lead, and if she made a cake of herself, no shame would be brought upon the Jenkin's name since she not only wore a mask to hide her identity, but no one knew her true identity in the first place.

Once inside, Katherine descended the stairs into the ballroom. People cluttered the floor like a swarm of colorful bees, buzzing in all directions. Dancers performing a minuet reminded Katherine of butterflies flitting from flower to flower in loops and circles, touching one petal after another but always coming back to the nectar of their choice. She'd witnessed similar displays when her parents had hosted the occasional ball at Steepleton Manor, but Katherine had been too young to attend at the time. She and Claire had snuck from their bedchamber in their nightgowns and stood peeking over the stair railing to watch the magical revelry.

Chandeliers blazed overhead, filling the room with light. Gilded mirrors hung along the walls and reflected the clusters of candles' brilliance. Heavy red velvet drapery added richness to the room and accented the open French doors leading to the terrace and gardens.

Katherine's body vibrated as she bit back a smile. She wanted to memorize the scene—lock it away to enjoy in future daydreams. People whispered and strolled toward the staircase as they realized the Hartington family had arrived. Despite his costume, the six-foot son of the earl was hard to miss. Guests hoped to increase their social status by befriending nobility and nudged their way to the front of the crowd. Overly eager mothers elbowed their daughters to stand up straight, hoping to catch the eye of the heir to an earldom.

Stephen met the converging crowd with the poise and confidence of a man who entered ballrooms with regularity. Julia latched onto his arm and raised her head like a proud swan, daring the young women in the room to compete with her beauty.

The costumes added a dreamlike quality to the ball. Strange beings approached and peered at Katherine's mask, trying to determine who could be the honored guest of Lord Hartington. If they peered deep enough, would someone recognize her? Her hair had been pulled straight into a tight and sleek coiffure. The weight of all the pins to keep her unruly curls in line, added at least a few pounds. She'd added dark feathers to her mask to cover more of her face, but there was no way to disguise the color of her eyes. She could only pray no one would look that close, especially with her cousin paying for information on a curly haired green-eyed woman.

Katherine forced her feet to stand her ground as jesters, mermaids, angels, Vikings, and even a lion, complete with a full mane, floated through her line of vision. None of them held the same statue as Cousin Horace. Did he attend these types of events? He'd become a loner since Madeline's death, but his recent behavior was unpredictable.

Abby glanced back at Katherine and waved for her to stand by her side. Katherine stepped closer. She'd come to support her friend, and if she eased dropped on the gossip to see if the word spread about the supposedly dead Countess or the happenings at Steepleton Manor, then all the better.

An aggressive Cleopatra and fairy princess nudged their way between Abby and Katherine to pay their respects to the earl's family but lingered in front of his unmarried son. A rabbit, knight, and shepherdess cut in, pushing Katherine to the fringe of the group near an eerie Grimm reaper. She shivered and backed up until she stepped on someone's foot.

She jumped. "I beg your pardon."

A man dressed head to toe in black stepped out from the shadow of the long draperies, his face covered by a long black domino instead of the more common loo-mask.

"Would you care to dance?" He didn't wait for her response but gripped her elbow and led her onto the dance floor.

"Wait." She floundered for an excuse to return to the safety of her group without causing a stir. "I haven't had an introduction nor permission to dance the waltz."

He chuckled and whisked her around the dance floor. "A masquerade is an opportunity to get away with all sorts of mischief."

Honestly, she could do with a little less of misdeeds, but the stranger's voice didn't sound familiar. To give him the cut-direct and walk away would not only prohibit her by propriety standards from dancing the remainder of the evening, but it would also create a scandal, drawing unwanted attention. She swallowed and followed his footwork. His excellent lead helped her to remember the steps. His gaze drifted to the front entrance to where Abby and Lady Felton stood and freed Katherine from conversing. She let the notes of the violin and cello meld with her body, and the strange faces faded into the background. The man in black slightly favored one leg but his sure steps reminded her of the waltz in the meadow—how the intensity of Stephen's gaze had left her breathless.

"Lord Hartington is to your right." The man in black inclined his head in Stephen's direction.

Her lips parted. How did he know? Yes, she had been stealing glances over his shoulder, hoping to locate Stephen, but she hadn't been obvious, had she?

"You're taken with him. It's written all over your face. I would wager you fancy yourself in love."

"You overstep." Katherine lowered her eyes to the buttons on his shirt front. *Fancy yourself in love*. Her feelings couldn't be trusted, especially if Stephen still believed her to be a horse thief.

She stumbled over the hem of her dress and stepped on his foot trying to recover her balance

His firm hold kept her from falling.

"Pardon. I haven't danced..."

He limped slightly with his left foot.

"Did I injure you?" She gasped. "I'm terribly sorry."

His mask covered his mouth, but a glint in his eye hinted at a smile. "You've done me no harm. I've had this limp for some time now."

Katherine, unsure how to respond, lapsed back into silence.

"I suppose you are the dawning of day?" he asked.

She blinked twice before understanding sank in. "You mean my costume. I believe I'm supposed to be twilight."

"How do you know the Hartingtons?"

Katherine opened her mouth to answer but hesitated. She hadn't thought of how to answer people's questions. "I-I'm a longtime friend of Abigail."

The man in black's eyes narrowed, and his steps slowed. "I've known Miss Hartington all her life, and I'm also a business associate of the Hartington family, but I don't recall Miss Abigail Hartington having such a lovely companion."

Katherine gulped and forced a weak smile. "You are too kind." She glanced at the orchestra. This dance set couldn't end soon enough.

"Why don't we take a turn about the room?" he said, raising his arm for her to take as the first song finished.

She tucked her hand into the crook of his elbow and resisted the urge to press her mask tighter about her face.

"Are you also from the Cotswolds?" He guided her beyond the onlooking guests to a less congested area away from the dancing. "Or did you meet Miss Hartington in finishing school?"

"Neither." Her thoughts whirled seeking a neutral answer to offer and the moment grew awkward. What could she say? What was safe? "I daresay, doesn't Abby prefer to go by Mrs. Emerson?" If he'd known her all his life, he'd know she'd been married.

"Being married for a day hardly counts as a marriage." He snorted. "Her husband left the next morning to get himself killed in battle, poor bloke. The townsfolk reverted back to what they'd been accustomed to calling her, myself included."

Kathrine licked her lips. It felt in poor taste to speak about her friend without her being present. "What kind of business dealings do you have with the Hartingtons?"

"Horses mainly. Not to bore you with business-talk, but I'm on the hunt for a pure blood, preferably a Lipizzaner for Lord Hartington to train."

Katherine perked up.

"Have you ever ridden one?"

"Yes indeed." An airy breathlessness laced her tone and she tried to tone down her excitement. "You won't find a more agile breed."

"You seem to know a lot about them."

"I grew up around..." She coughed and covered her mouth to hide her gaffe. "Pardon me." She'd revealed too much. "Oh look. There's Abby." She pointed to Juliet being led onto the dance floor by a man in a raven costume.

The man in black drew up short and since she still had hold of his arm, so did she.

"This may be poorly done of me,"—he placed his hand over hers— "but may I ask for you to put in a good word for me with Miss Hartington?"

"I thought you were friends?"

"We are..." He shifted his weight. "We were. It's merely been a while." His lips wavered in a half-smile. "I'm not certain she'd even recognize me."

For some reason, his nervousness touched her. Would there be any harm in Abby dancing with him? It might be good for her to have someone interested. Maybe it could redeem the disaster of Mr. Wilson's intentions?

She nodded.

Without another word, he ushered her to where Lady Felton stood. He bowed, excusing himself, and disappeared into the thick crowd. She stared at his retreating form. Was his interest a good thing or would she be making a mull of things for Abby or the man in black?

Another gentleman appeared at Katherine's side to request a dance, allowing her no opportunity to ponder the strange man in black. The night continued thus—one dance partner after another until she was breathless. Occasionally, she caught glimpses of Stephen, Julia, Fredrick, and Abby, passing her on the dance floor. Everyone appeared to be enjoying themselves.

Katherine asked her current partner, dressed as King Henry VIII, for a reprieve, and he led her to the refreshment table for a glass of lemonade and to catch her breath.

"I believe the next dance is mine." Stephen's warm fingers touched her elbow.

CHAPTER 22

Stephen refused to stand by and watch one more fop draw Katherine onto the dance floor. Even costumed, he recognized Lord Timsbury, a notorious rake whose greedy eyes had landed on Kate the moment she entered the ballroom, and his old friend from Eton, Simon McFarlane, who had a gambling problem. The only one he didn't recognize was the man dressed all in black, but the way he immediately pulled Kate onto the dance floor was proof enough that neither he nor any of the rest of them deserved even to lick Kate's dance slippers.

The melodious laugh that flowed from Kate stirred a possessiveness in his gut. "I don't recall you laying claim to any dances with me."

Cheeky little mite. Little did she know he'd claim all the dances if he could. "Tonight, propriety is thrown to the wind." He pulled her onto the dance floor, ignoring the affronted look of Henry VIII. The musicians struck up a waltz.

Her arms trembled, and he frowned. "Are you tired? I don't want to overexert you."

"I'm fine." Damp ringlets that had fallen loose framed her

face, and her cheeks were flushed, but her green eyes shone. "More than fine. I'm enjoying myself immensely. I merely wish..."

He swept her about the floor. If only he could shoo away the other guests and have her all to himself like in the open glen, where'd they'd previously danced the waltz in secret. She smiled in a dreamlike state, and a sigh escaped her lips.

"What do you wish?" With all his heart he wanted to grant it to her.

Kate's lips parted, but she hesitated and lowered her gaze. "I wish I could be this carefree."

He understood the weight of many responsibilities, but to what could she be referring? "You feel pressured?"

A shadow clouded her green eyes, and she looked away. "The guests here might be dressed as someone else, but they're certain their name was on the invitation. They may break the rules at a masquerade, but they understand and know what's proper. I don't know if I have an invitation, and I can't comprehend what's expected of me." She faced him. "It's as if everyone has the answers, and I'm still trying to grasp the question."

His fingers twitched with longing to pull her into his embrace. He understood what it was like not to be in the know. It had reached its peak with Daphne and her deception. It was one of the reasons he'd joined the Home Office, because he desired to have insider knowledge so he wouldn't be tricked again.

"I'm afraid to appear foolish." Her voice wavered. "I lack what others in the room radiate."

His brows furrowed. "What is that?"

"Confidence." She exhaled a sigh so deep it drew the breath from his lungs with it. Her flushed cheeks glowed with unaffected beauty, and his eyes followed the elegant curve of her neck and slender arm down to her gloved fingers. She had long, graceful hands. Funny how he hadn't noticed them before. He lifted an arm for her to turn, and when she floated back around, her gaze met his. His chest tightened to contain the wild beating of his heart.

To the devil with the spying and horse thievery. This woman held his heart. The last strains of the waltz died, but Katherine and he continued to sway to an inaudible rhythm. He couldn't will himself to let go. "Would you care for a stroll on the terrace?"

She nodded, and he led her past the guests, out the French doors, and into the cool night air. A breeze set her loose tendrils bobbing as they stopped at the railing and peered out over the torchlit gardens. The reflection of the fire danced in her eyes. "Isn't it splendid?"

"Indeed." He could sit and watch the expressions on her face all night. She, of all people, shouldn't lack confidence. "Kate."

She turned to face him, and the rest of the world fell away.

"You belong here as much, if not more, than anyone else. You have grace and poise that rivals anyone on that dance floor. You find delight in everything and help this bitter soul to see things in a new light. You believe the best of people. But above all, you have a heart for people. It's in the way you encouraged Abby to come tonight and live again. You helped Marisa to believe in herself and not be intimidated by the older kids. You listened to Mrs. McLaughlin and showed true interest in her life and hobbies. You've helped me to realize the importance of family." She was everything he wanted in a wife. "Those are rare but much needed qualities in today's society."

Her lower lip quivered until she captured it between her teeth. The cords of her slender neck tightened as she swallowed. He cupped her elbows to draw her closer.

Two young bucks in loo masks traipsed up the steps, laughing at something.

Stephen released Kate and stepped away so the men

wouldn't assume he'd been up to anything untoward and hurt her reputation. Spying Kate, one of the chaps slowed. "What do we have here?"

The other gent spotted Stephen and nudged his friend along.

The one on the right gripped the door frame and looked behind him. "Save a dance for me."

"You imbecile." His friend chuckled and shoved him inside.

"I'd be enjoying myself more"—Stephen gripped her elbow and led her inside through a different set of doors—"if I weren't so preoccupied with strangling every gawking male."

"Pardon?" Kate snorted in that adorable way of hers.

He tucked her hand into the crook of his arm and leaned his head closer for her to hear over the din of the music and guests. "I can't contain my urge to plant a facer in every man who pants after you like a lovesick puppy. Unfortunately for me, it's the whole lot of them. Every male in this dastardly place has asked me for an introduction."

Kate pinched her lips to cover her laughter. "You jest."

He arched a don't-doubt-me eyebrow.

"What about Julia?" She attempted to keep her tone to be light and flirtatious but her heart at the same time ached and braced for his answer.

"I admit. I had contemplated marrying Miss Napier, but after meeting you, I've reconsidered."

The cadence of her heartbeat sped as fast as a Viennese waltz.

His lips twisted into a playful grin. "I do believe a new day has dawned."

"I happen to be dusk, not dawn." Her shoulders shook with mirth. "And I think the costumes are playing tricks on your mind."

"I wish they were." He glared at an ogling man with such disdain that several dancing couples moved out of their path.

A Vesuvian eruption of laughter burst from Katherine's lips. "Oh, I am having a marvelous time."

The amusement sparkling in her eyes quickened Stephen's pulse.

"I believe the next dance is spoken for." A lion tapped him on the shoulder.

Stephen forced his arms to lower and his feet to step aside.

Kate flashed him an apologetic look, but the lion, whom Stephen recognized as the Lord Rutherford's spendthrift friend, eyed Stephen with a look of smug triumph.

But Katherine wouldn't be his prize for long.

---

*T*he set ended after two more songs, and the musicians stopped for an intermission. Katherine asked her partner, a court jester, to return her to where Abby sat enjoying a glass of lemonade.

"Here. Have a sip." She passed Katherine her glass. "Your cheeks are flushed."

Katherine sat on the corner of the settee and swallowed the lukewarm drink. "So are yours."

The crush of gathered guests and the warmth of body heat had turned the large room into a furnace. Despite the heat, Katherine couldn't remember having this much fun since she was a child playing princesses with Claire while Papa pretended to be a dragon.

Her throat tightened. Was it right for her to have a lovely time while her home was in upheaval because of wretched invaders?

Abby's gaze drifted over the crowd. Katherine refused to feel guilty about tonight if her friend was in high spirits. Abby deserved to have a similarly delightful time. "Are you enjoying yourself?"

"I am." But her smile faded.

"What's wrong?" Katherine wrinkled her brow. "Are people still uncertain what to say around you?"

Abby shrugged. "That's not it. At a masquerade, people can pretend to be someone else. It's allowed some to feel they can speak freely with me."

"What is it then?"

"There is a man over there next to the pillar—don't look."

Katherine snapped her gaze back to her friend.

"He keeps watching me. I'm probably being silly, but I can feel his eyes on me whenever I'm not looking. There is something familiar about him, but I can't place it."

Katherine flicked her gaze in his direction. It was the man in black. "I danced with him earlier." She flipped open her fan, but it only moved about the warm air. "He said he's known your family and is a business associate of Stephen. You'd probably recognize him without the full mask. He has a limp and a husky voice. Does that remind you of anyone?"

Abby shook her head and glanced in the direction of the man in black. Katherine did the same. He pushed off from the pillar and strode in their direction, his limp barely noticeable.

Abby clutched Katherine's arm. "He's coming this way."

"He's probably going to ask you to dance. In this crowded room, the worst he can do is step on your toes, and you won't have to worry. He's an excellent dancer."

Abby exhaled. "You're right." She squeezed Katherine's hand. "I'm so grateful you came."

"I'm the one who's grateful."

"Miss Hartington." The man in black looked to his left and right before settling his gaze on Abby. A long pause grew between them. Gone was the surety of the man who'd pulled her onto the dance floor. In his place stood a man who seemed as nervous as if he were asking for his first dance. "May I request the honor of a dance?"

"It's Mrs. Emerson." Abby rose. "Certainly."

He held out his palm, and she placed her hand in his. As he led her onto the dance floor, she glanced back at Katherine.

Katherine flashed what she hoped was her best smile of encouragement.

"Care to dance?"

A scream caught in Katherine's throat. She knew that voice and turned to face her cousin Horace. Long, white folds of fabric lead to a pair of Roman sandals. He appeared to be dressed as Julius Cesar or a Roman Soldier. It was difficult to discern while keeping her gaze lowered like a bashful debutante. She gripped her skirts, preparing to flee.

"Such a beautiful woman should never be left unattended." He lifted her hand and placed a sloppy kiss on the back of it. The smell of alcohol assaulted her nostrils.

Did he recognize her? Should she stay calm or make a scene? Would doing so put the Hartingtons in danger? Had she already put them in harm's way? She wanted to snap her hand back but kept it still.

"The music beckons. Shall we?" He attempted to tuck her hand in his arm, but she pulled away.

"I beg your pardon." She tried to imitate the lilt and pitch of Julia's voice. "But I must freshen up first."

"By all means." He lessened the hold on her hand only to grip it tightly again. "Hurry back."

Katherine yanked her hand out of his clutches and backed away until she reached a safe distance before turning to flee. Her heart rose in her throat, choking out her breath. She scanned for the nearest exit and, rounding a corner, skidded into a knight in full armor.

Katherine glanced over her shoulder to see if her cousin followed her, but he already held the hand of a young brunette dressed as a peacock. She escaped the ballroom into the hall that led to the retiring rooms, a set of drawing rooms, and the front foyer.

Katherine excused herself and darted around the knight.

Praise God, her cousin hadn't recognized her. Katherine rested against the wainscoted wall like a collapsed sail, limp with relief.

"I can't believe it." A shepherdess covered in ruffles and flounces with a large bonnet and shepherd's crook clung to Julia's arm as they exited the ballroom. "An earl. Your sisters will be so jealous."

Katherine ducked into the shadow of an alcove as they passed.

"My sister still lords over me that she'd married a viscount." Spite littered Julia's tone. "But I've done one better. I've landed an earl. I expect he'll propose tonight."

Propose? On the terrace, Stephen claimed he'd had other intentions. Katherine's stomach sank as if she had swallowed a lead ball. How could Stephen lead Julia on? Or was she the one being misled?

Katherine didn't want to face Julia in the retiring room, and she couldn't head back to the ballroom with her cousin. The stuffy air filled with French perfumes and alcohol raised bile in her throat. The need to find a place to hide drove her to a stairway that had at first looked like an alcove veering off on the right. She climbed, uncertain where it led. At the top, it opened into a narrow, unlit room with heavy draperies pulled back to reveal a small balcony overlooking the grand ballroom. She could remain hidden here until just before the unmasking. Then, if anyone noticed, she'd feign a headache and slip back to the carriage to await her group until it was time to leave.

She stepped closer and peeked over the balcony, seeking to stay abreast of the movements of the man dressed as Caesar. Had he given up searching for her or had he attended the ball to finish what the bandits failed to accomplish?

*S*tephen scanned the ballroom for Kate after dropping hints to every gent who'd listen that he was looking to purchase a Lipizzaner thoroughbred. He had pawned Julia off to Fredrick, and she'd had the gall to make poor Fredrick wait while she freshened up. Julia's haughty attitude wore on Stephen. Her behavior after the scuffle with the horse thieves opened his eyes to her true self. Had she always been so selfish and demanding of her way? Had he? He'd kept her company all this time. He ran in the same circles. Had he been *that* shallow? *God forgive me.*

He strode through the French doors and onto the patio, perking up in the cool night breeze. Couples strolled outside to gain relief from the oppressive indoor body heat. He couldn't find Kate anywhere.

Alarm poked at him. He scanned the gardens, but they were dimly lit, with only an occasional torch to light the path. Stephen knew what risqué behavior happened in the gardens and Kate would know better than to be lured there. He pictured her innocent eyes filled with wonder after their shared kiss. Wouldn't she?

He shouldn't have let her out of his sight. He should have told Julia the truth and sent her packing. His heart belonged to Kate. Who knew, maybe Julia and Fredrick could have a go at it. They seemed to enjoy each other's company.

Returning to the ballroom, he stepped into a wall of heat. People swirled around him, laughing and stumbling, many having imbibed on too much champagne. Masquerades were always the most uninhibited of parties. People made complete fools of themselves, thinking their masks protected their identities.

He stood just inside the doors and searched for a pair of striking green eyes in a dark violet costume. Twilight. The costume suited her perfectly. It was the most mysterious time of day, when the light played tricks on people.

An inebriated Napoleon Bonaparte tripped and slammed into Stephen's back. The force knocked his chin up. He lost his balance, stumbling forward several steps.

"So s-sorry, dear chap," came a slurred response.

The woman clinging to the man's arm burst into a fit of giggles.

A slight sway of the curtains above caught Stephen's attention, and he squinted to get a better look. In the recess of the balcony, Kate hid in the shadows, watching the revelry. Her high perch kept her safe above what was quickly becoming a ruckus. He breathed a sigh of relief and maneuvered his way through the crowd, trying to gauge which staircase would lead him to her sanctuary.

---

*T*he music glided over Katherine. She closed her eyes, enjoying each note as they swelled into a crescendo, only to open them again, not wanting to miss the dancing below. From her view, it was as if a stained-glass window had come to life, a kaleidoscope of colors mixing and swirling across the dance floor. Katherine caught sight of Abby dancing with the man in black, but it was difficult to tell from this distance if things were going well between her and the mysterious man. She scanned the room for Stephen, hoping to watch him from afar. She'd pretend she was the one on his arm, not Julia.

The dancers continued to ebb and flow like ocean waves to the minuet, the women's beautiful gowns flowing behind them. From her vigil, she disconnected from the part of society to which she should have belonged. If things had been different, if her parents hadn't decided to travel to Bath that day, she would have been part of this glittering society. She would have been among the young women who flirted brazenly and didn't have a care in the world. Instead, her life had slipped through the cracks. She'd missed her opportunity, and now she floated in limbo, where she didn't quite fit. She was a countess without a home, without people, and for the most part, without a family. She drew in a shuttered breath. It was past time she told the Hartington family the truth. They would be hurt, but hopefully, they'd understand.

Tomorrow, tomorrow I will put an end to this pretense.

Then she'd leave on the next coach to check on her sister.

The familiar scent of citrus and leather surrounded her like a warm blanket.

Stephen.

Her senses heightened, like someone with weak eyes looking through glasses for the first time. Everything grew vibrant when he was near.

Her stomach dropped to her slippers, knowing she would be leaving him. The pain would be unbearable. *Please don't let him hate me for all the lies.* She didn't want to be pushed out of his life like the forgotten gravestone of his dead aunt, but he would have Julia to turn to. The hardest part would be looking in his eyes as she revealed the truth. Like how Samson had borne the consequences for his actions, so too must she. It was time to set everything right with the Hartingtons.

His strong hands rested on her upper arms.

"Julia believes you're going to propose to her." The words spilled from her lips, begging for an answer. "I overheard her say as much to a shepherdess."

His fingers tensed. "I promised a sennight ago to escort her to the masquerade. That was all. I plan to send her and her mother back to London on the morrow."

She leaned back against his warmth, turning her head to rest upon his chest. He gasped a sharp intake of breath, and his bunched muscles flexed. His gloved fingers traced her hairline before gently turning her to face him. His fingers lifted her chin to meet his gaze.

With his other hand, he pushed his mask over the top of his head. "When I couldn't find you..." His voice sounded ragged. "God help me. My life has been turned upside-down since I climbed in through your window that night. I'm not the same man. My logic had been flawed, but it took you to help me to see it."

Katherine couldn't squeeze words past the lump in her throat. Tears blurred her eyes. When she left tomorrow, she'd be leaving her heart behind.

"I don't want to lose you. Not ever." His fingers moved to the back of her head and untied the knot to her mask. Startled, she raised her hands to hold the mask in place but froze as Stephen's heavy-lidded gaze moved to her mouth. His lips descended upon hers.

The party below became a distant memory as his lips molded against hers. Her heart thundered in her ears, and her skin heated as if she stood too close to a fire. She closed her eyes and melted into his arms. Her mask slipped through her fingers and fluttered to the floor.

His hands wound around her neck, slid into her hair. Pins scattered to the floor below. The caress of his lips left her breathless and filled with longing. His fingers ran over her arms and up and down her spine. She memorized the feel of his lips on hers and leaned into him, wanting to hold onto this moment and make it last a lifetime.

A boisterous laugh echoed off the ceiling. The noise of the crowd below increased, sounding a warning in the back of her mind. She stiffened, recognizing her cousin's hideous cackle. The crowd quieted. She broke free from Stephen's drugging kiss and jerked out of his arms.

The unveiling had begun. Everyone's identities were to be revealed at midnight.

"I must go," she said in a frantic whisper.

"Stay." He reached out to pull her back into his embrace. "I want you in my life—"

"But Julia." Her pitch raised an octave.

He stepped close and cupped her face. "I don't love Julia."

Her gaze flicked from Stephen's pleading eyes to the nearest exit. The crowd below chanted, *eight, seven, six.* Her stomach rolled with each counted number. "Tell your family I'll be waiting in the coach." She hitched up her skirts and ran down the stairs.

"Wait." Stephen called.

The confusion marring his face as she broke away haunted her as Katherine skidded around the turn into the foyer. She fled toward the front door.

Five, four...

She brushed past a guest. Two footmen prepared to open the doors for her.

"There you are." Julia blocked her path. "Have you seen Stephen?" Her narrowed eyes shot accusations.

Three, two...

Katherine glanced about for her cousin, but he was nowhere in sight. The Grimm reaper stood ominously in the corner, a shadow shrouding his face with darkness. Katherine trembled with foreboding and forced her eyes away.

"I have a headache," she said. "I'll be in the carriage." Katherine side-stepped the woman, bolted down the steps and out the front door to the waiting coach.

*S*tephen stumbled down the stairs, reeling from their kiss and the tangy-sweet taste of lemonade on Kate's lips. After nearly declaring his love, he couldn't erase her panicked expression. He leaned against the wall on the bottom step and rubbed his temple. What just happened? Had he misread her? How did Kate switch from passionately melting in his arms to fleeing his presence?

"Well, I never." Julia glared at Kate's retreating form. Her fingers clenched into fists. "I didn't spend an entire season vying for Stephen's attention to let some nobody step in and steal him away."

Her sharp tone drew him up short.

Kate darted through the front doors.

"Pardon me." A Grimm reaper glided to Julia's side. "Do you know the woman who just left?"

Something about the stranger set warning sirens blaring in Stephen's head, and he stayed in the shadows of the stairwell. He inched closer to listen without being seen.

"Her?" Julia's lips curled as she gestured toward the front door. "I'll warn you. She is a conniving little witch. I'd keep your distance. She's worse than a poor relation."

The man's lips cracked into a cunning smile. "That sounds like her. Remind me of her name?"

She inspected the man from head to toe. "Why do you want to know?"

"Let's say, she belongs to a friend of mine, and he wants her back."

Belongs to? What could he mean by that?

"Truly?" Julia straightened. The reaper now had her full attention.

"If you tell me the name she is going by and with whom she is staying, I can make certain she returns to where she rightfully belongs. I trust that would be useful to you?"

Stephen's muscles clenched. His training with the Home Office kept him from coming to blows. Who was this man, and what did he want with Kate? The only way to find out is to wait and draw him out. Premature action only led to the culprit getting away.

"Most definitely." Julia stepped closer and whispered into his ear.

Stephen had known Julia was jealous, but how could she offer Kate up as a sacrifice that easily?

"Splendid." The wicked grin returned to the reaper's face.

Julia turned to re-enter the ballroom, but the man grabbed her arm. She stared at his hand before slicing him with a scathing gaze.

The reaper merely chuckled. "This is to be our secret." He blasted her with a frosty glare meant to leave her quaking. "I wouldn't want my little bird to fly away before I can bring her home."

The color drained from Julia's cheeks, and she yanked her arm away. "Who are you?" She rubbed her upper arm as if his grip had left a bruise. "In case I discover any more information that could be...useful." Her lips quivered the tiniest bit.

The gentleman inside of Stephen desired to swoop in and help a woman in distress, but the spy in him hesitated, not willing to blow his cover until after hearing the man's response.

"So I know how to get in touch with you." Julia said.

The reaper released his grip and leaned forward in a mock bow. "Lord Pewitt, at your service."

CHAPTER 23

The following morning, Katherine arose early after a fitful sleep. Last night's scare proved she must tell the Hartingtons the truth. They needed to be aware of the danger she'd subjected them to by taking advantage of their hospitality. She'd tell Stephen first because he deserved to understand why she made a hasty departure. She rehearsed her words until they flowed from her lips as she strode down the stairs and through the hall to the breakfast room.

God, help Stephen to understand why I did what I did.

Her jumbled thoughts cleared, and her muscles relaxed. Was this the peace Lady Felton spoke of?

Weston, the butler, informed her that Stephen had broken his fast and was meeting with a new client and his stud. With Stephen unavailable and the rest of the family still asleep, she decided to settle down with a good book. She entered the library and scanned the bindings—poetry, Greek architecture, the complete works of Lord Byron.

The romantic poet's prose would never affect her the way Stephen's words had. *God help me. My life has been turned upside-*

down since I climbed in through your window that night. I don't want to lose you.

How would he feel about her once he knew she'd been lying about not knowing who she was all this time? Surely if he let her explain in full, he'd understand. Why then did she keep picturing his stony face as he glared at his aunt's grave marker?

A knock sounded on the front door, echoing throughout the sleepy house and jarring Katherine from her thoughts. Her ears strained for sound. Her cousin may be in the area, but he certainly hadn't seemed to be looking for her last night. He was too busy chasing a bit of muslin and was probably still sleeping off the ill effects of drinking. She moved closer to the door and heard the butler speak with the new visitor.

"One moment while I see if Miss Vernon is accepting callers."

"I'll await her presence." The voice's oddly familiar tenor tingled her spine, and Katherine's breath caught.

Lord Pewitt.

He'd found her. Had he been at the masquerade last night, too? An image of the Grimm Reaper standing in the corner flashed through her mind. Her mask had fallen off, and her hair had come loose as she'd fled. The reaper held the same build as Lord Pewitt. Had he recognized her and notified her cousin?

She pressed a fist to her mouth to hold back her scream.

God help me.

Should she hide? Run?

Think, Katherine, quick.

She snuck down the corridor and used the servant's stairs to get to her room. Someone climbed behind her. She peeked over her shoulder to find one of the Hartington footmen following.

"Would you like for me to get something for you, my lady?"

She flashed him a smile. "I'm merely going to go rest in my room." Forcing a regular pace down the hall to her chamber, she shut the door behind her and locked it. There must be a way to escape. The memory of Lord Pewitt's disturbed dark eyes sent a wave of shivers through her extremities. Her cousin was horrific, but Lord Pewitt had seemed like the devil himself.

She flung open the wardrobe and snatched her pelisse. Turning to the bed, she reached under the mattress and removed her saved pin money and the picture of her parents. Her eyes darted around the room. *What now?*

A flutter outside the window caught her eye. The wind blew, bobbing the cherry blossoms, which rained petals to the earth. Their cheerful beauty contrasted with the nightmare that had befallen her.

Hurry.

She hesitated, her breaths rising and falling in rapid succession.

Should she try to find Stephen and tell him the truth? He'd think the worst of her for leaving. A gravestone flashed in her mind. Lord Felton had tried to help his sister-in-law, and his aid resulted in injury. *If I brought them trouble—if someone gets hurt...*

Like Stephen had never forgiven his aunt, he and his family would never forgive her.

Katherine squeezed her eyes shut. She needed to think things through. She needed more time—time she didn't have.

A knock sounded at the door. Katherine remained silent, hoping the butler would assume she was elsewhere or still sleeping.

Get out now.

Her stomach twisted. She didn't even have a chance to tell Abby and Lady Felton goodbye, and they'd become like family. Only a few short weeks had passed since Stephen frightened her by crawling in through the window, but her life had changed entirely. The best way she could protect them was by leaving.

She whirled at the thought. *The window.*

If Stephen could get in that way, she could escape. She dashed to the glass pane and threw open the sash. Leaning her body halfway out, she craned her neck. The thick branch hanging a few feet from her window must have been how Stephen got onto the ledge. Its limbs branched out and veered off above the roof line but there was a clear shot to a sturdy part. Could she make it with one good leap and no running start?

She must.

Another knock sounded on her door.

Shrugging on her pelisse, she stuffed her pin money into her corset and tucked her parents' miniature portrait into her coat pocket. Then, she crawled onto the sill, pressing her back against the house. The distance to the ground tingled her hands and feet. She wasn't afraid of heights, but she'd never attempted a feat like this. The jump to the thicker part of the cherry tree's branch was at least half the length of a person. The ground swam below her. She inched to the right, closer to the limb, but her pelisse caught on the window frame. Teetering, she clutched the rough stone exterior, her palms dampened with sweat. With a quick yank, she pulled it free. Taking the tiniest of steps, she shuffled her way down the ledge, her thin-soled shoes helping her feel her way along. Small pebbles cascaded to the ground below and tapped against the side of the house.

She focused on her destination. The branches of the cherry tree bobbed in the wind and scraped against the side of the house, groaning their eerie forewarning. She bit her lower lip and concentrated on the swaying branch.

She must jump for it.

Crouching down, she inhaled in a deep breath, counted to three, and leapt into the air with all the strength she could muster. The thick cherry branch hit her across the stomach with a thud, knocking the wind from her lungs. She clung to the branch, her nails and skin digging into the rough bark as her legs dangled in the air.

———

Stephen strode in from the stables after introducing the new stud and speaking with its owner who'd arrived several days early. He'd instructed a footman to keep watch over Kate, caught Jacob up on last night's events, and sent Felix to gather intelligence regarding Lord Pewitt, who he is and how he's connected to Kate. Tired and dirty, Stephen grimaced at the carriage sitting out front. So much for a long hot bath. The last thing he wanted was to entertain another visitor. He'd hoped for a quiet moment to get God's direction.

His feelings for Kate were clear. He wanted her in his life and was willing to accept the risks and unknowns to marry her, but she still didn't trust him, not enough to reveal her secrets.

She belongs to someone. Lord Pewitt's voice clawed at the recesses of Stephen's mind. What could the blackguard have meant?

Stephen had prayed and prayed, and God seemed to confirm Kate as the right choice for him. Her life was shrouded in mystery, her faith infantile in development, and she refused to trust him, yet over and over again, God put her on his heart.

Logically, it doesn't make any sense.

For the first time that morning, God ended his silence with a simple whisper into Stephen's heart. *Faith requires trust, not logic.*

He entered the house and paused on his way up the main stairs. Did he hear God right? His ears strained for an audible voice and his heart for another impression.

The hall clock ticked its steady pace.

Murmurs resonated from the parlor. His mother would entertain their visitor while he cleaned up, and whoever it was would have to wait if they were looking to speak to him. He would check on Kate and ensure she was feeling better, and then they needed to have a long and hopefully fruitful discussion.

S till damp from his bath to remove the dust and dirt from getting in the ring to demonstrate how he trained the horses, Stephen shrugged on his jacket and exited his room.

"Stephen." His mother waited in the hall, clutching her hands at her waist.

"Is something amiss?" He frowned. "I was hoping to speak with Miss Vernon first thing."

"It's about Kate."

The fine hairs on the back of his neck rose.

A footman strode toward them. "My apologies, milady, but I'm afraid we are unable to locate Miss Vernon."

Stephen jolted. Kate was missing? "You checked the stables and the library?"

The footman nodded.

Mother gripped his arm. "A man arrived this morning looking for her. He said he was friends of her guardian."

"Did he give his name?"

She nodded. "Lord Pewitt. I'd never heard of him."

Stephen choked and gripped the back of his hair. The Grimm reaper had wasted no time in coming for her. His instincts had been right. "Is he still here?"

"He left when Kate wasn't in her bed chamber, and we couldn't locate her."

Stephen's stomach dropped. Had Lord Pewitt abducted her? He rounded on the footman. "You were supposed to keep watch."

"She'd been in the library, my lord, and I followed her up the servant's back staircase. She said she was going to rest in her room. I swear she didn't exit her chamber. The only time I left my post was when Lady Felton beckoned me."

Blast. "She might have gone for a walk. Did you check the grounds?"

"I have four groomsmen out checking the premises, milord."

His mother's expression mirrored Stephen's concern. "I'm going to wake Abby and see if she knows where Kate may be."

Stephen excused himself and strode directly to the stables. If she'd left the house, Jacob would have spied her. Stephen raised his hand to hail his boss, who rushed over. His cap was off, and his hair stuck out in all directions.

"She's part of a bigger operation, fer sure." He kicked the dirt. "And a good one at that, cuz she got away."

A searing pain sliced through Stephen's chest. "Are you certain?"

"Caused a big distraction by sneaking that new mare in with the new stud and others in the pasture." He set his jaw and shook his head. "While we're trying to keep the mare from biting and kicking, yer Miss Vernon ran off with Dominion."

Stephen rubbed his hand across the lower half of his face. "I believe she's running from that Pewitt fellow. I don't know why or who the man is, but I intend to find out. I'd place bets on him being involved in higher crimes because Kate's afraid to tell anyone what Pewitt's after or why he's after her. Send for me the moment Felix returns." He squeezed his eyes shut, hashing out a plan of action. "In the meantime, keep your best men out there. Search the town." His fists clenched. "Confound it. Search the whole countryside. We have to find her before Pewitt does."

"Agreed." Jacob nodded and issued commands.

Stephen stormed back toward the house and quashed the

desire to saddle up another horse and go after her himself. Lord Pewitt had to have a role in all this. Everything went to perdition with his arrival. Stephen's stride faltered as he remembered her face as she'd fled from him on Dominion, thinking someone was in pursuit, and her panic when she saw a strange carriage in the drive that turned out to be Julia. He raced into the house to interrogate the staff.

Several maids agreed Miss Vernon had been up and about that morning as usual. Another footman confirmed she ate in the breakfast room, and another maid passed her in the library, but no one saw her leave the house.

"Pardon me, milord." Jacob stood just inside the servant's entrance.

Stephen pivoted and focused his attention on the agent in disguise.

"Dominion 'as returned unharmed."

A breath whooshed from Stephen's lungs. Thank heaven. "Where's Kate."

Jacob shook his head. "She didn't return wit 'im."

Stephen clenched his hands to hold down the dread threatening to spiral his mind into panicked disarray. Kate was too good of a horsewoman to have been thrown, and he'd trained Dominion not to take risks with riders. It could only mean she'd climbed off the horse and continued her flight on foot, but to where?

Jacob backed out of the house and returned to the stables.

Stephen excused the maids and dashed up the stairs, hoping to find clues in her chamber. Propriety suffered him to knock first, but after several painful seconds of no response, he entered. Her familiar scent of lavender still lingered in the air, but the room was empty. Her bedchamber was tidy, just as Stephen assumed it would be. Everything about Kate was orderly, except her unruly hair, despite her attempts to tame it.

A breeze ruffled the writing paper on the nearby desk.

Stephen checked to see if she'd left a note. The word *dear* has been scribbled on the top of the page and dangled there leaving its readers wondering what she'd wanted to convey and to whom. He moved to the window, hoping to glimpse her strolling in the east field. Instead, a small piece of material, not even the size of his pinky finger, attracted his eye. It fluttered on a nail near the ledge. He pulled the pale green fabric from its hold.

He wished he'd asked the maids what color she'd donned this morning. Had she leaned out to test the weather before going for a walk? He scanned the distance for a glimpse of her. His forearms rested on the smooth sill. He'd slipped on small stones and almost fallen during his own crazy stunt of sneaking in through the same window. If he hadn't killed himself, he could have broken a leg. Strange that the ledge appeared dusted. He leaned out farther. A broken twig dangled precariously off the large branch.

A sense of dread seeped into his bones. She wouldn't have? She couldn't have? He held his breath before dropping his gaze to the ground below. A rush of air escaped his lips. There was no limp, broken body lying there.

She'd risked her life to get out unnoticed, but why? What would cause her to dare such a stunt?

All indicators pointed to Lord Pewitt's arrival.

---

*K*atherine eased her way up to the ticket booth. She tried her best to look inconspicuous, but it was difficult with her breath coming in gasps and a very unladylike sweat on her brow. She'd ridden Dominion to the end of the Hartington lands but refused to take the horse any farther. Katherine Jenkins—or Kate Vernon—was not a thief. She'd smacked Dominion on the backside and commanded him to go home. The horse had galloped off and stopped a few yards away to look back at her. "Go on," she'd yelled. The horse, seeming to understand, cantered in the right direction. A horse as well trained as Dominion would return to where it was fed.

She smoothed out her skirts and stepped up to the ticket counter. "When is the next stagecoach headed west toward Sherbourne?"

"Came and went on Tuesday," said the man behind the counter as he stamped tickets and filed them in a tin box. "Won't have another headed out that way fer a couple more days."

She jerked her head in a tight nod and stepped away. Dreaded tears threatened. She needed to think. Inhaling a deep breath, she sought the peace she'd seen in Lady Felton. What would Lady Felton do?

Pray.

"Lord." She closed her eyes. "What am I to do? Where do I go? Please make a way. I need You."

The rhythmic pounding of stamped tickets was joined by a fainter thudding sound. Her ears perked up as she realized the noise was horses' hooves thundering in the distance. Katherine opened her eyes, expecting Stephen or Lord Pewitt to bear down on her. She had no idea how quickly they had discovered her disappearance or how easily they could track her here.

A team of horses and a stagecoach rounded the bend.

"Thank you, Lord." She gazed heavenward to show her appreciation and stepped up to the ticket booth.

"Where is this coach headed?"

"Let's see. Ah, to London." He flicked open his pocket watch and glanced down at it. "Right on time."

She could visit her attorneys and get answers about her cousin's guardianship.

The stagecoach pulled up. Three hired men with loaded guns sat perched on top of it.

Katherine hesitated. "I'd like to purchase a ticket." She slid money over the counter, and the coins scratched along the metallic tray.

"Don't yer worry, ma'am. They're there for yer protection. One can never be too cautious, especially with all the recent attacks by highwaymen. There was a young woman who drown not that far from here after bandits chased her coach off the road into the river. But we make certain our stagecoaches are well protected. You'll be safe with us." He winked at her.

He picked up the change, counting them as he did so. "For you, miss." He slid a ticket her way.

She couldn't help but worry as she approached the stage-coach. While the stable hands hitched up a fresh team and after passengers disembarked, she took hand of one of the gunmen and slipped inside.

"No baggage?" he asked.

"No." Katherine fought against the sensation of being trapped in a nightmare and unable to awaken. Here she was again, running with hardly a plan in place and no one to help her. She sat between an Irish-looking man with red hair and freckles and a dark-haired man half hidden behind a newspaper. She exhaled a ragged breath and blinked away the hot tears building under her eyelids. A scripture Abby had cited entered her mind, *For God hath not given us a spirit of fear, but of power, and of love, and of sound mind.* She wrapped the words around her like a shawl as the stagecoach jerked into motion, bound in the opposite direction of Claire.

And far away from the Hartingtons—and Stephen.

---

*S*tephen checked Dominion for any signs of foul play, but found none, ruling out the possibility that Kate was lying somewhere injured. She had sent the horse back to the barn intentionally. Running a hand over the top of his head, he wished she'd stayed on horseback. Her soft-soled shoes would be much harder to track.

Where would she go? He needed to think fast. She held a head start, but now that she was on foot, he might be able to catch up. Town seemed the best option. Maybe someone would recognize her. He adjusted the stirrups, mounted his horse, and spurred Dominion willing him to move with speed, but kept an eye out for any sign of Kate. *I can't lose her. Please God, not now.*

CHAPTER 24

The green rolling hills of the countryside disappeared, replaced by London's charcoal-stained buildings. Katherine shifted on the hard stagecoach seat to ease her stiff muscles and ignored the doubts blaring in her head. *How are you going to survive on your own in a big city like London? You're setting yourself further away from your sister. What if something happens? How will you get to her?*

She would. She'd figure out a way to keep herself and Claire safe and return their inheritance back into their hands. The solicitor's office would have answers and then she could form a plan.

The idle chatter of the Irishman helped pass the time. He didn't ask her many questions about herself, just prattled on about his worries and homesickness for his country. Katherine rarely visited London. Her parents had brought her with them to the city as a child, but she only recalled a pale blue nursery where her parents, dressed in splendid formal attire, would come to kiss her and Claire goodnight before flitting off to various parties.

She must have drifted off somewhere along the road, for

she awoke when the coach jerked to a halt. Stepping into the hustle and bustle of the crowded streets, Katherine hugged her arms to her chest. Men in overcoats and women in traveling dresses brushed by her. They didn't ask her name or look her in the face, merely carried on as if she were a streetlamp in the middle of the sidewalk. Even though anonymity was what she needed, she swallowed the empty, unsettled feeling in the pit of her stomach. She hurried to the ticket counter and inquired about the next coach to Sherbourne.

"Leaves Thursday morning at half past nine." The man pushed his thin wire spectacles up to his winter-white brows.

"Thursday morning?" In four days? "There must be something sooner." She raised onto her tiptoes and leaned on the counter.

"I'm afraid not. It's a remote destination. Now for Petersham, we have a coach that leaves every hour."

"But I don't need to go to Petersham. I need to get to Sherbourne."

"Well then, miss, you'll need to wait until Thursday. Next!" He peered around her to the customer behind her.

Katherine stepped away from the counter and was swept into the crowd. She bumped along in the current like a toy boat set adrift down a rocky stream. She flagged down a hired hackney cab and directed the driver to the address of the Jenkins solicitors on Bedford Street. She gripped the bottom of the seat to keep from being jostled as the hack rode down the cobblestone street. The day had grown long during her travels and some of the street sellers started to pack up their wares or push their carts home.

The hack stopped in front of a paned glass store front with a painted black, wooden sign with gold lettering hanging above the door that read, *Whitmer and Collins Attorneys at Law*. A round man in a top hat and overcoat stepped outside and turned the key in the lock.

Katherine bounded out of the cab without waiting for assistance. "Wait."

The solicitor peered at her and straightened. "I'm sorry miss, but I'm late for an appointment." He patted the case he held in his other hand.

She dug through her reticule and paid the driver a few coins. "I'm Katherine Jenkins, the Countess of Dysart." She addressed the solicitor as she approached, stopping in front of him.

His brows pulled together "I don't know what kind of fool you take me for, but Lady Dysart passed several weeks ago in a tragic accident. It has been all over the papers."

"The papers were wrong. I survived—"

"Why didn't you make this known earlier?" His eyes narrowed. "Why come here and tell me?"

"Didn't you receive my letter?"

"I'm afraid not."

She pressed her fingertips to her temples. "I had to stay in hiding. My cousin was behind the attempt on my life. He's trying to get his hands on my inheritance and the Jenkins Lipizzaner horses."

His lips thinned into a tight line. "Why didn't you go to the local authorities?"

"The constable is a close friend of my cousin."

He glanced at the brim of his hat and exhaled, his frown displaying his annoyance. "Anyone can say they are the countess and there are few who wouldn't love to get their hands on her inheritance. How do I know who you say you are."

"Please Mr...." Was he Whitmer or Collins?

"Whitmer." His terse tone jolted through her. "Listen, I'm late for an appointment. I have my files with me. I'll look over it while I'm gone. You'll have to come back another time with proof you're the countess."

"Tomorrow?"

He shook his head and walked away, but she fell into step with him. He grunted. "I'm expected out of town along with my associate and won't be back until Thursday."

"Thursday?" She faltered a step. "What am I supposed to do until then?"

"*If* you are who you claim to be, then I suggested visiting Bow Street." He waved down a hack and climbed inside. "Good day, to you, miss." He tipped his hat, still frowning.

"Six for a penny." A match girl held up a few matches and peered at Katherine.

Katherine shook her head and the girl moved on. How would she prove to her solicitor who she truly was? There must be a way—something only someone from the Jenkins family line would know. But what? She hailed another hack and wracked her brain the entire ride to Bow Street.

She waited for the driver to help her alight and paid the man before entering the double wooden doors of the white stone building. Clusters of people stood gathered around in small circles pleading their cases to men dressed in scarlet waistcoats under blue greatcoats—the signature uniform of a Bow Street Runner. Katherine hesitated in approaching anyone. Should she wait a turn or elbow her way in as the young gentleman on her left had.

"May I be of service, miss?"

She startled and spun around to face a Runner who'd entered the building behind her. He stood tall in his uniform, but the boyish youthfulness of his full and rosy cheeks had her guessing he'd not yet seen twenty years.

"I'm here to report a crime." She explained the events of her cousin's making and the attempt he'd made on her life. The young man listened and interrupted only to clarify with questions and in the end went to his superior to plead her case. Katherine watched them discuss her circumstances from across the room and the lad's superior shook his head and frowned as her solicitor had done. The young runner's head hung as he approached, and a painful lump grew in Katherine's throat.

"I'm afraid it's out of our jurisdiction." The young man cleared his throat. "You'll need to speak with the local constable."

She'd already explained her conundrum with the local authorities. "But—"

"I'm sorry." He issued her a sad smile and held the door open for her to leave.

She tripped out onto the street in a daze. What would she do now? Where would she go? All of her plans had failed.

People scurried off in all directions to get home for the evening meal. And street vendors peddled their wares at a lower price to move them before the day was through. Men dressed in top hats with canes strolled with elegant women clinging to their arms. Women with little white caps on their heads hurried past with arms laden with groceries or other packages. Businessmen, like the one who'd sat across from her in the stagecoach, checked their watches and tucked their newspapers under their arms, intent on reaching their destination without delay.

Concentrate on one step at a time. Katherine's stomach rumbled. She must get some sustenance, then a place to rest her head tonight.

Different smells wafted through the air, some horrid and sulfuric, and others delicious, like the smell of bread rising or nuts roasting. She stopped to buy some bread and cheese at the cheesemonger's shop.

"I beg your pardon." She accepted the bread and cheese he handed her. "You wouldn't happen to know where I might be able to find a boarding house or other lodging? I'm new to the city."

The vendor, already starting a new transaction, cast Katherine a sideways glance, "Try Second Avenue and James."

He looked her over from head to toe. "I 'ope you're not on your own, miss. The boarding 'ouses around 'ere don't look kindly upon rentin' a room to a lone female."

She thanked him and headed in the direction he'd pointed her. She'd never considered she might not be able to find a room. A tightness formed in her chest, and the dark cloud of her thoughts hung heavy over her. She hugged her midsection. Perhaps if the boarding house owners wouldn't rent her a room, they could tell her someone who would.

After the fifth boarding house turned her out, she admitted that the street vendor had been correct. None would rent a room to a lone female. The man behind the counter at the most recent one sneered and told her to try down at Covent Garden.

Katherine wandered in the direction he pointed but stopped a couple of blocks away as men stumbled in and out of taverns, shouting lewd comments. The seedy avenue was littered with Courtesans and streetwalkers. She gasped and turned, hurrying in the opposite direction.

---

*S*tephen had looked everywhere. He slumped behind his desk at Willowstone Farm, probing his brain. Where could she have gone? He'd inquired at every storefront along the main road and practically threatened the man at the stagecoach ticket counter. A new shift had started, and the man had no idea if a petite woman with green eyes and curly light brown hair had purchased a ticket. He'd informed Stephen that three coaches had traveled through that day, one headed east to London, one west to Bristol, and the other north to Birmingham. The only direction Stephen could rule out was south, and a lot of good that did.

He demanded to speak to the employee who'd worked the previous shift, but again, the ticket salesman proved inept. He only knew the man's first name, John. The only way Stephen could question him would be to come back tomorrow during the morning shift.

He'd continued his frantic search the rest of the evening, unable to accept that Kate had disappeared. Defeated, he returned home to Willowstone Farm to find Julia's mother pacing the halls. Abby and his mother jumped to a stand, but he shook his head, and they sank into their chairs.

Julia remained seated but gnawed on an edge of her fingernail.

"I have half a mind to give you a stern tongue lashing, young man." Mrs. Napier huffed her frustration. "My daughter and I traveled here only to be blatantly ignored while you search for some little nobody who left of her own accord. Never has my daughter been treated so shabbily. She left a string of prospects behind in London all vying for her hand to chase you out here in God-knows-where."

Julia had the grace to look stricken by her mother's remarks, but probably because she still hoped to get her hooks into him.

He understood where she got her selfishness from.

"It is ungentlemanlike to string Julia along as you have," the woman continued. "I demand to know your intentions toward my daughter, or we'll pack our things and return to London this moment."

Stephen accepted the brunt of her anger, aware some of it was justified. He hadn't been fair to Julia. He should have known from the beginning that they wouldn't be a good match, but he'd disregarded what God had been telling him. He couldn't ignore it any longer. "I think that might be for the best."

Mrs. Napier stumbled a few steps and paled. That must not have been the response she'd expected.

"I've never." She placed a hand over her heart. "You'd prefer to chase after a vanishing woman who couldn't love you enough to stay?" Her caustic words sliced through him. "One who'd prefer to go back to being a governess or other lowly working-class girl rather than be with you." She spun on her heel. "Come along, Julia. We're leaving." She marched out of the room.

"I hope someday you will accept my deepest apologies." Stephen bowed to Julia, but her head remained lowered, and she didn't meet his eye.

Their carriage departed shortly thereafter.

The hall clock chimed the ten o'clock hour as Stephen sat alone in his study. How was he going to find Kate? Only twelve hours had passed since she'd gone missing, and already his heart ached for her companionship. He missed her smile, her eyes, inquisitive as if seeing everything for the first time. *God, why did You have me fall in love with her if she was going to vanish like a shooting star crossing the night sky?*

Stephen rubbed his face. He needed to let go and trust God. God had a plan, and only He could work all things for good. Staring at the wall would accomplish nothing, but prayer could.

He bowed his head and pleaded from the deepest recesses of his heart.

*K*atherine sat on a park bench and wiped her tears, fighting the urge to weep and failing. *Lord, I can't do this on my own. I thought I could handle Steepleton's upkeep, my cousin, and my wretched situation of faking amnesia, but I've made more than a mull of things. Please, I need your help.* Twilight cast long shadows across the building fronts, and the cool night air sent a chill down her spine. She pulled her pelisse tighter around her shoulders, and fat tears splatted onto her chest.

"Mind if I sit for a bit? My feet are paining me somethin' awful." A buxom woman carrying a large satchel of groceries plunked herself down on the bench beside Katherine. Her dark hair streaked with gray had been pulled into a loose bun, and her bonnet dangled behind her on worn ribbon ties.

"Name is Elise." An amicable smile crinkled the corners of her eyes. "Been runnin' all day without a single rest. If I don't sit for a moment, I think I may faint from exhaustion." She peered at Katherine. "Dearie me, what is the matter?" She fumbled around in her coat for a moment before pulling out a handkerchief and handing it to Katherine.

"Thank you." She wiped her eyes.

"Now, tell me what the matter is. Someone doesn't spill tears that big without havin' a real sad story to go along with them. Sometimes the best thing to do is to talk it out. Lifts the weight right off ya, and I'm a good listener."

Something about the woman reminded her of Lady Felton. Maybe it was the sparkle in her kind eyes, her sweet smile, or the way she took Katherine's hand and tenderly squeezed it, but the woman made Katherine feel comfortable enough to spill her entire story. She didn't hold back to the kind stranger as she spoke of her parents' deaths, her cousin's threats, the love she felt from the Hartington family, and her current dilemma of no one being willing to rent her a room.

When Katherine finished, Elise wrapped an arm around her shoulders and hugged her to her side. "I think God must be look'n out fer ya. Come with me."

Elise pulled Katherine by the hand out of the park and down the side streets near St. Giles like she might a small child. Lantern light shone off the cobblestones until they turned down a dimly lit alley.

"I'm not supposed to do this." She shoved a key into a door lock. "But as long as you can be up and out before dawn, I can give ya a warm bed by the fire fer the night. This won't solve all yer problems, but God's mercies are new every mornin', so we'll let tomorrow take care of itself."

Elise pushed open the creaky door, and they stepped inside a hearth-lit room. The air smelled of ale and stewed meat. Katherine's eyes adjusted to see a kitchen stove, a clean prep table, and a well-used stone fireplace. In the far corner, a young girl, probably three and ten, scrubbed dishes in the sink. Men's voices filled with revelry emanated from the other side of the kitchen wall. Katherine's eyes darted to the adjoining door where the laughter originated.

"Welcome to Hunter's Tavern." She spread out a hand as if displaying the Queen's quarters. "Don't worry, luv. I always lock the door at night once the kitchen is closed, which it shortly will be since it's been a slow night. Me and Gretta sleep in the storeroom right next to the door, so you'll be safe."

The girl at the sink shook the water off her hands and wiped them on her apron.

Elise handed Katherine a blanket and small pillow. "You'll be nice and warm here sleeping at the foot of the grate. I'll wake ya before sunrise because the owner doesn't take well to non-drinking guests."

Katherine's concern must have shown on her face because Elise chuckled. "Don't worry, dearie. The owner may be efficient and stingy, but the one thing he's not is punctual. If you're gone before the first customer arrives, he'll be none the wiser." She held a warm smile. "Now you go and get yerself some good rest. Things will look brighter in the morning."

As she spread out her pallet on the hardwood floor, weariness ate at Katherine's bones, and the day's events whirled in her mind. What must the Hartington's think of her sudden disappearance? The overgrown grave haunted her. Stephen may never forgive his aunt nor Katherine, but she would treasure their moments together. She lay on the pallet spread in front of glowing embers of the fire and rested her head on the pillow, imagining that she was back on the balcony overlooking the Rutherford ballroom leaning against Stephen's chest.

*T*he following day dawned, and Katherine had awoken to a hearty meal to break her fast thanks to Elise. The tavern owner didn't abide lone female guests unless the women were paid to warm his customer's beds, so Elise sent her on her way, but Elise's words echoed in her mind, "Remember, trust in the Lord. Approach his throne with confidence. Hebrews says if you do, you will receive mercy and find grace to help you in your time of need."

Katherine prayed as she walked the city for God to help her find a place to stay until Thursday, but who would take her in? London's vastness overwhelmed her, especially not knowing her way around. Could she work for room and board? Perhaps at a seamstress shop or habit maker? She was handy with a needle but doubted that they would hire her without a reference.

A maid swept dust out into the street. A carriage rumbled by, and Katherine dodged the splash of the puddle as it passed. Something tugged at her skirt, and Katherine spun around to discover a mother and child begging. The mother jostled the baby to soothe its whimpering. Dirt smeared their faces, and their clothes were torn. The woman held her hand out, and Katherine's heart broke. Reaching into her pocket, she opened her change purse and slipped them a half penny.

"God bless you, child," the woman said. "You just put food in the tummy of my little boy."

Katherine smiled weakly and continued. Three more nights until Thursday. Will she, too, be sleeping in some back alley like the beggar woman? No, Elise said to boldly approach God's throne of grace.

Please Lord, make a way.

A horse cart rumbled up the street, and a young man dressed like a chimney sweep bumped into her, tripping up her steps. "Pardon me, miss. Didn't see ya there." He helped steady her and went on his way.

Katherine continued to push one foot in front of the other until she wandered into Hyde Park. A park bench posed a refuge for her aching feet. Courting couples paraded by in luxurious open carriages. Her parents had once owned a house in the west end of London. In fact, her papa had resided there when he met Mama during her first season. Pity that Katherine had convinced the attorneys to sell it. The oversight and maintenance required of a large estate *and* a London townhome was too great. Little did she know that she would need a place to stay in the future.

That was it. She could prove she was the Countess of Dysart by listing all the financial transactions she'd had with her solicitors since her parents' deaths. Why hadn't she done so when she had the chance? She pursed her lips. Because he'd hurried off in a rush.

Katherine found her way to a safer part of town where she might have blended in with the elegant ladies strolling through Hyde Park if her shoes hadn't been worn and her gown wrinkled. The women wore fancy walking dresses, the men top hats and jackets. People in open carriages waved to others passing by. It was as Stephen had described his life in London on their morning rides. Stephen owned a townhouse on Mount Street not far from here in Mayfield. She was sure of it.

She peered down one of the streets. Nothing prevented her from walking by. Why not? She rose and stretched, hoping no one would notice her unladylike ways. Her leg muscles groaned in complaint, and her feet throbbed with every step, but she was determined to see her plan through. It was silly but seeing where he lived would make her feel a little less lost. She crossed a few streets, wandering until she located the sign for Mount Street. Turning right, she admired the beautifully maintained townhouses. She strolled down the street until a servant passed carrying a bundle of French bread loaves. Katherine stopped her and asked the number of the Hartington town house. The girl pointed to number fifty-four.

A smile tugged on Katherine's lips at the grand stone Julian-styled house. The four-story exterior was simplistic in style but had a masculine flair, with its bold Grecian columns and large windows.

A small inner voice urged her to knock on the door. It would be improper. Unmarried ladies never visited bachelor's lodgings. What would she say when the butler answered the door? How would she explain her presence?

It made no sense, but the nudge persisted. An unearthly pull drew her toward the house, but she couldn't override her fears. She passed the house several times as the tug at her heart grew. Unable to ignore it, she lifted her chin and ascended the front steps.

She had to summon the courage to knock. Elise's words rang in her head, *Approach His throne with confidence. If you do, you will receive mercy and find grace to help you in your time of need.*

She knocked and stepped back, squaring her shoulders.

Lord, make me bold.

Fighting the urge to run, Katherine forced herself to stay still. The door swung open, and a stately butler dressed in fine livery peered down his nose at her.

Katherine swallowed.

The butler raised an eyebrow in a silent inquiry. Under his unswerving gaze, she said, "I beg your pardon, but I've just traveled here from Willowstone Farm. I know I should have sent notice of my coming, but I was in a rush. Forgive me, I'm weary from traveling."

To Katherine's complete mortification, the butler stepped back and started to close the door.

A hand jutted forth and stopped it before it crashed against the frame.

"Wilson." A woman pried it open and addressed the butler. "Don't you remember your last conversation with his lordship?"

"Of course," he said through a pinched expression.

The female servant cleared her throat and straightened. "A lady has arrived from Willowstone Farm. She's apologized for not sending notice of her arrival." She nudged the butler, and the jingle of keys identified the servant as the housekeeper. "This may be *her*." The woman's hand flew to her bosom. "By Jove, the master's gone and done it." Her expression brightened.

The butler's brows drew together. "Surely, I would have been notified."

The housekeeper snorted and whispered in the butler's ear.

Katherine had no idea what they were talking about and only caught snippets of the conversation.

"It must be she... highborn ladies... bachelor's lodging... rude to leave her ladyship waiting on the front steps."

Heat flooded Katherine's neck. Her mother would be horrified that her daughter had been reduced to a beggar on the streets.

The door widened, and the butler, a trifle paler than before, placed an arm behind her back and ushered her into the foyer.

Katherine followed him in a daze.

"*My* lady, may I take your coat?" The butler grabbed her pelisse and slid it down her arms with the lightest touch.

The housekeeper escorted her into a sitting room and lowered her into a chair. "May I fluff the pillow for you, milady?" Without waiting for an answer, she fluffed the pillows around her.

LORRI DUDLEY

"Would you care for tea, Lady Hartington?" The butler yanked on the bell pull.

Lady Hartington? They think I'm married. They think I'm Julia.

Katherine stood quicky and extended her palms to ward them off. She was not going to get caught in another charade. "There has been a mistake. I'm *not* Lady Hartington."

The butler and housekeeper reared back.

The butler recovered the quickest. He nudged the housekeeper with his elbow. "I told you." He straightened and peered down his nose at Katherine. "Other than his immediate family, the master doesn't accept callers of the female variety to his bachelor's lodgings. I think it best for you to take your leave."

Heat flooded her body, culminating in the tips of her ears which burned like a hot stove. Did they believe she was some harlot looking to become Stephen's mistress? She backed up a step. It didn't matter how desperate her situation became. She still had some semblance of pride.

"You're mistaken." The housekeeper spoke the words before Katherine's tongue could form them. She peered at Katherine as if assessing her from the inside out. "She doesn't carry herself like a romp or some vixen, and we wouldn't allow the like around the master." There was no mistaking the warning in her tone.

"I am a friend of the Hartington family, and I came here seeking Lord Hartington's"—she swallowed and forced the word out—"help." Inwardly she recoiled. Ladies of the Quality don't knock on bachelor's doors, and they don't ask for help. Would her parents be ashamed of her? Had she let them down and the Dysart name? "I shouldn't have come here. I will see myself out." She turned and strode to the door, but the butler stepped ahead.

He placed a hand on the knob but didn't open the door. "Maybe we can be of service. What is it that you might need?"

Her cheeks burned like two red hot coals. "I'm in need of a

286

place to stay until Thursday, when the next stagecoach leaves for Sherborne."

"My sincerest apologies, miss." His face paled. "We cannot allow visitors without the master's permission. To do otherwise could cost us our employment."

"I understand." Katherine nodded for him to open the door, and stepped back out into the sunshine "When his lordship returns,"—she raised her chin in a highborn manner—"tell him the Countess of Dysart paid him a visit."

"Wilson." The housekeeper's voice held a pleading tone.

He hesitated in the doorway. "I don't know how dire of straights you are in, but I can send someone to see if any rooms are available in any of the inns."

Katherine pivoted to face the servants and tears stung the backs of her eyes. She didn't hold out much hope, but maybe they knew of some places she hadn't tried. "I appreciate your offer. If you would be so kind."

"If nothing is available, my sister lives over on the other side of town on Grange Road. She works with the church and will either take you in or find someone who will. Let me get one of the stable boys to ride a message over to her." The housekeeper's voice faded as she scurried down the hall.

"Very good. One moment while have a carriage brought around." He closed the door.

Katherine descended the steps and stopped at the street. Her lips trembled as she fought back tears. Blast her pride for stating her real name and not that of Kate Vernon. She'd wanted to set Stephen's servants in their place by using her title but in doing so she could have tainted her reputation and the Dysart family name, and Stephen would most likely not make the connection that Kate Vernon is actually Katherine Jenkins, the Countess of Dysart.

"Stay right here, Isaac." At the townhouse across the street, a blond woman and a small boy exited the front entrance.

The woman inspected her reticule. "Where did I put my parasol?"

Katherine stilled, praying the woman wouldn't spy her leaving Stephen's bachelor's lodgings.

The petite blonde glanced directly at her. She cocked her head before turning her attention to her child.

She willed the carriage to be brought around in a hurry and felt for her reticule in her pocket to offer to pay the Butler's mother for taking her in, but the bulge of her change purse was missing. She patted the side of her gown and gasped.

The chimney sweep.

She'd been pickpocketed.

Now, even if she found a place that would accept her, she had no way to pay. How would she purchase a ticket to Sherborne? Her knees threatened to crumble, and tears filled her eyes as she crossed the street.

The rumble of a fast-approaching carriage caused Katherine to glance over her shoulder, affording her one last look at Stephen's townhouse. A blur of something caught her eye. A small boy darted out into the road after a runaway ball. A carriage barreled toward him, and ice surged down her spine. She strained her legs to get to the boy in time. Opening her arms wide, she snatched him up, yanking him out of the way. Toppling on the side of the road, she banged her head on the cobble stone but clutched the boy to her bosom and tensed for impact. The gust of wind as the carriage passed blew her bonnet off her head to dangle by its strings.

A woman screamed, as the conveyance rattled up the street.

Lord, please don't let the child be hurt.

CHAPTER 25

*T*he little boy squirmed in Katherine's arms.

Her bonnet hung by its strings limply on her back, and springs of curls blocked her vision. With a quaking hand, she tucked them behind her ear and felt for any blood. Her white glove remained white, but the side of her head was tender. She rose to a stand hefting the child up beside her. Pain sliced her head, and she blinked back a wave of dizziness. She scooped up the ball and handed it to him. Keeping his hand firmly grasped in her own, she led the child across the street on watery legs.

Tears streamed down the blond woman's cheeks as she embraced her son. She kissed, scolded, and sobbed all at the same time.

The child clung to her, looking contrite. Tears shimmered in the woman's eyes as she met Katherine's gaze. "Thank you." She repeated the words over and over.

"I'm grateful I could get to him in time." Katherine blinked to clear her blurring vision. The dull ache where she'd hit her head spread to the front and the back.

The woman's gaze fell to the bottom of Katherine's dress. A black wagon wheel track had imprinted in the light fabric of her day gown, showing how close to a near disaster they'd come.

The woman burst into tears anew, flowing like a river down her cheeks, and she hugged her son tighter.

Katherine assured the woman her son was fine, before fumbling to fix her bonnet and be on her way.

"Wait," the woman cried. "You saved my son's life. How can I ever repay you?"

This was her chance. *Ask for help.* Katherine hesitated.

"My name is Ella Whitmore." The woman released her son and rose. "Are you a relative of Lord Hartington's?"

Katherine clasped her gloved hands, hoping it would stop her head from spinning as it had the first morning, she'd awoken at the Hartingtons. "A pleasure to meet you, I'm Katherine Jenkins, Countess of Dysart." Fog clouded her brain, mushing her thoughts. Should she have referred to herself as Kate Vernon?

Mrs. Whitmore studied Katherine's expression. "The pleasure is all mine, heaped with gratitude for saving Isaac's life. Please come inside, and I'll ring for tea and scones and have my staff clean and fix your pelisse."

Katherine tried to examine the sleeve where she'd fallen but blackness crept into her periphery. *Do not dare faint and further embarrass yourself.*

Isaac tugged on his mother's gown.

"You won't be going to the park until you learn your lesson not to dart into the street. Carter will take you to your room, and I will send your papa up to speak to you."

Carter?

A man dressed like a butler stepped into her narrowing line of vision and held out his hand to the child.

Katherine startled and her head throbbed harder as blood coursed through her temples. She exhaled in an attempt to dispel the darkness.

Isaac's head lowered.

Do. Not. Faint.

"Are you all right, Lady Dysart?" Mrs. Whitmore's face floated in the dimming light. "You look pale."

"I might need to lie down." Katherine wavered on her feet.

"Oh dear." Mrs. Whitmore took her arm and instructed Carter to take the other. They led her up a flight of steps and into the townhome.

Katherine fought against the dark tunnel narrowing as she was guided down what felt like a hall. They turned and Katherine winced at the bright light streaming in through the window.

"Lay down here." Mrs. Whitmore's voice sounded distant and as if speaking to her through a pillow.

She was lowered onto a cushy service.

"Fetch Andrew and hurry."

"No need to fuss." Katherine refused to succumb to the darkness. "I rarely faint and just need a moment. I'll be hail in no time."

"*I*f Agent Scar discovers we're using Home Office resources to look for your ladylove," Jacob said, "the secretary is going to terminate us both, and I need this job."

Stephen gripped the arms of the shabby chair perched in front of Jacob's desk. His friend was right, but the Home Office was his last hope. He rubbed his temples and blocked out the smell of cheap pipe smoke and the colleague in the next office eating lox at high noon. He'd returned to London yesterday because the ticket collector recalled that Kate had purchased a ticket here. He'd inquired around the London station, but no one could remember a woman fitting her description. He'd stopped by his Mayfair apartment to shower and shave and sleep but knowing she could be on the streets had him up before dawn. All yesterday and today, he'd walked London's alleys and rat runs. He spoke to every nightwatchman, leaving his address and a reward for anyone who could locate a woman with curly hair and green eyes.

Kate was gone, lost in the largest city in all of England.

"There's not much to go on here." Jacob's feigned accent had disappeared. He stood and perched his hip on the corner of his desk with a frown. "Are you sure she didn't give any clues as to where she might go? People she knows in London?"

Stephen relayed the entire story again in case he'd missed a clue as to where he might find her. His voice grew tighter with each retelling.

Every so often, Jacob jotted down a note or two. He released a loud whoosh of air. "I hate to ask him, but Agent Scar might have a suggestion."

"We have to find her." Though it felt impossible. "See if any of his sources have heard of this Lord Pewitt fellow. He's why she ran. I just know it."

"Felix discovered Pewitt is Welsh, and not from this area." Jacob flipped back a few pages in his notebook. "We don't have much intelligence yet, but he used to frequent Tattersalls and was asked to leave. About three years ago, he disappeared and this is the first the Home Office heard about his reappearance."

Jacob slapped his notebook shut. "I don't mean to sound negative, but if she doesn't want to be found, London is the perfect place to hide. Keep thinking about conversations you shared. She must have let something slip. Send for me if you think of anything else." He clapped Stephen on the shoulder. "It pains me to see you like this, but don't worry. I have eyes and ears in every rookery and bawdy house in the city. I will put all my contacts on the alert for a petite, green-eyed, curly haired woman."

Stephen thanked his friend and exited the building. He should head home and try to slumber for a few hours, but his thoughts still whirled, and his limbs twitched to do something. He turned in the direction of Covent Garden to search there, and then he'd head to Whitechapel.

God willing, he'd find her.

Katherine awoke in a strange bedchamber adorned in blue papered walls and cream fabrics. She winced at the pain in her head and at the remnant of daylight still streaming in the window but at a lower angle.

Drat. At least she hadn't fainted this time. She'd laid down to rest—there's a difference.

"Oh, thank heaven, you're awake." Mrs. Whitmore rose from her chair near the door. "Let me get my husband." She darted out into the hall.

Katherine eased herself up into a seated position, careful not to jar her head. The evening hour approached, and she hadn't found a place to stay the night. Perhaps the Whitmores would be kind enough to allow her to stay the night until she could make other arrangements. She frowned. Did Stephen's butler and housekeeper have any luck in finding lodging for her or had they given up? Did they even know where she was, or did they think she disappeared?

A tall man with jet black hair knocked lightly on the door and entered with Mrs. Whitmore following close behind. She stopped at his side. "Lady Dysart, allow me to introduce my husband, Doctor Andrew Whitmore."

Dr. Whitmore bowed and offered her a kind smile. "I must first thank you for saving our son and apologize for putting you through such an ordeal." He pulled up a chair and sat next to the bed. He held up two fingers. "How many fingers do you see?"

"Two."

"And now?" He added an additional two.

"Four."

"Very good." He folded back all but his index. "I want you to track my finger." He moved it left and right. "Good." He leaned forward and held his palms near the sides of her head. "Do you mind?"

She shook her head and winced.

He dipped his fingers into her hair and probed her scalp. "You've got a bump on the right side of your head, but the swelling has gone down already. Can you stand?"

She flipped back the covers, and he aided her out of the bed. The dizziness had subsided a little.

"Walk a straight line for me."

She did as she was told while Dr. and Mrs. Whitmore watched.

"Hmm." The doctor scrunched his lips to one side.

Mrs. Whitmore exhaled and the stiffness in her shoulders eased.

"Please lie back down." He gestured to the bed.

Katherine complied but remained sitting up in the bed.

"I'd like for you to stay the night for observation but if you feel up for it you may join us for our evening meal, or we can have supper brought up to your chamber."

Katherine's breath caught. Who would have thought her having fainted would have been an answer to prayer?

Dr. Whitmore excused himself, but Mrs. Whitmore

lingered. "Is there anything I can get you or ring a servant to bring?"

"Actually." Katherine held back a smile at her good fortune. "Would you be kind enough to post a letter to my sister in Sherborne? It was one of the tasks I needed to undertake today."

"Most certainly." She moved to the rolltop desk on the opposite side of the room and removed several sheets of paper. "Would you like me to bring it over to you?"

Katherine raised her palm. "I'll write it at the desk. I don't want to accidentally spill any ink."

Mrs. Whitmore lingered. "I saw you leave Lord Hartington's apartment. Are you a relative?"

It was time she told the truth. Katherine swallowed. Why did her throat clog every time she needed to be open and honest about her situation?

Because others will realize how lacking you are.

Because you failed in keeping Steepleton Manor up to the Dysart standards

Because you allowed your cousin to march in and steal your inheritance.

Because you ran and hid instead of facing your problems.

Katherine opened her mouth to speak but the words refused to come.

Courage is a habit.

"I'm not a relative."

Mrs. Whitmore's eyes widened, and Katherine could almost read her thoughts. *Had she just allowed some lightskirt into her household?*

"I am a friend of the Hartingtons." She inhaled a shaky breath. "They have been very kind to me, and I had hoped to infringe upon their kindness, once more, while I wait for my solicitors to return from their trip. I hadn't expected to arrive in London so soon, and I needed help finding lodging."

"Ella." Andrew bellowed from below. "Let the countess rest for a bit."

"I must leave so you can heal." Mrs. Whitmore sidestepped toward the door. "But I trust Lord Hartington's judge of character, so you are welcome to stay as long as you like."

Katherine's jaw dropped. Mrs. Whitmore didn't question Katherine's character after being seen leaving Stephen's bachelor's lodging? She didn't ask why Katherine didn't carry any luggage? Or even why she'd come to London. She trusted Stephen and therefore trusted Katherine. The concept seemed so foreign after the disappointment of Alfred and the invasion of Cousin Horace. Her ability to trust had dwindled to just her sister, but then she met the Hartingtons and now the Whitmores. Maybe there were people out there she could count on after all.

With a compassionate smile, Mrs. Whitmore left the room and started to close the door behind her.

"Mrs. Whitmore."

She paused and peeked her head back in. "Please, call me Ella."

"Thank you, for your kindness, Ella, and I'd love it if you called me Katherine or Kate."Her smile widened. "Have a good rest, Katherine." She closed the door and the latch clicked.

---

*W*here could Kate have gone? Stephen had inquired at every boarding house in the city and searched the stews and back alleys, praying she'd turn up. He'd gotten into a fist fight with men who didn't like him asking questions. The men were in their cups and itching for a fight, and he reacted in self-defense but might have taken out a bit of his frustrations in the process. He sent up a prayer for forgiveness, and his bruised cheekbone and bleeding knuckles served as punishment.

Before dusk settled in, Stephen knew he needed a better strategy. He notified Bow Street about a missing woman with curly hair and green eyes. One young runner believed she'd come in the day before, but he didn't know where she went and only remembered that her complaint was out of their jurisdiction.

"Did she mention a Lord Pewitt?"

The young runner shook his head. "I can't recall. Bow Street was a mad house yesterday."

Stephen ground his teeth and told him to contact him if she was located. It was only out of a lack of knowing where else to search that he climbed onto his horse and rode to his townhouse in Mayfair. He needed to clear his head and devise a better plan. He blocked out some of the horrific sights he'd seen, like emaciated children and women who sold their bodies in exchange for a warm place to sleep and meager food. The thought of Kate being alone out there chilled him to his core.

Stephen strode up the front steps, and Wilson swung the door wide, offering his usual curt greeting, but stood a bit stiffer than normal.

"Inform the cook that I'm in need a of hot meal. I'll be in my study."

Stephen stalked into his office and sat behind his large mahogany desk. He rubbed his temples. Where else could he look? The image of Kate cradling the McLaughlin baby in her arms, and her standing at the top of the steps wearing the gown for the masquerade flittered through his memory. *God, I should have told her I love her. I can't lose her. Please, I need Your wisdom for what to do, how to find her.* Stephen leaned his head on the chair's backrest and stretched his long legs beneath the desk. If only he had wise counsel.

Andrew and Ella. They were precisely to whom he should

speak. If Andrew didn't know how to find her, then Ella might have some input from a woman's perspective. They'd pray for Kate if nothing else, and God's divine intervention was most needed.

A knock sounded on his study door. "Enter."

Wilson opened the door and stood in the entrance. Mrs. Bevel, the housekeeper, peeked over his shoulder. "My lord, you may prefer more time to get settled, but I thought it imperative to inform you that you had a visitor today who didn't leave a card."

He jerked upright. Had one of the Bow Street runners located her? "Did he leave his name?"

"She, my lord, and yes, the Countess of Dysart."

The Countess of Dysart had died in a carriage accident. The story had been all over the papers.

Kate.

He jumped to his feet. "What did she look like?"

"Curly, brown hair." He held up a hand near his chin. "About this height. Quite lovely if I may be so bold to say so."

Stephen skirted his desk to stand in front of Wilson. "Were her eyes green?"

"I believe so."

"Indeed they were, my lord." Mrs. Bevel spoke up behind Wilson.

Stephen gripped Wilson's elbows and beamed a smile at him. "Huzzah! God is good. Kate is here. Where is she? In the guest chamber?"

Wilson paled. "I'm afraid she left."

"Left for where?" Stephen gripped Wilson's elbows and sobered.

"I'm not certain, my lord." Wilson's Adam's apple bobbed, moving the knot in his cravat. "We told her we needed to seek your permission for her to stay, but we believed you we're still visiting with your parents at Willowstone. I'd offered to help her find a place to board, but she disappeared while we were having a carriage readied and brought around."

"Where did she go? We have to find her. Gather the staff. Someone must have seen at least which direction she went."

Mrs. Bevel wrung her hands in her apron. "I told her about my sister on Grange Road, perhaps she didn't want to put us out and hailed a hack to take her there?"

"Have a carriage readied. We can ride out there and see for ourselves unless the staff saw where she went." Stephen ran a hand down his face. Kate had been here. She'd come to find him, which either meant she missed him or was in desperate trouble.

Why would she disappear? It was like Kate to try to figure things out on her own, but why use the countess's name? Was Kate the dead countess whose body they believed had floated down river. Or had she taken up another alias, because Lord Pewitt had followed her to London, and she feared for her life?

Stephen gripped his hair.

Did she disappear because Pewitt had her in his clutches?

*K*atherine penned another letter to Claire, informing her sister about her plan to travel to Sherborne on Thursday. Her trip, however, was based on convincing her solicitors that she truly was the Countess of Dysart, and them allowing her to withdrawal enough funds.

A knock sounded on the door and Katherine opened it to find a petite maid standing there with a dress in her hands.

"Good evening, miss. The evening meal is almost ready, and my mistress has offered one of her gowns to borrow if you'd like to join the family. The mistress, also, said you may have a letter in need of posting.

"Indeed." Katherine retrieved the letter she'd written to Claire from off the desk.

The maid accepted the letter and stepped back out into the hall. "John." She waved the envelope above her head as a footman trotted over. "Find a messenger to post this letter."

The maid stepped back into the room and helped Katherine change for dinner into a pale green taffeta gown. It hung a tad loose on her frame, but the maid added a few stitches that could be removed after, making it look as if the gown had been made for her.

"I've never seen such a mass of curls." The maid fingered the springy bunch as she pinned them up into a spray of ringlets on top of her head. When she finished, she showed Katherine the way to the dining room. The hall clock struck eight and Katherine's stomach grumbled since she hadn't eaten since early morning. She'd also grown accustomed to the Hartingtons dining at country hours instead of city hours as the Whitmores followed.

Dr. and Mrs. Whitmore stood outside the reception hall talking to young Isaac. Dr. Whitmore kneeled on one knee. Katherine had never seen a man speak to a child on their eye-level. Isaac nodded at what his father said and threw himself into his papa's arms. The display drew a smile to Katherine's lips but also a stabbing pain to her heart, missing her own parents.

"All right, young man, you run along, back up to your room." Dr. Whitmore rose and tousled his son's hair. "It's past your bedtime. Go to your room and sleep."

"Yes, Papa." The boy raced up the stairs.

Ella sighed and smiled as Katherine approached. "He's a handful, that one, but such a treasure. I keep thanking God for bringing you along when He did. You were Isaac's guardian angel."

Had God brought her here for that reason, as He'd brought

the Hartingtons to discover her on the side of the road. What if rescuing Isaac had been God's plan all along? She inhaled and the weight of all that she'd endured the last few days lifted. She had been lost, wandering throughout this big city, but maybe God's hand had guided her with the intention for her to be in Mayfair at the proper time to save young Isaac. All her worries had come to naught. Elise had taken her in and now the Whitmores. God had provided. Maybe she needed to trust God. Stop fighting to go it alone in the way she thought best and allow Him to lead.

"Come. Dinner is ready to be served, and I can't wait to hear more about you." Ella guided the way into their formal dining room.

Katherine sat in the chair a footman pulled out for her. Candlelight danced from the tiered candelabras in the center of the table, and the highly polished silver shined in the light.

Ella and Andrew seated themselves near Katherine, leaving a huge expanse of the table untouched.

"I prefer a more intimate setting. It's much too difficult to communicate from the far ends of the table." Ella patted Andrew's hand before turning to Katherine. "Tell us about Dysart and your family?"

Katherine hesitated. She'd held the pretense of amnesia for so long that she hesitated before relaxing in the freedom to speak of her childhood. The footman served the first course, as she spoke, "I was born and raised in the outskirts of Laverton. I'd rarely left my small town until I came upon the Hartingtons."

"Truly." Ella sipped her soup. "I grew up similarly, in the small fishing town of Weymouth. My father was a sea captain and always out to sea. My grandmother and all of the townspeople looked after me, often teaching me their trades."

Andrew shook his head with a teasing glint in his eye. "And because of it she thinks she knows everything."

Ella flicked her napkin at him, pinching back her grin. Obviously, they were a love match. Katherine bubbled with laughter at the exasperated look Ella flashed her husband. A lazy half smile graced Andrew's lips, and his eyes glowed with warmth as Ella told of their first meeting and happily-ever-after ending. Ella said it was God's divine intervention that brought them together. Katherine longed for Stephen to look at her the way Andrew gazed at his wife.

Ella bombarded Katherine with questions, and she barely touched her first course before the plates were taken away. *Did she have any other siblings other than the sister she mentioned? Did she enjoy growing up in the country? Has she been to the city before?* She asked about Katherine's parents, and Katherine mentioned they had passed in a carriage accident.

"How dreadful." Ella's eyes clouded. "I'm so sorry." She leaned forward over her glazed ham and asparagus. "I know how devastating it is to lose a parent. My mother died when I was young. It was a tragic time, but my papa and I mustered through."

"My sister and I sustained each other, at least at first. She's been away at finishing school for the past year and a half."

"And you've been alone since then?" Ella splayed a hand over her heart.

"There's still the staff, and the running of the house and our stables keeps me occupied."

Dr. Whitmore speared a root vegetable. "You said your last name was Jenkins and that your parents passed. Are you related to the Jenkins' legacy of Lipizzaner horses?"

Katherine's chest swelled at the name her family had made for themselves—the same one she'd failed to preserve. "Indeed, I am."

His eyes narrowed. "You're the Countess of Dysart, but I read that she died recently in a carriage accident."

Katherine braced for him to react the same as her attorney

had. Would they believe her an imposter and throw her out on the street? Her breathing shallowed. Why did she tell them her real name? She should have stuck with plain unknown Kate Vernon. She exhaled a deep breath. No. She would speak the truth. It was time for her to trust God and let him lead.

"I survived the accident thanks to—"

A pounding resounded on the front door.

The butler bowed and exited the room to see to his duty, and Dr. Whitmore rose with a sigh. "It never fails that one of my patients needs tending whenever I'm in the middle of a meal."

Ella squeezed her husband's arm.

He peered at Katherine. "I beg your pardon. Ella will have to fill me in on the rest of your story later." He stepped out of the room and closed the door behind him.

She could stay? He'd believed her without even hearing her out? A strange giddiness tingled Katherine's stomach. Once again, God had provided.

*S*tephen sagged against the door frame, nauseous from the thought that he might never find Kate. His staff had witnessed Kate leave but they had resumed their duties and didn't see the direction she went. After a trek out to Grange Road on the outskirts of the city, Mrs. Bevel's sister hadn't had any visitors and hadn't seen anyone fitting the description of a curly-haired green-eyed woman. He'd returned to Mount Street and started knocking on doors to see if his neighbors had seen anything and was now making his way down the opposite side of the road.

What if Pewitt had her, or some ruffian out to lighten her pockets and have his way with her? What if her lifeless body is found in some rat run or floating in the Thames. The image of

Daphne's pale skin and dull bulging eyes bulging turned his stomach. He couldn't bear Kate to suffer a similar fate.

"God, please intervene," he whispered his prayer in a hoarse voice. "I will never forgive myself if Kate dies."

The Whitmore butler swung the door open. "Good evening, Lord Hartington."

"Stephen?" Andrew stepped around the butler. "I thought you might be a runner for one of my patients." He frowned. "You look knackered." He stepped aside. "Please come in."

Stephen shook his head. "I mustn't. I'm looking for someone. Her name is Kate Vernon." His voice cracked, and he rubbed his chin to get a hold of himself.

A deep frown puckered his friend's face. "As your physician, I think you should come in and rest a bit."

"I can't." Stephen backed up a step. "I have to find her." His friend would understand. "I love her. Just tell me if you've seen her. She was here on Mount Street this afternoon. I missed her." He no longer was making sense. All he could see was Kate's beautiful face crying out for help, and him not being there.

Andrew hooked his arm around Stephen's and led him into a drawing room adjacent the foyer and sat him in a chair. He signaled to the butler and said, "Bring a glass of brandy."

Stephen raised his palm and shook it. "No. I need to keep a clear head."

"What was the woman's name again?" Andrew stood over his still frowning.

"Kate. Kate Vernon." The weariness of the day hit him as if he'd run into a brick wall, but if Andrew hadn't seen her then he'd need to keep moving.

"I'm afraid I haven't met anyone with that name but—"

"Can you ask Ella?" There wasn't much time. Twight had already set, and the lamplighters were lighting the poles.

Stephen pushed to a stand. "Your staff, too. See if they've seen a woman with curly hair and green eyes."

Andrew's head drew back as if he'd been slapped.

The sound of a door across the hall opened and Stephen pivoted around.

Ella exited the dining room and turned to smile at a woman following behind her.

Stephen gripped the back of the chair to steady himself.

Kate.

CHAPTER 26

Stephen's brain struggled to function. Kate was alive, well, and looking lovely, in his best friend's dining room. His skin tightened with the overwhelming need to touch her, feel her, and make certain she wasn't a vision of his imagination.

"Kate?" He stepped forward and banged into a side table. A lamp wobbled but Andrew's hand steadied it. Trapped by the chair and table between them, he stood transfixed, praying she wasn't a figment of his imagination. He feared that if he blinked, she'd disappear.

Her gaze met his and she gasped. "Stephen." Her lips trembled into a smile and his knees weakened. She looked well. More than well, she looked magnificent. Her aqua dress brought out the green in her heavily lashed eyes.

"You're here,"—she blinked and her brow furrowed as if confused— "in London."

"You didn't think I'd come looking for you?" He skirted past Andrew and around the chair. "I've turned over half the city searching for you."

Ella stepped out of his way and strolled to her husband's side.

Stephen strode to stand in front of Kate, stopping at arm's length and using every ounce of his remaining energy not to sweep her into his embrace in front of present company.

Kate scraped her top teeth over her bottom lip in that endearing nervous way of hers.

Did she realize what she'd put him through? He wanted to shake her and make her promise to never leave him, ever.

"Ah, new love." Andrew's voice broke into his thoughts. "That must be how I looked when I first met you, darling." He slid his arm around Ella's waist.

"Why don't we have a seat?" Ella gestured toward the sofa into the drawing room. "Katherine had finished telling me about the accident and how you met, but I promised to fill in Andrew."

Stephen nodded but didn't take his eyes off Kate. Ella calling her Katherine rang in his head. Kate had referred to herself as Katherine after playing cricket with the children. Was she the countess? Wasn't the Dysart family affiliated with the Jenkin's Lipizzaner horses? There was much he needed to know and understand. He held out his arm for Kate to take. She threaded her hand through, and he placed his other palm over her hand as if it could prevent her from running off again.

She raised her chin, reminding him of the fiery wildcat he'd first encountered when he climbed in her window.

Ella and Andrew lowered onto the sofa while Stephen and Kate sat in high back bishop's chairs near the hearth.

An awkward silence filled the room as Stephen shifted in his chair to face Kate. His brain raised a thousand questions, but it was best to start with the basics. "Are you the countess?"

"You didn't kn—"

Andrew placed hand on his wife's knee and silenced her blurted statement.

"My real name is Katherine Jenkins, Countess of Dysart."

"You never had amnesia, did you?"

She shook her head.

Stephen's jaw clenched. "Why did you lie to me—to my family?"

"I was frightened." She sat on her hands as if to keep them from fidgeting. "If I told you who I truly was, I feared you'd have no choice but to send me back to my guardian."

"Who is your guardian? Why would you not want to return to their care?"

"Because he sent men to kill me."

Stephen's fingers dug into the wood of the chair's armrests to the point of snapping them in half. At several points in Kate's story, he stood up and paced raking a hand through his hair. If only she'd told him her predicament. Surely, she would have known he would have protected her. He swallowed. Or had she picked up on his accusations of thinking she might be involved in the horse thieving ring.

Stephen stopped pacing.

"He's after me because he wants possession of my father's Lipizzaner horses with official documentation. They're worth six times more than a regular stallion's price with the proper paperwork."

"And you wouldn't sign the papers over to him, so he threatened to kill you. That's why you ran?"

"He tried to force me to the altar, and that's why I ran."

"Why not just have you sign over the papers?"

"I assume not to raise questions, my father's attorneys and bankers would need to approve the signing since they manage the Jenkins fortune until I turn five and twenty or marry. I have to document all of the expenditures on the property for reimbursement and receive a monthly allowance. Less questions would be raised if he received the horses through marriage."

. . .

*W*ere the horse thieves that the Home Office had wanted him to lure out of hiding really fraudulent hucksters shaking down an innocent woman to take her inheritance? It certainly fit. They might have gotten away with it too, except they'd tried to kill her, which made them attempted murderers.

He hailed a footman. "I need a runner to locate Jacob Warren. The Home Office will know where to find him. Tell him I sent for him and that it's urgent." His gaze slid to Kate. "And tell Mr. Warren that an escort is to be sent to retrieve a Miss Jenkins from the Sherborne Finishing School for..."

"Young Ladies Decorum. A Miss Claire Jenkins." Kate's eyes misted and she flashed Stephen a thank-you look. "They'll need to speak with Madame Lamoureux and let her know they have my permission."

Ella grabbed a paper and pen from a nearby desk and passed it to Kate who jotted a note to the headmistress giving her authorization. She handed it to the servant.

The footman bowed and scurried off to do his bidding.

Ella returned to her seat and Andrew curved an arm about her shoulders, but addressed Stephen, "You're getting the Home Office involved? Not Bow Street?"

"This is bigger than Bow Street's jurisdiction." He sat on the edge of his chair and faced Kate. "I need you to relay your story to Jacob. You'll recognize him as the head groom, but he's my associate."

"Associate?" From Andrew's tone, he'd already discerned the truth.

Stephen glanced at the hoovering servants.

With a wave of his hand, Andrew dismissed them, and the butler and remaining footman filed out of the room.

Stephen released a long breath. If his cover wasn't already

blown, it would be once Jacob arrived. "I'm a domestic spy for the Home Office."

"*I*t's them. It's got to be, the unsavory rascals."

Stephen nodded his agreement to Jacob's statement. He held a better grasp on Kate's situation which should have brought relief, but he understood the professionals they were up against.

Jacob propped a boot up on the grate and rubbed his lower jaw.

Kate's gaze shifted from one man to another while Ella rang for another refill of tea.

"But Lady Dysart is right. Until we know if Bainbridge is officially her guardian, we can't charge them with anything. He has control of the funds and could have the parental authority to marry her off to whomever he chooses."

Andrew crossed his ankle over his knee. "Even himself?"

"The church requires that both parties must be willing." Jacob shrugged. "But Bainbridge can find a priest or reverend who'll look the other way as many have."

"How wretched." Ella waved in the butler carrying the fresh tea set.

Stephen waited for the man to leave before speaking, "And we can't bring him up with charges of attempted murder unless we have witnesses."

"Indeed." Jacob pushed off the grate and flopped onto Stephen's empty chair. "It will be a woman's word against Bainbridge's and he's well-connected."

Stephen pounded his fist into the palm of his other hand. "Blast."

"I can send my man to slip into the law office tonight and

inspect the files." Jacob laced his fingers behind his head. "We can have an answer by morning."

Katherine shook her head. "He took the will with him to review. We won't know until he returns."

Stephen paced behind Jacob. "The status of his guardianship won't put the fiend behind bars, and I want him locked up tight in Newgate for what he did to Kate."

"Then we'll need to stage an operation with Lady Dysart as bait." Jacob twisted his head to peer at Stephen. "But this time we'll have witnesses."

"Absolutely not." The boom of Stephen's voice startled Ella who spilt tea into the saucer.

"I'll do it."

Stephen's head jerked in Kate's direction.

She met his gaze with her familiar wildcat look. "I'm tired of running. If we don't stop him, who becomes his next prey? My sister? Another unsuspecting woman?"

He saw her as she'd stood down by the river, the breeze bouncing her curls, her wide smile brimming with laughter that she flashed over her shoulder as they raced, and his heart pounded just as it had when she'd cuddled the McLaughlin baby in her arms. The urge to protect her coursed through his veins, pulsing with every beat of his heart. He'd never let her go before some scoundrel.

He glanced in Andrew's direction for guidance. What would he do if it was Ella? Ella had curled her legs up onto the sofa and leaned against her husband's side. Andrew's arm rested across her shoulders. They'd played a key role in leading Stephen back to God and their marriage in inspiring him to leave bachelorhood behind and pursue Julia. But Julia hadn't been the right one. He'd known inside Kate was the woman for him the night she attacked him after crawling in her window.

"It's too dangerous." He still tried to dissuade her even

though what must be done clarified in his mind with increasing sharpness.

A wobbly smile flittered on her lips. "Then I'll leave it up to you and God to protect me."

He addressed the room, but his gaze stayed honed on Kate. "I need to speak with Kate."

"Alone."

---

*T*he room fell silent.

Katherine moved to sip her tea, but her hand shook so she set the cup and saucer down on the side table. Had she been hasty in her decision to face her cousin?

God would be with her. She didn't have to face this alone.

The fire popped beside her, and she jumped. *Lord, Give me courage.*

Stephen's gaze riveted in Dr. and Mrs. Whitmore's direction. "It will only take a moment."

Ella's mouth opened. Propriety's rules didn't allow two unmarried people to be left alone in a room together. She peered at her husband. Dr. Winthrop nodded his approval. "We'll leave the door open."

Stephen's dark expression left a foreboding presence. Katherine's palms burned, and her insides tingled. She loved Stephen but would he forgive her for all the mistruths? She was through with secrets. Falsehoods only caused pain and sorrow. From now on, she would trust in the One who controlled her destiny and not be blown around by circumstances like the cherry tree's petals in the wind. She prayed for strength. If only she could atone for her mistakes.

Stephen drew a chair in front of her, the same way he had the night he'd broken into her bedchamber. Katherine searched his face, but his expression remained aloof. At least the muscle in his jaw had stopped twitching. His gaze locked with hers, and the silence in the room grew deafening. Just when she started to squirm, Stephen said, "All the secrets must stop. From now on it's imperative that we be open and trust each other."

"Stephen, I..." It was too much—his nearness, the intensity of his eyes, his scent. She wanted to throw herself into his arms and weep, beg for his forgiveness. Instead, she squeaked out a pathetic, "I'm sorry."

She gripped the armrests and slid to the edge of her seat until their knees almost touched. "I'm sorry for the pain and embarrassment I have caused you and your family. It was never my intention. You have shown me kindness, and I have repaid you with regrets. I let fear rule my life, but I'm tired of being afraid. I believed I had to solely be responsible, or I'd be controlled by my circumstances, but God ultimately controls my fate, and from now on, I'm going to put my trust in Him. I am truly sorry and pray someday you will be able to forgive me."

He placed a hand over hers. "I'd better." He cleared his throat, and when he spoke again, his voice was strong and confident. "Otherwise it's a bad way to start a marriage."

Katherine blinked. "Pardon?"

"God has been nudging me and this confirms it. The only way that scoundrel of a guardian can no longer force you into marriage is if you're already married." He scooped her hand between both of his and rested his forearms on his knees. "I'll leave in the morning to obtain a special license."

"What?" Her mouth dropped open. "You don't hate me like you do your aunt? I was going to tell you the truth that day in the field when we saw the deer, but then I spotted her grave, and you were so angry. You said her secrets destroyed your family. I couldn't tell you after that. I feared you'd hate me like you did her."

"What she did to our family was different." The sorrow in his eyes, constricted her chest.

"Darling, you are not my aunt." He pulled her into his arms. "It will never be that way between us." His thumb stroked her back. "My aunt's selfishness hurt others, but you've helped me to see that I didn't know her story. There were likely factors beyond my knowledge that led her to make unwise choices and ultimately take her life and the life of her child. My parents had forgiven her. Maybe it's time I did too." He squeezed her hand. "You did what you had to do to protect yourself and your sister. I probably would have done the same."

Her heart inflated like a balloon, but reality's sharp pin burst it. "I don't want you to marry me out of a sense of duty or an obligation to protect me."

A crooked grin curved one side of his mouth. "I'm not marrying you out of obligation. I love you, and if anything, your disappearance proved my ardor."

She peeked up to confirm his sincerity.

"Do you know where I've been the past two days? After waking up long before sunrise, I visited every rooming house, searching for you."

He'd searched for her? For two days?

"I turned the city on its ear, combing through the scum and mire of every alley and rat run in the stews looking for you." He snorted "If only I'd thought to look next door."

Stephen hadn't arrived in London by happenstance. He'd come for her.

"I love you, too." She whispered the words to his taut profile. "I lost my heart to you by the river when you told me my hair was the color of barley." A strangled laugh sounded from her lips.

He cupped her face with both hands. "Then Kate" —he gave his head a little shake— "I mean, Katherine Jenkins,

Countess of Dysart, will you do me the great honor of marrying me?"

"Yes." She smiled past the tears of joy blurring her vision. "Of course, I will marry you."

He pulled her to a stand, and his lips swooped down on hers. Wrapping his arms around her, he cocooned her in his embrace.

"How lovely." Ella's breathless sigh sounded from the foyer. "Andrew, they're to be married."

Dr. Whitmore grunted. "I figured as much the moment they laid eyes on each other."

Stephen smiled against her lips, and she grinned back.

CHAPTER 27

*S*liding her feet out of bed and onto the cool floor,
Katherine stretched. A gentle breeze blew through
the crack in the curtains of the Whitmore's guestroom and
early daylight peeked through. Sleep had been long coming.
Thoughts raced through her head as she replayed last night's
sequence of events.

Despite the mess she made of things, God was bringing her
and Stephen together as man and wife. It was a miracle. She
would pledge her life to Stephen. She would no longer need to
make decisions on her own or feel as if all the weight rested
upon her shoulders. She'd cast her cares on God and know that
He cared for her. And now Stephen would walk by her side as
they navigated life together.

She could only pray that facing her cousin wouldn't land
her in an early grave. She wiggled out a shiver. God had
protected her so far. She would trust that He'd continue to
do so.

Her mama and papa would be pleased to have Stephen as a
son-in-law. If only they could be there for the wedding. At least

Claire will be at Willowstone Farm for the wedding. What a relief it will be to see her and know she is safe.

The same maid from last evening entered to help Katherine dress and escorted her to where Ella awaited in the breakfast room.

"How is the bride this morning?" Ella rose, beaming a bright smile as Katherine entered the dining room.

"Splendid." She sat in the chair the footman pulled out for her. "I feel like I'm dreaming, and I don't want to wake up."

Ella resumed her seat and sliced a strawberry with her knife. "When Stephen first saw you yesterday, I thought he was going to hurdle the end table and chair to get to you."

"Are you certain he wasn't considering strangling me after what I put him through, searching all of London?"

Ella laughed. "Definitely not."

Katherine smoothed her napkin in her lap.

"Isaac's nanny has taken him to the park and plans to keep him occupied for the day." Ella waved over a footman. "We have a lot of planning, and a short time to do it, so we'd better get started. I have an early wedding present for you." Ella turned her wedding ring on her finger. "I know that you won't have access to your trousseau and only have borrowed clothing at the moment, so I'd love for you to wear the gown I wore at my own wedding."

The footman held up a lavender taffeta gown with capped sleeves and a lace overlay.

Katherine gasped. "It's lovely." She fingered the high quality fabric. "But what about your future daughters? Won't you want them to have it?"

"Pish posh. It will be terribly out of fashion. If I have any future daughters, they most likely won't want to wear a relic."

"Are you certain?"

"I hope you like it."

"I love it." Katherine hugged her new friend. "I'm so grateful."

"I've already arranged for my maid to make a few alterations." She rose. "Before you break your fast, if you come this way, I'll have her place the pins so she can get started right away."

Katherine stood and put a hand to her stomach to calm her nerves. "This is really happening."

Stephen followed the butler into the Whitmore's dining room, smiling at the laughter flowing from within. Katherine and Ella sat at the table while a footman removed their empty plates. His pulse raced at the sight of the woman who'd become his bride the day after tomorrow. "Good morning, ladies."

Ella glanced up and waved him in. "Stephen, do join us. Andrew is with a patient but I'm certain you're here to visit someone else." She eyed Katherine. "Katherine was just telling me about some of her childhood adventures."

A pang twinged his heart for having missed out on hearing her tales. There was so much he wanted to know about Kate, but he knew her heart and that was what mattered most. He sat down in the chair across from her.

She peered at him with a silent question.

He patted his breast pocket. "I obtained the special license." It took some convincing of the poor archbishop he'd roused out of bed to grant him the license, but once he understood that a woman's life was in danger, he consented.

Katherine issued him a shy smile and a bit of color tinged her cheeks.

Ella didn't seem to notice. She clasped her hands together.

"Do go on. You're about to tell the story of your rock skipping abilities."

Stephen arched an eyebrow and the color in her cheeks deepened.

"It's actually a trifle embarrassing when I think back upon it." Kate glanced between him and Ella. "My parents decided to have a soirée." She laced her fingers in her lap. "My playmates and I stood on a small bridge over a little pond, seeing who could get a rock to skip the most times. I had been practicing and discovered a technique to bounce six times, beating the boys' record." Her shoulders straightened over her feat, and he could see the glow of pride in her face.

"The oldest boy, Alfred Turner, was infuriated, because it had been his record I'd bested. I was a silly young girl and tried my hardest to impress him with my abilities. As it turned out, Alfred didn't like losing, especially to the fairer sex. His face turned as red as a tomato. He told me that I couldn't do anything that mattered and pushed me into the water."

"The brute." Ella's jaw dropped. "How dare he."

"Instead of popping back up and crying for my mama like everyone expected me to do, I exacted revenge. At that age, I was good at holding my breath. Alfred's laughter died, and the other kids grew nervous when I didn't come out of the water. They all knelt on the bridge and peered down as I watched them from my position under a lily pad. Alfred panicked and leaned low to try to find me. My parents had chosen that moment to introduce Alfred's parents to my sister and me. Like a deranged sea monster, I lunged out of the water, grabbed Alfred by the ear, and pulled him headfirst into the pond."

Ella pressed a hand over her mouth, and a chuckle escaped from Stephen's lips, impressed by his wildcat.

"My parents were mortified." Kate stared at the space on the table where her plate used to rest. "Lord and Lady Turner were stunned as their son stumbled out of the water sputtering and howling. I stood, dripping wet, while Lady Turner ranted about my inexcusable behavior. I was sent to my room while my parents apologized for my conduct."

"I would have cheered you on." Ella crossed her arms. "I've never liked bullies."

"My parents might have, except they'd just finished signing paperwork betrothing me to Alfred."

Engaged? His jaw clamped so tight his molar felt like it might crack. What was this? Where was the cad now? Did he cry off? The dishonorable lout. Thank heaven, he didn't pull through. Stephen forced his mouth to relax.

"Did they call it off right then? Don't tell me you're still engaged to that bully?" Ella's eyes widened.

"They didn't call it off." Katherine's smile faltered. "Not then, but Alfred's father passed a few years later, and after my parents died in their accident, Lady Turner arrived on my doorstep and announced that, since no one remained alive who'd agreed to the silly engagement, there was no point in upholding it."

Ella gasped. "They backed out on their word when you needed support and comfort. How dreadful." Her voice softened. "God saved you from a life of marital heartache. You have my deepest sympathy for your parents. When my mama passed, I thought the world had ended." She smiled at the portrait of their family in the gilded frame on the far wall. "God, however, had other plans."

Stephen eyed the glass in his hand, fighting the urge to call out Alfred Turner. Picturing her as a small girl trying to defend herself against a childish brute burned the back of his neck. Her lack of trust could stem from her fiancé's rejection—especially at a time when she would have needed a husband.

He wanted to stand up and vow to her that he would be there for her. He wasn't some coward that backed out of his word, but those sentiments would be best proven by his actions instead of words.

Kate sipped from her teacup with the elegance of nobility. How had he not realized she was the countess? Maybe it hadn't occurred to him, because the countess was considered dead and because the sunken carriage was found two towns over which equated to about eighteen miles away. "There's one thing I keep trying to calculate. How did you find your way to Vernon Road?

"The carriage drifted down the river. I was still in Laverton when the bandits attacked." She set down her teacup.

"You walked a long way." His nerves pricked at the thought of her lying on the side of the road. "Alone?"

"I was too frightened to ask for help. I didn't know who could be trusted."

What if his parents hadn't come along when they did. His chest tightened.

Kate tilted her head. "How far do you think I traveled?"

"From Laverton to Vernon Road is still about twelve miles. Anything could have a happened if the wrong person came along." He puffed his cheeks and blew out the air. "I still can't believe you did it by yourself."

Kate chuckled.

"What's so funny about that?" Ella tilted her head.

"It's merely that Lady Turner, when she visited to ensure I was holding up to the standards of her son, told me I couldn't do anything on my own or without help." She shrugged a shoulder, but her eyes clouded, and he could see the hurt the contemptable woman had caused. "Growing up, I tried to prove Lady Turner wrong and do everything on my own, but I had a lot to learn. I failed often and she would point it out. Doing things without help made for a lonely life. The irony is that she and her son leaving me to fend for myself made me figure out how to accomplish things." She sighed. "But she'll never know it."

"You not only walked at least twelve miles, partially in the rain, you evaded a forced marriage to an evil wretch, protected your sister, endeared yourself to my family and me, and traveled to London and found shelter for two nights all on your own."

Her brow furrowed for a second before her chin lifted. "I did, didn't I."

"I could arrange a soiree after our wedding and we could invite Lady Turner and her coward of a son, and I'll use the moment to tell of your accomplishments."

"Make certain I'm on the invite list." A sly grin twisted one side of Ella's mouth. "I want to be present to see the look on Lady Turner's face."

"That won't be necessary, but I wouldn't mind running into Lady Turner at a ball where we can glide past her, proving I know how to dance the minuet." Kate pursed her lips. "I made one misstep due to Alfred's inability to properly lead, and Lady Turner sent a dance instructor so I wouldn't further embarrass my future mother-in-law. In front of my parents, she presented her critiques as a nice gesture, but when she cornered me alone, her sharp tongue would flay me alive. She'd tell me 'You'll never know how to pour tea without spilling. You'll never be able to manage a household if you don't understand what wines pair well with fish. The Turner name will be tarnished forever if you can't organize a seating chart. You should know Lady Otto despises Lord Colton and not to seat them next to one another."

Ella shook her head. "People like that aren't worth trying to please. Nothing can ever make them happy."

"Agreed." Stephen rose. "We'll leave her and her son to their miserable lives, but it is time for us to return to Willowstone and celebrate our future together."

*K*atherine leaned back into the plush velvet cushions of Stephen's carriage as it raced along the road to Willowstone Farm in Notgrove. Her life had taken so many turns recently she felt dizzy. After bidding farewell to the Whitmores, she and Stephen rushed off in his carriage.

A young Scottish lady's maid dozed off across from them who Stephen brought along from his own staff to assist Katherine. Unanswered questions begged to be voiced, like what had happened to Julia, why he spied for the Home Office, and a thousand more about their future together, but they weren't alone.

Katherine swallowed the butterflies in her stomach. She loved the Hartington family, but would they feel the same about her after disappearing without a note, explanation, or even a goodbye. She chewed her bottom lip.

"What is the matter?" Stephen asked.

She turned to face him, unsure if she should voice her concerns.

"You're worried about facing your cousin."

She exhaled a deep breath. "I'm deliriously overjoyed about marrying you, but the weight of what I must do hangs over me."

"We." He scooped up her hand and kissed the back of it. "You're not facing your cousin alone. We are in this together."

"That in itself is a relief but also a burden. I have been doing things on my own for so long, it seems surreal to have someone on my side. Claire would have been, but she was at school for the most part. The only thing is..." She stared at the buttons on his shirtfront.

He cupped her chin with his index finger and raised it until their gazes met.

She swallowed. "I don't want to lose you. I fear now not only for Claire but for you."

Stephen glanced over at the lady's maid, as if to ensure she was asleep, and pulled Katherine closer to his side. "God will protect us."

"I know." She sagged against his warmth. "I merely needed to hear it spoken."

She listened to the clopping of the horses' hooves and deep breaths of the young maid. "There's one more thing." She hesitated. "Your parents probably think I'm wretched running off the way I did."

"My parents adore you, and they will continue to do so for the same reasons that I do."

She searched his eyes to confirm the truth of his words.

He brushed his lips over hers.

Her fingers moved to feel the clean-shaven line of his jaw. He lowered his mouth once again to hers. His arms slid around her waist, drawing her closer still. Protected in the cocoon of his strong arms, she sagged against him. His kiss deepened, and a warmth spread through her stomach as if she'd taken a large gulp of tea.

The maid coughed and stirred.

Katherine jerked away and slid into her original spot on the cushion.

One side of Stephen's mouth rose in a grin, but his eyes smoldered as he held her gaze.

She swallowed and straightened her skirts, ignoring the flushed heat of her skin. Their separation did little to calm her rapidly beating heart. Breathless and containing a longing she didn't understand, she stared out at the passing moors to collect herself. This was to be her life. She bit back a smile but failed. After Alfred had cried-off and she was left to manage Steepleton manor, she'd believed that she'd missed her opportunity for love. She'd been happy to focus on her sister and see her happily married. After she'd settle for a gentleman who'd still have an off-the-shelf spinster or remain unwed. But God had turned her horrid circumstances around for His good and in the process gave her the secret desires of her heart.

God would protect them through the encounter with her cousin, but her stomach refused to settle until this unsavory business was behind them.

CHAPTER 28

$\mathcal{A}$s the carriage turned down the lane of Willowstone Farm, Kate shifted in her seat, crossed, and uncrossed her ankles, opened her fan, waved it twice, then folded it back up again.

Stephen laced his fingers with hers to ease her worry. If she was this nervous about confronting his parents, how would she be able to confront Bainbridge and Pewitt? He'd have to convince her and Jacob to resort to another plan.

He alighted from the coach and aided her descent but was loathe to release her gloved fingers. He didn't want to let her go —not to face her cousin, not even to see his parents. It had only been yesterday that he got her back, and he wanted to keep her for himself. Safe by his side.

A curtain rocked back and forth in the drawing room window, and seconds later, Abby flew out the front door and crashed into Stephen's side in her enthusiasm. "Hurrah. You found Kate."

Abby flung her arms wide and wrapped Kate in a tight hug until both women were wiping tears from their reddened eyes. Abby had already dealt with the sorrow of her husband having gone missing. Had Kate's disappearance added to her pain?

"Forgive me." Kate's tears splattered on the collar of her pelisse. "I can explain why I left without leaving a note."

Abby grinned and gripped both of Kate's hands. "I'm just glad you're safe."

Gentleman's training had Stephen reaching into his inside pocket and dangling handkerchiefs for both of them. Abby snatched hers and chuckled at their tear-soaked faces while Kate mopped her eyes.

The heavy oak door hinges squeaked, and the butler stepped aside for Lady Felton to pass. Spying Kate, she clasped her hands in front of her bosom. "Praise God. You found her." She called into the house, "Charles, he found her. God heard our prayers. They're both back safe and sound."

Stephen pressed a kiss to his mother's cheek, but she pulled him into a tight hug.

"Mother," Stephen laughed. "In the past, I've been gone for months and haven't received a reception like this."

She let go and swatted his arm. "I fretted over the unsavory places I knew you'd be searching. My knees are worn out from praying, but I'm grateful you're both home safe." She turned and opened her arms to Kate.

Choking back a sob, Kate fell into her embrace. "I'm sorry I caused you such a fright."

"I knew God would bring you back to us—back home." Mother hugged her so tight that fresh tears trailed down Kate's cheeks.

Home. Had God also been speaking to his mother's heart?

Pulling away, Mother grabbed both of her hands and held them. "Let me look at you. Thank God you are in one piece." She put a hand on Stephen's and Katherine's backs, guiding them toward the house like a mother hen. "You can explain everything over tea and sandwiches."

Stephen winked at Kate. "We have splendid news."

"Oh?" His mother and Abby skidded to a stop.

"Kate has her memory restored."

Abby gasped.

"She's Katherine Ainsley Jenkins, Countess of Dysart."

Mother placed a hand over her heart. "The countess everyone believed had drown?"

"The very one." Stephen nodded. "But very much alive."

"Good heavens." Abby stared at Kate as if seeing her for the first time.

"And we're to be wed, as soon as her sister arrives tomorrow." He casually tossed out the momentous information.

Abby gasped. "Truly?" Her pitch rose several octaves.

Kate froze and her gaze slid to his mother.

Mother pressed her clasped hands to her chest. "It's about time."

---

*A*fter all the hullabaloo settled and a celebratory meal was eaten, Stephen caught sight of Jacob strolling past the window towards the servant's entrance in the back and excused himself from the wedding chatter.

Jacob stood in dusty head groom clothes with a crooked smile on his face, leaning against the kitchen doorframe with his ankles crossed and his hands in his pockets. Giggles emanated from inside the kitchen as one of the scullery maids succumbed to Jacob's sweet-talk. He reached forward and accepted something wrapped in cloths. He sniffed it. "It smells almost as delicious as you."

More giggles followed.

"I'd like to hear about the horses." Stephen's voice boomed in the small dimly lit back hall. "Have a moment?"

"Evenin' gov'ner." Jacob winked at the maid. "I 'ave all night."

He answered Stephen's question, but his tone sounded like a proposition to the kitchen maid. Stephen snorted with a shake of his head and ushered Jacob into his office. "Please, take a seat." Stephen gestured to a leather chair and sat behind his mahogany desk.

"I met with Agent Scar this morning, before returning with your coach" Jacob's accent fell away and his expression sobered as the cavalier head groom switched personas. "He received word from Felix that this Lord Pewitt fellow has had underhanded dealings in Wales, and he's thought to have been involved three years ago in a scheme where false horse pedigree papers were pawned off as originals. The fake purebloods were sold at Tattersalls and created a stir among the horse breeding community."

Jacob set the wrapped treat aside and laced his fingers across his stomach. "It can't be confirmed but it's believed, that before Pewitt went underground, he'd swindled London's nobility out of fifteen thousand pounds."

Stephen whistled.

"Up until,"—his comrade leaned forward—"a man brought the forged documents to Richard Tallersall and the repository's attention—one Lord Gerald Augustus Jenkins, the Viscount of Dysart."

Stephen jolted. "Kate's father."

Jacob nodded. "And it can't be purely coincidental that her parents died in a carriage accident and the countess was attacked and thought to have drown in a carriage accident too, after Pewitt resurfaces."

"How was not more made of this? Why wasn't Lord Pewitt hunted down?"

"You know how the nobility can be." He shrugged his shoulder. "They'd prefer to land in debtor's prison than be

made to look a fool. It all became hush-hush for no one's reputation to be sullied."

"But Kate's parents were killed."

"There was no proof, because their deaths were made to
look like an accident, and that's what the nobility wanted to
believe."

"Confound it." Stephen pounded his fist on the armrest.
"We must bring in this ne'er-do-well or he could continue to
murder innocent people." Stephen shook his head. "I don't
want Kate involved in the operation. It's too risky. There must
be another way."

"Let's hear it?" Jacob leaned his elbow on the arm of the
chair and rested his chin on his fist.

"There's a local horse fair at Stow-on-the-Wold in two days'
time. We could bait Pewitt and Bainbridge there as potential
buyer and have them illegally sell us a horse."

"If Bainbridge has guardianship, then it wouldn't be a crime
for him to sell a horse and gift Pewitt the proceeds or use it to
pay down debts owed to Pewitt." Jacob rubbed his upper lip
with his index finger. "I have some interesting intel on Mr.
Horace Bainbridge, too."

"Go on."

"Mr. Horace Bainbridge was married to Madeline Jenkins,
the eldest daughter of the viscount's brother. In lesser circles
Lady Dysart's cousin one removed was referred to as Bain or
HB Bain."

"Bain." Stephen leaned over his desk. "Not the same Agent
Bain who used to work for the Home Office?"

"Now you're catching on." A smile broke out on Jacob's face.
"The very one."

"Didn't he turn rogue and become a mercenary no longer
working for the Crown?"

"Last I heard"— Jacob shifted to the edge of his seat—"he

stormed out of the office before he could be terminated, threatening to take matters into his own hands."

"What matters?" Stephen drew his brows together.

"Bainbridge has been unstable since the death of his wife." Jacob turned his palms up.

"If I recall correctly, Agent Bain went undercover as a horse thief to infiltrate a horse-stealing ring. From what I understand, things went bad quickly."

Jacob lowered his voice. "This isn't fact, but the whispers were that Agent Bain's wife slipped information to her brother-in-law, who we now know was Lord Dysart. Lord Dysart exposed Bainbridge's actions and was slated to be terminated— if he hadn't stormed out first."

Stephen fell against his chair's backrest and stared at his friend. "A few days later, Bainbridge's wife turned up dead, and a month later, Lord Jenkins and his wife died in a carriage accident."

"But was the culprit Lord Pewitt, Bainbridge, or both?"

"Kate won't be stepping foot into that pit of vipers." Stephen spoke through clenched teeth.

Jacob exhaled a long low sigh and lowered his gaze. "I don't know of another way." He locked gazes with Stephen and remorse darkened his eyes. "Lady Dysart should be the one to decide. It was her family members who were killed, and it's her life and that of her sister's that's being threatened."

Stephen pounded the side of his fist into his palm. "Thunder and turf."

---

*S*tephen pulled Kate into the library, desperate to get her alone. His parents had gone off to bed sleepy from all the excitement and the only way he could get Abby to give them a moment was to send her on a mission to pick out his attire for tomorrow. He turned up the oil lamp on the table next to the highbacked leather reading chair, and he leaned against the mantel of the adjacent fireplace. The rows of bookshelves and warm marble-surround hearth framed a cozy atmosphere.

"I confirmed with our local reverend that he will marry us tomorrow." Stepping close, he tucked a curl behind her ear. He'd once fancied himself in love with Daphne, but what he felt for Kate wasn't merely intrigue, fascination, or attraction. No one had captured his heart as Kate had. He wanted to spend the rest of his life loving her, teasing her about her competitive spirit, laughing at her frustration with those beautiful but unruly curls, and learning everything about her.

He had some catching up to do with her past, but he knew enough about her heart to vow to love and cherish her for the rest of their days. Anyone who would risk her life to save a young boy from being trampled by a carriage, manage an estate with little guidance other than the servants input, and who'd fight to save her holdings from a tyrant, all the while protecting her sister by keeping her whereabouts secret, was someone he could respect. And when wrapped in a lovely feminine package with the most beguiling green eyes, he couldn't prevent his heart from falling hard. Leaning in close, he brushed her velvety lips with a kiss. The slightest touch opened a spicket of ardor he struggled to keep under control. "Tomorrow can't come soon enough."

He deepened the kiss, wrapping her in his arms. She fit perfectly against him, and the warmth of her skin set his own ablaze. Two days ago, he drove himself to the brink of madness thinking he might not ever see her again. His arms tightened, and his fingers slid into silky curls at the nape of her neck. He couldn't let her go—not into the lair of potential murderers.

He broke off their kiss and gasped for breath. His chest rising and falling along with hers.

Her cheeks blushed with a lovely pink hue.

He reluctantly stepped back and gestured for her to have a seat. "There is more brewing regarding the Pewitt fellow with whom your cousin is involved."

The color drained from her cheeks as she slid into the chair.

Stephen crouched in front of her and placed a hand on her knee. "I hope you realize now that I would never let anything happen to you."

She nodded.

"Jacob pulled me aside earlier. He and I are still working on another plan to put your cousin and his accomplices behind bars. I don't want there to be any more secrets between us, so you need to know what we're up against. Your cousin used to be an agent like myself."

Her lips parted in a silent gasp, "How could that be? Madeline never said anything."

"Madeline wouldn't have known."

Kate quieted and a crease formed between her brows. "He threatened me, struck me with his own hand, and tried to have me killed. Why would the Crown trust a man like him?"

"This line of work can alter a man. The things we see and are asked to do..." The image of Daphne's unseeing gaze haunted him, and he swallowed down bile. He'd been the one to acquire the list of French spies and hand it over to the Home Office. At the time he'd been in denial that Daphne's name would be on that paper, but his sentiments for her had blinded him to the signs. His resolve deepened to protect Kate at all costs.

"Lord Pewitt is a professional swindler, manipulator, and thief. He and your cousin are suspected of being involved in both Madeline's murder and that of your parents."

Kate's lower lip trembled, and he covered her hands with his own.

"What I need from you is a detailed schematic of Steepleton Manor, a list of every servant's name, age, and description, and everything you can remember about your cousin and her husband."

She exhaled and nodded.

"We've put Steepleton Manor under surveillance, and it's only a matter of time before they make a mistake. Time is on our side, and God willing, they will never cause you an ounce of worry again."

---

*T*he next morning Kate entered the sunlit breakfast room. Footman buzzed around the table refilling cups and serving food. She could hear Lady Felton and Abby's chatter before she even entered but her gaze fell upon Stephen and the rest of the room blurred. Today she would become his wife. A giddiness welled up that she tried to suppress. She shouldn't feel this happy, should she? Not when her cousin still held her home hostage and her sister was yet to arrive.

Spying her, Stephen's lips spread into a leisurely smile as intimate as the kiss they'd shared last evening, and warmth flowed into her cheeks. "Ah, the blushing bride has awoken." He rose and pulled out the chair next to him and seated her.

Abby gripped the edge of the table, and her voice hummed. "Today I gain a sister." She leaned over her plate. "And I'm so grateful it's you."

And not Julia. Katherine heard the unspoken relief in Abby's phase.

"We couldn't have a lovelier day for a wedding." Lady Felton patted Katherine's hand in that motherly way of hers. "What do you think, Charles?" She peered at the corner of the room where Lord Felton sat in his favorite chair, but the paper lay on his chest and his eyelids had closed. He'd dozed off, but instead of waking him, a softness lit her eyes.

Katherine glanced at Stephen's profile who turned to nudge his father awake. She would she and Stephen over the years hold a love as deep as Lord and Lady Felton?

Lord Felton jolted upright at his son's prod and answered a question he most likely hadn't heard. "Yes, dear."

Abby and Stephen chuckled.

The day was indeed lovely. Warm sunlight streamed in through the windows and only tiny white puffy clouds floated by.

A footman cleared his throat behind Stephen. "A Mr. Warren is outside, my lord. He's asked to speak with you and insists that it's urgent."

"See him to my study." Stephen rose.

Kate gripped his arm certain it involved her cousin's doings. "I'm coming with you."

Stephen didn't protest as she pushed back her chair, and instead, Stephen aided her to rise.

"But you haven't eaten." Lady Felton frowned.

"It should only be a moment." She bobbed a curtsy to Lady Felton and Abby, excusing herself and followed Stephen out of the breakfast room and down the hall to his study.

Mr. Warren slouched in a leather chair, rubbing his chin as they entered and jumped to a stand. "I have sensitive news." He offered his seat to her and moved to stand near the wall with his arms crossed and legs in a wide stance. His face appeared haggard and his natural savoir faire lacking. "The escort has returned."

"My sister?" She squeaked the words past the tightness in her throat.

Stephen placed a hand on her shoulder, and Katherine hugged her stomach to guard against the bad news written in Mr. Warren's expression.

"Miss Jenkins didn't return with the escort."

Katherine gasped.

"She stayed at the school?" Stephen's other hand came to rest on her other shoulder, but whether it was for comfort or to restrain her from jumping out of her chair and absconding with the Hartington carriage to locate her sister, she wasn't certain.

Mr. Warren winced. "Not exactly."

"Why don't you start from the beginning."

"The man we sent to be her escort, Agent Felix, returned this morning after traveling most of the night. He was told that Miss Jenkins had left earlier that day, and they could not disclose where or with whom she had gone. He demanded to see Madame Lamoureux, but she too was absent, and the staff was unable to say where she'd gone or if the two women were traveling together. The school was locked down tighter than Newgate prison and not welcoming of visitors especially of the male variety, but he slipped in as a servant and found that indeed, Miss Jenkin's bags had been packed, and she'd left the premises."

"My sister's gone missing?" Katherine tried to rise but Stephen's firm hold kept her seated. She covered her mouth with her hand. "He has her. Oh Lord, please no."

"We don't know if it was Bainbridge. There was no sign of a struggle." Mr. Warren shook his head.

"With his cunning there wouldn't be." She doubled over, her stomach heaving. If Cousin Horace had her... All she could see was Claire's innocent tear-filled eyes staring up at her the day they learned of their parents' accident and asking, *who's going to take care of us?* Katherine had pulled Claire into her arms, hugging her tight. *I will. I will always take care of you.* She was going to retch. She should have gone straight to the Sherborne School. She should have tried harder to find a way. Why did she believe Claire was safe at school? *God, I failed. I failed at the most important thing—keeping Claire safe.*

"Our men are looking into it," Mr. Warren said.

"Don't fret." Stephen rubbed her arms. "We'll find her." She felt him straighten and address Mr. Warren. "Has Agent Scar had any activity at Steepleton Manor? Any carriages coming or leaving?"

"I sent an agent to find out." Mr. Warren pulled a pocket watch out of his breast pocket and flicked it open. "He should return by early afternoon."

Stephen moved to crouch down in front of her and cupped her face in his palms. His gaze held hers sure and steady. "We're going to find her. You're not in this alone anymore."

Katherine wrapped her arms around his neck and clung to him.

———

A knock sounded.

Stephen pulled away, hating to do so when Kate needed his comfort. "Come in." He rose.

Weston stood in the doorway. "My lord, a visitor has arrived to see the Countess of Dysart."

"Did they give their card?" Who knew Kate had returned? A jolt ran through his body. Besides his family and the Whitmores, who knew Kate was Lady Dysart?

Weston handed Stephen the card.

The name Horace Bainbridge was written in elegant script.

It couldn't be. Not yet. He stared at the name willing it to change to someone else. He and Kate hadn't exchanged vows, nor finalized the plan. They weren't ready.

Jacob peeked at the card over his shoulder and stiffened. "Blast."

"Who's here?" Kate's eyes widened, her face ashen. She clutched Stephen's forearm. "It's my cousin. He's found me."

A fierce protectiveness blazed through Stephen. With great effort, he maintained an outer calmness that he didn't feel. "This will be the last time he disturbs you. Give me one minute to tend to him."

Jacob blocked his exit. "This could be our only chance."

Stephen pushed past him.

"What about her missing sister?"

Kate jumped up and yanked him back with a strength he didn't know she had. "We can't let them hurt Claire."

"We'll have to play along with his plan," Jacob's tone rang with authority. "Men are in place. We can bring them down from the inside."

"I don't see how throwing Kate into the mix aids our position."

"We need her to get them to reveal their intentions in front of witnesses." Jacob stepped closer and set his jaw. "It's the best way."

"I won't allow it." Stephen crossed his arms, and his tone lowered to a deadly growl. "If anything happens to her..." His chest tightened. "I won't allow Kate alone with that monster for a single moment."

"Claire's my sister." Katherine pleaded with her eyes. "You'd do whatever it would take to save Abby. I must do the same."

His shoulders slumped.

"God will protect me." She placed a hand on his chest and smiled a weak grin. "Besides, I won't be alone."

Stephen entered the drawing room after he and Jacob had worked through a sketch of what Stephen deemed a shaky plan. A pit opened in his stomach, but thanks to years of training, he forced an easy stride and a neutral expression. Three men had gathered there. The local constable, a middle-aged man with thinning hair and gray at the temples, and a man with beady eyes he recognized as the Grimm reaper. He must be Lord Pewitt, which meant the middle-aged man was Bainbridge. Stephen gritted his teeth. "What can I do for you, gentlemen?"

The dandified Bainbridge stepped forward with what Stephen deemed as misguided self-assurance. "Ah, Lord Hartington, I'm sorry if our unannounced visit has caused you any inconvenience."

The man exuded the air of a power-hungry politician who would say or do anything for position and money.

"As soon as I heard my wife had arrived in town, I made haste before she discovered a chance to run again."

"Your *wife*?"

Mr. Bainbridge flashed him a sympathetic smile. "She is the former Lady Katherine Ainsley Jenkins of Dysart, now Lady Bainbridge."

"I believe you're mistaken." *Lies, all lies.* Stephen forced his expression to remain devoid of emotion.

Bainbridge strutted around the room, his hands clasped behind his back and his gaze occasionally meeting Stephen's. "Soon after our marriage, Katherine decided married life didn't agree with her." He waved a hand in the air. "Women let emotions rule their lives, so she left, without any notice, to be with her sister. She had barely gone as far as the edge of town when roadside bandits attacked her carriage. I'm certain you've heard about her disappearance in the papers. It wasn't until recently that my good friend"—he clapped Lord Pewitt on the shoulder—"discovered her alive and residing here. From what I've heard, I fear her memory hasn't been serving her correctly."

Stephen clenched his teeth and sucked in a deep breath,

fighting to remain calm and not plant a facer onto Bainbridge's haughty nose. He didn't believe one bit of Mr. Bainbridge's Canterbury tale, and yet the scoundrels looked at him as if he were wet behind the ears.

"I understand my wife's deceptive ways. She probably lied to you as she has to me. I understand any hesitation, which is why I brought the marriage certificate signed by Lady Bainbridge and myself."

If Pewitt had forged horse breeding documents, he could falsify a marriage certificate. Yet a wave of cold terror ran up Stephen's spine. Was Kate married to this man? Surely she would have confessed when he proposed, but she'd lied before. The possibility weighed like a rock in his stomach, but he shook it off.

Bainbridge held out the document for him to take. It had to be a forgery. Of course, it was.

In the Borough of Dysart in the county of Wiltshire, it is hereby known to one and all that Mister Horace Fredrick Bainbridge and Lady Katherine Ainsley Jenkins, Countess of Dysart were united in the bond of holy matrimony...

The words blurred. Stephen squeezed his eyes tight and then opened them to refocus on the signatures at the bottom of the page. There in slanted, feminine script, was the name *Katherine Ainsley Jenkins*.

Blast. It looked real, and its mere existence, even forged, chilled his core. He and Kate were to have been married this afternoon, but Bainbridge appeared the day after their arrival as if he'd staked out Willowstone Farm, waiting for them. Could he force Kate's hand, or did he even need to do so with the fake certificate?

Stephen could feel the weight of Mr. Bainbridge's stare as if his eyes burned holes into his head.

"I'm looking for you to return what is mine." Bainbridge widened his stance. "Lord Pewitt is here as a witness to the ceremony, and the constable has joined us to ensure my wife's transition back into my care goes smoothly."

He was supposed to summon her—act angry at her lies and tell her to pack her bags—but he couldn't do it. Kate's heartshaped face floated in his mind's eye. He heard the tinkling of her laugh as they raced across the meadow, her hair loose in the wind. How could he surrender the woman he loved? *God, please, there must be another way.*

---

*K*atherine shook out her cold fingers and swallowed. She wasn't facing her cousin alone. God was with her, as were Stephen and the entire Hartington family. Her cousin held no power over her.

She turned toward the drawing room. *God can save me from this, and even if He doesn't, I will not bow down to criminals.* Katherine lifted her chin. *I put my trust in God.*

She quietly pushed open the door to the drawing room. Her eyes landed first on Stephen, whose face was overly pale.

Lord Pewitt grinned at her with a sickly smile of victory.

"My love." Horace extended his hand toward her. "There you are."

Love?

Like a panther smelling weakness, he maneuvered around Stephen and came to stand in front of her, blocking her view. "I'm so glad you are alive. You have no idea how much I missed you." He kissed her cheek and wrapped his arms around her. To Stephen, it probably appeared as a lover's embrace, but Horace's fingers entangled themselves in her hair at the nape of her neck, drawing tight and forcing her ear to his lips. "If you go along with what I say, no one will get hurt, especially not your sister."

It was true, then. They had Claire.

His other hand pressed on her lower back, and something steely and cold poked into her stomach.

A gun.

Horace pulled away but clasped her elbow. She held back a scream. Doing so could end in someone getting shot. Her mind whirled in a thousand directions. *God is with me.*

A light tap sounded at the door. Lady Felton entered the room, followed by Abby. "Lord Pewitt, I'd say it was a pleasure, but your last visit caused quite a stir. I'm afraid we must ask you to leave."

Had Lady Felton and Abby been apprised of the situation?

Lord Pewitt's lips twitched. Katherine wasn't sure if he enjoyed inflicting people with pain or relished the challenge. "Good afternoon, Lady Felton, I'm afraid this visit is of a similar nature, but we'll be on our way." He gestured for them to leave, and Horace pushed Katherine toward the door. "Your son will explain everything."

That muscle twitched in Stephen's jaw—a telltale sign he was doing everything in his power to keep his temper under control. A pained expression crinkled the corners of his eyes. Her name written on a certificate lying on the table caught her eye as she passed. She scanned the contents—a marriage certificate. Stephen would know it's a fake, wouldn't he?

"I'm not—"

Cold steel pressed into her back

—married. She swallowed the crucial word.

Cousin Horace stepped closer, his fingers gripping her waist as a married couple would. Doing so hid his weapon from view.

"She stays here until we can verify all the witnesses." Stephen's deadly calm voice sliced through the air.

Horace turned to face Stephen. "I was hoping it wouldn't

come to this, for our sakes and yours, I was hoping to avoid a scandal." With a dramatic pause, he shook his head. "But by British law, my wife is my property. If you are going to be unreasonable, the constable will have no choice but to intervene."

Stephen's face reddened and the constable stepped toward him.

"No." Her voice punctured the tension in the air. "I will go."

Cousin Horace snorted his approval. "We shall take our leave, then. Good day." He grabbed the certificate from off the table and stuffed it into his coat pocket, but not before Katherine glimpsed her sister's name as a second witness.

God, please protect Claire.

"Lord Pewitt, lead the way." Horace shoved her from behind.

She peeked over her shoulder for one last look at Stephen. Lines of strain hardened his face as his sister and mother bombarded him with questions.

Would this be the last time she looked upon their faces? Tears blurred her vision, and she stumbled as her cousin half dragged her down the hall and out the door to their coach. Jacob opened the coach door dressed in the Jenkins livery. She tried not to stare. How was he able to trade places with a Jenkin's footman? He tipped his hat and his reassuring gaze met hers.

She wasn't battling alone.

Horace shoved her inside. He and Lord Pewitt sat across from her, and the constable settled beside her. Katherine didn't say a word, only tilted her chin high so the burning tears wouldn't fall.

Lord Pewitt rapped on the ceiling, and the driver set the horses into motion. "Better start accepting your destiny, my dear, because we won't be so kind if something like this happens again." He flashed a wicked grin. "Lies can be sticky, can't they, Lady Bainbridge?" He laughed at his wit—a hideous, callous laugh that made Katherine's insides cringe.

Horace squeezed just above her knee hard enough for her to wince. "You are going to become much more biddable now. Aren't you, my dear?"

She wanted to shrink into the cushions and curl herself into a tight ball, but Abby's words rang in her mind, *courage is a habit.* The scripture Abby used to face her fears popped into her head. *God did not give me a spirit of fear, but of power, love and self-control.*

"I demand for you to take me to my sister."

Lord Pewitt snickered an evil laugh. "You aren't in a position to be demanding anything."

Katherine refused to give Lord Pewitt or her cousin the satisfaction of seeing her afraid. Even though her future looked bleak, she knew Shadrach, Meshach, and Abednego had faced a furnace seven times hotter, but they trusted God. Confronting her cousin was *her* fiery furnace, and she knew God had the power to rescue her. But if He didn't save her for reasons she might not be able to comprehend?

Would she marry her cousin to protect Claire?

Bitter bile churned in her stomach, knowing what she could have had with Stephen.

She'd undergone a lot of strain, but in the end, God led her to be in the right place to save Isaac. Her cousin thinks he can get away with cheating and maybe dealing from the bottom of the deck, but there were consequences. The Home Office was on to him, and the winning hand would ultimately be God's.

CHAPTER 29

*K*atherine kept her breathing steady as the coach rocked. Unable to stand the sight of Lord Pewitt eying her like she was Christmas dinner, she pretended to be sleeping. Memories of Stephen dancing with her in the field, refereeing the children's cricket game, and tucking a strand of her hair behind her ear shredded her heart.

"I daresay she's asleep." Lord Pewitt whispered. "Let's run through your objectives once again. My buyer is eager for those stallions, and I'm eager to take his purse."

Katherine strained her ears to comprehend Lord Pewitt's hushed tone.

"If for some reason the Hartingtons weren't persuaded by our little farce, and lover boy comes sniffing around for her, then you'll need to make his death look like a jealous lover situation gone extremely wrong."

Katherine's insides turned to sludge. *Oh God, Stephen was in danger*. She must tell Jacob to warn him. Their voices lowered even more, and Katherine could no longer make out what they were saying.

God, don't let Stephen come for me—not if he could end up dead. Protect him, please.

Lord Pewitt cackled, and Katherine startled. The hairs on her neck stood on end.

"You woke her." Horace frowned. "Just as well, since we are pulling up the drive."

Katherine peered out the window to where Sugar grazed in the pasture. Steepleton Manor looked the same, and memories of her happy childhood flooded back. If the situation had been different, her homecoming would have involved bringing Stephen here to visit. He would have loved the pastures, and they could have ridden side by side together as she showed him the house and land where she'd spent all of her childhood days. He'd be delighted with the expanse and quality of their stables, and he could even have set up another training ground and doubled his business. However, Stephen wasn't with her, and she dreaded what lay ahead.

The carriage drew up in front of the house. Horace, Lord Pewitt, and the constable exited the coach before her. She would be more vulnerable within the house—at the complete mercy of her cousin.

Her legs refused to move.

I am with you.

Those small words were spoken into her heart. She could feel God's presence like a steadying hand. Her shoulders relaxed and her breathing slowed. Everything was going to be fine. She had no idea if their plan would work, but God was bigger than her circumstances.

She descended from the carriage, and her cousin tucked her hand into the crook of his arm. His haughty gaze changed as their eyes met. Suddenly, he looked uncomfortable—vulnerable, and he looked away. He escorted her toward the house, but he didn't speak or glance in her direction until they entered the foyer.

Denton, her faithful butler, stood with his head high and chest puffed out, but broke his stern demeanor with a broad smile when he greeted her.

Her cousin brushed by, but Katherine stopped in front of her longtime friend, wrenching her arm out from her cousin's grasp. Horace continued to her father's office, shutting the door behind him.

"Denton, it is good to see you."

The butler bowed, and his eyes sparked. "It is good to see you in good health, m'lady. We believed the worse had happened." His gaze filled with concern.

"Enough talk." Lord Pewitt gestured for her to move along. "We are starving. Make certain the noon meal is served in fifteen minutes." Turning, he bellowed for a servant, and several appeared, tripping over themselves and each other to form a small line about ten feet in front of him. They each bobbed a curtsy, and Katherine noted they all stared at the floor, their fear of him evident.

"You." Lord Pewitt pointed to a small girl on the end. "Assist your mistress to her room to change. Do not let her out of your sight. If she is not in the dining room in fifteen minutes, your son will not eat for a week." He eyed Katherine with a smug expression, leaving no doubt that this was to display his control. "Do I make myself clear?"

"Yes, my lord." The maid bobbed several curtsies.

He turned and strode down the hall with the constable. Their footfalls slapped the hard marbled tile.

"I demand to see my sister," Katherine yelled.

Lord Pewitt raised a hand but didn't stop or look back. "All in good time."

Katherine tried to offer the ladies' maid a smile of courage, but the poor girl continued to stare at the floor. She turned to Denton and lowered her voice to a whisper. "Where are they keeping Claire?"

Denton's body jerked. "Miss Jenkins?" He offered the lightest shake of his head. "Not here, my lady."

God, I must save Claire. Where could she be? How will I find her now? What shall I do?

He whispered, "And I daresay it's not safe for you here either."

Katherine's feet turned to ice.

"*I* can't stand here while these scoundrels have Kate." Stephen raked a hand through his hair as he paced the length of the drawing room.

His mother rubbed her temples. "Our headgroom—an agent—Agent Warren—he told you to wait until dusk?"

His heart softened toward his mother whose fingers gripped the velvet armrests of the highbacked chair of the rose drawing room. He'd thrown a massive amount of information at his parents and sister in the last half hour. At least she'd recovered from her shock of learning he'd been a spy for the crown. His father appeared proud of Stephen's service, but unable to cheer him due to the wretched circumstances, and Abby remained speechless, staring at him as if being introduced to her twin brother for the first time.

He checked the wall clock and the minute hand had barely moved since the last time he checked. "I can't sit back and wait while the charlatan either marries my fiancée or worse kills her."

"You mustn't do anything rash." Abby finally spoke but her gaze remained distant as if speaking from experience. "Use your head because your heart is too intimately tied to Kate to make rational decisions." Anguish lined her eyes, and his heart twisted, knowing she referenced Nicholas.

The sound of a carriage approaching perked his ear up.

Abby rose and moved to the window drawing back the curtain with her index finger. "Were we expecting anyone?"

Father glanced at Mother.

"Not that I recall." She shrugged. "But with the wedding and today's events I've been out of sorts."

"It's an unmarked carriage." Abby stepped aside for Stephen to look.

Groomsmen scurried out of the stables to care for the horses that panted as if having been ridden hard. A footman hopped off the back, lowered the steps, and opened the door.

Two women emerged from the conveyance at the assistance of the footmen. One older woman held herself with a stiff posture and opened her parasol, while the other petite blonde shook the wrinkles from her gown.

"I don't recognize them." Abby spoke over his shoulder. "I'll send them away. We don't have time for social calls right now." She left the room.

Stephen squinted for a better look. There was something oddly familiar about the blond, but it didn't matter. There was no time for distractions. He'd already ordered his horse readied, and Henderson packed Stephen a bag. He needed to focus on getting Kate back.

"What would you have us do?" His mother shifted forward in her seat and his father nodded.

What could they do from here? He lowered his gaze, and one word rang in his mind, *Pray.* "Pray for Kate's safety."

The light clicking of Abby's kid boots on the hardwood flood, followed by her bounding through the door. "You won't believe who's here."

She stepped aside and the two women from outside entered the drawing room.

His father struggled to rise, but the austere older woman with a spine so straight Stephen feared it might snap, waved for him to remain seated. The younger blond entered behind her, clutching her reticule in between her gloved hands. Her face didn't look familiar, but there was something about the way she moved that triggered an alert in Stephen's head.

Abby stared wide-eyed at Stephen. "May I introduce Madame Lamoureux, the head mistress of The Sherbourne Finishing School for Young Ladies decorum, and her pupil, Miss Claire Jenkins."

Kate's sister? Stephen jolted. "Claire?" Shock allowed the informal use of the woman's name slip through his lips, but that was how Kate had referred to her sister.

Miss Jenkins's face lit, and she stepped forward. "I was hoping to visit with my sister. May I see her?"

Heaven help him, how was he going to explain? "Please be seated." He gestured to the sofa where Abby had sat. "I'm Lord Stephen Hartington and this is my mother and father Lord and Lady Felton, and you've already met my sister Mrs. Abigail Emerson.

Madame Lamoureux nodded her head after being seated. "A pleasure."

"You must be weary from traveling." Mother rose and yanked the bell pull. "Let me ring for tea and finger sandwiches."

Stephen rubbed his brow. Claire was here, but Kate believed her cousin had her. He must get word to Kate —quickly.

"Please." Miss Jenkins's lips turned up in a half-smile. "I'm quite desperate to see my sister."

As was he. Stephen shook his head. "I'm afraid your sister is no longer here."

Miss Jenkins's face fell, and her shoulders drooped, but Madame Lamoureux nudged her to straighten. "Do you know where I might find her?"

Abby stepped next to her brother. "Your cousin came and collected her."

Miss Jenkins shot out of her seat, but Madame Lamoureux pulled her back down.

"He brought a constable, insisting they were married, and that he was bringing his property back home." Stephen studied Miss Jenkins's reaction.

"She wouldn't marry the likes of him." Miss Jenkins pressed a gloved hand to her stomach. "Not of her own volition. Not without telling me."

Any miniscule niggling of doubt that Kate might be married to Bainbridge evaporated. "You're being here proves as much." Stephen started to pace once more as he worked out the implications. "I'm assuming you weren't present at the wedding and didn't sign as a witness."

"Certainly not."

Forgery would put Bainbridge and Pewitt away for at least a year. It wasn't the life sentence for murder they'd hoped for, but it was enough for now. Claire was known to be safe. He could get Kate out of there, marry her and Bainbridge would lose guardianship.

Miss Jenkins dug through her reticule, producing a folded piece of paper. "She wrote a letter to Madame Lamoureux—"

"Which was badgered out of me." Madame Lamoureux pursed her lips.

"—stating that Horace attempted to have her killed. She asked for me to be kept under the protective care of the school grounds and to never allow admittance for our cousin or any strange men."

Stephen extended his hand. "I'd like to have a look at that letter, if you don't mind, Miss Jenkins."

"Of course, read it yourself." She handed the paper to him.

Stephen held the note so he could read it. Katherine wrote in small feminine handwriting, not the slanted long script he'd viewed on the marriage certificate.

"Keep this as evidence." Stephen handed her back the

letter. "Why did you come here when you were instructed to remain at the school?"

"I told you we should have stayed." Madame Lamoureux eyed her pupil. "I never should have caved to your persistence."

"I couldn't bear not knowing if she was safe, and my fears were correct. If only we'd come earlier." She clasped her hands. "Lord Hartington, I beseech you. My sister is in serious danger. We must act before it is too late. I pray it isn't already."

To perdition with waiting until dusk. "I'm going after her." He turned to his sister. "Entertain our guests until I return."

"I'm coming with you." Miss Jenkins rose this time evading Madame Lamoureux's reach.

"Absolutely not." Stephen shook his head.

"Indeed." Madame Lamoureux rose. "You were left in my care, and I won't have you putting yourself in harm's way when you're supposed to be under my protection."

Miss Jenkin raised her chin the same way Kate often had. "Then you'll just have to come along also."

"If they're going than so am I." Abby crossed her arms.

"No." Stephen barked, but their stubborn expressions suggested he'd lost command over the room.

Miss Jenkins rounded on her headmistress. "I know the grounds and all the servants trust me. I can be of help."

"We're wasting time." He turned to Miss Jenkins. "Can you ride?"

"Of course."

He took her arm, and they made for the door.

Madame Lamoureux's stern voice called out, "Miss Jenkins, you are not properly attired for riding. You will travel in the coach."

Claire let out a frustrated sigh. "Do you know the way?"

Stephen nodded. Jacob had described to him the roads and markers to look for.

"Ladies do not express frustration, and please remember

your posture." Madame Lamoureux clucked her tongue. She rounded on Stephen. "Lord Hartington, you may ride with us, or you may take your own mount and ride alongside our coach —whichever meets your fancy. Miss Jenkins was left in my care, and she will stay under my close watch for her protection."

Stephen considered strangling the headmistress. Not only would a carriage slow him down, but also precious time would be wasted swapping out their exhausted horses.

"Ride ahead." Miss Jenkins pleaded with her eyes. "We'll catch up. Save her before it's too late."

Stephen raced to the stables. He barked orders at the groomsmen, who handed him Dominion's reins. In one motion, Stephen grabbed the horse's mane and kicked his leg up, propelling himself into the saddle with ease. He clicked his tongue, and his horse burst out of the barn in full gallop.

He glimpsed his mother climb into Madame Lamoureux's coach followed by Abby. He heard Abby yell, "We'll be right behind you."

He raced down the lane. *Lord, help me get to Kate before that blackguard lays a hand on her.*

The sun slid behind the hills stretching long shadows of trees across his path as Stephen approached Steepleton Manor. He pleaded the entire ride for God to protect Kate. He would never be able to forgive himself if he failed to rescue her. He snapped the reins, uncertain how far behind the cumbersome coach had fallen. He'd been riding full out for three-quarters of an hour, but Dominion could handle it.

Stephen squinted at an object taking shape beyond the setting sun on a far-off hill. Fences and horses dotted the countryside. As he got closer, he made out a large estate overlooking well-groomed grounds. He turned down the lane, riding over a stone bridge toward the large Greek revival-styled mansion. As soon as he was on the far side of the creek, he veered to hide under cover of a line of trees. *Lord, be our front and rear guard. Get her out of this mess unscathed.*

---

*K*atherine endured the evening meal and the snide comments from Lord Pewitt but could only pick at the roasted duck. While the constable and Lord Pewitt fell into a discussion, she set down her fork, and addressed her cousin in a low voice. "Where is my sister? I want to see her, I won't cooperate until I know she hasn't been harmed."

Horace stared at her above the rim of his glass, his eyes clouded.

"I know you loved Madeline, and she adored her family. She wouldn't have wanted anything to happen to Claire or me."

The amber liquid in his glass started to shake. He tossed it back and swallowed.

Was he nervous?

Katherine leaned toward him. "Madeline loved you with all her heart and spoke highly of you. How can you besmirch her memory this way?"

Her cousin pushed away from the table, having eaten only part of his meal and murmured about business needing to be finished. He pulled a piece of paper out of his pocket and strode toward her father's study.

She rose to excuse herself. Perhaps if she spoke to her cousin alone, she could get him to change his course.

Lord Pewitt lifted a finger, and a footman rushed to his side. "I can't abide droll company. See the countess to her room."

A footman she didn't recognize gripped her arm and hauled

her out of the dining room and up the stairs. He escorted her to her chamber and whispered, "Agent Warren sends his regards."

She gasped. He was with the Home Office. Thank Heaven. She gripped his arm. "I must get a message to Agent Warren. Please tell him that Lord Hartington is in danger. Lord Pewit plans to kill him."

"I will do my best." He gestured for her to enter.

She wanted to clutch his lapels and shake him. "It's imperative."

"Pardon, but it must be done for affect." He slammed the door and strode back the way they came.

Katherine paced her room and prayed her warning would reach Stephen and that he would heed it. How was she going to get Lord Pewitt or her cousin to confess in front of witnesses? First, she must discover where they were keeping Claire.

Footsteps echoed up the stairs and continued in her direction. Katherine grabbed a candlestick and retreated to the far corner of the room.

A banging noise pounded on her door. It wasn't someone knocking. It sounded more like someone hitting the frame with a hammer. Her entire door shook, and bits of plaster dust broke off the wall and crumbled to the floor. The noise stopped, followed by the sound of metal sliding into place. Footsteps retreated down the hall.

Katherine put down the candlestick and approached the door. She lifted the latch to peer out, but it wouldn't budge. She pulled harder, even putting her knee up against the adjoining wall, but to no avail. Someone had installed a lock.

She was trapped.

Her knees hit the wooden floorboards but the pain barely registered. How was she supposed to full fill her part of the plan when she was locked up like a prisoner? She crawled her way back to the side of the bed and pressed her face into the mattress. When her tears ran out, she turned her head to the side for fresh air.

She was supposed to find Claire, but all she'd done was put herself and Stephen in danger. *God, my circumstances look bleak. I can't see a way out. Help me to trust You.*

Pushing up onto shaky legs, she moved to the bookshelf and removed the Bible her mother had given her. She blew the dust off and gently opening the pages, turning to the book of Daniel to reread the story of Shadrack, Meshach and Abednego. The quaking in her limbs ceased before she'd finished reading about the fiery furnace and was halfway through the story about Daniel being thrown in the lion's den when a light tap sounded on her door.

"My lady," Denton whispered. "Are you all right?"

"I need your help." She set down the Bible and moved to lean against the doorframe. "I must find my sister. Can you unlock the door?"

"I don't have the key."

"You must get it."

"I will try my best. Bainbridge drinks hard in the evenings. I might be able to sneak the key off his person once he drinks himself into oblivion. In the meantime, don't worry. I will do everything I can to protect you."

"Be careful." His loyalty touched her. Was Denton's visit and Agent Warren's message God's way of letting her know He was with her. "The footman who escorted me up here, he's on our side. He can help."

"I must go, but I will keep my ears open regarding Miss Jenkin's whereabouts, and I will return if I can get the key."

She listened to his steps retreating down the hall. "Lord, thank You for loyal friends." She prayed the rest of the evening for God's protection over Stephen, her sister, the agents, and staff involved. After exhausting all words, she turned to read more of her Bible, and the next verse spoken by the angel Gabriel stuck out as if it had jumped off the page. *"Do not be afraid, Daniel. Since the first day that you set your mind to gain understanding and to humble yourself before your God, your words were heard, and I have come in response to them.*

Had God already dispatched His angels on her behalf?

---

*D*arkness had settled by the time Stephen heard a shrill whistle that could have been mistaken as a bird. Stephen reined up short and slid off his horse. He stashed his horse down a path in the woods. The whistle sounded again, and Jacob strode out from behind an old wood cutter's cottage. Hidden in the twilight stood a man of good height and powerful build dressed in all black. His hat was tilted, and its brim shadowed his eyes and face, but in the faint light, Stephen could make out a mass of puckered and bunched skin from a burn on one side of his lower jaw.

"Lord Hartington, this is the handler I spoke of. We fondly call him Scar. He's been monitoring the premises and relaying messages to the agents inside." He pointed to two other men standing at windows with spyglasses held up to their eyes. "You know Felix, and he's Higgins."

Stephen offered a curt nod, which Agent Scar and the men returned.

"She's safe for the moment." Agent Scar's scratchy voice sounded as if he were fighting an illness. "We haven't located the sister."

"There's new information." Jacob and Agent Scar turned their full attention to Stephen. "Miss Jenkins is safe. She's traveling here by carriage with my mother, sister, and the headmistress of the finishing school." He eyed Jacob. "Someone will need to intercept them and bring them here, so they don't ride up to the main house. Miss Jenkins is willing to help, but must be protected at all costs."

"They misled Lady Dysart into thinking they held her sister." Jacob grunted. "I saw the pistol they had pointed into her back as they forced her into the carriage."

Heat filled Stephen's face. He couldn't jail these men fast enough.

Agent Scar unrolled a sketched layout of the grounds. "We need to get Lady Dysart out of there quickly. My deep cover agent says that Pewitt is anxious and becoming unpredictable. I have a plan, but, Hartington, your part will be risky."

"I'll do anything. I want Kate out of that nightmare."

"You are going to need to put your feelings aside."

Easier said than done, but he nodded.

"From what I've learned from the butler, Bainbridge sleeps in the master's chamber, Pewitt in the west wing." Agent Scar pointed to the areas on the drawings. "They have her locked in her room on the second floor of the main house. We have intel that Bainbridge is going to bring her into the library, within the hour, to write a missive to her solicitors informing them of her nuptials and that financial control has been handed over to her so-called-husband. Jacob is going in, but she'll trust and listen to you better, so you'll be going with him. However, you can't be spotted by Pewitt or Bainbridge. They'll recognize you immediately."

Stephen ached to wring the necks of the men who dared imprison her. The image of Kate's pale face as Bainbridge escorted her from Willowstone, and now knowing she had a gun pointed at her back soured his stomach. "What would you have me do?"

"The butler will get you inside," Agent Scar said. "I need you to go in and not get shot."

CHAPTER 30

Katherine awoke with a start, her heart pounding and her Bible still open on her chest like a shield covering her heart, both figuratively and literally. Setting it aside, she stood and walked to the window, breathing in the cool night air. If only her window had a cherry tree.

Courage had become a habit for Daniel and his friends, and so, too, it must be for her.

"God is with me." She whispered to the night air.

The hall clock chimed the hour, and she counted nine dongs. Her cousin and Lord Pewitt argued below, but their words were indecipherable. A door slammed and footsteps thudded up the stairs. She grabbed the candlestick and ran to the far side of the bed. Her pulse thundered.

The footsteps stopped outside her door, and all the normal nighttime sounds halted. She could hear heavy breathing on the other side. Her mind screamed as the exterior lock clicked and the bolt slid. She gripped the candlestick tighter, ready to defend herself. The door opened to reveal her cousin.

"We have some business for you to attend to." He nodded to the candlestick. "You won't be needing that."

She raised the candlestick higher.

"Everything is going to be fine." His eyes softened, and he appeared more like the man Madeline had married. "Just do what I ask, and you won't get hurt. In fact, if you obey me, things can go back to the way they were before my arrival."

"What have you done with Claire? I want to see her."

"Claire is safe and unharmed."

"Why should I believe you?" She didn't want things to go back to how they were before. She wanted to be Stephen's wife and wake up every day in his arms. God willing, she wanted children and a family.

"I'm not the monster you think me to be."

"Why should I believe you?"

"I know it doesn't seem like it, but I've tried to protect you all along."

"By striking me and sending men to kill me?"

He winced. "I needed you to run. I didn't know he'd send men after you."

She shook her head. "I don't understand."

"It's best if you don't. You must fear me or he'll catch on, but I need you to do what I tell you." His gaze held a look of desperation, and his fingers curled into fists as if pleading.

"Why are you doing this?"

"For Madeline." His voice broke with emotion. He skirted the edge of the bed, stepped toward her, and gently pried the candlestick from her fingers. He closed his eyes and gritted his teeth. "For my wife." His tone turned menacing, though she couldn't imagine why.

He took her arm and guided her down the stairs and through the main hall into the library, where Lord Pewitt sat at her desk as if he belonged there.

He didn't look up from the documents he was perusing, merely gestured to be seated.

Horace led her to a chair and took the adjacent one.

"You will sign this letter to your solicitor. There's no need to go through all the pomp and circumstance of a wedding. I've already obtained the priest's signature." He turned the document to face her and lay the quill next to the spot where she was to write her name. He pushed another set toward her cousin. "These documents go to your husband, signing over the Lipizzaners and the Jenkins' fortune to me as payment of debt."

Katherine notched up her chin. "If I refuse?"

"You don't understand the gravity of your situation." Lord Pewitt's piercing eyes bore into her own.

"Enlighten me." She spoke the words as a dare to his ego.

A wicked smile tugged at the corners of Pewitt's lips. "Bainbridge and I have a hobby involving the sale of horses—prime bits of blood. Your father stuck his nose in my business and notified Tallersalls and the authorities that the certificates were forged." Pewitt shrugged. "He, of course, was correct." Years of hatred hardened his eyes. "I lost my livelihood thanks to your father, but I am a patient man. I knew when and how to exact my revenge."

"You killed my parents."

He chuckled. "Don't you remember? It was a carriage accident." Thick sarcasm laced his tone. "Your father got his due, but your mother was collateral damage."

Her periphery darkened until all she saw was the scornful grin on Lord Pewitt's face. "Is my life to be collateral damage too?"

"If it serves my purposes."

Horace flashed her a warning glare. "Do what he asks."

"The truth will get out." She would no longer be a victim of her circumstances. "I won't cooperate until I know my sister is safe, and if you kill me, you won't be able to lay a hand on her because any more accidental deaths will make the authorities suspicious."

"My, aren't we brave?" Lord Pewitt cackled with laughter, a

wheezy, unholy sound. "I don't fear the authorities. Not when a little payoff or cut of a sale will keep them quiet. Don't you realize your life is in the palm of my hand? I can snuff you out easier than I would a candle."

"You can do only what God allows." She kept her gaze steadfast.

"Such an idealistic girl." He snorted. "Your death will merely be one of a long string of accidental deaths." His tone oozed with pride.

Horace whipped a revolver out of his jacket and pointed it at Pewitt. "That's enough to bring you in. You're under arrest and will be tried by the House of Lords. May they and God not take mercy on your soul."

Pewitt's chin drew back, and he laughed a hollow cackling sound. He raised his own gun from behind the desk and Katherine peered into the end pointed directly at her.

"You'll do what we say, or she'll die as Madeline did, with her pretty eyes still holding out hope of rescue until her lifeblood drains onto the floor."

Horace flew across the desk, catching Pewitt by the throat and knocking his weapon beneath the desk.

Katherine crouched on the floor and tried to locate where the gun landed but the skirt of the desk blocked her view. The men wrestled for control of Horace's revolver. She tried to crawl around them to run to the door but screamed as Lord Pewitt slammed her cousin into the desk, nearly toppling it over on her. Spittle and blood sprayed on the rug.

She backed against the wall and stood.

Horace hit Lord Pewitt in the jaw. Pewitt fell back on his side but rolled and rose holding his gun.

Both men pointed their weapons at each other, trapping Katherine who couldn't get by without stepping into their crossfire.

Peripheral movement caught her attention. Stephen's face reflected in the mirror. He stood in the partially open doorway.

Katherine gasped, and she wanted to yell to him, but Lord Pewitt's words from the coach ride stopped her. *If Hartington shows up, we'll just make it look like a jealous lover's quarrel and kill him.* She raised her palms to signal for him to stay.

Stephen's eyes widened, but he didn't move.

She inched her way toward the door as her cousin and Pewitt began to circle each other.

Horace lunged and someone's gun spun across the floor and ricocheted off the baseboard.

Katherine darted toward Stephen.

A muffled shot rang out from underneath the two men, and Katherine screamed.

"Where do you think you're going?" Pewitt yelled as he rose pointing his gun at her.

Katherine froze halfway across the room.

Horace moaned, grasping his leg as blood poured from a bullet wound in his thigh.

Lord Pewit stepped closer and wiped the blood dripping from his nose away with his sleeve. "Another inch, and I'll put a bullet in your head."

Stephen stepped around the corner and cocked his revolver. "And I'll put a hole in your chest."

"But will your bullet reach me before my bullet reaches her?" The barrel of Lord Pewitt's gun rose to within inches of her temple.

---

*S*tephen seethed with anger. "Your time is up, Pewitt. The Home Office has you. You may get leniency for forgery, but you won't for murder."

Kate's face was pale, and her hands trembled by her sides.

"If you want your sister to live, you'll come with me." Pewitt reached for her, but she backed just beyond his reach.

"Your sister is safe." Stephen stared at Pewitt's trigger finger. "She's with my mother."

Kate's gaze flew to his, a spark of hope in her eyes.

"Your sister is doomed unless you come with me." Pewitt's eyes grew wild. "I'm your only option if you don't want anyone getting killed."

*K*atherine shook to the point her legs could barely carry her. Fear had controlled her, but no longer. *God is in control.*

She stepped toward Stephen. *Lord, I trust in You.*

Pewitt gripped the gun's handle with both hands. "Not another step."

Stephen tensed and drew back.

Mr. Warren and Denton appeared behind Stephen each held a weapon pointed at Lord Pewitt.

Pewitt glanced toward the window, but Jacob slipped along the perimeter of the room and blocked his escape.

Katherine took another step.

"I said, don't move." Rage shook Pewitt's voice.

A gunshot pierced the air.

Pewitt stumbled toward her and discharged his gun.

His heavy weight landed on top of her, pushing her to the floor. She failed to get her arms up to catch her fall. Her head hit the corner of the desk, sending white sparks of light in front of her eyes. *Not again. Not now.* She fought to stay conscious, but the dizziness returned, nausea threatened, and darkness overtook her.

*S*tephen lunged for Kate as the gun went off but couldn't reach her before Pewitt. He yanked the man away. Kate's gown was covered in blood and more pooled around her. Pewitt didn't move. Stephen lowered his weapon.

God, don't take her from me.

He dropped to his knees and cradled her body. A guttural groan screamed from his throat.

During the chaos, Agent Scar must have found his way inside through the window, by the look of the open sash. He pointed his weapon at Bainbridge, who sat against the wall, blood pouring from his thigh, still holding a smoking gun. Scar ripped the weapon from Bainbridge's fingers and tended to the wound.

Stephen heard Jacob step behind him and caught the gleam of his raised gun. Jacob rolled Pewitt's body over and examined the entrance wound. He crouched by Stephen's side.

Stephen clutched Kate closer. "I should have been there. I should have protected her."

Jacob reached for Kate.

"I won't let you take her." Stephen knocked his hand away.

"Easy." Jacob held up his palms and nodded to her hand.

Stephen forced his arms to relax and allowed his friend to touch her wrist.

"There's a strong pulse. She's alive."

Stephen felt for himself. Sure enough, a steady rhythm surged against his fingers. He looked for a bullet wound, running his hand along her midsection and sides. Finding nothing, he turned her to inspect her back.

"Well?" Jacob asked.

"I can't find a bullet wound." Could it be?

Katherine moaned. "Oh God, thank you." Stephen pressed her head against his chest.

Bainbridge, Jacob, and even Agent Scar slumped in relief.

Stephen brushed curls off of her face, and her eyelids fluttered open. His hands trembled. "Kate?"

Her lips curved into a weak smile, and she asked in a soft voice, "Who's Kate?"

He chuckled, and her mouth twitched into a broad smile. He crushed her against him, holding her tight. "Don't you ever do this to me again. I love you too much."

Kate cupped his cheek. "I love you too."

Denton draped a tablecloth over Pewitt's body, and Stephen aided Kate to her feet, but he kept her close to his side. Pewitt's blood had stained both of their clothes, making them a hideous sight, but he didn't care.

"I questioned your methods, but in the end, you got him." Agent Scar tied a tourniquet around Bainbridge's leg.

Jacob straightened. "Bainbridge was the deep cover agent feeding you intelligence?

Bainbridge grimaced as Agent Scar aided him to a stand.

"So deep we had to hire you to lure him back out of hiding. I don't agree with his unconventional methods, but he took the villain down and avenged his wife's death." Agent Scar looped Bainbridge's arm over his shoulder.

"For Madeline." Kate stared at her cousin.

"That monster deserved to suffer a worse fate." His growl punctuated the air. "What he did to my Madeline was unfathomable. I hope he burns for all eternity."

"I hate to do this to you, friend, but until things are sorted out, you're placed under His Majesty's custody." Agent Scar started for the door.

Bainbridge pulled away and addressed Kate. "For what it's worth,"—He grit his teeth and grimaced holding his leg— "I'm sorry for my ruse and the pain I put you through." He exhaled. "My threats were empty, and the so-called priest who witnessed and signed the documents never existed." He snorted with a crack of a smile. "You were fearless."

She rested her head on Stephen's shoulder.

Stephen tilted his head up in a silent, *Thank you, Lord.*

Claire and Abby ran into the room with Madame Lamoureux shouting at them from behind. Claire gasped at the blood and skidded to a halt.

"Claire." Kate hugged her sister. "Thank heaven, you're all right."

"Me?" Claire's hands tightly gripped the fabric of her sister's gown as if never intending to let her go. "It's you who's covered in blood."

"I'm fine." Kate leaned back to see Claire's face. "I could stand a little less excitement, though."

Agent Scar pulled his hat down and nodded to the women as he shuffled his prisoner out of the room.

Abby's gaze tracked the agent with a puzzled expression. "Was he the man from the masquerade?"

Kate turned to look, hooking an arm through her sisters before she shrugged. "I'm not certain."

His mother stepped into the doorway and gasped.

"Everybody's fine, Mama," Abby said.

Mother sagged against the frame. "Thank God."

The entire room seemed to exhale a collective sigh and weak but grateful smiles wobbled on everyone's lips.

Stephen nudged Kate. "Look at all the people who came to your aid, even Bainbridge. You were never alone."

Jacob pointed to a bullet hole in the wall. "This must have been the second shot we heard."

Kate released her sister and moved to Stephen's side.

Stephen's heart stopped. The second bullet pierced the spot where Kate had stood only seconds before the gun exploded. If she hadn't stepped forward... Bile rose in his throat, and he hugged his intended with renewed fervor.

Kate clung to him and whispered against his cheek, "I trusted God and stepped out in faith."

EPILOGUE

*K*atherine kissed the head of the chubby little toddler wriggling in her arms and set him on the floor among his toys.

Little Benjamin pulled himself to a standing position on his papa's pant leg. She crouched down and held her arms out to him. He smiled and stuck out one pudgy arm as if to say, *You come to me.*

"You can do it, Benjamin." She waved, beckoning him over. "Come to Mama."

His face puckered up as if to let out a wail.

"Mama's right here. I won't let anything happen to you."

He bent his knees, clearly planning to crawl.

Katherine shook her head. "No, Benny," she said softly, "you can do this. Mommy has you."

Emotions splayed across his face. She'd knew that feeling. It had taken her a long time to step out in faith. She fell many times at first, but the more steps she took, the easier it became to walk by faith. She still stumbled here and there, but God strengthened her. He'd walked her and Stephen through the premature birth of Benjamin, a whole five weeks early. Their little baby had been so small and fragile. But, despite the midwife declaring that he wouldn't make it through the night, she and Stephen had disregarded her words and prayed until the wee morning hours. God was faithful, and Benjamin survived.

Stephen smiled at their son. "You can do it, Benny." He was a proud papa, and she was blessed with a new family and a wonderful husband. God had brought them together despite all the obstacles set against them. She and Stephen grew in their faith and love of the Lord, and she'd moved from baby steps into a deep and wonderful walk with their Savior.

Benjamin let go of his father's pant leg and took one wobbly step. He frowned and almost lost his balance, but he stepped again and steadied himself.

He looked at his mama with a big grin and, with another wobbly step, fell into her outstretched arms.

Did you enjoy this book? We hope so!
**Would you take a quick minute to leave a review where you
purchased the book?**
It doesn't have to be long. Just a sentence or two telling what
you liked about the story!

Receive a FREE ebook and get updates when new Wild Heart
books release: https://wildheartbooks.org/newsletter

FROM THE AUTHOR

Dearest Readers,

I'm so excited to start another series journey with you. I hope you enjoyed Katherine and Stephen's story and with a little intrigue mixed with romance. Thank you for choosing *Revealing the Truth*. It would be lovely if you could post a quick review. Also, get ready for Abby's story in *Reclaiming the Spy,* the second book in the series, coming out next.

My deepest gratitude goes to my publisher Misty Beller at Wild Heart Books, and her amazing team. Misty, thank you for being such a joy to work with, a publishing and marketing guru, and believing in me. Thanks to your incredible team, Sherri, Sarah, Robin, and all the others behind the scenes who help make my stories come to life. Robin Patchen, I can't thank you enough for your wisdom, calling out my mistakes, and urging me to rethink scenes from a different perspective. I am a better writer and person because of your guidance and friendship.

I can't thank my launch team enough for posting reviews, telling their friends, and generating all-around excitement. Also, thanks to my beta reading team for finding all the little things that slipped through the cracks. Lori, Kristen, Shannon, and Liz, you are dear to my heart. Special thanks for your keen eyes and encouragement. And a shout out to the Louisville ladies who've been such support not only to my mother but also to my writing.

I'm blessed with the most genuinely awesome family. I'm so

appreciative of the notes my aunts, cousins, and second cousins send me to encourage my writing. Mom and Dad, thank you for fostering my creativity over the years and bringing up the topic of my books every chance you get, including on the praise reports of our Sunday school class. I love you. To my beloved husband, John, you're one handsome, God-fearing man who makes the best specialty coffee drinks to keep me writing.

But most of all, to God be all the glory!

If you love historical romance, check out the other Wild Heart books!

Marisol ~ Spanish Rose by Elva Cobb Martin

Escaping to the New World is her only option...Rescuing her will wrap the chains of the Inquisition around his neck.

Marisol Valentin flees Spain after murdering the nobleman who molested her. She ends up for sale on the indentured servants' block at Charles Town harbor—dirty, angry, and with child. Her hopes are shattered, but she must find a refuge for herself and the child she carries. Can this new land offer her the grace, love, and security she craves? Or must she escape again to her only living relative in Cartagena?

Captain Ethan Becket, once a Charles Town minister, now sails the seas as a privateer, grieving his deceased wife. But when he takes captive a ship full of indentured servants, he's intrigued by the woman whose manners seem much more refined than the average Spanish serving girl. Perfect to become governess for his young son. But when he sets out on a quest to find his captured sister, said to be in Cartagena, little does he expect his new Spanish governess to stow away on his ship with her six-month-old son. Yet her offer of help to free his sister is too tempting to pass up. And her beauty, both inside and out, is too attractive for his heart to protect itself against—until he learns she is a wanted murderess.

As their paths intertwine on a journey filled with danger, intrigue, and romance, only love and the grace of God can overcome the past and ignite a new beginning for Marisol and Ethan.

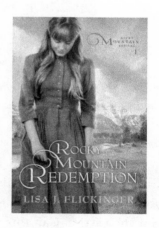

Rocky Mountain Redemption by Lisa J. Flickinger

A Rocky Mountain logging camp may be just the place to find herself.

To escape the devastation caused by the breaking of her wedding engagement, Isabelle Franklin joins her aunt in the Rocky Mountains to feed a camp of lumberjacks cutting on the slopes of Cougar Ridge. If only she could out run the lingering nightmares.

Charles Bailey, camp foreman and Stony Creek's itinerant pastor, develops a reputation to match his new nickname — Preach. However, an inner battle ensues when the details of his rough history threaten to overcome the beliefs of his young faith.

Amid the hazards of camp life, the unlikely friendship growing between the two surprises Isabelle. She's drawn to Preach's brute strength and gentle nature as he leads the ragtag crew toiling for Pollitt's Lumber. But when the ghosts from her past return to haunt her, the choices she will make change the course of her life forever—and that of the man she's come to love.

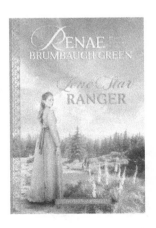

Lone Star Ranger by Renae Brumbaugh Green

Elizabeth Covington will get her man.

And she has just a week to prove her brother isn't the murderer Texas Ranger Rett Smith accuses him of being. She'll show the good-looking lawman he's wrong, even if it means setting out on a risky race across Texas to catch the real killer.

Rett doesn't want to convict an innocent man. But he can't let the Boston beauty sway his senses to set a guilty man free. When Elizabeth follows him on a dangerous trek, the Ranger vows to keep her safe. But who will protect him from the woman whose conviction and courage leave him doubting everything—even his heart?